Already Dead

Supernatural Collection

Holly Copella

ISBN: 0997106476
ISBN-13: 978-0997106473

For Charles A. Koch
"This We'll Defend"

CONTENTS

ACKNOWLEDGMENTS

Copella Books: First Paperback Edition 2016
Cover Artist: Shardel
SelfPubBookCovers.com/Shardel
Printed by CreateSpace, An Amazon.com Company

PUBLISHER'S NOTE

Bloodletting

Holly Copella

Chapter One

The tropical white sandy beach lent a romantic backdrop for young lovers taking a long walk on a breezy, summer evening. Beyond the gently crashing waves, a thunderstorm was seen approaching in the distance. Not far from the beach, an attractive blonde woman leaned against the open door of a dark sports car and watched the romantic couple holding hands as they disappeared past a large rock formation. Jersey LeBelle was dressed nightclub savvy in a revealing, formfitting dress and high heels. She sighed with boredom then removed her small compact from her purse and fixed her make-up by the glow of the car's interior light. Two men conducted business in the shadows nearly fifty yards away from Jersey and the sports car. Neither man was clearly identifiable from the location of the car, not that Jersey actually cared. She closed her compact and looked toward the two men, sighing with annoyance. One of the men finally turned and approached Jersey and the sports car. She returned her compact to her purse and looked at the handsome, finely dressed man with some impatience.

"Can we go now?" she whined.

Tony smiled as he paused before her and flashed a large wade of cash. "Honey, we can go wherever you want."

Jersey smiled with renewed enthusiasm at the sight of the bundled one hundred dollar bills and clung to his arm. "Someplace with dancing."

"Anything you want."

Tony leaned on the open passenger door and suavely extended his hand for her to get inside. She slid onto the seat in a somewhat sexy manner, although her actions had more to do with the tightness of her dress restricting her movement. He shut the door and

5

rounded the car to the driver's side. Once comfortably seated, Jersey immediately lowered the visor and looked into the mirror while applying an additional coat of lipstick. When the driver's side door opened, Jersey didn't bother looking at Tony; instead, she fused over her appearance in the visor mirror.

"I think we should rent one of those cabin boats," she announced with giddy delight. "You know the ones you can sleep in."

When there was no response, she looked at the open car door where Tony remained standing in the doorway. Jersey stared with a curious look.

"Tony? Are you listening to me?" she asked then leaned on the driver's seat and attempted to look at him beyond the car roof.

Tony suddenly collapsed to his knees before the open car door. His face was drained of all color and he had a large gash on the side of his neck, which revealed little blood considering the size of the wound. Jersey suddenly screamed with horror and surprise. She fumbled with the car door, threw it open, and half fell onto the ground. She scrambled to her feet, hindered by her tight dress and high heels, and looked for her boyfriend's attacker. To her surprise, there was no sign of whomever had silently attacked Tony. She breathed heavily a moment then reached inside the car for her purse. From the corner of her eye, she saw the outline of someone moving within the darkness near the car. She bolted away from the car, leaving her purse within it, and ran for the beach.

Jersey lost traction once she hit the sand in her high heels and nearly fell down. She regained her balance and flung off her shoes as she ran. She looked behind her, but there was no one there. Jersey slowed and turned, looking back at the sports car only lit by its interior light. She didn't see anyone and it didn't appear as if anyone was following her. Jersey finally stopped and surveyed the area while breathing heavily. She clutched her chest and held back her sobs. When nothing moved, she caught her breath and was finally able to relax. She was too frightened to return to the car and her dead boyfriend. Jersey then saw some beach homes in the distance. As she turned, she suddenly collided with a man in a black trench coat. Jersey screamed with surprise at the appearance of a man who hadn't been there just a second earlier. She leaped backwards, lost her balance, and fell onto her backside.

The man, whose face was cloaked in darkness, closed in on her. Jersey scrambled backwards on her backside, frantically kicking up sand. She finally scrambled to her knees and slung a handful of sand at the man as he approached. He stopped and clutched his face, blinded by the sand. Jersey screamed, finally made it to her feet, and ran across the beach without looking back. Not far from the beach homes and just beyond the large rock formation, she saw a bonfire with several teenagers camped around it while drinking and laughing. As she got closer, she could hear the loud music coming from their small sailboat pulled onto shore. Jersey's eyes lit up at the sight of the kids and their party. She ran faster for the people on the beach just beyond the large rocks.

"Hey! Over here! Help!"

Jersey approached the rocks dividing her from the small group of teens. A shadow loomed over her along with a small gust of wind. She barely saw the dark figure before colliding with him. The man in the trench coat was suddenly standing before her even though he had just been behind her. Jersey let out a horrified scream as he grabbed her shoulders to keep her from falling. Although she didn't see his face, she saw his vampire fangs and his blood covered lips. A low, gurgled growl escaped his throat as he lunged for her neck with his teeth. Jersey screamed loud and shrill. The teens surrounding the bonfire turned down their music and looked toward the rocks. There was no one there except rocks, shadows, and darkness.

Chapter Two

Two weeks later. The city of Boston was alive with Friday night activity. Residents and visitors flooded the sidewalks and cars filled the streets. It was a beautiful summer evening and most wanted to enjoy it. Not everyone was taking advantage of the gorgeous evening outside though. In an apartment building above the bustle of the city streets was a tastefully decorated, two-bedroom apartment with bright, plush furniture and plants seemingly growing out of the walls. Beyond the bright, cheerful living room, there was a dark bedroom with a slightly gloomy atmosphere, unlike the exterior room. The bed headboard was black wrought iron, matching the dark comforter and throw pillows.

A young, attractive woman in her early twenties sat on her bed with her laptop computer. Cybil Brooklyn was a raven-haired beauty with a milky completion and sinfully dark eyes. She typed on the keyboard then paused and stared at the screen with a look of great interest. The bedroom door open partway and a shadow fell over the busily working woman. She was so engrossed in her laptop, she hadn't noticed someone entering the room. Heidi Desmond cast herself onto the foot end of the bed, causing it to bounce, and startled Cybil. She glared at her friend, not appreciating the surprise attack. Heidi was a lively redhead with an unusually dark complexion for her hair color. Most men considered her attractive and her spirited nature made her practically irresistible.

Heidi remained playful despite the look she received from her overly serious friend. "Well, are we going out or are you planning on an evening of cybersex with the Count?"

Cybil frowned, returned to her keyboard, and continued to type. "He's an interesting guy," she announced then muttered, "and we don't have cybersex."

"Yeah, interesting," Heidi scoffed. "If you're into the tall, dark, creepy type."

Heidi stood and paced the dimly lit room. She looked at the dismal furnishings and frowned her distaste.

"Actually, I am," Cybil replied while avoiding looking at her attractive friend.

Heidi rolled her eyes and groaned softly. "It's not normal. Your interest in the macabre."

"It's my dark side."

Heidi flopped down on Cybil's bed and immediately rolled into a seductive position. "You're certainly one of the more interesting roommates I've ever had." There was an awkward moment of silence as she stared at Cybil's face practically hidden behind her laptop screen. "So, are you going out with me tonight or not?"

"I don't know. It depends."

"Depends on what?"

Cybil finally looked up at her friend. "The Count wants me to come back on-line tonight so he can tell me about the Bloodletting Ritual."

Heidi appeared disgusted and sprang upward on the bed. "Bloodletting? How sick is that?"

"There's an entire history surrounding that island and the legend of vampires inhabiting it," Cybil informed her with enthusiasm. "You know that stuff fascinates me."

"Island?" Heidi suddenly asked, her eyes now sparkling. "He lives on an island?"

"Yeah. There's a small village near the island resort. It's not far from the abandoned castle," she replied. "It was believed the vampires inhabited the castle in the late 1400's."

Heidi frowned and slid off the bed. "Well, that ruined the whole island thing for me," she muttered. "Forget the Count. Get your ass into a revealing dress and let's get going. You're going to have a good time even if it kills me."

Heidi left the room without waiting for a response. Cybil considered not going out with her friend, but she probably wouldn't get a moment's peace all evening if she didn't. It was best to just suck it up and give into Heidi's whim.

✝

The popular city nightclub was buzzing with crowds of men and women dancing on the large dance floor, while others hung around the long bar and pub tables drinking and socializing. Cybil and Heidi squeezed through the crowd in their sexy, flattering dresses. Cybil was forced to wear one of her friend's dresses, per her insistence. She hated dressing as if she was out on the prowl, but Heidi enjoyed the free drinks Cybil refused to accept. Cybil was disinterested in the entire club scene and possibly a little subconscious about her revealing dress. Heidi, on the other hand, appeared lively and overly enthusiastic. She checked out the handsome men, who in turn checked her out as well.

They approached the bar and attempted to squeeze through to get drinks. A man in his late twenties approached them from behind and grabbed Cybil around the waist, holding her against him. Cybil jumped with a startled cry then looked over her shoulder to the grinning man. Josh Albright was a fairly attractive man with a modest build to compliment his 6'2" frame. He wasn't the sort of man women were magnetically drawn to, but he was able to secure dates with some frequency. Despite that, he seemed to prefer spending his time hanging out with Heidi and Cybil rather than finding viable companionship of his own. Cybil attempted to relax after her 'attack' and patted his hand.

"I didn't know you were going to be here tonight, Josh," she announced cheerfully to her friend. "You didn't return my call."

Josh laughed and finally released her, allowing her to breath. "I got your message late," he announced then grinned. "It's so unusual for you to be out, I just couldn't resist." He gave her a quick once over and nodded his approval. "Looking hot, Cyb."

Heidi appeared less than impressed with Cybil's friend and almost went out of her way to ignore him when they were together. Cybil didn't understand the contempt Heidi had for Josh. He was always nice to her and *rarely* made inappropriate remarks. Josh returned Heidi's unenthusiastic look and smirked.

"Heidi," he grunted a greeting.

"Josh," Heidi snarled back.

Heidi immediately returned her attention back to the bar and ordered some drinks. Josh eyed Cybil and raised his brows in silent question. Cybil managed a slight shrug.

†

Josh, Heidi, and Cybil walked on the sidewalk just outside the nightclub heading back for their apartment. It was already after one o'clock in the morning, and Heidi was once again drunk. She sang loud and terrible while following a few lengths behind Josh and Cybil. The couple did an amazing job at ignoring her horrible singing though several people shouted from bedroom windows.

"So when are you going to meet this mystery man, the Count?" Josh asked his friend.

Cybil laughed at the question. "Meeting men on the internet isn't big on my priority list. He's just fun to talk with." She considered her comment then sank into thought. "Though the history of that island is so fascinating. I'd love to visit a place so rich in culture and superstition."

He chuckled softly, mocking her. "You are one bizarre girl, Cyb."

Heidi clung to Cybil's shoulder from behind and half leaned on her while giggling drunkenly. "We should go to that island and hang out on the beach. Wouldn't that be fun?"

Josh eyed Heidi clinging to Cybil from behind. Her drunken condition didn't improve his feelings for her. Josh sank into thought then looked at Cybil and grinned almost deviously.

"You know, that's not a half bad idea," he announced with enthusiasm. "We could all go. Island resort, sandy beaches, girls in bikinis. Sounds like a blast." He then eyed Cybil and grinned. "And then you could meet this internet love of yours."

"I already told you, I don't want to meet him," Cybil insisted. "I'll admit I'm into other cultures and the darker side of humanity, but I think the Count would be a little darker than my comfort zone."

"Then don't tell him you're going," Heidi offered while giggling. "You can seek him out, get a good look at him, and then decide if you actually want to meet him. It'll be fun." She became drunkenly enthusiastic. "I think we should go."

"I don't know--" Cybil softly protested.

11

Josh half pushed Heidi out of the way and placed his arm around Cybil's shoulder. Heidi gave him an offended look then hurried to catch up with them.

"Oh, come on, Cybil," Josh announced cheerfully. "Where's your sense of adventure? The three of us have never been anywhere together. You two could share a room and save some of the expense. I haven't had a real vacation in years. I'll even spring for the airfare."

Heidi suddenly clung to Josh's free arm and nearly fell to the sidewalk. Her eyes immediately sparkled. "What time does the plane leave?"

Cybil looked at Josh and Heidi with some surprise. "You two are serious? You really want to go to this island?" she nearly gasped. "Do you have any idea what you're in for?"

"I'm open to new things," Josh replied without care. "Probably not much different then visiting Salem during Halloween. What do you say?"

Cybil stared at the two smiling faces staring back at her. She laughed softly and shook her head. "This should be a very interesting trip."

Chapter Three

The Night Crawler Resort was a beautiful, tropical resort comprised of a large main building, which was three stories tall and several smaller bungalow style buildings attached to it with enclosed walkways. Outdoor cabanas and a large pool added to the elegance and native appeal. The white sandy beach was well-maintained with lounging beds beneath canvas cabanas. Despite being a beautiful, warm morning, the beach was practically deserted. Josh, Heidi, and Cybil entered the main building lobby with their bags. All three looked around the rustic, tropical lobby containing mostly wood features, carved furniture, and fans lining the entire cathedral ceiling. The lobby appeared deserted as well.

Josh looked around with a slightly concerned look on his face. "This place looks dead."

Heidi giggled softly. "All the vampires must be in their coffins."

Cybil refrained from commenting. They approached the front desk tended by a young, female desk clerk. Angelica Tramaine stood behind the desk flipping through a magazine with the look of complete boredom. As her name suggested, Angelica had a certain 'girl-next-door' beauty with flowing golden-brown hair. They paused before the front desk and nearly startled the young woman. Angelica appeared embarrassed then smiled.

"Good afternoon," she chirped cheerfully. "Checking in?"

Josh smiled warmly at the attractive young woman and leaned casually on the desk. His suave attempt at flirting nearly had Cybil and Heidi laughing. "Yes," he announced in a voice deeper than usual. "We have reservations for two rooms. The name's Albright."

She checked the computer and smiled cheerfully. "Yes, I have your reservations right here."

"What's up with this place?" Heidi asked while again looking around. "Where is everyone?"

Angelica laughed softly. "Must be your first time here," she teased. "Everyone's asleep. The party lasts until the early morning hours. We're approaching our two hundred year anniversary of the Bloodletting Ritual. You'll see this place come to life somewhere around six o'clock tonight." She then took on a more serious tone. "If you're planning on attending the ritual, which I'm sure you are, you'll need to speak to our hotel manager, Brandon Carrington. He's in charge of arranging for guests to attend. He'll tell you about the rules."

"We'll be sure to catch up with him," Josh suavely announced and leaned a little further across the desk and read the name on her ID badge.

"He'll be here around seven tonight," Angelica announced. "Most of our staff works the evening shift, since that's when most of the hotel guests are up and about."

She handed them their room keys, which were old and rustic, similar to skeletons keys.

"You'll find your rooms down the corridor in the third bungalow on the second floor. Rooms 210 and 211," she announced cheerfully.

Josh took their keys and smiled with added charm while straightening. "Thank you very much, *Angelica.*"

They collected their luggage and walked back across the lobby.

✝

Heidi and Cybil walked along the beach, having changed into their bathing suits. Despite being almost noon, they were still the only guests on the beach. It seemed odd having the entire beach to themselves, although Cybil liked the solitude. Heidi wore her red skimpy, thong bikini while Cybil wore a less revealing black bikini with a sarong tied around her waist. They could see a breathtaking castle just off the beach nearly half a mile away. Both eyed the castle with some surprise and plenty of marvel.

"Who do you suppose lives there?" Heidi asked.

"The castle has been abandoned for over two hundred years," Cybil informed her friend. "Legend has it the vampires live there. It's the final destination of the Bloodletting Ritual. Locals believe if they donate blood to the vampires, they won't kill to acquire it."

Heidi glanced at Cybil and grinned teasingly. "You have too much time on your hands."

"The Count told me all about the island history," Cybil informed Heidi despite her possible lack of interest in history and facts. "Legend has it that evil vampires nearly destroyed the entire village on a vicious killing rampage. Several good vampires warded off the bad vampires and saved the village. The ritual is to show their continual gratitude to the vampires who saved them and to keep them in their good graces."

Heidi hid her smile and had to keep from laughing. "So the people on this island actually believe there are vampires living among them?"

Cybil nodded.

Heidi finally had to laugh. "Oh, this is going to be one hell of a week." She eyed her friend. "So what is the ritual like?"

"Similar to Spring Break, I'm told."

Heidi suddenly appeared pleased as her eyes nearly sparkled. "Like one big party?"

"Pretty much."

"You know, I may have been wrong about you."

✝

The lobby remained quiet and lifeless even toward evening. It seemed surprising that so many people didn't even show up for dinner. A handsome man in his early to mid-thirties, Brandon Carrington, stood behind the front desk with a large, well-built African-American man in his late twenties, Harford Mann. Brandon was ruggedly handsome with nearly black hair kept business short and the darkest eyes. Despite being average height, his broad chest and shoulders suggested he was somewhat muscular. Harford was a big man in both height and build. He had to be at least 6'4" and built like boxer. Despite his imposing build, his round face and baldhead gave him a boyish appeal. Josh, Heidi, and Cybil approached the front desk to finally meet the manager, who would arrange for them to partake in the ritual that evening. All still appeared amazed by the lifelessness of the lobby and the resort itself. They paused before the front desk and the two men, who appeared rather attentive.

"Angelica said we have to register with Brandon Carrington for the ritual celebration tonight," Josh announced to the men behind the desk.

Brandon pleasantly extended his hand to Josh. "I'm Brandon Carrington," he announced cheerfully. "Angelica mentioned the three of you would be stopping back." He released Josh's hand and offered a curious smile. "How much do you know about the Bloodletting Ritual?"

Josh chuckled lowly and appeared slightly embarrassed. "Not much, I'm afraid."

"I'd be happy to explain it to you."

Brandon walked around to the front of the desk and joined them on the other side. They walked with him across the lobby and sat on the handmade, tropical furniture.

"A little over two hundred years ago, legend has it a group of vampires saved the town from a bloody rampage of evil vampires," Brandon began. "To show their appreciation, the town gathered on the beach for a ceremony and a feast. To please the vampires, everyone would donate blood and present it to the good vampires as, well, sort of a sacrifice. In return, the good vampires would live in peace with the villagers and ward off any evil vampires. I guess, back then, it was the town's idea of health insurance." Brandon remained cheerful while continuing with the story. "So the ritual was continued over the years on a weekly, sometimes nightly basis. We begin with a bonfire and ceremony on the beach in front of the resort. The donated blood is then carried to the old castle and deposited within the courtyard. We then return to the beach for a buffet feast in honor of the good vampires." He had to hide his humored smile. "It's more of a party than anything."

Heidi appeared giddy with delight. "Sounds good to me. Where do I sign up?"

Brandon chuckled softly and maintained his cheerful mood. "We'll get to that shortly. First, there are some rules you must abide by before you're allowed to join the ritual."

All three listened with great interest. Cybil wasn't aware that there were rules regarding the ritual. Something the Count had failed to mention.

"Photography is not permitted," he informed them in a firm tone. "Supposedly it angers the vampires or some nonsense like that. And most importantly, you will be required to donate blood before you're allowed to attend." He was quick to answer their question before they could ask. "And before you ask, the reason behind that is a belief that the vampires look unfavorably upon those unwilling to participate fully. The villagers also fear they will show their displeasure by attacking the non-participant. Therefore, anyone not willing to donate won't be permitted to participate in the ritual. The people around here are very superstitious, and it's best not to offend them."

"Has anyone ever seen a vampire?" Heidi asked, although it was hard to tell if she was serious or mocking the ritual.

Josh and Cybil glared at Heidi, coming to their own conclusion for her asking. She continued to smile at Brandon and ignored them. Brandon returned the smile and appeared almost humored by her bold question.

"I couldn't say," he replied, "but I doubt they'd ever reveal themselves. So you never know." Brandon stood while maintaining his enthusiasm. "If there are no objections to the rules, I'd be happy to begin the donation procedure."

Josh appeared surprised and stared at the hotel manager. "You collect the blood?"

Brandon held back his laugh and grinned. "Not to worry, Mr. Albright. I'm also the local doctor. I just manage the resort as a side job. Many of us have more than one specialty." Brandon smiled slyly and raised his brows. "I could show you my license to practice. It's on the wall in my office."

Josh suddenly fidgeted and appeared embarrassed. "I didn't mean to offend you."

"You didn't," he replied without hesitation. "If you're ready, we should get started right away. The ritual is only a few hours away."

Chapter Four

Cybil uncertainly entered the doctor's office, being the last of her friends to offer her donation. Brandon, dressed in a white lab coat, stood by the counter in the office set up for exams, minor injuries, and light surgical procedures. Brandon hung an empty bag on the short pole alongside the exam table and looked at Cybil. He noted her tense look and smiled reassuringly.

"Make yourself comfortable," he announced. "This won't take long, I promise."

Cybil appeared uneasy as she shut the door behind her. Rather than approach the exam table, she nervously leaned against the door. "I think there's something I should tell you before we go any further."

Brandon turned, giving her his full attention, and appeared curious.

"I have a blood disorder," she gently informed him. "I'm not allowed to donate blood because of it."

Brandon smiled reassuringly and chuckled. "You have nothing to worry about, Ms. Brooklyn. I promise your blood won't be used for any sort of transfusions."

Cybil uncertainly moved onto the exam table and remained sitting. "Just so you understand. I wouldn't want anything to happen."

Brandon continued to smile and sat in the chair alongside the table. "Even if the blood were to be used for donations, it would be tested for any disorders or disease," he informed her then appeared curious. "What sort of blood disorder do you have?"

Cybil uncertainly lowered herself to the table and closely watched while he prepped her arm for the needle.

"I'm not really sure," she informed him. "I just know that I'm not supposed to donate blood."

"That's very responsible of you," he replied. "Small pinch."

Cybil watched as he inserted the needle into her vein. Surprisingly, she didn't flinch.

"Must be amusing to a doctor," she announced. "People celebrating something so unusual and bizarre."

"Not anymore unusual than celebrating Halloween or Mardi Gras. Mexico has their All Soul's Day," he offered. "It's my belief that the customs of other cultures should be embraced and not snickered at. You'll have a chance to meet many of the villagers tonight. They're wonderful, well-balanced men and women."

"Do you believe in vampires, Dr. Carrington?"

Brandon looked at her and chuckled softly. "I can't remember the last time someone's called me doctor." Brandon sat back in his chair and smiled gently. "Culture beliefs are very intriguing. When you're within a certain culture for any length of time, you tend to feel what they feel and believe what they believe," he informed her. "So, yes, I suppose I do believe in vampires." He shifted in his chair while studying her. "Have I ever treated anyone with a vampire bite? I can't say I have." He maintained his good sense of humor. "Beliefs are a very personal thing. I'd prefer you formed your own opinion during your stay here."

Cybil watched the blood run through the tube and into the bag. She glanced back at Brandon.

"I'm open to most beliefs and theories. I find it very fascinating."

"Then you should be in for a good time this week. I haven't seen many guests leave dissatisfied. Most enjoy the Mardi Gras type atmosphere." He sighed deeply. "Plenty of drinking and going wild."

Cybil laughed softly and looked up at the ceiling. "Well, that's not the type of atmosphere I'm looking for, but I'll take the good with the bad."

"So what did bring you here?"

"Just a general curiosity," she replied and met his gaze. "Things outside the norm have always fascinated me. My friends think I'm a bit odd."

"I have yet to meet someone who isn't."

Brandon stopped the blood flowing through the line and removed the needle from her arm. He applied a cotton ball with some pressure then applied a Band-Aid.

"You may want to remain still for a few minutes," he informed her. "You could become light-headed."

Brandon disconnected the tubing and carried the pint of blood to the refrigerator. Cybil slowly sat up and rubbed her arm. Brandon returned to her and watched as she stood with little difficulty. He gave her a slightly bewildered look.

"You seem to handle that blood loss rather well," he announced. "Most donors experience some dizziness."

"Must be that blood disorder."

Brandon smiled pleasantly. "Must be. Enjoy the festivities tonight."

Cybil smiled and left the office. Brandon shut the door behind her. He paused a moment, pondered something, and then sank deep into thought. He approached the nearby counter with the tubing still containing some blood, drained a few droplets of blood onto a hemoccult slide, and placed it beneath the microscope. He made himself comfortable on a nearby stool and examined the slide through the microscope. Something caught his attention. Brandon straightened while deep in thought and tapped his fingers on the counter. He finally removed the hemoccult slide from the microscope, hesitated a moment, and then dabbed his index finger into the blood on the glass. He licked the blood from his finger. He raised his brow with a curious look and then licked the glass slide clean.

†

Cybil walked along the lobby and looked around for her friends, but Heidi and Josh were nowhere to be found. She turned and suddenly collided with someone. A handsome man in his mid-thirties captured her elbows to keep her from losing her balance. Simon Vander stood before her with a pleasant smile. He was a Prince Charming sort of handsome with silky light brown hair and a boyish, baby face. He had a lean, sturdy build, suggesting he was athletic. Sapphire blue eyes finished off the complete Prince Charming package.

Cybil appeared mildly startled then embarrassed as she stared at the handsome man. "Oh, I'm so terribly sorry."

Simon appeared hesitant to release her and continued to smile. "Don't be." He finally released her, and they exchanged pleasant looks. "It's not every day a beautiful woman runs over me."

Cybil hid her embarrassed smile and blushed from the compliment.

Simon extended his hand to her. "I'm Simon Vander."

Cybil accepted his hand and politely shook it. "Cybil Brooklyn."

Simon's smile brightened considerably. "Cybil? What an interesting name."

"Named after my great-grandmother."

"I wasn't holding out much hope for this vacation, but it's starting to look up," Simon announced and studied her with great interest. "Will I see you at the ritual tonight?"

"My friends and I will be attending, of course."

Brandon appeared behind the front desk and looked toward the couple with more than a passing interest. Their encounter seemed to annoy him.

"Great," Simon announced cheerfully. "I'll look for you there."

Simon released her hand and continued to stare at her even as she turned and walked away. Simon stared after her, smiled warmly, then turned and approached the desk with his overnight bag. He set his bag on the floor and smiled at Harford.

"Simon Vander checking in."

Harford smiled pleasantly and checked the computer. "Yes," he announced politely. "You've reserved our Presidential Suite."

Brandon continued to study Simon from his position toward the back of the desk. He appeared annoyed and returned to his office down the hall.

Chapter Five

That evening, the entire beach was lined with bamboo torches staked in the sand. A huge bonfire was set ablaze in the center of the beach while several hundred people gathered for the Bloodletting Ritual. Village men and women were dressed in brightly colored, tropical clothing. The women wore fresh flowers in their hair, and the men wore flowing robes. As spectators arrived on the beach, they were each given a flower and garlic leis to ward off evil vampires. Each guest was given a candle in a cross-shaped candlestick holder to carry on his or her journey to the castle courtyard. Most of the guests wore casual beachwear, sundresses, or colorful outfits, and the women were also given flowers for their hair. The ritual began with the villagers dancing around the bonfire to the lively tropical music. The women chanted and tossed powder into the fire, which caused the flames to erupt briefly upward. The guests cheered each time the flames erupted.

The blood donations were contained within a large elegant, carved wooden box. It was carried out on a stretcher of sorts with six men carrying the stretcher, almost like a casket. The chanting continued along with the music and dancing. The candles were now lit and the procession proceeded toward the old abandoned castle in the distance. Everyone traveled in pairs behind the donation. Two men leading the procession carried large crosses and candles. Attractive, young village women tossed flower petals just behind the lead men, littering the beach with the fresh petals. Josh walked alongside Angelica, which suited him just fine, while Cybil walked alongside Heidi. Heidi made faces several times and nudged Cybil with a humored look, refusing to take it seriously. Cybil attempted to ignore her friend's humored looks.

The entire procession entered the castle courtyard. Flower petals from days and weeks past remained scattered along the courtyard floor. As the group entered, the newcomers looked around the spooky courtyard with concern and possible fright. Cybil was just as curious as most. Shadows seemed to lurk in every corner, almost as if they were being watched. They placed the donation box into the center of the courtyard, where a small ritual was performed, adding to the tensions of the newcomers. Once the ritual was complete, they filed out in the same order. Cybil continued to survey the courtyard and the castle walls, causing her to shiver. Her candle suddenly extinguished. Heidi glanced at her then her candle. None of the other candles had extinguished. Heidi lit Cybil's candle with hers as they continued from the castle.

Once they returned to the beach, the cross candlesticks were returned to a nearby table. A buffet feast was laid out on a table near the pool along with the open bar. Everyone now ate, drank, and danced to modern music provided by a DJ. The party was filled with fun and laughter. Angelica returned to the hotel, leaving Josh moderately disappointed. Heidi finished her large drink and was already working on her second in record time.

"Well, that was bizarre and twisted," Heidi remarked and held back her drunken laugh. "Could that castle be creepier?"

"I have to admit," Josh announced, "even I got an uneasy feeling inside that courtyard."

"And what was with your candle, Cybil?" Heidi almost demanded. "Do you suppose the vampires have chosen their virgin sacrifice?"

Cybil glared at her friend with a slightly annoyed smirk. "Very funny, Heidi."

Josh looked around the beach then saw Brandon talking with some of the other tourists. "There's Brandon," he announced while grinning slyly. "I think I'll just go over there and ask him."

Cybil felt her cheeks redden at the suggestion. The virgin jokes came out at least once a week, and they were getting old. "Do and die."

A voluptuous blonde woman wearing a sexy flower print bikini and matching sarong stood near the bar with a large, exotic drink in her hand. Josh took in an eyeful of the woman and nearly choked on his drink. As she looked in his direction, he smiled almost helpless to her nearly perfect body. Jersey flashed a smile at him, indicating her interest as well. Her lavish, flower only leis hung at just the right length to draw attention to her ample breasts barely contained within her bikini top.

"Check out that hot number," Josh nearly gasped. "If you ladies will excuse me--" Josh hurried across the beach.

Heidi watched him make a fool of himself while practically running to join the sexy woman at the bar. She shook her head. "He's such a little lapdog."

Cybil hid her smile, knowing Josh and Heidi were almost identical in their behavior around the opposite sex, even though neither would ever admit it. Brandon joined them and smiled pleasantly. Heidi appeared a little more than pleased to see the handsome man. In her nearly drunken condition, any handsome man would do.

"Are you ladies enjoying the festivities?" he asked.

"I'm having a great time," Heidi announced cheerfully while holding up her drink. "I don't know what they put in these drinks, but they're excellent."

Brandon chuckled softly. "Better watch. They can sneak up on you."

Heidi giggled in a flirtatious manner, placed her hand on Brandon's lower arm, and smiled seductively. "I don't mind. I'm going to have a good time even if it kills me."

Brandon continued to smile but didn't comment. He then glanced at Cybil. "And what about you, Miss Brooklyn? Are you enjoying the festivities?"

Heidi continued to flirt with Brandon by clinging to his shoulder and playing with his jacket. Cybil appeared slightly embarrassed by her friend's flirtatious behavior. She managed a smile and tried to ignore Heidi's hands on the good doctor.

"Yes, I'm having a wonderful time. Thank you."

Brandon casually maneuvered himself away from Heidi while maintaining his pleasant smile. "If you ladies need anything, just let me know."

Heidi suddenly appeared drunkenly humored and was about to comment when Cybil grabbed her arm, stopping her from embarrassing herself further.

Cybil smiled at Brandon. "We'll be sure to do that."

She pulled Heidi away from Brandon before she caused a scene. Heidi giggled while staggering alongside Cybil.

"Oh, Cybil," Heidi announced almost too loudly. "Always trying to protect my reputation. When will you ever give it up?"

"When you're married and no longer care to flirt."

Heidi suddenly laughed. "And you think that would stop me?" She waved off her friend. "Besides, I'm never getting married. A husband would just get in the way of my loose lifestyle."

"At least you admit it," Cybil muttered. "Come on. Let's sober you up."

"This is a party, and I don't have to drive," Heidi suddenly announced and glared at her friend. "Lighten up, will you."

Heidi finished her drink then looked around the hustling party of villagers and tourists alike dancing around the bonfire. She giggled and joined the dancing. Cybil groaned and shook her head while watching. It was going to be a long night. A shadow fell over Cybil, causing her to turn and look behind her. Simon stood alongside her with a charming smile on his handsome face.

"So, we meet again," he teased.

Cybil couldn't help but admire his radiant smile and hid her grin. "I thought you'd changed your mind about the festivities. I didn't see you earlier."

"I hadn't changed my mind, I just don't care for their bizarre tradition," Simon informed her. "I can handle the aftermath party. I'm actually just here to get away from the hustle of city life."

"So you don't believe in vampires, Mr. Vander?" she lightly teased.

"Please, call me Simon." His mocking smile almost answered her question. "I'm afraid I'm the type who has to be able to see and touch something to believe it's real. Makes me a bit dull, I suppose."

Cybil had to admit, she was taken by the handsome man. He was almost too suave to be true. "Nothing wrong with keeping your feet planted firmly on the ground. Rational people help keep the dreamers from getting too far out of touch with reality."

Simon laughed then casually captured her hand, taking her by surprise. "I like that analogy. Would you care for a drink?"

"I've had one, thanks. They're a bit strong."

Simon guided her toward the bar near the swimming pool and appeared intrigued. "A woman who likes to keep her wits about her? I like that."

"I'm the responsible one." Cybil nodded toward the happily dancing Heidi. "Someone has to look after Heidi. She tends to drink excessively and get herself into bad situations."

Simon affectionately squeezed her hand and smiled charmingly. "We'll have to see about you having some fun for a change."

Cybil hid her smile as they approached the bar. Brandon watched them pass from a distance. His look was almost harsh and evil. As it grew later, Cybil and Simon had fun dancing around the bonfire with the rest of the tourists and villagers. Cybil appeared more carefree then earlier, suggesting she may have been on the verge of being drunk herself. One of the female villagers showed her interesting, ethnic dance steps. Cybil imitated the woman's movements until they had the entire dance sequence.

Everyone cheered and laughed along as the women danced and put on a slightly sexy dance show. One of the male villagers stole Cybil away to dance with her. She found it very entertaining. Simon didn't appear the least bit threatened and ended up dancing with the aggressive village woman. When the village man released Cybil for a moment longer than he should have, Simon pulled her into his arms, stealing her away, and danced with her. The village man appeared disappointed but quickly found a replacement. Everyone seemed to be having a great time. Cybil laughed while dancing the fast song with Simon. A woman bumped into Cybil, knocking her off balance. She fell to the sand anticipating a soft landing but felt a sharp sting instead. She suddenly let out a painful cry, more than that of surprise. Cybil clutched her thigh then lifted her hand to reveal a large amount of blood. Simon lowered himself to her side and looked at her bleeding leg with concern.

"Are you okay?" he asked. "What happened?"

The village woman saw the blood on Cybil's hand, stopped dancing, and gasped loud enough for others to hear. "You're bleeding!"

Simon helped Cybil to her feet to reveal broken glass tinted with blood in the sand. Some careless person left their glass or dropped it, making for a disastrous situation. Cybil's thigh contained a two-inch gash that bled freely down her leg. Simon briefly examined the cut with growing concern. Several others took notice and appeared horrified when they saw the blood.

The village man quickly approached. "You must see the doctor immediately," he informed her with a frightened look on his face. "You can't be out here bleeding like that." He looked to the sky. "It's like being in the ocean with sharks. The scent of blood may attract the vampires."

Josh saw what had happened and hurried toward her. He too observed the freely bleeding cut then removed his handkerchief and applied it to her thigh.

"Let's get you inside and take care of that," Josh announced.

"I'll take her to the doctor," Simon insisted. "No reason for you to keep your date waiting."

Josh remained concerned for Cybil and took her arm as she held the handkerchief to her leg. He glanced at Simon and attempted a smile. "That's okay. She's my friend. I'll take care of her."

Josh didn't even give his date or Simon a second thought.

Cybil gave Simon a sympathetic look and grimaced slightly. "I'm sorry if I ruined your evening," she announced timidly.

Simon smiled and waved her off. "Don't be silly. I'll see you in the morning."

Josh helped Cybil limp away from the bonfire and toward the resort. Jersey appeared annoyed, huffed at the unfolding situation, and stormed down to the water.

Chapter Six

Brandon stood behind the front desk with Harford, having what appeared to be quite the conversation. Whatever their discussion, it didn't stop either man from accomplishing their paperwork. Josh helped Cybil across the lobby while she clutched the bloody cloth to her thigh and limped severely alongside him. Both men looked at them from the desk. Brandon rushed out from behind the desk and hurried to assist.

"What happened?" he asked, immediately noticing the bloodied cloth. "Are you all right?"

"She fell onto someone's wineglass on the beach," Josh informed him with a hint of annoyance. "I don't know who the hell had a glass container on the beach in the first place."

Brandon removed the bloody cloth from her thigh and glanced at the cut. "Better get her into my office," he announced. "There's still some glass fragments stuck in there. She's going to need stitches."

Cybil cringed at the thought, but she knew it was probably necessary the moment she saw all the blood.

†

Cybil attempted to relax on the exam table while Brandon removed the bloody cloth to examine the cut. It wasn't bleeding nearly as badly as a few minutes ago, but the gash was gaping and oozing.

Josh remained near the door looking slightly pale. He fidgeted then pointed to the door. "I'll, uh, just wait in the lobby."

He bolted from the exam room without awaiting confirmation that they'd heard him. It was possible he intended to purge his dinner. As Brandon cleaned sand from the wound, Cybil cringed and endured the pain. She thought she could watch, but it only made her nauseous. She finally had to look away.

"I see the glass fragment," Brandon announced then glanced at her and attempted a sensitive smile. "I'll numb the area first, since I need to suture it anyway."

"I appreciate that."

Brandon approached the nearby counter and drew some liquid anesthetic into a needle. Cybil half watched him then groaned disgusted with herself and the evening.

"Well, it was fun for a while," she muttered just loud enough for him to hear.

Brandon smiled and chuckled softly while returning to his stool alongside the exam table. He injected the needle around the wound. Cybil cringed from the first prick but barely felt those that followed. It didn't take long to numb the area.

"You still have a few more evenings to enjoy the festivities," he informed her while working on removing the glass fragment with a sterile tweezers. "--and your new friend."

Cybil glanced back at him while he worked, saw the bloodied tweezers in his hand, and quickly looked away.

"Nothing like needing medical attention on your first date," she remarked. "That and my overly protective guard dog, Josh."

"I know women who would die for that sort of attention."

"Perhaps, but it makes dating for either of us very difficult," she informed him. "I wouldn't doubt his date ran off with my date."

Brandon chuckled softly then dropped the bloody glass fragment into a small bowl. "That wasn't so bad, was it?" He resumed cleaning the wound with a certain seriousness. "You're lucky this wasn't any deeper."

"Yeah, I would have attracted every vampire in the neighborhood," she announced with a soft chuckle. "You should have seen how freaked the locals were."

"I can imagine," he announced without looking up from the gash on her leg. "A small cut sends them into a state near panic. We go through vampire scares like thunderstorms."

Brandon finally finished cleaning her wound then proceeded to suture the gash.

"So there have been suspicious incidents?" she asked with some surprise.

"Usually just dog bites," he replied casually. "I know what a dog bite looks like, and I can't be convinced a dog bite is a vampire bite. The town tends to believe the dog bite victim lied so they wouldn't have a stake run through their heart." He shook his head with disgust. "Maybe if they'd keep their mutts on leashes, we'd have less problems."

Cybil laughed softly while attempting to relax. "It's always fun to imagine a whole world out there that we know nothing about, but that changes the moment we realize it's actually real."

"I suppose the thought of dying takes some of the fun out of it, but--" he began then hesitated a moment to grin while closing her wound, "--we have yet to lose a single tourist to a vampire bite." He smirked and withheld his chuckle. "Causalities to careless drinkers though are plentiful, but I think you'll live."

He finished the last stitch then proceeded to dress the wound. Cybil propped herself up on her elbows and resumed watching.

She then teased, "But will I be safe from those thirsty vampires who may have caught the scent of my young, virgin blood?"

Brandon didn't look up, but he chuckled low in his throat. "I can't make any promises," he teased. "I have very little malpractice insurance." He patted her leg, although she didn't appear to feel it. "All better."

Brandon stood and removed his gloves, tossing them into the red biohazard bin.

Cybil slowly stood as he washed his hands. "Can't wait to see that bill."

Brandon dried his hands and turned back to her with a pleasant smile. "This resort is all-inclusive, remember? I wouldn't dream of charging for my medical services." He then reconsidered the comment. "Unless I'm woken from my sleep, then I tend to be a bit cranky."

Cybil appeared surprised and delighted by the free of charge medical service. "That's very noble of you, Dr. Carrington."

Brandon remained humored and smiled pleasantly. "Please, call me Brandon. Whenever someone calls me doctor, I fear flocks of lawyers will start to swarm. Personally," he announced with a sigh, "I prefer the company of vampires over that of lawyers."

Cybil laughed softly and found herself smiling at him. Not only a handsome man, but also he had quite the personality as well. "I really appreciate the medical attention--Brandon. If you won't accept payment, I'll just have to think of another way to repay you."

"Completely unnecessary," he announced then hesitated. "Unless you're offering to have dinner with me. In which case, I'd probably reconsider."

"Dinner it is," she replied cheerfully. "Tomorrow night?"

"I just happen to have an empty spot on my calendar from eight o'clock until the turn of the century," he remarked. "I think I can fit you in."

Cybil smiled then studied him with great interest. "You're very easy to talk to. I usually have a difficult time around people I don't know well." She suddenly laughed. "That drink I had must've been stronger than I thought."

Brandon continued to smile and casually leaned against the counter. "Those drinks do tend to bring out the demon in most."

Cybil suddenly sank into thought then appeared embarrassed. "I seem to recall some risqué dancing. Guess I'll be feeling some embarrassment tomorrow." She laughed softly. "Oh, well. If you can't make a fool of yourself from time to time, who'd want you?"

She turned toward the door and limped with some discomfort. Brandon joined her and walked her to the door while supporting her by her elbow.

"Should I find your friend in the lobby to help you?"

Cybil paused by the door and glanced at him, pleased with his bedside manner. "No, that's okay. It's not that far to the lobby. I can make it."

"I'll walk you out."

Cybil looked back at Brandon and stared a moment longer then she should have. She felt herself blushing slightly. "Thanks again for tonight."

Brandon chuckled softly. "Thanks for not vomiting in my office."

Cybil laughed softly then studied him once again. A warm smile suddenly crossed her face. "A free dinner hardly seems thanks enough." She moved closer and kissed him warmly on the lips.

Brandon either was taken by surprise or was resisting her affection. She felt a little subconscious and pulled away. She'd never been that forward with a man before, so it had to be the drink. Before she could apologize, he took a quick step closer, pulled her into his arms, and returned the kiss, startling her. As his hand slipped behind her neck, the garlic and flower leis suddenly broke and fell to the floor between them. Cybil seized the opportunity and returned the kiss, increasing Brandon's desire. He kissed her passionately and with a little more aggression. His foot casually pushed the leis across the floor and away from them. As she felt his

31

rising desire, Cybil realized she needed to put on the brakes before it went too far. She gently broke off the kiss and attempted to hide her blushing face.

"This really isn't like me," she gently informed him.

Brandon quickly pulled away with embarrassment and released her. He looked down while fidgeting, rubbed his temple, and then turned away. "My fault; I'm sorry."

Cybil shifted uncomfortably and managed a tiny smile. "I just had too much to drink, that's all," she informed him gently. "I'm not blaming you for my actions."

Brandon kept his back to her, unable to face her after his behavior. He attempted to control his heavy breathing then ran his tongue over his exposed fangs. As his tongue brushed over the sharpened teeth, he frowned almost painfully.

"Don't apologize," he announced gently. "It's okay, trust me."

Cybil remained embarrassed and didn't like that he was too ashamed even to face her. "Are you sure it's okay?"

Brandon finally turned to face her and smiled pleasantly, his fangs once again gone. "Of course I'm sure," he announced then gently cleared his throat. "I'll escort you to the lobby. You should really have your friend take you to your room and get off that leg."

Cybil managed a smile although she remained embarrassed. "We're still on for dinner tomorrow night, right?"

"Absolutely."

Brandon opened the office door and extended his hand to the hallway.

†

Josh helped the limping Cybil along the hallway toward their rooms, which they now regretted the second floor view. The steps were a joy and the walk was painfully long. As they approached her room, she finally looked at her friend.

"Are you going back down to the party?"

"I don't think so," Josh replied now lacking enthusiasm. "Somehow I doubt I'd enjoy myself much. Jersey's probably mad at me for taking off like I did." He groaned softly. "I don't need to deal with an irate woman, especially one I barely know." He cast a look at Cybil. "It's bad enough when familiar ones yell at me. I don't need it from strangers."

"You didn't have to dump her to help me," Cybil protested. "Simon was willing--"

"Simon was willing all right," Josh scoffed with annoyance. "Trying to get you drunk from what I was seeing. I saw you two carrying on and the way you were dancing with him like that. That's not like you at all."

"It wasn't his fault," she protested. "That drink was strong. I only had the one, you know."

"No matter. I don't trust the guy."

Cybil rolled her eyes and shook her head. A shadow moved along the ceiling near them from behind. She suddenly stopped and looked around them with an odd feeling of concern.

Josh became alarmed and looked around as well. "What? What's wrong?"

Neither saw anything.

Cybil insecurely rubbed her arms. "It was nothing. I just got this odd feeling--" Cybil nervously looked around and felt chilled. "Almost like we were being watched."

Josh groaned lowly and refrained from rolling his eyes. "Not again. You go through this every so many months." His stare was demanding. "Starts to creep me out after a while."

"Sorry."

They finally approached her bedroom door. Cybil removed her key, unlocked the door, and looked at her friend.

"Good night, Josh."

"See you in the morning."

Cybil smiled her gratitude then entered her room, shutting the door behind her. A shadow rolled along the corridor ceiling. Josh hesitated then tensed and nervously looked around him. He appeared uneasy a moment, brushed it aside, and then continued for his room next door.

Chapter Seven

Cybil slept peacefully on her handmade, bamboo-framed bed while the beach party was still going strong outside her open bedroom window. There was no telling what time Heidi would be coming to bed, and Cybil wasn't letting that interrupt her sleep for a change. She'd spent too many nights worrying about her friend and tonight Heidi had made it perfectly clear she didn't need Cybil or Josh interfering in her good time. A shadow moved past the open window bringing about a slightly cool breeze. Cybil's eyes suddenly opened as if for no apparent reason. She looked at the partially open window and the light outside filtering in from the all-night beach party.

For some reason, she felt compelled to sit up partially in bed and stare at the window a moment longer. She finally glanced at the bedside clock and saw it was nearly five in the morning. She glanced at the empty bed next to hers. It was still made from that afternoon. Despite her insistence she wasn't going to interfere in Heidi's poor decisions, she groaned softly and got out of bed anyway.

†

Cybil limped into the brightly lit lobby while still half asleep. She was now dressed casually in shorts and a sweatshirt, for some reason feeling slightly chilled despite the tropical island location. Harford stood behind the desk while reading a book and appeared completely absorbed in the medical thriller. A shadow rolled along the wall behind Cybil, but when she turned to look, there was nothing there. She stared in the direction of the elevator for a long, nervous moment. It was odd, but she almost felt as if she were being watched. She let the feeling pass, uncertainly turned, and collided with Brandon. Cybil gasped with surprise and jumped away from him while dramatically clutching her chest. Brandon managed a slightly humored smile at her reaction.

"You gave me quite a scare," he teased.

Cybil felt her beating heart through her chest while gasping. "Me?"

Brandon looked past her toward the elevator then met her gaze. "Something back there?"

Cybil appeared slightly disoriented. "No," she quickly replied then hesitated. "Well, I thought I saw something." She shook her head and attempted a tiny smile. "I woke up and discovered Heidi hadn't returned to our room, so I thought I should check on her. You know, make sure she didn't pass out on the beach."

"Believe it or not, we have someone who does that," he announced.

Cybil couldn't help but laugh even though she knew he was serious. "Still, I'd like to have a look for myself."

"It gets pretty raw out there at this hour," he admitted. "I'd better walk along. No telling what you might see. You're liable to get one hell of an education."

✝

The beach had a completely different mood in the early morning hour. The bonfire smoldered while several couples were seen making out beneath blankets. It was quite possible some were doing more than just making out. Drunken men and women stumbled about, clinging to objects, arguing with others just as incoherent, and cursing at one another. In addition to that, there were others who randomly vomited wherever the mood struck them. Security guards appeared as plentiful as the clean-up crew. Cybil was amazed at the sheer number of guests passed out on the beach, half-expecting to find Heidi among them. She saw several men and women, who were barely dressed, one man who was obviously urinating into the surf, and a couple engaged in oral sex near a distant rock formation. Cybil looked around with some embarrassment and slight discomfort. She attempted a tiny smile while barely looking at Brandon.

35

"I see what you mean."

"It's what some people come here for. Our security team does a fine job at keeping control." He managed a soft laugh. "Can't force morals on anyone. There comes a point when everyone needs to take some responsibility for their own actions." He then appeared curious. "Do you think your friend may have gone off with a male friend?"

Cybil attempted to hold back her laugh at his polite way of asking if Heidi had 'hooked up' then smiled shyly. "It's very likely. Heidi tends to share male company with amazing frequency. I'm able to save her from herself one out of ten times," she admitted. "Josh takes bets on which guy in a crowd she'll take home."

Another drunk man urinated just before them. Brandon placed his arm around her shoulder and immediately redirected her, so she wouldn't have to witness it.

"This is the less glamorous side to the festivities," Brandon announced with moderate embarrassment himself.

Cybil avoided looking at a couple groping each other while lying on the beach and making out. Brandon kept his arm around her.

"Not all of our guests go to this extreme," he insisted. "Most just enjoy a good time then go to their rooms around three or four in the morning. After four, well, those are our hardcore, Woodstock types. The same ones nearly every night."

Both looked around the beach before them. A man chased a playfully screaming, half naked woman. Brandon didn't even flinch at the sight of her happily jiggling breasts.

"That young lady came here quiet and reserved," he informed her. "Been running around wild and naked ever since."

An excessively drunken man approached them and smiled at Cybil. "Hey, babe. Why don't you lose the straight-arrow and go with me. I'll show you a good time."

Cybil appeared uneasy and clung to Brandon.

Brandon glared at the man and showed no emotions. "The lady doesn't want to be bothered. Now leave us."

The man stopped and stared at them with surprise. They walked past at a casual pace and easily ignored him. Cybil didn't release Brandon's midsection.

"Now I see why you have so much security."

The man suddenly appeared alongside them and caught Cybil's arm, despite Brandon's arm around her. Cybil appeared alarmed and let out a startled cry. Brandon suddenly whirled Cybil into his right arm and against him then blocked the man with his left arm. He stared him down with a calm but threatening look.

"Don't--" Brandon snarled lowly. "That's your last warning."

The man became angry and made a motion to punch Brandon. Two security guards approached, startling the man. He took one look at security and ran off. Security followed him at a slower pace. Brandon casually returned Cybil to his left arm. She attempted to look back at the activity then returned to clinging to Brandon.

"I think I've seen enough for one night."

Brandon casually turned her back toward the resort. She continued to cling to him then buried her head into his chest to avoid looking at a naked man passed out on the beach.

"I suppose you did try to warn me." As they neared the hotel, she looked up at him and attempted a smile. "Thanks for walking along. Had I been alone, I'm sure I would've caused a scene."

"I never would have let you go out there alone," he insisted. "I would hate to see you corrupted for life after all that."

Cybil and Brandon entered the lobby together from the beachside entrance. He gently rubbed her shoulder then removed his arm from around her.

"I'll see you back to your room."

Cybil smiled gently and continued to cling to his arm as they casually walked in the direction of her bungalow. They walked at a leisurely pace along the hallway.

She glanced at him and smiled warmly with some embarrassment. "I really feel I must ask--"

Brandon glanced at her with a smile and great interest.

"How is it possible that you're still single?" She suddenly hesitated and blushed. "I mean, are you the ultimate confirmed bachelor? A closet playboy? I just can't figure you out."

Brandon hid his smile. "Actually, I was married very happily for many years. Very sweet, gentle lady, but she died a few years back."

Cybil became unusually uncomfortable and sympathetic. "Oh, I'm sorry. I didn't mean to come on to you, I mean, had I known."

Brandon patted her hand warmly and smiled as they stopped just outside her room. "Don't apologize. We eventually have to move on."

"But in your office--"

"Around here, women make passes all the time. If it bothered me, I would have made it known."

Cybil attempted a smile. "I still feel bad."

"I don't." Brandon leaned closer and gently kissed her on the lips. He pulled away and smiled warmly. "Pleasant dreams, Cybil."

She smiled warmly then watched him walk away. She sighed and allowed her head to fall black against the door. There had to be something wrong with him. He seemed too perfect.

Chapter Eight

The sun was rising over the horizon on the nearly deserted beach. A majority of the guards had finished their shift, since most of the guests had gone to bed. A young couple made out near the rocks in the shadow, kissing and groping each other. Heidi was lowered to the beach as she moaned softly with her eyes shut. The man lying partially on top of her kissed her neck then along the revealing neckline of her sundress. It wasn't long before their silhouettes came together in the missionary position. Their sexual acts were clear even despite the shadows.

Heidi clung to the man on top of her and moaned drunkenly with pleasure as he pressed against her. He aggressively kissed her mostly naked chest just above her tan line. Heidi continued to moan beneath his writhing body. As he picked up the pace, she moaned louder. As he kissed her above her breast, his lips parted to reveal his sharp vampire fangs. Without missing a stride, he sank his fangs into her bosom. Heidi gasped with surprise and pain, winced as if momentarily paralyzed, and then clung to him while moaning. He continued grinding his hips against hers while sensually sucking blood from her body.

†

The morning sun brightened the entire bedroom, waking Cybil and nearly blinding her. She stumbled from her bed and shut the curtains with a weary groan. Despite having gone to bed much earlier than most, she was still exhausted. She glanced at Heidi's bed and saw her friend buried beneath the covers including her head. Cybil was relieved her friend had made it back to their room and approached her bed.

"What time did you get in last night?" There was no response. Cybil sat on the edge of Heidi's bed and gently nudged the massive lump beneath the covers. "Come on, Heidi. It's your own fault if you're hung over."

There was still no response. Cybil tapped her with a little more vigor. She still didn't move. There was a moment's hesitation then Cybil uncertainly reached for the covers over her head.

"Heidi?" she gasped softly with concern.

Heidi whipped the covers from her head, startling Cybil, and glared at her friend through bloodshot eyes. Her hair and make-up were messed, and she looked like hell.

"Will you just let me sleep?" Heidi scoffed. "I feel like shit! Are you happy?"

She pulled the sheets back over her head and curled up in a small blanket cocoon.

"Serves you right for making me worry," Cybil announced and sprang up from the bed. "Who was he this time?"

"Don't know; didn't ask; don't care," she muttered from beneath the covers. "I just want to sleep. Don't wake me until dinner."

"Well, it's just going to be you and Josh," she informed her friend. "I'm having dinner with someone tonight."

Heidi suddenly poked her head out from the covers and gave her a strange look. "You? With who?"

"I'm not telling," Cybil taunted. "You'll just have to get your sad ass out of bed and find out."

Heidi covered her face and groaned. "You're too weird to be true."

†

A little later that morning, Cybil approached the outdoor pavilion on the patio just outside the dining room. She looked around then noticed Josh sitting at a table with the excessively voluptuous Jersey. She looked absolutely stunning in her strapless bikini, and Cybil was certain Josh took in more than an eyeful of her ample breasts attempting to spring free from the bikini top. Despite having brunch plans with Josh, Cybil considered leaving them to their privacy then reconsidered and approached the couple.

"I hope you don't mind that Jersey joins us," Josh announced cheerfully.

"No, of course not."

They exchanged pleasant smiles as Cybil joined them at the table.

"Have you two made any plans for today or do you mind a third wheel?" Cybil asked.

"You're the ones traveling together. I'm the third wheel," Jersey insisted. "If you don't mind my tagging along, I'll join you."

"Well, I actually wanted to take a walk," Cybil replied. "Check out the old castle."

"Acht," Josh reminded. "That's off-limits, remember?"

"Says who?" she demanded.

"Says the sign on the beach," he retorted.

"I didn't see that sign." Cybil grinned slyly. "I just want to have a quick look around."

"That sounds like fun," Jersey chirped.

Josh groaned lowly. "Great. Now it's two to one on the side of danger."

✝

Josh, Cybil, and Jersey walked along the beach toward the castle in the near distance. The flower petals were now dried and wilted from the previous night's festivities. The castle was just up ahead, and it looked almost as spooky during the day as it had at night; perhaps even more so.

Josh frowned and made an effort to stop their approach. "I'm not sure I like this idea."

Cybil grabbed his arm and pulled him along. "Come on, you wuss. All the vampires are tucked away in their coffins, remember?"

Within a few minutes, all three entered the castle courtyard through the latched, iron gate. Jersey and Cybil now joined Josh in his tense state. The flower petals remained on the stone courtyard floor, but the decorative chest containing the blood donations was gone. All three looked around the courtyard and then to the creepy castle.

"This place is even creepier during the day," Josh announced.

Cybil looked at the castle windows and saw a shadow move away. She appeared puzzled by what she possibly saw. There certainly couldn't be anyone within the castle. It was abandoned; except for the vampires. Josh noted her stare, looked around nervously, and became even more paranoid.

"What is it?" he nearly gasped.

"Just mother," she muttered under her breath.

Josh looked confused. "Huh?"

She shook her head. "I thought I saw someone in the upstairs window. It's just my imagination."

Josh grabbed Cybil's arm and immediately panicked. "Then we'd better get out of here before we get into trouble."

Jersey laughed softly, catching their attention. "Don't tell me you're actually afraid of some mythological creature that can't even come out in the daylight."

Josh glared at her and appeared insulted. "Of course not," he scoffed. "It's just that we're not supposed to be here. We could get kicked off the island."

Cybil glanced at Jersey and grinned slyly. "Should we check it out?"

Jersey returned the smile and eagerly nodded. Both women approached the castle doors, forcing Josh to bring up the rear. Josh was becoming more skittish by the minute as he nervously followed. Jersey and Cybil attempted to open the door, but it wouldn't budge.

Jersey frowned with disappointment. "Not part of the show. I suppose they'd prefer if we stayed out."

"This area is off-limits," a man gruffly announced from behind them.

All three turned to see a security guard standing just within the courtyard entrance. Victor was a menacing looking man with a military buzz cut and a muscular build. He was almost certainly one of the guards Cybil had seen patrolling the beach last night.

"Let's go," Victor ordered.

They shamefully walked away from the castle and joined the guard by the entrance. The castle door slowly opened as they left the courtyard. A low, soft growl was heard from the dark opening.

Chapter Nine

Victor approached the front desk with his morning catch of the day. Josh, Cybil, and Jersey shared the same look of shame, mostly because they'd been caught. They stopped before the desk where Angelica was working. She eyed the security guard in silent question.

"I found these three trespassing on the castle grounds," Victor informed her in a serious, gruff tone. He certainly wasn't about to let them off with a warning. "Where's Brandon?"

"He asked not to be disturbed," Angelica informed the guard, "but I'll notify him when he returns."

Victor wasn't satisfied with the answer, but he finally nodded then left. Josh frowned while hiding his embarrassment and avoided looking at Angelica.

"Pretty serious guy, huh?" Jersey huffed while folding her arms across her ample bosom.

Angelica appeared slightly irritated while eying Jersey then focused her hostility on Josh. "He's just doing his job," she snapped. "There are signs posted everywhere about staying off the castle property. The village police tend to deal harshly with tourists who feel the need to poke around the castle." Her eyes narrowed slightly while glaring at the three. "The villagers believe it invokes the vampires."

Josh glared at Cybil and muttered lowly, "Told you so."

"I'm sure Brandon will overlook the first offense," Angelica announced with little kindness in her tone, "but I wouldn't attempt it again or you could be looking at a hefty fine and a night in jail if the village police get involved."

Josh attempted an uneasy chuckle, grabbed Cybil's arm, and flashed a smile at Angelica. "Tell Brandon we're sorry and it won't happen again."

Josh practically pulled Cybil away from the front desk, his embarrassment showing. Jersey was quick to hurry after them.

"You're on my shit list, Cyb," he snarled softly.

✝

Jersey, Cybil, and Josh had the hot tub to themselves late that afternoon. The hot tub was connected to the swimming pool allowing easy access from one to the other. There was no one else around the resort grounds and little signs of life, except the occasional resort worker. Cybil sat on the edge of the hot tub and soaked her legs up to her knees but avoided getting her injured thigh wet. The hot, jetted water from the Jacuzzi would not be a healthy environment for a fresh wound. Infection could easily set in. Jersey nearly busted out of her skimpy bikini top, leaving little to the imagination. Josh attempted to be a gentleman, but his eyes kept falling to her barely contained breasts. The blonde bombshell wore a patch near her ear just below her hairline. Since her hair was now pulled up, Josh noticed the patch and appeared interested.

"What's the patch for?" he asked. "Quit smoking?"

Jersey uncertainly touched the patch then smiled and laughed softly. "Motion sickness," she replied simply. "It was a long flight here."

Cybil glanced at the clock on the wall near the cabana and realized it was nearly seven. "I didn't realize it was that late. I'd better wake Heidi and get ready for my dinner date." She hesitated and sighed softly. "I suppose I'll have to hear about this afternoon all through dinner."

"You have the option to walk out on him," Josh informed her. "Just remember that. Don't let him treat you like a child."

"Yes, I do have the option of walking out, but he also has the option of turning me over to the village police," she insisted. "I'm better off just making nice."

"I'm sure you can sweet talk him," Jersey announced while grinning deviously. "Most men melt with just the right amount of flirting."

Cybil attempted a smile, although not totally agreeing with Jersey's suggestion, and got out of the hot tub. Once she dried off her lower legs, she slipped into her shoes and entered the lobby, which was finally coming to life. She nearly collided with Simon. Despite her surprise, he appeared delighted to see her.

"Cybil, I've been looking for you all afternoon," Simon announced cheerfully.

"Josh took me and a friend to the village shopping," she informed him. "We've only been back an hour."

"How's your leg?" he asked. "I was worried."

"Oh, it's just fine," she replied. "Dr. Carrington took care of my cut. He had to stitch it."

"Oh, I'm sorry to hear," Simon replied then attempted to lighten the mood. "I was hoping to have dinner with you tonight, if you haven't already eaten."

Cybil appeared uneasy and fidgeted. "I'd love to, Simon, but I promised Dr. Carrington dinner. You know, to thank him for the medical attention and all."

Simon appeared disappointed but smiled nonetheless. "I understand," he replied although he seemed a tiny bit jealous. Perhaps she was wrong though. "How about the ritual this evening? We could try again."

"Thanks, but I'm taking the night off. I didn't sleep much last night, and I'm exhausted," she announced but then felt bad for brushing off the handsome man. "But I'm free all day tomorrow."

"Then I'll settle for all day tomorrow," he teased. "I'll get to bed early, so I don't sleep the entire day. Perhaps we could take an afternoon picnic."

"That sounds--" She suddenly hesitated and smiled gently. "Uh, romantic."

"Sort of the point," he teased. "I'll meet you in the lobby around noon tomorrow."

Cybil nodded then passed through the lobby and headed for the long walkway toward her bungalow.

Harford hurried after her. "Ms. Brooklyn."

Cybil stopped and turned just before the walkway. Harford stopped near her and smiled pleasantly.

"I'd heard about what happened this afternoon," he announced, surprising her.

She hid her embarrassment and attempted to look him in the eyes without blushing. "Gossip spreads fast, huh?" She then grimaced. "Is Brandon mad?"

"Actually, I haven't seen him," Harford replied then shifted slightly as if uncomfortable. "I was wondering if you were still interested in touring the castle."

Cybil appeared surprised by the offer then immediately fidgeted. "I'm interested but not at the price of a night in jail."

"No one's ever gotten into that sort of trouble, even those who've made it into the castle," he informed her. "I can give you a brief, guided tour. I know my way around the guards and the castle."

She eyed him suspiciously. "At what cost?"

"Twenty bucks," he replied. "I'm paying off a ring for my girlfriend, and I need some extra cash."

Her mind was already reeling with the information. She wasn't sure if her curiosity was great enough to risk being caught again. "I'll get back to you on that, okay?"

Harford nodded.

✝

Cybil entered her bedroom a few minutes later and noticed that the mass still remained beneath the sheets in the dimly lit room. She couldn't believe her friend was still in bed. Even after an all-nighter, she thought Heidi would be up by now.

"Come on, Heidi. Rise and shine," she announced in an overly cheerful tone meant to annoy her friend. "The moon's up."

The sheets moved followed by a female moan. "Let me die in peace."

"You've been in bed long enough," Cybil scolded then shook her head. "That must be one hell of a hangover you're battling."

Heidi groaned and sat up, allowing the covers to fall from her body. The bite mark above her left breast was briefly revealed, although Cybil didn't see it. Heidi scratched it then allowed her nightgown to cover it. She was beyond disheveled, needing more than a mere shower, and looked at Cybil with limited recall.

"Did I hear you say you have a date tonight?" she questioned. "Or was that just some weird dream?"

"You heard correct," Cybil announced then considered. "I almost had two dates. One for dinner and one for the festivities, but I didn't think that would be right."

"Have them fighting over you now, huh?" Heidi teased, managing a tiny smile. "Why didn't you accept the second date?"

Cybil removed a simple yet sexy black dress from the closet and took a moment to study it.

"That's mine, you know," Heidi announced.

46

"I know. I just want to borrow it," Cybil informed her. "I didn't want to make the second date, because I don't think it's right seeing two men in one evening."

"I do it all the time."

"Well, I don't," Cybil insisted. "Besides, maybe my dinner date will run into the evening's festivities. That would be very awkward if I made a second date."

"You're always one step ahead of the game," Heidi remarked with limited enthusiasm. "I've no doubt you'll make a good wife someday. Devoted and a complete pushover."

With her back to Heidi, she slipped into the dress and zipped it with little effort. She turned to face Heidi and fixed her hair.

"I like the thought of one man for the rest of my life," Cybil insisted.

"Most men don't share that dream," Heidi muttered. "Speaking of dream men, whatever became of the Count?"

"I can't check my e-mail from here," Cybil replied then drifted out a moment, almost allowing guilt to consume her. "Apparently, the hotel doesn't have internet access, if you can believe that." She shrugged it off. "Maybe I'll look into it for my last day, you know, just to meet him. It's not as if we were engaging in internet romance or anything. Besides, right now, I have two very cute guys to get to know. I don't intend to introduce a third."

"He sounded creepy anyway." Heidi seductively lay across the bed and smiled. "Will you be needing the room tonight if things go well?"

Cybil glared at her then offered a teasing smile. "I don't intend to let my date go that well," she easily reported. "And I'm turning in early, so you'd better behave tonight."

"Don't worry; I'm pretty much partied out," she announced and collapsed to the bed. "I can't believe how tired I am."

Chapter Ten

Once she had finished changing, Cybil went downstairs and entered the outdoor dining patio. She looked around, somewhat surprised by how crowded it was for the late hour. A storm appeared to be brewing in the distance and the evening's festivities were suddenly in doubt. The guests obviously sensed the same by the limited enthusiasm they displayed and their frequent looks toward the dark horizon.

The host approached Cybil and offered a pleasant smile. "Good evening. I was asked to seat you at the private cabana when you arrived," the host informed her. "Dr. Carrington is running late with new arrivals, but he'll be along shortly."

Cybil followed the host across the patio where she was seated at a private cabana. It was further away from the restaurant in a less traveled section of the outdoor dining area. The lighting was dim and romantic with a view of the beach unobstructed by the pool. The host poured her some wine then hurried away to tend to others now arriving. Cybil admired the view of the beach and the approaching storm. A shadow fell over her, startling her. She looked alongside her and saw Brandon standing near the table with a pleasant smile.

"Sorry to have kept you waiting," he announced.

She wasn't sure if it was just the romantic dining location or the handsome doctor, but she swore his voice had gotten sexier. "I wasn't here long."

Brandon joined her at the table and admired her attire. "That's a stunning dress. Black suits you."

"Black is mysterious," she informed him. "I like to keep people guessing." Cybil casually leaned on the table and smiled with

48

some embarrassment yet remained bold. "Perhaps we should get the unpleasantness over with, so we can enjoy the rest of dinner."

Brandon eyed her suspiciously then managed a strange smile. "Unpleasantness?"

Cybil casually leaned back in her chair and studied him. "Aren't you going to rant and rave about this afternoon?"

Brandon stared at her a moment with a strange look then smiled while chuckling softly. "I rarely rant and I never rave," he announced with humor. "You're referring to your little stroll to the castle, I assume. The place is pretty much a rattrap. I assure you, there's little to see. It's cold, dirty, damp, and creepy." He continued to stare at her and showed little reaction. "If you're hell-bent on seeing the place, I'll take you there myself. Not exactly my idea of an entertaining tour though."

Cybil appeared surprised. "You're not mad?"

"Should I be?" he teased. "Dozens of guests attempt to check out the castle on a weekly basis. It's quite common." He sighed softly. "Touring the castle would distract from the power of the ritual." He considered his comment. "And possibly invoke some hostility from the village."

Cybil appeared relieved and laughed softly. "Here I thought I'd hear about it all evening."

"That's hardly my style," he casually replied. "Besides, this is my first date in five years. I hardly think a lecture would be a very good start."

Cybil smiled warmly and sipped her wine. "You really wouldn't mind giving me a tour?"

"Of course not," he announced then turned serious. "Not at night though. There's no electric."

She laughed with a certain note of uneasiness. "You wouldn't get me in there after dark anyway."

His smirk mocked her. "I thought you didn't believe in vampires."

"I never said I didn't believe in them. I'm keeping an open mind, remember?" She managed a tiny laugh. "Besides, I wouldn't want to risk realizing I was wrong."

Brandon laughed softly. After dinner, the waiter cleared away their dirty dishes and was quick to give them their privacy. They heard faint music filtering to their table within the cabana. The breeze had picked up considerably, the clouds appeared threatening, and lightning flashed in the distance.

Brandon looked at the sky and sighed softly. "Looks like the ritual will be canceled tonight. Bad weather is bad for business."

"I need to catch up on my sleep anyway," she reminded him.

Brandon stood without warning, approached her, and extended his hand. "Would you care to dance?"

Something about his romantic yet rugged appeal tonight made her heart skip a beat. She was reminded of their passionate kiss in his office last night. Something stirred in her. Cybil accepted his hand and, without hesitation, danced with him in their own private cabana. They danced to the slow, romantic song with a little more closeness than strangers should.

"You're not like most of our guests," he informed her softly with his lips close to her ear. "You don't seem to fit into the party atmosphere for a young woman. What really brings you here?"

Cybil rested her head on his shoulder and smiled, even though he couldn't see it. "Incurable curiosity to what is real and what isn't. I've never really fit into the *norm* of society." She considered her life a moment. "My mind often wanders, and I dream far too much. Maybe, among strange customs, I may find a place where I fit in."

Brandon chuckled lowly, catching her attention and forcing her to look up and meet his gaze. "That's why we're here. This is the island of misfit toys," he teased. "We tend to place importance on unimportance. Think outside the box, so to speak. It takes a special breed to live on such a secluded island with bizarre customs, no cell phones, and limited internet access. It really sucks, because I'm addicted to internet shopping." He smiled dashingly. "Maybe you'd like to fill out a job application."

Cybil laughed softly, clung to his neck, and again rested her head on his shoulder. "It's difficult to find what you're looking for when you don't even know what that is."

Brandon nuzzled her neck. "I've never had that problem. Knowing what I want is the easy part," he informed her then held his breath. "Obtaining it is what gives me the most trouble."

He allowed his lips to brush past her neck, his fangs nearly touching her skin as they passed. He moaned softly and shut his eyes. Just then, someone approached and gently cleared his throat.

"Dr. Carrington, I hate to disturb you--"

Brandon and Cybil quickly pulled away to see Harford standing within the cabana opening. Brandon turned toward Harford and attempted to regain his composure.

"What is it? Has something happened?"

"A couple of guests decided to wander up to the castle," Harford announced. "Security found the man and woman, but a second man is missing." He appeared tense. "The woman sustained an injury. They're worried about their friend. I guess he was pretty drunk."

Brandon became curious. "What sort of injury?"

"A large cut to her shoulder," Harford replied. "She said she fell against a tree. The villagers saw them when the guards brought them back." He hesitated and appeared nervous. "There's some panic among the villagers about her injury."

Brandon groaned and shook his head. "Tell them there's nothing to worry about," he announced. "I'll have a look at the girl in my office. Let me know when they find the missing man."

Harford nodded and waited just outside their private cabana.

Brandon turned toward Cybil, sighed deeply, and offered a timid smile. "I'm off to save the world against the evil tree vampires. I hope you don't hold it against me."

Cybil returned the pleasant smile. "I won't. I understand."

Brandon walked past her to join Harford then paused and backed up a step. He met her gaze with a warm smile. "Thank you for your company," Brandon announced warmly. "I really enjoyed tonight."

She smiled with some embarrassment. "I suggest you just kiss me before that poor girl bleeds to death."

Brandon hid his embarrassment and kissed her quickly but passionately on the lips. He pulled away, smiled warmly through closed lips, and then hurried to join Harford. Harford cast an odd glare at Brandon then led him across the patio.

†

Cybil entered the crowded lobby as rain poured down outside, ending any chance of continuing with the festivities. The storm raged in full force with gusting wind and sporadic thunder and lightning. The guests hung out in the lobby with their drinks and enjoyed the village band as they played a lively beat to entertain the guests. Cybil worked her way through the crowd and approached Josh, who stood near the lobby desk where Angelica was working. Angelica appeared disinterested, although that didn't seem to stop him.

Cybil paused near Josh and looked around the lobby. "Where's Heidi?"

Josh rolled his eyes and nodded across the room toward the fireplace. Heidi stood within a crowd of five men. She was already drunk and flirted like a high priced prostitute.

Cybil frowned and shook her head. "What's gotten into that girl? I've never seen her like this."

"Must be the alcohol they use in their mixed drinks. Makes the natives horny," Josh announced. "I have my own vixen dogging me."

She gave him a surprised look. "Jersey? I thought you were interested in her."

Josh appeared less than enthusiastic. "I guess you hadn't noticed I was trying to get rid of her all day. She has a ton of sex appeal but nothing beyond that. Far too wild for me. It'd be like going out with Heidi only worse."

"You could try breaking it to her gently, so she stops wasting her time."

"I told her I wasn't interested," he announced with conviction. "She doesn't seem to care. I even tried being rude." He frowned and waved her off. "I think I'm turning in early tonight too. Angelica won't talk to me, and Jersey won't leave me alone. It's going to be a retched evening."

Cybil glanced back toward the fireplace and Heidi. "Perhaps we can kidnap Heidi as well."

Josh looked back at Cybil with an odd look. "I thought you had a date? It couldn't have been too good if it's over already."

"He was called away on a medical emergency," she announced then smiled in a somewhat dreamy manner. "I like him, Josh. He's so *charming*. There's something about him, almost as if I've known him forever. I'm not usually comfortable around strange men, but he's different."

"And a doctor too."

Cybil laughed softly and patted his lower arm. "Don't get too excited. Being a doctor around here isn't any more prestigious than being a gas station attendant," she teased. "Low pay and not very glamorous, I'm afraid."

Josh laughed at her comment. His smile suddenly faded when he saw Jersey enter the lobby. "Let's grab the lush and make a hasty exit."

Chapter Eleven

Josh and Cybil practically dragged Heidi along the corridor toward their rooms. As her protests continued, Josh finally slung her over his shoulder and carried her barbarian style into her guestroom. Despite being completely wasted, she was fairly feisty and a little more than annoyed that they forced her to leave the party. Cybil shut the door behind them as Josh approached the bed. Without regard to her pounding on his back with her tiny fists, Josh dumped Heidi onto her bed. She landed on her back with a bounce and attempted to jump back up but changed her mind when she nearly fell back down.

"You two are absolute party poopers," she cried out. "What the hell's wrong with you? Can't a girl get laid in peace around here?"

Josh and Cybil ignored her ranting and casually made plans for the following morning.

"Morning stroll on the beach?" Cybil asked Josh.

"Followed by brunch on the patio?" Josh added.

"Sounds perfect," Cybil agreed.

Heidi stared at them in disbelief. "I don't know who the hell you two think you are," she launched hotly. "If you'd get lives of your own, maybe you wouldn't feel the need to ruin mine!"

She attempted to spring up from the bed. Josh casually placed his hand to Heidi's shoulder and pushed her back onto the bed. She let out a startled scream as she again bounced onto the bed. She attempted to pull herself from the bed but was too drunk to make it into a sitting position.

"Bastard!"

Josh casually walked away from Heidi's bed and approached the door. He paused before the door then turned while glancing from Heidi to Cybil.

"If she gets out of hand, tie her to the bed," he announced simply.

Cybil managed an uneasy laugh. "Goodnight, Josh."

Josh left the room but not before casting a glare at Heidi. She was too busy attempting to sit up to even notice. When Cybil looked back, Heidi was sprawled out on the bed already passed out. Thunder cracked loudly, reminding Cybil of the raging storm just outside. She approached the balcony doors and looked outside. Outside lights remained lit around the resort but the only thing Cybil could see was pouring rain. It came down so hard it resembled a waterfall. Thunder cracked loudly but it was barely heard over the deafening sound of the pouring rain. Lightning flashed, lighting up the sky over the ocean. As dark corners of the resort were lit by the flashing lightning, Cybil swore she saw someone moving around. If guests or employees were out in that mess, they had to be insane. Cybil allowed the curtains to fall back into place then turned and looked back at Heidi's bed. Heidi, in her slinky eveningwear, looked like the poster child for some party college while passed out on top of the bed's comforter.

✝

An hour or so later, the thunder and lightning had ceased, but the rain continued to pour, allowing Cybil the perfect opportunity to enjoy the garden style bathtub in their bathroom. She relaxed beneath a layer of bubbles with her hair pulled up to keep it from getting wet. She shut her eyes and attempted to relax after her rough two days. Within their shared bedroom, Heidi slept peacefully in her skimpy party dress, although she was now curled in the fetal position. A shadow mysteriously appeared before the balcony doors. For some unknown reason, Heidi stirred in her sleep and looked at the glass doors beyond Cybil's empty bed. She drunkenly smiled and beckoned to the shadow on the other side of the door.

Within the bathroom, Cybil drifted to sleep within the tub. As her head slowly fell to the side while she lounged within the warm sudsy water, she forced herself awake. She didn't need to drown in the tub while on vacation. She then heard a clunk from within the bedroom beyond the bathroom door. Cybil quickly sat up in the tub and looked toward the door.

"Heidi?"

There was no response, although she didn't exactly expect one. Cybil climbed out of the tub. Without bothering to dry off first, she slipped into the plush hotel bathrobe hanging on the door. She opened the bathroom door to the dimly lit bedroom, allowing some light to escape and brighten the room slightly. A large mass moved beneath the covers on Heidi's bed almost resembling a couple engaging in sexual activity. Heidi moaned softly from beneath the covers. Cybil stared with bewilderment at the bed.

"Heidi?"

It appeared as if a shadow raced out the partially open balcony door, sending a gust of air across the room. Cybil stared at the open balcony doors and the pouring down rain just beyond them. She hurried to the balcony door, stared at it a moment with confusion, and then shut and locked it. Cybil took a step back from the balcony doors with a confused and moderately concerned look. She knew the doors had been closed, but she couldn't attest that she'd personally locked them. She finally looked back at Heidi, who remained motionless beneath the covers.

"Heidi, was there someone in the room?"

There was no response. Cybil didn't like her lack of response, especially when she was positive she'd seen a lot of movement just a moment earlier. She approached the bed, sat on the edge near her friend, and gently nudged her bare, exposed shoulder.

"Heidi--?"

"Leave me alone, will you," she moaned softly from beneath the covers and pulled them over her head.

Cybil straightened with defeat then uncertainly looked at her wet fingers. Through the dim lighting from the bathroom, she could see what almost certainly looked like blood on her fingertips. Cybil felt a shockwave of alarm sweep through her and quickly reached for the bedside light. The room brightened considerably. Cybil stared at the blood on her fingers then noticed Heidi's scattered dress and panties on the floor. She knew it broke all the boundaries of their friendship, but she no longer cared. Cybil pulled the covers from Heidi's head, exposing her naked body down to her waist. Heidi cried out with irritation and grabbed the covers to pull them back up. That split second was all Cybil needed to see the set of deep puncture marks just above her breast. As the covers flew back over Heidi's head, Cybil gasped with horror while springing to her feet. She darted frightened looks around the room, momentarily fearing she wasn't alone then reached for the bedside phone. She punched in Josh's room number.

"Come on, Josh--" She listened to the phone ring several times without being answered then slammed down the receiver and nervously ran her trembling fingers through her hair. "Shit!" Cybil hurried across the room, shedding her robe as she ran.

Chapter Twelve

Only a moment later and now fully dressed, Cybil hurried to Josh's room alongside hers and promptly pounded on the door. There was no response, which she didn't understand. He made it a point to mention he was turning in early as well. Her frustration continued to rise rapidly. She ran back to her room and briefly looked inside to check on her friend. When she was sure Heidi was still okay, she ran down the long corridor toward the lobby. Cybil entered the lobby with its crowds of people and loud music as the party continued in full swing. People drank, socialized, and danced to the live band. Cybil pushed and shoved her way through the crowd and toward the front desk. To her horror, there was no one there. She looked back across the lobby with a distraught look. Harford made his way across the crowded lobby with the guard, Victor, glued to his side. Cybil felt a slight pang of relief and hurried through the crowd toward them. Her heart was racing and her breathing was heavy as she stopped before Harford.

"Where's Brandon?" she gasped breathlessly. "I need to see him right away."

Harford appeared concerned to the urgency in her tone. "He's not back yet. They're still searching for that missing man." He was now on high alert. "Is there a medical emergency?"

"Yes, my friend needs medical attention."

"Should I call for a nurse?" Harford asked.

She wasn't sure why, but she felt uncomfortable with anyone but Brandon seeing Heidi. "No," she practically cried out. "I'd rather she be seen by Brandon."

Harford and Victor stared at her with bewildered looks that immediately made her feel uncomfortable. Harford turned to the guard and indicated his handheld radio.

"Do you suppose you could reach him on that?" Harford asked.

As Victor reached for his handheld radio, Cybil felt a tiny bit of relief. Before Victor could even make contact, Cybil saw Brandon enter the lobby from the outside entrance. He was soaked from the pouring rain despite his black trench coat. Cybil pushed past Harford and Victor and hurried across the lobby, recklessly bumping into people. She approached Brandon as he removed his soaking wet trench coat. He was slightly surprised to see her, since she had gone to bed a few hours earlier. She startled him as she clutched his wrist and stared with a look of dread.

"Something's wrong with Heidi," she gasped softly. "You need to see her right away."

Brandon didn't even question the request. He grabbed her hand and pushed his way through the swarm of guests while pulling her behind him.

†

Within minutes, Cybil and Brandon entered the dimly lit bedroom. Cybil immediately realized that the bedside light had been turned off. Brandon turned on the main room lights by the switch alongside the door. Both looked at Heidi's bed, but she was gone. Cybil stared at the empty bed then looked around the room while Brandon immediately headed for the bathroom and looked through the open door.

Brandon looked back at her. "Where is she?"

Cybil's eyes fell upon the balcony door, which once again was partially open. She hurried to the balcony, threw open the door the rest of the way, and looked outside onto the dimly lit grounds within the pouring rain. She quickly turned back toward Brandon as he approached her.

"What's the emergency?" he asked with noted concern.

Cybil uncertainly looked around the room with her mouth hanging open as every horrible thought raced through her mind. As she looked back at Brandon, she was now beyond rational thinking.

"She had a bite mark on her chest," she gasped while staring at him with wide, horror-filled eyes. "I swear to you it was a vampire bite."

Brandon stared at her with a strange, hard to read expression. "A vampire bite?" he slowly repeated.

She knew he was thinking she was insane or paranoid. She didn't have time to convince him she wasn't a whacko like the others who claimed such things. Her anxiety was rising rapidly.

"I know what you're thinking, but I know what I saw."

Cybil ran to the bed and pulled back the sheet to reveal a small amount of blood near the top of the cover. She pointed at the spot of blood.

"There! It's fresh blood," she announced close to shouting.

Brandon approached the bed and eyed the blood, but it was obvious a small spot of blood was inconclusive. She knew he was thinking that and felt as if she had to defend herself.

"I thought I heard something while I was in the bathroom. When I came into the room, I saw something moving on the balcony." Cybil was rapidly becoming animated. "That's when I saw the mark on her chest. Two puncture wounds. She was bit by something or someone."

Brandon appeared uncomfortable and moved closer to her while staring into her eyes. "You need to calm down, Cybil."

Those were the wrong words, which had the opposite effect on any woman. Cybil felt her entire body jolt with adrenaline. "You calm down! My friend was bite by a vampire and now she's gone!"

Cybil ran from the room. Brandon bolted after her. She ran just a few feet down the corridor to Josh's bedroom door and pounded on it. Brandon paused behind her and stared with surprise as she began slamming her shoulder against the door to break it down. Brandon stopped her before she could strike it again and revealed his master key. She remained still a moment while holding her head as he unlocked the door. Brandon opened the door and immediately turned on the bedroom light. The room was empty. Cybil ran to the bathroom, glanced inside, and then looked back at Brandon.

"We have to find them," she announced now bordering on hysteria.

As she ran for the open bedroom door, Brandon grabbed her arm and stopped her. She spun toward him with surprise, which quickly turned unstable.

Brandon remained calm while staring into her eyes. "We'll look for your friends, but I want you to get yourself together first," he announced firmly. "You can't be running around the resort crying vampire. The repercussions would be astounding."

She knew he was right, realizing she was ranting and raving like a mad woman. She took several deep breaths to appease him and met his gaze. "Okay, I'm calm."

Brandon eyed her with a look of disbelief and shook his head.

Chapter Thirteen

Cybil walked quietly alongside Brandon through the crowded lobby as his hand firmly clutched hers. She looked around the congested room with great interest and plenty of concern. They weaved through the crowd and approached the front desk where Harford had resumed his post. Cybil watched the horde of partygoers with distrust. She felt as if they were staring at her. Perhaps they were, considering she was dressed in shorts and a sweatshirt. Her emotions had run away with her, and she feared any of the guests could turn on her at any moment.

Brandon paused before Harford, appearing casual, and leaned on the desk. "We're looking for Cybil's travel companions. Have you seen either?"

Harford considered the question, gave it some thought, and then snapped his fingers. "Yes," he announced. "I saw the man, Josh. He came down here about an hour ago and got into a tiff with Angelica just as her shift was ending." He sank into thought. "I can't be sure, but I think they went off together."

Brandon looked back at Cybil and raised a brow in silent question. She appeared slightly relieved at Harford's response, because it sounded plausible. Josh liked Angelica, and he may have returned to the party in an attempt to win her over. Brandon looked back at Harford.

"Will you call Angelica's room and see if he's there with her?" Brandon asked. "It's important that we know."

Harford nodded and dialed an in-house number. All three waited for the reply. Harford lowered the phone and shook his head. "No answer."

Cybil felt concern sweep over her and immediately looked at Brandon's profile. "They got her too!"

Harford glanced at Cybil and appeared bewildered by the comment. Brandon didn't bother looking at her, although he firmly squeezed her hand in response, silencing her.

"Get security to locate her whereabouts," Brandon announced. "Have them check her room. If they're there, I want to be informed immediately."

Harford nodded and called the number for security.

Brandon turned and casually looked around the lobby. "While security is doing that, we'll check the lounge," he announced. "Maybe they went for a drink together."

†

Brandon and Cybil entered the lounge and looked around the crowded room from their position near the entrance. Buffet tables were lined along the far wall offering the same sort of feast they had after the nightly ritual. Both scanned the room for Heidi and Josh, but the crowd made it difficult to identify any one person. Brandon stopped a passing waiter.

"Have you seen Angelica?" Brandon asked.

The waiter shook his head then continued on his way.

Cybil remained close to Brandon while clutching his hand. "We should check the castle."

Brandon suddenly looked at her with surprise then turned oddly irritated. His tone was low and firm. "Now why on earth would either be in the castle?" he almost demanded.

Cybil continued to glare at him. She raised her brows as her eyes narrowed. "You *know* why."

"You are not going to that castle in the dark and especially during a storm," he firmly insisted. "There's no electric, remember? No one, and I mean absolutely no one, would consider traveling to that castle with you on a night like tonight."

Cybil's look was harsh and cold. "Then I'll go by myself."

His glare was almost frightening. "You're absolutely out of your mind," Brandon growled lowly then straightened proudly. "I'm going to get you a drink. I want you to calm down and attempt to regain some rational thinking."

"I don't want a drink," she protested a little louder. "I want to find my friends."

62

Cybil attempted to walk away from him, but he refused to release her hand. She met his gaze. Despite her own harsh look, his was far more intimidating.

"For your own good, you'd better calm down," he announced in a mildly threatening tone then attempted to show some compassion. "We'll find your friends, I promise."

Cybil glared at him with a look of hostility as her eyes narrowed. She hissed, "Unhand me or I scream vampire."

Simon suddenly appeared before them and glared at Brandon with his own threatening look. "I think you'd better unhand her."

Brandon glared back at Simon. The exchange was frightening. For a moment, Cybil almost envisioned them drawing swords. Both men had a look of mayhem in their eyes. Cybil was moderately surprised when Brandon actually released her hand, although he didn't take his eyes from Simon. Simon captured Cybil's wrist and pulled her closer to him, putting distance between her and Brandon. Neither man looked away from the other. Brandon was the first to collect himself. He casually placed his hands in his pockets and looked at Cybil in a calm manner.

"I strongly suggest you remain with me to search for your friends," Brandon announced in a calm voice.

Simon's agitation increased as his body stiffened, preparing for a fight. His eyes remained locked on Brandon. "And I strongly suggest you stay the hell away from her."

Brandon returned Simon's glare. Cybil didn't like the look in either man's eyes and felt incredibly uncomfortable. She was almost certain there was about to be bloodshed.

Cybil backed away from both men and attempted a smile. "I think both of you need a time-out," she announced timidly. At least Brandon had succeeded in knocking rational thinking back into her head. "I'll be at the bar if you need me."

Cybil hurried across the crowded lounge and made her way closer to the bar. Simon finally turned away from Brandon and followed her through the crowd. Brandon continued to glare at him but didn't follow. Simon joined Cybil at the bar and ordered a drink for both of them. She remained slightly uncomfortable but tried to relax. She glanced toward the doorway, but Brandon was gone. She looked back at Simon and accepted the drink.

"I'm glad you were both able to walk away," she announced with some relief. "I'd hate to think I caused a fight."

"I'd hate it even more if he'd harmed you," Simon remarked then shook his head. "Some men just can't handle rejection, I suppose."

"That's not what that was about," she informed him then hesitated a moment. "I'm looking for my friends, and he's trying to keep me from going to the old castle."

Simon stared at her with surprise. "Why would you look for your friends at that castle? It's off-limits."

Cybil sipped her drink and nervously shook her head. "There's something more going on here," she replied. "I'm afraid that castle has the answers."

Simon studied her a moment in awkward silence, but his bewilderment was quickly replaced by curiosity. "Don't tell me you think your friends were abducted by vampires."

Cybil didn't look at him. She couldn't look at him. She knew how it sounded and what he must be thinking about her sanity.

Simon continued to stare a moment longer then moved closer to her. "So you think the vampires came down here, abducted your friends, and took them back to the castle?" he asked softly then straightened and seemed oddly serious. "Defeating a vampire would be difficult enough without attempting to defeat them at night."

Cybil eyed him with surprise. "You actually believe me?"

"Why not?" Simon asked.

She then took another sip of her drink. "You're right. It would be foolish to enter a vampire's lair at night," she replied softly. "But if I wait, they could be dead by morning."

Simon remained unusually close then looked around to make sure no one was listening. "Just between us," he announced softly, "I came here to write the sixth segment in a series of twelve books about superstition and ancient curses."

She suddenly looked at him with surprise to his announcement.

"I've always wanted to prove the existence of vampires," he continued. "So far, I haven't been able to prove or disprove any of it."

She didn't take her eyes off him but refrained from commenting.

"I think that Brandon character is threatened by my presence," Simon continued. "I think my reputation is out. I can help you find your friends." He met her gaze and remained serious. "I've been studying vampires, myths, and superstitions for years. I know more than most about them, their habitat, and how to kill them effectively."

Cybil continued to stare at him then leaned closer with great interest. "Would you be willing to go to the castle with me and help me find my friends?"

"Of course I'd be willing to go with you," he announced with enthusiasm. "I've been dying to find a way into that place, but it's always being watched. How would we get in? There are guards hidden all around that place."

She drew a deep breath while staring at him. "I think I know a way."

Chapter Fourteen

Harford stood behind the front desk with a look of horror in his eyes as he adamantly shook his head. Cybil and Simon attempted to remain calm from their position on the other side of the desk. There were so many people crammed into the lobby it would be almost impossible for anyone to hear their conversation.

"No way. Not happening," Harford protested and continued to shake his head. "That's one spooky ass place at night. You want in; I'll get you in but not before sunrise."

"By then it could be too late," Cybil protested.

Harford stared at Cybil a long, silent moment then raised his brows. "You look like an intelligent woman, Cybil," he announced. "There's nothing to this whole vampire charade. Honestly, your friend is probably just having a little fun at your expense. Guests love to prank their friends. Trust me. There's no such thing as vampires."

"Then why won't you go in until sunup?" Simon suddenly demanded.

"Rats," he lashed out and gestured with his hands. "Big, hairy, mutant rats. They'll tear your leg off, man." He then fidgeted. "Besides, it's pitch-black in there at night. Lend a classic thunderstorm as a backdrop, and you have every possible reason why I won't go in there at night."

"One hundred dollars," Simon offered. "One hundred dollars just for you to tell us how to get into the castle undetected."

Harford shook his head. "Brandon will have my ass."

"Please," Cybil begged. "My friends could be out there."

Harford stared at the pleading look on Cybil's face. He rolled his eyes, groaned softly, and then looked back at her.

"I'll take you in." Harford suddenly glared at Simon. "And just her."

Simon straightened defensively and shook his head. "No way. I'm not leaving her out of my sight."

Cybil looked back at Simon with some surprise. "Simon--"

Simon continued to glare at Harford then looked back at Cybil. "You don't know this man," he interjected. "He could take you in there and just leave you there. Or worse."

Harford glared at Simon with a tough, offended look. "Seriously? You think I get my kicks from luring women into creepy rattraps to get my sexual jollies. The hell with you, man!" He then turned to Cybil and raised his brows. "Let me know what you decide, but I'm not taking rich boy along for the ride."

As Harford walked to the far end of the desk, Cybil turned to Simon. "I have to go, Simon," she pleaded. "My friends could be in danger."

"It's a bad idea, Cybil," he announced. "You're completely at his mercy. We'll find another way inside. You don't know that man."

"I don't know you either," she insisted while folding her arms across her chest.

Simon stared at her with some surprise, seemed to realize she had a point, and then groaned softly. "Fine," he huffed. His look turned serious. "You have one hour. If you're not back here in one hour, I'm coming in after you, even if it means punching a few out of shape security guards."

Cybil smiled her appreciation. "Thanks, Simon."

†

Harford hurried along the beach in the pouring rain with Cybil running directly behind him. Both were drenched before they even made it fifty yards from the resort. Despite the torrential downpour, Cybil wore one of the flower and garlic leis and carried a wooden cross candlestick. The flowers were already drenched and flattened against her sweatshirt. They entered the woods, causing Cybil some concern.

"Where are we going?" she shouted just so he'd hear her above the rain.

"Trust me," he called back.

67

They approached a cave entrance near some rocks. Cybil looked around the dark, damp cave as Harford stepped just inside the opening to get out of the rain. Harford turned on his flashlight and shined it down the tunnel then looked back to see Cybil still outside the cave.

"Well? Are you coming?"

She entered the cave with some uncertainty. It felt good to be out of the pouring rain, but she was suddenly cold from the cool air inside the cave hitting her soaked body. As Harford shined the light through the tunnel, a few rats scurried away. A steady dripping sound seemed to echo loudly within the tunnel. She wasn't even sure where the sound came from.

"What is this cave?"

"The backdoor to the castle," he informed her. "Few people know about it." He motioned with the flashlight. "Come on."

She uncertainly followed him while shivering from the cold and her wet clothes against her body.

Chapter Fifteen

A thick wooden door, possibly centuries-old, creaked open. Cybil followed Harford into what appeared to be a cold, damp basement and looked around. As Harford shut the door, she realized it wasn't a basement but an actual dungeon. He shined the light around the dungeon, allowing her to see old shackles hanging from the walls and iron cell doors leading to abysmal cells where most were probably left to rot. For a brief moment, it dawned on her that Harford could easily lock her down here and no one would find her remains for years. She drew a deep breath and put faith in him being as nice of a guy as he seemed.

"This was the old dungeon," he informed her.

The light from his flashlight skimmed past old rotting objects she could almost positively identify as torture devices.

"Charming," she muttered softly while shivering.

If Harford was as cold as she was, he certainly didn't act it. Harford shined his light into each cell as they passed through the dungeon. Their shadows from the flashlight were cast upon the wall, giving an eerie appearance. Cybil hated to admit she was suddenly frightened by her own shadow.

"If they were brought here against their will, this is where they'd be," he informed her.

Cybil shivered from more than the cold and held her breath. She was almost afraid they would find them inside one of the cells. A shadow moved along the wall behind them. It appeared to be out of sync with the shadows she'd been eyeing since they entered the dungeon. Cybil nervously looked around but whatever she had seen wasn't there.

"Let's look a little faster," she announced and continued to shiver. "This place really gives me the creeps."

They continued along the maze of rooms and corridors. Doorways seemed to lead to other cells and more doorways. They all started looking the same to Cybil. Harford seemed to walk with purpose, so she assumed he knew where he was going. Actually, she prayed he knew where he was going. They passed several stone staircases. Their shadows danced along the walls and appeared almost alive with movement. Cybil was almost certain there were more shadows than there should have been. They heard a low snarl echo through the dungeon. Harford's eyes widened as he quickly waved the flashlight around the area.

"What was that?" she suddenly gasped.

"Rats?" Harford suggested, although his tone lacked conviction.

"An awfully big rat."

Something large passed through the light in front of them. Both jumped with alarm. Harford scanned the corridor and the ceiling with the flashlight while forcing her to back up as he nearly backed into her.

"Shit," he cursed softly while looking around. "I think we should get out of here."

Although concerned for her friends, Cybil was frightened enough to agree with the suggestion. Something large suddenly tackled Harford into a nearby cell. The flashlight flew across the corridor, spinning light out of control and casting more shadows. Harford let out a startled scream, followed by a shrill cry, a growl, and then a hiss. Cybil listened to the frightening sounds, momentarily frozen by them. Harford continued to scream then silenced.

"Harford!"

Something whizzed past her face, causing her to scream. Cybil snatched the discarded flashlight from the floor and shined it into the cell. The flashlight did a poor job lighting the large cell.

"Harford!"

There was no response and she couldn't locate him with the flashlight. The dungeon became completely silent with the exception of the dripping water and the sounds of rats scurrying about. Thinking she was mistaken about the cell he'd been thrown into, Cybil nervously shined the flashlight into the nearby cells as well, but there was no sign of him. She turned around several times becoming disoriented.

"Shit--"

Cybil moved slowly along the dungeon corridor. A shadow swept past her, forcing her to cry out and run along the corridor. She reached several dead-ends and had to keep turning back around until she had no idea where she was heading or where she had been. Despite the flashlight, it was too dark to get a fix on her location. Her breathing was heavy and frightened. She ran along another corridor and collided with someone. Cybil screamed hysterically while jumping back and shined the light in front of her. Simon attempted to calm her down while shining his own flashlight on her.

"It's just me," he kept saying in a reassuring tone. "It's okay. It's just me."

Cybil stared at Simon a moment in disbelief while attempting to catch her breath and slow her urgently pounding heart. She let out a relieved sigh and threw her arms around him.

"Simon," she gasped. "Thank God!"

He only briefly held her then pulled away and looked at her while shining his light on her. "Are you okay?" Simon asked. "I heard you screaming."

She attempted to relax then eyed him with surprise. "How'd you get down here?"

"Naturally, I followed you," he replied. "I certainly wasn't about to allow you to come out here alone with that guy." He shined his light around the corridor. "What happened? Where's Harford?"

"I don't know," she gasped while holding her head and trembling at the thought. "Something grabbed him, and then he was gone. I think we should get out of here. We're at a disadvantage down here in the dark with all these corridors."

Simon produced a water pistol, nearly shocking Cybil. As he handed it to her, she gave him a puzzled look.

"I came prepared," he informed her. "They're filled with holy water. If a vampire comes after you, give him a squirt right between the eyes."

Cybil uncertainly nodded and clutched the water pistol. "We need to find Harford and get out of here."

He shined his light around the area. "Where did you last see him?"

Cybil shined her light around as well. A helpless look crossed her face. "Damn it, all the corridors look the same."

Several rats scurried past as if on their own mission. Simon attempted to avoid stepping on them.

"I vote we move for higher ground," he informed her. "This place is too cold and damp even for vampires. I think your friends would be upstairs somewhere if they're here."

"Are you sure?" she suddenly asked. "Harford didn't think so."

71

"Harford's already missing," he replied. "I think we should use my plan now."

She couldn't argue with that and reluctantly nodded.

Chapter Sixteen

Cybil and Simon climbed the first set of stone steps they found and finally ended up within the castle's grand hallway. It was dark, cold, and roughly the size of the resort lobby. The castle was even bigger than she had imagined. It would take hours to search the entire castle for her friends. She suddenly shivered and not just because of her damp clothes against her chilled body. Cybil scanned the area with her flashlight.

"I don't like this," she almost whispered. "I feel like I'm being watched."

They heard the castle groan, possibly due to airflow. Cybil gasped with surprise. Every torch within the castle suddenly erupted into flames, brightening the entire hallway and startling both. The enormous grand hallway had marble flooring and a fifty-foot ceiling lined with old-fashioned, candle chandeliers. A massive, hand carved staircase seemed to rise straight to heaven. Both looked around with nervous anxiety.

"What in the world--?" Simon gasped, marveling at the lit torches.

"At least we can see," Cybil nervously replied while looking around.

Simon indicated the staircase with a slight nod, obviously anxious to proceed up them.

"Are you sure?" she asked while eyeing the stairs with tacky red and gold carpet runners down the middle.

"Vampire hunting isn't an exact science, but I'd be willing to bet their caskets are upstairs," he announced. "Perhaps that's where we'll find your friends."

Cybil appeared uncertain while staring at the stairs. If they knew the vampires were upstairs, going up there didn't seem like the best plan. It was night, and the vampires would have the advantage as well as the home playing field. If it meant finding her friends, she knew she needed to investigate. She clutched her holy water squirt gun and reluctantly nodded. They slowly walked up the stairs, keeping watch all around them. Once they reached the top, they saw light coming from the partially open bedroom door on the right. Simon slowly pushed open the door the rest of the way.

The huge room was heavily furnished with centuries-old furniture, complete with an enormous four-post bed that towered to the ceiling. There was a marble walk-in fireplace at the opposite end of the room, which immediately caught Cybil's attention. Toward the back, there were rows of stained glass windows surrounding a rounded wall. The room was breathtaking. Cybil's eyes then fell to the old, decorative casket mounted on a pillar surrounded by the stained glass windows. Simon and Cybil remained frozen as they stared at the casket.

"He wouldn't be in there, would he?" she gasped softly.

"No, it's far too early for that," Simon informed her then walked across the room, silently approaching the casket.

She had to wonder; if he didn't think the casket was occupied, why did he feel the need to sneak up upon it?

Simon looked back at her and grinned slyly. "I have an idea."

Cybil eyed him, uncertain if she even wanted to hear him out. She nervously followed him from a distance. He approached the casket and slowly opened the lid. Both jumped back at the same time as they peered inside. They were relieved it was empty.

"A little surprise for our fanged friend," he announced deviously. "Put your garlic leis and cross into his casket. He won't be able to touch them, and then he won't be able to get into his sanctuary when the sun comes up."

Cybil eyed him then uncertainly removed her garlic leis and placed it along with the cross into the casket on the satin liner. Simon shut the lid, took her arm, and guided her across the room toward the door. She was happy to be leaving. Simon suddenly stopped her and looked around, alarming her.

"What is it?" she gasped.

"I heard something."

Both nervously looked around as Cybil stood partially behind Simon while clinging to his arm.

"I think we have a problem," he whispered.

"What is it?" she gasped. "Do you hear something?"

Simon turned toward her and smiled charmingly with his exposed vampire fangs. Cybil's eyes widened with horror as she cried out. Simon suddenly grabbed her around the waist and by the back of her head, grasping her hair.

"I want you for myself," he snarled.

Simon pulled her head back by her hair, arching her neck, and lunged for her throat with his fangs. Cybil screamed and shot him in the face with the squirt gun. Simon hesitated and looked at her while licking the water from his lips. She stared at his reaction with horror.

"What's wrong?" he teased. "Did the mean vampire lie about the holy water?"

He once more dived for her throat. Cybil screamed and thrust her knee into his groin. Simon gasped with agony and released her hair but still kept his arm securely around her waist. He glared at her and growled through exposed fangs.

"Careful," he snarled then grinned, "you'll probably want some of that after I convert you."

Cybil rammed her forehead into his nose. Simon cried out, released her, and clutched his nose. He glared at her with annoyance, but she was already darting across the room. Simon mysteriously appeared in front of her, cutting off her path. Cybil stopped and stared at him with alarm. She quickly turned and ran for the casket and her weapons. Before she could open the lid, Simon was on top of her. He grabbed her around the waist and attempted to bite her from behind. Cybil screamed and, with one swift movement, darted out from under him. Simon growled and turned. As she ran, a gust of wind blew past her. A shadow fell before the door and instantly formed into Simon. He gazed into her eyes as he moved toward her. His look was hypnotizing. Cybil stared into his eyes with a look of concern and backed up.

"You will be mine, Cybil," he announced. "It was meant to be. Come to me now and feel my immortality run through your veins."

Cybil suddenly appeared motionless as she stared helplessly into his eyes. Simon smiled through exposed fangs and moved closer.

Her eyes suddenly narrowed. "Your pick-up line needs work."

Simon appeared surprised by her ability to overcome his hypnotic gaze. Cybil punched him in the mouth, tossing him several feet across the room. She bolted for the door, running from the room and down the stairs. As she ran along the grand hallway toward the front door, she heard movement from upstairs. She somehow knew he'd be on top of her any minute. While running, Cybil looked toward the staircase for signs of shadows following her. She suddenly collided with someone between her and the door and let out a horrified scream. Brandon stood before her with a stern harsh stare.

"What are you doing out here?" he demanded.

Her heart was racing, and she wasn't sure if she should be relieved or not. Brandon wouldn't be any match for a vampire. He'd just be a diversion to slow him down.

"He's after me," she cried out. "We'll argue about it later."

A shadow moved along the ceiling causing both to look up. Panic filled her.

"We have to get out of here!"

Brandon grabbed her hand and guided her toward the door. The shadow moved along the wall then dropped down in front of them. Simon materialized before them and hissed while Cybil screamed. Brandon slung Cybil behind him and snarled at Simon, revealing his own vampire fangs. Cybil jumped away from both with a look of horror in her eyes. They lunged at each other and crashed into the stone wall with force and speed. They viciously bit and clawed at each other.

"Fuck this!" Cybil ran out the main door into the courtyard and into the pouring rain.

Chapter Seventeen

Cybil ran the entire way from the castle to the resort in the pouring rain. She ran along the beach despite the sand filling her shoes, but she wasn't about to stop and take them off. The hotel was just up ahead. She could see a couple outside beneath one of the private cabanas. Through the dim outdoor lights, she could make out Josh on the lounge bed with a blonde woman. She ran for the cabana and saw her friend with Jersey. They passionately kissed and groped each other. Cybil barely slowed as she entered the beachside cabana.

"Josh," she cried out. "We have to get out of here!"

Josh pulled away from Jersey and looked at Cybil with drunken disorientation. He appeared so wasted; he could barely even focus on her. Jersey turned her head and looked at Cybil revealing exposed fangs. Jersey suddenly hissed her disapproval to the interruption. Cybil cried out with surprise, grabbed Josh's hand, and pulled him into a sitting position. Josh appeared to come to life before Cybil's eyes and looked at Jersey, who now lunged for him. He saw her fangs and screamed as well. Cybil pulled him off the lounge bed and nearly dragged him to the hotel. As they ran through the rain, Josh appeared to mysteriously sober, indicating he may not have been drunk after all.

"What the hell--?" he cried out. "Did I just see that?"

"No time to explain," Cybil cried out as they ran into the hotel lobby.

As they ran through the lobby soaking wet and leaving a trail of wet sand, they received several stares from the party goers still gathered there, although the crowd had decreased. Jersey casually entered the lobby and followed them at a leisurely, seductive pace.

Cybil looked back while pulling Josh toward the connecting corridor and their bungalow.

Josh didn't look back and started pushing her. "Don't look; just go!"

Cybil and Josh ran along the corridor that was now mysteriously darker than it had been. The shadows on the wall began to move, forcing Cybil to look at the ceiling. She stopped suddenly, causing Josh to run into her from behind. He pushed harshly against her back.

"What the hell are you doing?" he cried out. "Go!"

Josh grabbed her hand and pulled her along the hall. The shadow on the wall suddenly fell down to the floor before them. Josh cried out and pulled Cybil past the shadow that quickly formed into Simon. He attempted to grab her as they passed. Cybil screamed and eluded his grasping hands. Josh pulled Cybil into her room, being the closest, and slammed the door behind them. He locked and bolted the door then fell against it while gasping and wheezing from their impromptu run. The room was once again only dimly lit between the glow of the bathroom light and the light from outside. Cybil hurried to the glass balcony doors and ensured they were locked. She was about to close the curtains when she saw Jersey standing before the glass doors. She motioned for Josh with a devious, seductive smile. Cybil screamed and shut the curtains. Josh appeared alarmed and backed into the center of the room with Cybil. Both looked from door to door.

"What are we going to do?" Josh cried out. "This can't be happening."

She suddenly spun to face him and glared at him. "Take your shirt off."

"What?" he cried out with surprise.

"I need to be sure she didn't bite you," Cybil lashed out. "Now take off your fucking shirt!"

Josh ripped his shirt off and held out his arms to reveal his bite-free body. She let out a sigh of relief and shed her wet sweatshirt on the way to her dresser. Josh fidgeted slightly at the sight of his friend wearing only her bra. He scratched his temple and looked away. Cybil slipped into a dry shirt and ran her fingers through her wet hair while looking around.

Josh grabbed a sweatshirt from her drawer as well and changed into it. He attempted to calm down while staring at his friend. "What's going on, Cybil? Is Jersey really a vampire?"

"Yes, she's really a vampire," she replied while trembling. "And it wasn't just your girlfriend."

"Whoa," he cried out. "She's not my girlfriend. I don't even know how I ended up out there with her."

"Not the point, Josh," she groaned softly. "They're crawling all over this place. We don't know who we can trust."

They heard a casual knock on the bedroom door. Josh gasped and jumped with fright. Both stared at the door while clinging to the others' arm.

"No one's home," Josh cried out.

"There's no place to go, Cybil," Simon announced through the door. "You can't escape me forever."

"There's more than one way to kill a vampire, Simon. Remember?" she yelled back. "You can't escape *me* forever either!"

There was a moment of silence followed by a low snarl.

Josh looked back at Cybil with increased concern. "I'm not sure you should be upsetting the vampires."

They heard the terrifying sound of claws scratching deep into the wooden door. Both jumped back with surprise and alarm.

"Can he get in here?" Josh gasped.

"I don't think so," she replied softly although not looking away from the door. "If he could, he would've entered by now."

The corridor became silent. They no longer heard any movement outside their door. Cybil approached the balcony doors and peered out from alongside the curtains. She looked back at Josh with some surprise.

"I think they're gone," she whispered.

Josh sighed with relief and collapsed onto Heidi's bed. "What do we do now?" he asked. "We need to get off this island." Alarm suddenly crossed his face. "Where's Heidi? We have to find her."

"I think it's too late for Heidi," she announced gently. "I saw a bite mark on her chest earlier. When I came back with the doctor, she was gone."

"Heidi was bit by a vampire?" he choked on his words then shook his head. "This isn't exactly the thrill I was hoping for, you know." He stood and paced the length of the room. "So Simon and Jersey are both vampires?"

Cybil groaned lowly. "It gets worse. Brandon's one too," she informed him. "And if he can be a vampire, there's no telling how many of the others are."

"We're really in for a bumpy ride," he muttered while running his fingers through his wet hair. Josh then looked at her and pointed a warning finger. "First ray of sunlight, we're out of here." Josh appeared to consider something then looked back at Cybil with confusion. "Wait a minute. Jersey was out in the sunlight all day. I thought vampires couldn't be out in the sunlight. Was she just converted tonight?"

"Doubtful," Cybil replied. "Maybe that's just one of the misconceptions about the whole vampire gig."

Josh appeared horrified while staring at his friend. "But if they're able to come out during the day, how will we ever get off this island?"

"We're just going to have to wait it out," she replied with an exhausted sigh. "See what the morning light brings."

"So this whole ritual thing is just a ploy to get people to the resort so the vampires can feast upon unsuspecting guests? To just pick us off one at a time?"

Cybil collapsed on her bed and attempted to relax. "It sure looks that way." She sank into thought then sat up with enthusiasm. "We need to get our hands on some more of those garlic leis and some wooden crosses used in the Bloodletting Ritual. Simon didn't come after me until he tricked me into parting with them. They must have some power over the vampires."

"Why do I get this funny feeling we're never getting off this island?"

She stared at the dismal look in her friend's eyes and wished she could say something constructive. There was a soft knock on the door. Cybil sprang up from her bed and exchanged looks with Josh. They looked back at the door. Cybil slowly approached the door and moved alongside it to see if she could hear anyone.

"Cybil, are you in there?" Brandon asked through the door.

Josh and Cybil exchanged concerned looks.

"Cybil, I know you're in there. I know you're feeling a little confused and frightened," Brandon continued. "Just let me know that you're all right, and I'll leave you alone."

Josh looked at Cybil, smirked, and made a 'jerking off' motion near his crotch.

"Go away," she called out. "We're not letting you in!"

There was no response. Both looked at each other, sharing the same concern. They heard a soft tapping on the balcony door. Both jumped and let out startled cries. Cybil slowly approached the balcony door and opened the curtains to reveal Brandon. He appeared sad and defeated.

"You don't have to be afraid of me," he said gently. "I would never hurt you. I can explain everything, if you just give me a chance."

"He must think we're completely stupid," Josh muttered.

Cybil moved in front of the glass doors leaving several feet between her and the glass.

"You're a vampire," she announced. "What more do I need to know?"

"I know how it must seem, but that's not how it is," he informed her. "I don't know what to say to make you understand, but it wasn't supposed to be this way." He stared at her a moment through the glass doors. "It all goes back to the legend of the island. Evil vampires had slain the villagers and nearly wiped them out. A group of good vampires came in and saved them from annihilation." He gave her a sympathetic gaze. "We don't harm people. It's not in our nature. We're not all the same."

Cybil wasn't the least bit convinced. "Then explain Heidi's disappearance and the bite mark I saw on her," she demanded. "Explain what happened in the castle tonight. Harford was attacked, and he's probably dead." She felt her hostility rise. "Simon tried to convert me. Explain how there's no harm in that."

"Simon isn't one of us," Brandon insisted. "There are still evil vampires out there even today. I tried to keep you away from him, but you wouldn't listen to me."

"If you knew he was bad, you should have warned me," she snapped. "You should have warned the other guests."

"It's not always that easy to tell who's good and evil," he informed her. "I didn't figure it out until you were convinced your friend had been bitten. Simon was the only possible suspect." He hesitated then groaned softly. "I know it's not easy, but you have to trust me. Somewhere in your heart, you know I'm telling the truth."

Cybil stared at him a long moment then looked back at Josh. He made more faces. Cybil looked back at the balcony door with a weary, worn look.

"I don't want to trust you, Brandon," she announced. "Josh and I just want to get the hell off this island. If you really meant what you said, you'll let us leave."

"Of course you're free to leave anytime. When the sun comes up, you can catch the next boat off the island." He fidgeted slightly and gently scratched his dark brow. "There's absolutely nothing I can do to stop you. I can't be out in the sunlight."

"Then explain how Jersey was able to spend the entire afternoon in the sun with us."

He didn't seem to have an answer but attempted to offer an explanation. "Second generation vampires aren't as sensitive to sunlight, but she shouldn't be able to tolerate the direct sunlight either." Brandon sank into thought a moment. "I'd heard rumor of some sort of patch that would allow vampires to tolerate the sun, but I've never actually heard of any vampire willing to risk it."

Cybil looked back at Josh and tilted her head in silent question.

He stared back with surprise. "She wore a patch below her hairline, remember?"

"You must realize I'm sincere, Cybil. I don't want you to leave here hating me," he announced. "And I'm fairly certain you don't want to leave here hating me either."

Cybil leaned against the doorframe, rested her head against the wall, and stared blankly at the ceiling.

"Nothing short of a leap of faith could convince me to trust you, and I'm not willing to sacrifice my life for it," she informed him. "Of course it hurts. I want to believe you. I'm just really scared."

"I understand that," he insisted. "But if I wanted to devour you, don't you think I would've done it before now? I had several opportunities. It's not as if I'd need to set a romantic mood to do you in." He stared at her through the glass and pleaded with his eyes. "Vampires and mortals have been living on this island together for centuries. Most of the workers within the hotel are aware of who we are; what we are." There was a brief pause as if something seemed to cause him some emotional pain. "Vampires and mortals have even married over the years. None feared being harmed ever. It's not in our nature." He shifted uncomfortably. "My deceased wife, rest her soul, was a mortal woman. She was 92 years old when she died. She never wanted immortality, and I was fine with that. It was tough watching her grow older and sicker, but it was her wish, and I respected that."

Cybil looked at him with surprise, held her breath, and then looked back at the ceiling. There were tears in her eyes.

Josh stared at her with concern and hurried to her side. "Don't tell me you're going to fall for his sob story."

Cybil didn't look at Josh. She slowly moved back in front of the balcony doors and stared at Brandon.

"Simon had me put my garlic leis and cross in one of the caskets in the castle," she informed him. "You may want to exercise caution, if that's where you sleep."

Brandon stared at her in silence through the glass doors. A tiny smile crossed his face. "I appreciate the warning."

Cybil stared at him a long moment. Neither looked away. Brandon smiled warmly.

"Think about what I've said," he announced softly. "Goodnight, Cybil."

Cybil watched Brandon walk away from the balcony.

Josh approached her from behind. "Whatever you're thinking, get it out of your head. He's a vampire."

Cybil turned toward Josh with a stern look. "Don't you think I know that?"

She returned to her bed, cast herself upon it, and stared at the ceiling. Josh frowned and pulled the curtains closed.

Chapter Eighteen

Sunlight poked through the curtains and shined into the Cybil's guestroom. Cybil slowly woke and looked at the sunlight attempting to brighten the room. She groaned softly and rolled onto her back then looked at the second bed. Josh slept on Heidi's bed with his head beneath the pillow and both legs sticking out from under the covers on either side of the bed. Cybil slowly sat up and ran her fingers through her severely mussed hair. She couldn't stop thinking about their situation and what she feared became of their friend. There was a knock on the balcony door causing Cybil to jump and let out a startled gasp.

Josh sprang up in the bed with a startled scream and darted looks around the room. "What happened? What's wrong?"

Cybil climbed out of the bed and approached the curtains covering the balcony door. She hesitated the slowly pulled open the curtain. Angelica stood in the brilliant sunlight just outside the doors and held two garlic leis. She wore one around her neck as proof she wasn't a vampire.

Angelica forced a smile, although it was obviously insincere. "Brandon asked me to bring these to you."

Josh uncertainly got out of bed, still fully dressed from last night, and approached the balcony door. He couldn't take his eyes off Angelica. Cybil noted the sad look on his face.

"What do you think?" Josh asked softly.

"It's daylight and she's wearing garlic," Cybil replied then sighed. "She's probably not a vampire."

Josh uncertainly unlocked and opened the door, allowing Angelica to enter the room. She smiled at Cybil and flashed the cross necklace she wore around her neck.

"I think we're all safe." Angelica handed Cybil a garlic and flower leis. "Brandon asked that I escort you to the boat dock and see you off."

Josh suddenly appeared annoyed and sneered at her. "Oh, so you can be civil when we're fleeing for our lives, huh?"

Angelica frowned and slung the leis at him. He jumped having been smacked with the garlic. He caught the leis then glared at her.

"That hurt."

Angelica glared at him with limited patience and sympathy. "I heard what happened with your little blonde bombshell playmate," she snapped. "That's what happens when you play with fire."

"Is that what all this is about?" he demanded. "You're jealous over some cheap tart?"

Angelica didn't even respond to his remark. She looked at Cybil and got back to business. "The boat leaves in half an hour. I'll walk you to the dock when you're ready. Brandon said he'd notify you when he finds out anything on your other friend."

Angelica turned toward the open balcony door and was about to leave when Josh suddenly grabbed her arm, stopping her.

"I wasn't interested in Jersey," he announced a little too eagerly.

Angelica pulled her arm from his hand and glared at him. "No? Is that why she nearly sucked the life out of you while the two of you were making out in the cabana?"

Josh appeared horrified. "That wasn't my fault," he protested. "I was telling her to leave me alone. The next thing I knew, she was trying to make a blood withdrawal. I don't even *remember* kissing her."

"Only a weak man falls for the hypnotic look." Her eyes narrowed while glaring at him. "And besides, I live among the vampires. That must make me some sort of vampire sympathizer; the enemy." She folded her arms across her chest. "The vampires are my friends. You came here to exploit the legend and mock an entire way of life. They just want to live in peace among mortals."

Angelica turned and left through the open balcony doors. Josh and Cybil exchanged looks.

"You and I certainly know how to pick them, huh?" Cybil muttered.

†

Angelica led Cybil and Josh, each carrying their bags, along the dock toward the small passenger boat waiting for them. A man in his late fifties approached the boat railing and looked down at them as they prepared to board.

"I'm afraid we won't be sailing for a few hours yet," the captain informed them.

Josh stared at the boat captain and appeared alarmed. "Why not?"

"Mechanical difficulties, I'm afraid," the captain informed him. "Tried to turn her over this morning, but the old lady's being a little cranky today."

Angelica's expression turned concerned. She approached the ramp and clutched the railing. "Brandon gave specific instructions to get these two guests to the mainland this morning," she insisted. "You need to radio for another boat."

The captain shook his head. "Sorry to disappoint Brandon, but we're experiencing multiple problems today. Radio's on the blink as well," he informed her. "I'm sure we'll have the problem fixed by this evening."

"We can't wait until this evening," Josh squawked.

The captain laughed in his throat. "Afraid the vampires might get you?"

Josh mumbled, "Something like that."

The captain continued to laugh with some amusement. "Well, we'll do our best. We'll contact the front desk when she's ready to sail."

Angelica glanced back at Josh and Cybil while attempting to cover her frown. "We'll telephone the mainland and have them send someone out to get you--by plane if necessary."

"I hope this isn't some sort of trick to keep us here," Josh snapped.

Angelica glared, rolled her eyes, and then walked back to shore.

Cybil gave Josh a stern look. "And you wonder why she doesn't want to talk to you."

"Sorry if I'm a little more worried about my neck right about now, if you know what I mean."

They grabbed their bags and followed Angelica back to the resort.

†

Once they returned to the lobby, Angelica approached the desk and picked up the phone. Something seemed to be wrong. She hesitated then repeatedly struck the same button, obviously attempting to get an outside line.

"What the hell--?"

As Angelica tried again to get an outside line, Josh and Cybil stared at her with concern.

"What's wrong?" Cybil suddenly asked.

Angelica hung up the phone and looked back at them. Her expression was worrisome. "I'm not getting a dial tone for an outside line. I can make in-house calls but not beyond the resort or to the mainland."

"What about the village?" Cybil asked. "Can we make a call from somewhere in the village?"

"Very few people in town even own telephones, and none of them have lines to the mainland," Angelica informed her. "We can call the village police and the hospital on the radio, but that's the limit to their communication."

"I can't believe no one in the village owns a phone," Josh remarked. He then considered something else. "This is an island. There has to be another boat around here somewhere."

"Sure, there are boats," she informed them, "but none that could make it to the mainland. The villagers own fishing trawlers, but most of them will be out fishing all day until late evening. Even then, I don't know if any of their boats are in good enough condition to make it to the mainland. There's nothing remotely modern in the village."

Josh threw his hands in the air with disgust. "So we're trapped here. Perfect." He suddenly pointed an accusing finger at Angelica. "He did this. Brandon did this on purpose. He wanted to make us think he was trying to help us so we'd trust him and then he could trap us here."

Angelica became agitated and folded her arms across her chest while glaring at Josh. "You're wrong about Brandon. He wouldn't harm anyone."

"And if you're wrong?" Josh demanded.

"I've known Brandon for six years. If he wanted to suck my blood, he'd have gotten around to it by now," Angelica insisted. "The phone lines often go down. They'll get them fixed. It's all a coincidence." She allowed her arms to fall to her sides. "I suggest you go wrap yourself in garlic, arm yourselves with crucifixes, and lock yourselves in your room until the boat's ready to sail." She then stormed away from the front desk.

Josh watched her leave and shook his head. "Temperamental thing, isn't she? Wouldn't doubt she's one of them."

"Obviously, she's not," Cybil muttered then sighed with defeat. "Now what?"

"We get something to eat," Josh announced. "I'm starved."

As Josh turned and headed toward the restaurant, Cybil groaned softly and followed him.

Chapter Nineteen

It was already evening. Cybil alternated pacing her guestroom and looking out the balcony doors every few minutes while watching the slowly setting sun. Josh was stretched out on the bed looking almost relaxed for a change.

"I can't believe we're still stuck here," Cybil launched hotly. "No phones, no boat--it's like a bad nightmare."

"And your bloodsucking boyfriend is behind all of it," Josh muttered.

She spun to face him. "We have to do something."

"Like what? We could go to town and tell the local law that a vampire ate our friend and is coming after us," he casually remarked. "I'm sure they'd gladly lock us in a cell and prep us as a human sacrifice for tonight's ritual."

Cybil continued to pace and shook her head. "I feel so helpless."

Josh sank into thought then eyed her. "Was it my idea to come here? Because I'm thinking I really got ripped off on this vacation." He frowned and placed his hands beneath his pillow while he stared at the ceiling. "Molested by a blonde vampire vixen, running for my life, one friend vampire bait--"

A thought suddenly hit Cybil. She spun on her heels and looked at Josh. "My God, I can't believe it didn't come to me sooner." Cybil hurried for the door and looked back at him. "Stay here. Don't do anything until I get back."

Josh quickly sat up and stared at her with surprise. "Where are you going? Vampire sundowner syndrome isn't an exact science, you know. They could be out and about already."

Cybil looked back at him while opening the door. "This is important. Don't go anywhere."

"Cybil--" he protested.

She hurried from the room without further explanation. Josh frowned and groaned lowly.

†

Guests were milling about the lobby after dinner as they prepared for the outdoor festivities. Cybil hurried into the lobby and glanced at the front desk. Angelica was busy with a guest and didn't even notice her. Cybil quickly slipped past the desk and into the back, employee corridor. She hurried into Brandon's office, shut the door behind her, and then hurried for the desk toward the back. Cybil flopped into the chair before the computer and clicked on the internet icon. It reported there was no connection, which was probably due to the phone lines also being down. She frowned then sank into thought. Cybil then rolled the mouse over the documents folder and searched through random files. She suddenly hesitated, slowly sat back in the chair, and stared at the computer screen with disbelief while shaking her head. She heard the door quietly shut behind her. Cybil spun around in the desk chair and saw Brandon standing by the door with his hands in his pockets.

"I suppose I should be upset to find you poking around on my computer, but I guess I'm just glad you decided not to leave," he announced. "What changed your mind?"

"Being held captive had something to do with it," she remarked.

Brandon appeared confused while removing his hands from his pockets. "I don't understand. I gave Angelica specific instructions."

"The boat--dead. The radio--dead. The phones--dead."

Brandon practically lunged for the phone on the desk near her. Cybil rolled in the chair a few feet away from him and watched. He listened for a dial tone then practically slammed it down on its base.

He looked at her with surprise. "How long has communication been cut?"

"Since sunup."

It was obvious Brandon's mind was racing with the information. He again looked at her. "Did anyone take the motorboat to the mainland?"

"Angelica said it was too far."

"It's a trek, but it's been done before." Brandon studied her a moment longer than fidgeted. "I'll send someone out right away. I always keep my promises."

Cybil nodded then stood but refrained from moving further away from him.

Brandon seemed curious. "Showing a little faith? I really didn't expect to find you behind enemy lines." He indicated her bare neck. "And unarmed."

They exchanged silent stares. He seemed to know something was going through her mind, but he didn't call her on it. Cybil drew a deep, nervous breath and slowly took a step closer to him.

"Angelica said something this morning and it didn't sink in until just a few minutes ago," she informed him.

He tilted his head and appeared curious. "What was that?"

"She said no one in town has phones or any modern technology."

"That's true," Brandon replied. "It's a small, old-fashioned village. They barely have electric. What about it?"

Cybil stared into his eyes despite her anxiety and concerns. "Well, that makes you one of the few people with internet access."

Brandon still appeared puzzled. "I'm guessing I'm the only one with internet access," he replied. "I don't understand where this is going. If the phone line is down, I can't connect to the internet either. You know that."

Her body trembled slightly from his words. She uncertainly took another step toward him while keeping her eyes locked on his. "I was sitting in my room trying to think of who could help us out of this situation. Someone I trusted. There was only one person who kept popping into my mind." Cybil studied him a long moment with a strange look on her face. "I have to take that leap of faith, because there's only one person who could possibly help me now. It's you, *Count*."

Brandon's expression suddenly dropped as he stared at her. His eyes almost lit up with surprise. "You're *Witchy Woman*?"

Cybil attempted a smile and slowly nodded.

Brandon couldn't stop staring at her then suddenly appeared offended. "Wait? You planned a trip here and didn't tell me?"

She was surprised by his offended tone. "That hardly seems important right now."

"You're right," he snapped. "I'll be pissed later." Brandon studied her a moment and gave her a strange look. "You seem more *normal* then I'd expected."

"Well, I assumed you were different too," she remarked, "but not this different."

Brandon's mood softened considerably as he stared at her, a tiny smile across his face. "So, perhaps you can trust me after all?" he asked gently. "All those hours chatting on-line. You must realize I'm not the monster you think I am."

Cybil took another step closer and stared into his eyes. They stood only a foot apart now. Brandon remained ridged and didn't move.

A tiny, nervous smile crossed her face. "I'm ready to take that leap of faith." She slowly moved closer to him and placed her arms around his neck while staring into his eyes. "I have to trust you."

Brandon gently pulled her into his arms and groaned softly. "You don't know how much I wanted to hear that."

He lowered his mouth to hers and gently kissed her. Cybil uncertainly returned the kiss while attempting to relax. It was difficult at first, but the more passionate his kiss, the more relaxed she became. Brandon slowly broke off the kiss, almost disappointing her, but didn't release her.

He brushed his cheek against hers and whispered softly in her ear. "Now don't become alarmed--"

Brandon slowly pulled back to meet her gaze, revealing his sharpened fangs. Cybil tensed slightly at the sight of them but didn't pull away. She studied the new look and attempted to relax. It was difficult, but his warm smile beyond the fangs was reassuring.

"Just a side effect of over-stimulation," he informed her. "It doesn't mean I'm preparing to devour you or anything."

Cybil continued to stare then managed a tiny smile. "I'll trust you on that."

She uncertainly leaned closer and kissed him gently on the mouth. He gratefully returned the kiss, allowing it to turn more passionate and slightly aggressive. His mouth left hers as he warmly kissed her neck and throat. Cybil tensed slightly, gripping his shoulders out of reflex, but she didn't stop him or pull away. Brandon eagerly returned to her mouth and continued kissing her. She easily returned the kiss with renewed passion and trust. There was an urgent knock on the office door, startling them. Cybil jumped away from Brandon. He fidgeted slightly and kept his back to the door to keep anyone entering from seeing him in full vampire mode.

"Come in."

As the door opened, he glanced over his shoulder and saw Angelica. Brandon turned to face her despite his exposed fangs. She eyed both with a look of surprise then allowed her gaze to fall upon his mouth. His fangs were again gone.

Angelica appeared slightly embarrassed. "Did I, uh, interrupt something?"

Brandon attempted a pleasant smile. "No, Cybil and I were just making amends." His look then turned serious. "Is something wrong?"

Angelica appeared concerned and slightly distraught. "One of the guards found that missing man in the woods."

"His status?" Brandon asked with concern.

Angelica frowned and shook her head. Brandon shut his eyes with a low, painful groan. He looked back at Angelica and immediately took charge.

"What's the status on the transport boat?" Brandon asked.

"I haven't heard from the captain for a few hours," she replied. "Last I'd heard he wasn't able to correct the problem."

"Get one of the guards to check the dock," he ordered. "I'm not sure I like the situation."

Angelica nodded and hurried from the room. Brandon looked back at Cybil and the concerned look on her face.

"Do you think Simon's behind all of this?" she asked while fidgeting.

"I'd prefer not to take any chances," he replied. "We know he has one of his brood with him, but there's no telling if he's converted others."

"His brood?"

"Vampires like Simon always have several female converts surrounding them. It's like a symbol of status for his kind," Brandon informed her then frowned with distaste. "Unfortunately, they're often used as drones to protect him from destruction. Sort of his frontline defense. They're willing to die for him. Cowardly and sick, if you ask me."

Cybil appeared concerned. "What about Heidi? Have you found her?"

"We searched the castle from top to bottom, but she wasn't there," he replied although his look told a more unnerving story.

"You suspect she's one of his female converts, don't you?" Cybil asked, although she already knew the answer since yesterday.

"It would be the only explanation for the bite mark you found on her."

Cybil slowly sat on the edge of the desk with a defeated look. "Oh, Heidi." She then looked back at Brandon. "So what do we do now?"

"There's nothing more you can do," he replied. "I'll walk you back to your room. As long as you don't allow him to enter, he can't get to you and your friend. We'll advise all the hotel guests and mortal staff to return to their rooms." He released a soft sigh. "The rest of us will begin our own vampire hunt."

Cybil sprang to her feet and stared at him with concern. "That sounds dangerous."

"We can't allow evil vampires to roam our island," he insisted. "None of the villagers will ever be safe again. He has to be chased out or destroyed."

She fidgeted and remained sympathetic. "Are you sure there's nothing I can do to help?"

"You're the one he wants," Brandon informed her. "You're at risk everywhere but within your own room."

"What makes my room so safe? Heidi was attacked in our room."

"She must have invited him inside. He can't enter without your permission," he insisted. "I'll see you safely back to your room."

"What if something happens to you?" she asked softly.

Brandon smiled gently and touched her face. "I appreciate the concern, but I can handle myself."

Cybil stared into his eyes, smiled warmly, and kissed him. Brandon returned the kiss with more aggression but restrained himself.

He pulled away with a pleased, fanged smile. "I hope this means you'll consider staying here on the island with me once this is all over."

Cybil smiled warmly and gently caressed his chest. "I think it would be worth looking into."

Brandon smiled and kissed her quickly on the lips. "Let's get you back to your room."

Chapter Twenty

Security guards patrolled the resort in great numbers like a military strike force. Guests were politely rounded up and directed back to their rooms. Many grumbled about the mandatory lockdown but did as instructed with little incident. A few became agitated but eventually returned to their rooms as well. Cybil and Brandon hurried across the lobby and witnessed security guards attempting to coral the last of the guests.

"We have to ask that everyone returns to their rooms for the entire evening," a guard announced to a small crowd that had collected in the lobby. "We have reports of a swarm of infectious bugs heading this way. For your own safety, we ask that you remain in your rooms until you are advised it's safe to leave." He seemed to have their full attention now. "This is a high risk bug with the potential to cause death within hours. For your own health and welfare, we must ask that everyone return to their rooms and remain inside with the doors and windows shut."

Cybil looked around the lobby as Brandon rushed her through. "You're very efficient."

"Infectious bugs sounds better than a killer vampire on the loose," Brandon replied. "Too many of our young guests would probably want a selfie with the killer vampire."

As they headed toward the connecting corridor leading to Cybil's bungalow, Heidi entered the lobby. Cybil saw her friend, held back her gasp, and clutched Brandon's hand, stopping him. Brandon stared at Cybil's friend, who looked perfectly normal and healthy. Heidi appeared relieved to see Cybil and quickly approached them.

"Cybil, I was looking everywhere for you!"

Cybil stared at her friend and never felt so terrified to see her. Brandon flung Cybil behind him and glared at Heidi. Heidi appeared slightly surprised and mostly confused as she attempted to look past Brandon to her friend.

"What's going on?" Heidi avoided looking at Brandon and attempted to talk to Cybil past him. "Cybil--?"

Brandon continued to stare at Heidi and kept her from making contact with Cybil. There was a low growl within his throat. Upon hearing the growl, Heidi met Brandon's gaze. Once their eyes met, Heidi backed up a step and trembled with fear.

"Cybil, don't let him hurt me," Heidi begged.

Cybil watched the exchange and felt sympathy for her friend. What if she hadn't been converted? She couldn't let Brandon hurt her. Brandon took a step toward Heidi and stared her down. Heidi suddenly cowered and hissed while covering her face with her arm. Cybil felt her heart sink. It was true! Heidi had been converted. She was a vampire! Two guards suddenly rushed toward them. Heidi attempted to escape them and ran for the front doors. The guards cut off her path. She plowed through them and leaped into the glass doors. The glass doors shattered as she crashed through them. A few remaining guests were heard gasping with alarm then exchanged frightened words as they looked toward the broken glass. Heidi was already gone. The other guards rushed the remaining guests across the lobby and toward their rooms. Brandon hurried Cybil for the connecting corridor leading to her room.

✝

Josh nervously paced the length of Cybil's guestroom before the open curtains leading to the balcony. It was already dark outside, which didn't help ease his tensions any. Heidi suddenly appeared on the balcony while screaming and pounding on the glass. Josh turned and looked at the glass doors.

"Josh, help me," Heidi cried out. "She's going to kill me!"

Josh turned slightly pale as he nervously approached the doors while staring at his friend with distrust. Jersey appeared on the balcony behind Heidi and approached her with her fangs exposed. Heidi continued to pound on the door in terror.

"Josh!"

Josh unlocked the door and opened it, allowing Heidi inside. She bolted into the room past him. Josh quickly shut and locked the door behind her.

"Oh, Josh, I was so worried," Heidi gasped.

Josh stared at Jersey through the glass doors then quickly moved away from them. He turned toward Heidi about to speak when he saw her fangs beyond her slightly twisted grin. Heidi snarled and leaped for Josh. Josh cried out and bolted from her path. He leaped across the bed, ran for the guestroom door, and screamed as he threw open the door. Josh bolted into the corridor to escape his friend and nearly collided with Harford. Josh saw him and leaped backwards while screaming. Heidi lunged from the room and leaped for Josh. Harford let out a loud snarl while revealing his own vampire teeth while stepping between her and Josh. Heidi gasped with alarm and jumped away from the large, intimidating man. Josh saw Harford's fangs, screamed again, and ran down the hall. Heidi attempted to bolt away from Harford. He grabbed her by the throat and lifted her into the air. She hissed and thrashed to free herself from the hulking man.

Jersey suddenly appeared in the hallway, cried out, and leaped onto Harford's back. He tossed Heidi across the hall like a rag doll and easily slung Jersey from his back. She struck the floor and rolled several times before crashing into the nearby wall. Cybil and Brandon appeared in the hallway, saw the commotion, and ran toward them. Brandon attempted to keep Cybil behind him as they approached. Jersey saw Brandon and became enraged. She hissed at him, cried out, and leaped for him. Brandon suddenly produced a sharpened, wooden stake and thrust it forward as she leaped for him. The stake impaled her in the chest, stopping her in midair. As he released the stake, she dropped to the floor, writhing in pain and clutching the wooden stake in her chest.

Harford looked around the hall for Heidi, but she was gone. He looked back at Brandon. "The other one got away."

Cybil stared at Jersey lying dead on the floor. She wasn't sure why she expected to see more blood surrounding the stake through her chest. It was a grim reminder that the young woman wasn't human anymore. She controlled her emotions and looked back at Harford with some surprise.

"You're not dead?" she gasped.

His look was hard and cold. "No, just pissed."

"What happened to Josh?" Brandon asked.

"He took off down the hall," Harford replied. "Security will get him."

Brandon looked back at Cybil and frowned with defeat. "You'd better stay with me for now," he announced. "We'll find your friend then put you in a room with one of the mortal staff."

✝

Angelica walked along the pier toward the docked boat with Victor. The dock was well-lit with rows of lights leading the way. The boat had a few lights on as well, but there didn't appear to be any signs of life onboard.

"Captain," Victor called to the boat.

There was no response.

"He must be below in the engine room working on fixing the problem," Angelica announced.

Victor walked up the ramp toward the deck with Angelica following. As they approached the control room, Angelica glanced over the side of the ship into the dark water. The captain suddenly appeared from the control room, alerting Victor, who abruptly stopped. Angelica collided with the guard's broad back. Victor was about to speak when the captain reached out for him while gasping. The captain's throat has been slashed and blood soaked the entire front of his shirt. Angelica held back her startled scream as the captain fell into the guard. Victor caught him and lowered him to the deck.

"What the--?" Angelica cried out but the guard immediately silenced her.

Victor hurried her back along deck toward the loading ramp. An alarming gust of air blew past them, causing Angelica to look around with concern. Victor suddenly stopped and whirled Angelica behind him, nearly throwing her to the deck. By the time she caught her balance, Simon was already on top of the guard. Victor's fangs appeared as they clawed at each other while growling and hissing. Simon grabbed Victor by his throat and kept him at arms distance away. Despite the guard's muscular build, Simon appeared to be stronger than he was. Simon used his free left hand to break the nearby wooden railing. With one swift motion, Simon cast Victor backward onto the jagged wooden railing, impaling him through the heart. Victor cried out and clutched the jagged end of the railing protruding through his chest. It only took a moment for him to stop struggling and cease to breath. Angelica screamed at Victor's horrifying death then ran along deck away from Simon.

98

Simon casually followed after Angelica as she ran along the deck before finally reaching the bow. She looked over the railing then back in the direction she had just come. Simon was no longer behind her. Angelica continued to breathe heavily and nervously scanned the area for Simon. A shadow moved along the deck beneath her feet. Angelica looked toward the deck, gasped when she saw the shadow, and jumped around wildly to avoid it. She leaped over the shadow and ran back for the loading ramp, briefly glancing at the dead guard still dangling from the railing. Angelica ran down the ramp, leaped the last few feet, and collided with someone. Angelica screamed and thrashed while wildly throwing punches.

Josh attempted to stop her from hitting him. "Angelica, stop it!"

Angelica stopped swinging and stared with a look of fear yet relief. She suddenly looked behind her toward the ship then back at Josh. "We have to get to safety. He's after me!"

As they turned, Heidi approached them from the other end of the dock.

Josh stared at Heidi and grabbed Angelica's arm. "And *she's* after me."

They were trapped near the end of the dock, so Heidi appeared to be in no particular hurry. She smiled almost lustfully and licked her fangs. Angelica stared at Heidi and panicked. A shadow approached them from the boat. Josh pulled Angelica along the dock further away from shore and Heidi. As the shadow closed in on them, he forced her to run. The end of the dock approached fast.

Angelica stared at the end of the dock and suddenly gasped, "Josh--"

Josh and Angelica both screamed as they ran for the end of the dock.

"Just jump, damn it!"

The shadow flew past them and formed into Simon at the end of the dock before them. Both screamed but didn't slow. Josh shoved his shoulder into Angelica, casting both off the side of the dock and into the water. They screamed on the way down just before splashing into the dark water.

†

Several minutes later, Josh and Angelica stumbled from the water and walked onto the dimly lit beach. Both bent over and gasped for air. Josh looked around while hunched over. Angelica appeared ready to collapse.

"Do you think we lost him?" Josh panted.

"I don't think he was following us," she replied while gasping for air.

Josh saw the dark entrance to a cave just before them and gave a weary nod. "What's that?"

"It's a back entrance to the castle," she replied and slowly straightened. "It leads into the dungeon."

"That's not the way we want to go," Josh muttered then looked around. "Which way to the resort?"

Angelica pointed across the beach in the distance. Heidi walked along the beach toward them.

Josh suddenly straightened and shook his head with defeat. "She always hated me."

Angelica stared at the approaching woman and pulled on Josh's arm. "If she knows we're here, so does he. We have to seek refuge within the castle."

Josh stared at her and appeared horrified. "Are you out of your mind? That's where the vampires sleep! You don't escape the lion by hiding in its den!"

"It's Brandon's home," Angelica announced while pulling on his arm. "I know where there are some useful items. Garlic, crosses, things like that. We have to go."

Josh reluctantly ran with Angelica for the cave entrance.

Chapter Twenty-one

Cybil and Brandon hurried through the lobby as several guards and one or two hotel workers kept the area secure. Harford saw them enter and hurried toward Brandon.

"One of the guards reported the convert woman chasing Angelica and Josh into the castle cave," Harford announced. "He went after them to help."

Cybil held back her frightened gasp then looked at Brandon. "Simon's after him because of me, I know it."

Brandon didn't respond to her comment, instead keeping his attention on Harford. "I want you to take Cybil to one of the staff rooms and keep an eye on her. I'll take some of the guards and go to the castle after them."

She stared at Brandon and immediately resisted. "No, I'm going with you."

Brandon glared at Cybil with limited patience. "You're staying here with Harford," he scoffed. "I don't need you putting yourself in danger and compromising my ability to act."

"Josh is my friend," she protested. "Isn't it enough that I've already lost one friend to that monster? I want to help." Her eyes pleaded with his. "I can help you, I know I can."

"Absolutely not," he snapped without even considering it. "This is no place for a mortal."

"Well, at least it doesn't have anything to do with my being a woman for a change," she snapped back then took a firm stance. "He wants *me*. Like it or not, he's going to find me, so I may as well be with the undead SWAT team."

Brandon nodded to Harford. Harford nodded, took Cybil by the arm, and attempted to lead her toward the staff wing. Cybil fought the large man attempting to remove her. The mild flames within the fireplace suddenly erupted upward, startling several guards as well as Brandon. They looked around with concern, attempting to locate the source of the phenomenon. The doors and windows suddenly flew open and a strong, gusty wind blew harshly throughout the room. Objects were caught within the wind and jetted across the room. Vases crashed against the opposing walls and furniture was thrown across the floor. Everyone took cover and looked around for signs of Simon. Brandon suddenly hesitated and looked behind him. Cybil had managed to pull free from Harford and stood within the center of the gusting wind with her hands in the air and her eyes closed. The guards now stared at her with alarm as well, realizing the source. Cybil opened her eyes and dropped her hands. The wind flew forward, throwing every guard and Brandon across the floor by ten feet. They slowly picked themselves up and looked at Cybil with amazement. Cybil met Brandon's surprised gaze.

She folded her arms across her chest while glaring at him. "You boys aren't the only freaks around this place."

†

Cybil followed Brandon and several guards through an underground cavern beneath the resort. It seemed to extend forever. They finally paused before an old, iron door. Brandon opened the door and looked back at Cybil.

"This is a secret passageway to the castle," he informed her. "It's how those of us who are pure vampires move around during the day. Converts and second and third generation vampires aren't as sensitive to sunlight as we are."

Two guards entered first with Cybil and Brandon filing in behind them. The remainder of the guards and Harford brought up the rear. Cybil quietly walked alongside Brandon and kept a close eye on the walls. Torches were lit along the entire corridor, casting concerning shadows. She kept an eye on the shadows even though Brandon and the other vampires would sense if Simon were near. As they walked, Brandon glanced at her several times.

"What happened back there in the lobby?" he asked almost timidly. "It's nothing I've ever encountered before."

Cybil appeared slightly ashamed and fidgeted. "A few years ago, I discovered the man who raised me wasn't my real father. My mother had a very brief and unusual relationship with a man who claimed to be a magician." She tensed slightly. "When I did more research, I'd discovered he wasn't a magician at all. He was a warlock. I always knew I was different." She managed a slightly uneasy laugh. "When I met you on-line, I felt I'd found someone who could maybe understand what I was going through. I thought I'd be able fit in if I was with others who saw beyond what's supposed to be normal."

"So Witchy Woman wasn't just a screen name?"

Cybil allowed a slight laugh escape her throat. "No, I'm afraid not. My powers are very limited," she informed him. "My research indicates it could stay that way, or I may develop them in later years. Honestly, I really don't fit in anywhere."

Brandon studied her while they walked. A tiny smile crossed his face revealing his vampire fangs as he chuckled softly. "Well then, welcome to the club."

✝

They finally reached the main castle and entered the grand hallway. The four security guards removed small crossbows from beneath their jackets and looked around the darkened hallway. Cybil was slightly uncomfortable within the darkness and her limited visibility. She insecurely rubbed her chilled shoulders.

"So how do you intend to defeat Simon?" she finally asked while they waited in the grand hallway for the guards to sweep the surrounding area.

"The crossbows the guards carry are loaded with wooden arrows," Brandon informed her.

"Must be creepy," she remarked. "Vampires hunting vampires." She again looked around the darkened hallway. "A little dark in here, don't you think?"

"We're nocturnal, remember. We have little need for artificial light," Brandon informed her. "Simon has no advantage over us."

"What about Josh and Angelica?" she asked. "They'll never see him coming."

"I'm hoping Angelica went where I think she went," Brandon replied.

Cybil appeared concerned while looking around. "Still, I'd rather stack the odds in Josh's favor."

103

She nervously waved her hand along the hallway. Every torch erupted into flames, lighting the entire hallway and every room within the castle. The guards, Harford, and Brandon looked around then back at her with some surprise.

She attempted a tiny smile. "I have a flare for fire."

Once the guards finished their sweep of the main area, they continued along the now brightened hallway. Someone moved within the shadows where the torch light didn't quite reach. The guards aimed their crossbows into the shadows then scanned the area.

"Convert," Harford announced, alerting them.

"Heidi?" Cybil gasped.

"Hard to say," Harford replied while smelling the air. "Definitely female."

"There's no telling how many he may have converted," Brandon informed her. "There's a chapel toward the back of the castle. It was blessed by the village priest in the event of a vampire invasion. It contains anti-vampire devices." Brandon looked at Cybil and offered her a reassuring look. "Angelica knows of its existence. If they're able to reach it, she'll take your friend there."

They heard more movement along the walls. Brandon took Cybil's arm and pulled her closer to him as they searched the walls and ceiling. The guards kept their crossbows aimed. Four female vampires came at them from the ceiling. The guards found their targets and fired their crossbows. One convert was struck in the shoulder while a second was hit in the chest, immediately falling to the floor. The guards attempted to reload, but the remaining three converts recovered too fast, forcing them to resort to physical combat.

Brandon pulled Cybil away from the battle. "This isn't going to be pleasant," he informed her. "The guards will handle them. Harford and I will take you to the chapel. Hopefully your friend and Angelica are there."

Brandon and Harford hurried Cybil along the hallway past the fight. The guards swiftly overpowered the converts in a bloody battle of teeth and claws. Cybil grimaced and looked away.

✝

Brandon and Harford led Cybil toward the chapel near the back of a small connecting hallway. Shadows appeared to move along the walls and ceiling, putting them on high alert. Brandon kept Cybil close and hurried her toward their destination. Harford looked around while aiming his crossbow at the ceiling. They were almost upon the door when a shadow leaped across the hall and knocked Brandon into the next room. Cybil screamed. Harford grabbed Cybil by the arm, slung her behind him, and approached the room. Heidi suddenly leaped on top of Harford and knocked the crossbow from his hand. Harford easily tossed Heidi off him. She recovered a little too quickly and shoved him harshly into the chapel door with a tremendous thump. Harford appeared slightly dazed from the hard hit. Cybil stared at her friend with shock and horror.

Heidi slowly approached Cybil with a fanged smile. "We want you to join us, Cybil. It's your destiny."

She backed up a step and nervously shook her head. "I don't think so."

Cybil then turned and ran for Harford and the chapel door. She struck the door and attempted to open it, but it wouldn't open. She turned just in time to see Heidi running for her. Cybil screamed and leaped away from the door and out of her path. The chapel door suddenly opened to reveal Josh. He cried out with horror when he saw Heidi running straight for him. Unable to stop in time, Heidi hit the open doorway and was repelled at the threshold as if being struck by lightning. She was thrown backwards twenty feet through the air, struck the floor, and slid another ten feet along the hall. Heidi lay on the floor motionless. Cybil looked at Josh in the doorway then both looked back to their motionless friend on the floor. Harford pulled himself to his feet, reclaimed his crossbow, and slowly approached the motionless woman. He pushed Heidi onto her back with his foot and aimed the crossbow at her.

Heidi suddenly grabbed his ankle and pulled his feet out from under him. Harford struck the floor, cracking the stone. Heidi leaped to her feet, snatched the discarded crossbow, and aimed it at Harford. Cybil gasped with horror and ran toward them. She tackled Heidi to the floor, knocking the crossbow from her hand. Heidi grabbed Cybil around the waist and attempted to bite her on the neck. Harford jumped to his knees, grabbed Heidi around the neck, and attempted to keep her teeth away from Cybil. Heidi bit Harford on the arm, causing him enough pain to release his hold. Cybil attempted to hold Heidi back, but she had gravity working against her with Heidi on top of her. Cybil heard the distinct sound of parting air. Heidi suddenly gasped while releasing Cybil and looked at her blood-soaked chest. The tip of the crossbow arrow stuck out of her chest directly through her heart. Heidi appeared frightened as she looked at Cybil then gasped and collapsed to the floor.   Cybil scrambled into a sitting position and looked at Josh, who stood only a few feet away while lowering the crossbow.   Cybil exhaled with relief.

Simon suddenly bolted from the nearby room, grabbed Cybil around the waist, and leaped along the wall and down the connecting hall, taking Cybil with him.   Cybil screamed the entire way.

"Cybil," Josh cried out with horror.

Angelica ran toward him with her own crossbow and extra arrows.   Brandon staggered from the room while bleeding freely from several injuries on his neck, shoulder, and side.   He looked around with concern.

"Where's Cybil?"

Josh grabbed extra arrows from Angelica and ran down the hall in the direction Simon took his friend.

Harford had just finished reloading his crossbow and saw him take off down the hall.   "Josh, no!"

Chapter Twenty-two

The damp, dimly lit dungeon had only a few torches lit to brighten the corridors. Rats squealed and scurried along the wet stone floor. Simon leaped from the shadows on the wall with the still thrashing and screaming Cybil under his arm. He landed on the floor and immediately pinned her to the wall. She gasped with surprise and stared into his eyes with apparent concern. Simon smiled and exposed his sharp fangs.

"I'm sorry it has to be this way, my dear," he announced in a suave, moderately lustful tone, "but I promise you'll feel differently about our eternity together by dawn."

Simon seductively moved his fanged mouth toward her neck despite her attempt to hold him back. She let out a scream, causing every torch within the dungeon to erupt into flames. Simon pulled back and appeared momentarily startled, looking for signs of trespassers. He looked back at Cybil and the nearly blank look in her eyes. He smiled beyond sharp fangs.

"That's you. You're the one doing that," he gasped with renewed pleasure. "Well, what do we have here? So much more than a pretty face."

Cybil didn't look away and her harsh expression didn't change. The flames from a nearby torch suddenly erupted into Simon's face. He cried out and leaped backward while covering his face. Cybil bolted down the corridor and away from him.

Simon lowered his arms and smiled mockingly as he watched her attempt to run away from him. "Come back here, Cybil," he called after her with a laugh. "You can't escape me!"

As Simon attempted to run after her, every torch burst into massive flames and blocked the entire corridor.

Simon leaped backward and stared with surprise. "Wow, she's good."

✝

Cybil ran from the cave onto the moonlit beach. The night was calm, clear, and warm. She ran across the sand in the direction of the resort. As she neared the resort, she suddenly stopped. The beach was filled with guests drinking, dancing, and having a good time. She stared with horror as the guests partied despite being told to stay in their rooms. A shadow suddenly fell over her. Cybil tensed then slowly looked behind her. Simon stood just a few feet away from her. Cybil let out a startled cry then ran for the crowded beach and the resort in the near distance. Once she reached the guest packed beach, Cybil ran through the crowd, receiving several looks from drunken guests. A shadow loomed overhead. Cybil skidded to a stop and looked back, but Simon was nowhere to be found. She knew he could be anywhere. Cybil turned toward the resort and saw Simon standing only a few feet in front of her with a seductive smile upon his face. He casually approached her as she nervously backed up through the crowd of half drunken guests. She eyed the unsuspecting crowd while backing through them.

"Quite the dilemma, isn't it?" Simon teased. "Your compassion for others is your weakness. At any moment, my followers could have a feast of their own, and you don't even know how many of these people already belong to me." His eyes pleaded with hers while he maintained his lustful grin. "Just give in to me, Cybil, and these foolish, drunken mortals can have their fun, I promise. It's only you I want." He stared deep into her eyes. "And if you look deep within yourself, you know you want to join me for all eternity as well. Our time together was special, so much more than with any other, I assure you. Surely you've felt it too."

Cybil continued to back slowly through the crowd. She nervously eyed everyone, now suspicious of them. Several men and women appeared to be watching her as well. They had that glossed

108

over, vampire drone look in their eyes. Cybil nervously looked back at Simon then it dawned on her.

"You came here to take over the resort," she gasped. "You intend to use the Bloodletting Ritual to bring unsuspecting victims to you and your minions."

"It's the perfect set up, Cybil," he announced cheerfully. "Once you're converted, you'll understand the necessity of why I need what Brandon has here. It's perfect." He attempted a sincere smile. "I know you have mortal feelings for that one, but he's holding our kind back, making us into working class, subservient beings. You'll see everything much more clearly once you join us; join me." His smile turned mocking. "You'll see how weak and oppressive Brandon and his followers really are. And as a wedding gift to you, I'll allow you the privilege of killing him."

Cybil suddenly stopped and stared at Simon with a look of surprise, chilled by his words.

"It will be quite an honor for you, my dear," he informed her. "By killing him, you will achieve something beyond your wildest dreams. By drinking his blood, you will be a queen worshipped by all. Together, we can rule this island and the entire vampire order."

Cybil continued to stare at him, her expression oddly blank.

Simon smiled and took a step closer. "What do you say, my dear? Shall we rule this island together?"

He extended his hand to her. Cybil looked at his hand then slowly extended her hand toward him. Simon's smile brightened with satisfaction. As Cybil raised her hand, the wind suddenly whipped harshly and clouds rolled fiercely across the once clear sky. Thunder rumbled loudly and lightning flashed. Both human and non-human guests appeared startled. Simon appeared surprised as well then looked back at her and frowned.

"Is that your final answer?" he snarled. "Must this turn into a blood fest?"

Cybil's look was harsh as her eyes pierced through his. "No, *this* is my final answer."

Cybil threw her hands into the air. The wind suddenly shot past her, knocking over tables. Objects flew through the air and people were thrown to the sand. The thunder cracked loud and steady as lightning shot violently all around the beach. Human guests screamed and ran for the hotel as his followers attempted to grab the fleeing guests while dodging flying garlic leis. Simon attempted to grab Cybil but the wind and sand kept him at bay. Several locals saw Simon's vampire followers and became horrified.

"Vampire!"

Massive screams and widespread panic filled the running guests. Simon struggled against the wind and sand and leaped for Cybil. She suddenly pointed at him with rage in her eyes. Lightning flew from her fingertips and struck him, casting him backward and through the air. He harshly struck the pavilion and crashed through the flimsy wall.

Running guests continued to scream and grabbed flying garlic leis and candle crosses while heading for the hotel. Simon's converted vampire guests continued their pursuit. Cybil spun around and pointed at them. Lightning flew from her fingertips and struck several vampires, throwing them backwards through the air. She waved her left hand. The sand whirled together in the form of a sand tornado and sucked up two more of Simon's followers. They were cast across the beach. Simon leaped from the pavilion and through the air. As Cybil looked up, Simon was gone. She uncertainly looked around. The only people remaining on the beach were fallen vampires from Simon's army. Cybil continued to look around. Simon suddenly swooped down and tackled Cybil to the sand. She was momentarily stunned by the hard hit. When she looked up, Simon was on top of her, about to bite her neck. Cybil appeared alarmed and gasped.

A large, black object suddenly struck Simon in the face and tossed him off Cybil. The huge, fifty pound vampire bat was attached to Simon's body while biting his neck. Cybil scrambled to her knees and watched as Simon struggled against the vampire bat. He finally ripped the bat from his neck, revealing two deep scratches where its fangs had been embedded. He cast the bat several feet but it caught itself before striking the ground. It transformed flawlessly into Brandon. Simon sprang to his feet and glared at Brandon. Brandon stared back with a cold and hardened look. Simon growled then cried out and lunged for him. Brandon cast himself to the sand and flipped onto his backside as Simon leaped downward to land on him. Brandon grabbed a candlestick cross with a broken shaft and thrust it upward as Simon came down upon him. Simon struck the cross candlestick, piercing his chest as he landed on Brandon. Brandon pushed Simon off him and gasped as he fell onto his back.

Simon gasped and spit up blood while looking at the wooden candlestick cross protruding from his chest with the cross proudly displayed at the very end. Simon gasped again as his followers slowly gathered around him with looks of horror. Simon eyes rolled back as he turned to dust. All his followers suddenly collapsed to the sand. Brandon stumbled to his feet. Cybil jumped up from the sand and leaped into Brandon's arms. He held her against him a long moment before she finally pulled back and met his gaze.

"How did you know where to find me?"

"All vampires have a highly developed sixth sense." Brandon offered a tiny, sly smile and laughed. "Actually, your little lightning event gave away your location."

Cybil smiled warmly and resumed hugging him. The fallen followers uncertainly picked themselves up from the sand and looked around with disorientation.

Chapter Twenty-three

The following night, the Bloodletting Ritual continued as if nothing had ever happened. For those unwittingly converted, it *was* as if nothing had ever happened. None remembered the incident. Ironically, the other guests thought it was just part of the show and easily forgot about it. The villagers knew the truth, but it was their belief in their continued protection from the good vampires that allowed them to continue with the ritual and show their appreciation. Angelica and Josh enjoyed a romantic beachside cabana for two while taking in the festivities from a distance. They'd been inseparable since last evening after barely escaping evil vampires with their lives. Brandon and Cybil walked along a secluded section of beach together while the guests, villagers, and staff danced and partied around the Bloodletting bonfire. Cybil and Brandon stopped near the large rock formation and stared into the ocean together while in each other's arms. Lit torches from the nearby party lent a moderately romantic glow.

"So what now?" Cybil asked while glancing at him.

"We live happily ever after in our tropical paradise for the rest of eternity," Brandon teased.

Cybil smiled timidly while staring into his eyes. "I'm not sure I want to live forever, Brandon. I hope you understand."

"I understand, but it's not easy outliving wives."

Cybil smiled slyly and placed her hands on his shoulders. "You know, your average witch lives approximately three hundred years or longer." She informed him. "I'm not promising anything, but why don't we see how the first two hundred years go and take it from there."

Brandon studied her a long moment with a strange look of surprise. He then offered a pleased smile. "If I can't talk you into eternity before then, I suppose I'll just have to join the sunbather's club."

She grimaced slightly. "Hmm, sounds extra crispy."

Brandon laughed softly then smiled warmly. "I meant what I said. No pressure on converting. I'll cherish whatever amount of time we have together."

"You're quite the smooth talker--Count."

Brandon smiled and dipped her backwards, surprising her. He leaned closer and kissed her warmly but passionately on the mouth. As she returned the passionate kiss, the torches along the beach slowly dimmed.

The End

Holly Copella

Reaper of Souls

Chapter One

The charming country tavern was alive with cheerful, drunken locals, who were line-dancing, playing pool, and socializing. A lanky man in his late twenties, Dylan Rampert, played pool with another man, Oscar. Dylan was cheerful as he was about to win another game. His young, attractive sister in her early twenties, Regina, watched the game from the sidelines. Dylan won the game, gloated some, and collected his money.

"One more game," Oscar insisted.

"Just one more," Dylan replied. He approached Reggie, picked up his bottle of beer from the table, and studied her. "Are you sure you don't want to go someplace else? I mean, this is your college graduation night. I'm feeling guilty about getting off so cheap."

"You don't have to go overboard, Dylan," she informed him.

"Mom and dad would have. They'd be proud of you," he informed her then hesitated. "I'm proud of you."

Reggie smiled warmly and placed her hand on his lower arm. "Thanks, Dylan."

"You're the only sister I've got," he replied then teased, "Thank God. And if Brady doesn't stop checking you out every time I turn around, I'm going to knock him on his ass."

"He's a harmless pervert."

"Not from what I've heard," Dylan muttered.

"Come on, Dylan," Oscar called. "Winner breaks."

"Let me beat this guy one more time, then we'll go home."

She smiled and nodded. As Dylan returned to the pool table, she finished her drink then headed toward the restroom. A man in his late twenties, Brady, approached her as she passed.

"Heard you're officially a college graduate tonight," Brady announced. "Congratulations."

Reggie offered a smile but didn't stop to talk. "Thanks, Brady."

Brady cut off her path, forcing her to stop. "Since you won't be tied up with your studies anymore, maybe we could pick up where we'd left off," he said cheerfully.

"As I recall, we'd left off with me telling you if you ever touched me again, I'd cut your childbearing years in half," Reggie replied.

Brady chuckled. "I know you weren't serious."

"You tackled me to the ground--"

"I was just playing with you," he teased.

"You stuck your hand up the back of my skirt," she scoffed.

"So I grabbed your ass," Brady said with a shrug. "It was all in good fun."

"Yeah, so was my punching you in the mouth," she replied.

"Actually, that stung."

"Let's get something straight," Reggie growled. "I have no intentions on going out with you again. And you're damned lucky I fight my own battles and didn't tell Dylan what happened." She attempted to walk around him.

Brady caught her around the waist and playfully pulled her against him. "Okay, you can stop playing hard to get now."

She attempted to push him away. Her look was unpredictable. "Get your hands off me or we *will* pick up where we'd left off."

Brady laughed as if it was a joke.

"Hey!" Dylan cried out.

Brady and Reggie looked toward the pool area. Dylan was already standing before them with a look of mayhem on his face. Without warning, he punched Brady in the face. Brady released

Reggie and fell onto a nearby table. Several glasses fell to the floor and shattered. The entire tavern fell silent and stared.

"Keep your hands off my sister, prick!"

Brady held his mouth and slowly straightened with hostility. "What's your problem? We were just talking!"

Reggie grabbed Dylan's arm. "Time to go."

†

The beautifully restored Victorian home was located on a secluded back road far from anyone. Several lights were still on within the house. Dylan sat on the sofa while flexing his sore hand. Reggie entered with an ice pack and tossed it to him. He caught it and held it to his fist.

"Thanks," Dylan muttered.

"My overly protective, big brother," she said with a sigh. "I can take care of myself. You don't have to beat the crap out of every guy who talks to me."

"Brady wasn't talking to you."

Reggie sat on the sofa next to him and smiled warmly. "I know you feel you need to look after me, but you have to stop beating yourself up over it."

Dylan studied his hand and avoided looking at her. "I don't know what you're talking about."

"I know you feel guilty because you weren't home the night mom and dad died in the fire. It wasn't your fault. If you'd been home, you may have died too."

Dylan still didn't look at her and frowned. "By all rights, I should have been home."

"It wasn't your fate, just like it wasn't mine. Accept it."

"It was my fate," he insisted. "Going out at the last minute altered what should have been."

"Fate spared you if for nothing more than to look after me."

Dylan uncertainly looked at her.

She smiled gently. "I never could have made it on my own back then," she said. "I needed you to keep me sane."

He stared a moment longer, appeared to relax, and smiled timidly. "You're stronger than I ever was, Reggie. It's me who needs you, not the other way around." He playfully slapped her leg and grinned. "I have something for you."

He jumped up from the sofa, removed a gift-wrapped box from the end table drawer, and proudly handed it to her.

"What's this?" she asked.

"A little graduation present."

He sat alongside her as she opened the box. It was an opal ring with diamonds on either side. Reggie smiled happily and hugged him.

"It's absolutely beautiful, Dylan. But you shouldn't have."

"Of course I should. It's symbolic," he informed her. "That's the opal from mom's surviving earring that dad gave her on their tenth wedding anniversary. The two diamonds are from dad's watch that stopped when he had to unexpectedly deliver you on the kitchen floor, and the gold band was melted down from my class ring that I never wore."

Reggie stared at him a long moment with surprise. "Well, aren't you the sentimental big brother."

"Well, at least I'm good at something."

Reggie smiled and playfully patted his leg.

Dylan sighed and stood. "Do we have any Twinkies?"

"Of course we have Twinkies," she said with a groan. "You'd starve to death if we didn't."

"I'm a Twinkie addict, I know. But I'm just not ready to quit."

"You feed your addiction. I'm going to bed," she remarked and stood. "Don't leave the wrappers scattered about again. It's like a trail of Twinkie wrappers from the kitchen to your room."

†

Two A.M. Reggie slept peacefully beneath the covers in her dimly lit, second floor bedroom. Low, muffled voices were heard from the bedroom next door. There was a moment of silence followed by a loud clunk. Reggie suddenly woke with disorientation and looked around. There was another clunk from Dylan's bedroom. Reggie gasped and jumped from her bed. Dylan suddenly cried out in terror and possible agony. Reggie ran from her room. She slid before Dylan's door and attempted to open it. It was locked. Dylan cried out. The sound was horrifying. Reggie pounded on the door.

"Dylan! Dylan, open up!" she screamed. "Are you okay?"

He continued to cry out. There were more loud thumps and crashes associated with a struggle. Reggie was now terrified. She rammed her shoulder into the door. It didn't budge. She stepped back as Dylan's scream faded and kicked the door inward with one violent thrust. As she stood in the doorway, horror swept over her. There were broken objects, furniture was overturned, and the bed was covered with blood. Reggie was frozen with terror as she stared at the blood on the floor and surrounding the broken window. A bloody Twinkie wrapper lie on the nightstand.

Chapter Two

Two weeks later. Reggie sat on the porch, stared blankly at the woods, and spun the opal ring on her finger. She was lost in her own world. She actually hadn't been right since Dylan's abduction. She knew calling it an abduction was wishful thinking, but she didn't want to give up hope. A police car pulled up to the house. Sheriff Martin got out and walked onto the porch with a tiny, pleasant smile.

"Evening, Reggie," Martin said.

Reggie attempted a smile. "Hey, Sheriff." She shifted in her chair. "Anymore leads on my brother's abduction?"

Martin casually sat on the railing facing her. "No, Reggie, I'm sorry. I know you're dealing with this the best that you can," he said, "but you know he couldn't have survived that sort of attack."

"I broke into the room only seconds after the attack ended," she insisted. "Whoever did this wouldn't have had time to remove his body--especially from the second story window. He has to be alive."

"I don't know what to think, Reggie," the sheriff said with a defeated sigh. "We didn't find any blood outside the house. There's not enough evidence to support any theory."

The faint sound of a creature was heard wailing from somewhere within the woods. Martin looked toward the nearby woods.

"What's that?" the sheriff asked.

"A wolf, I think," she replied and rubbed her chilled arms. "It started a few nights ago."

"Sounds like it's sick. You'd better be careful," he announced. "If it comes around the house, call me, and I'll put it down."

✝

Two days later. Reggie sat at the island counter while eating dinner alone. She stared at the wineglass in her hand as Dylan's screams from that night echoed through her mind. Her emotionless expression suddenly hardened. Reggie threw the glass across the kitchen, and it shattered against the back, French doors. Red wine ran down the glass. Brady stood on the other side of the door with a look of surprise. Reggie saw him, rolled her eyes, and groaned softly. Brady opened the door without being invited and offered a tiny, sympathetic smile.

"Did I pick a bad time?" he asked.

"Yes, a very bad time," she replied while standing then indicated the broken glass. "If you don't mind, I have some cleaning to do."

"I thought I'd see how you were holding up," he said, sounding moderately drunk. "I guess I was right to be worried about you."

"Are you drunk again?" Her look was harsh as she approached and pushed him back toward the open doorway with a firm hand to his chest. "Out, Brady. I'm not in the mood to deal with you."

Reggie pushed him out the door and onto the patio. She was about to take a step back inside when he caught her arm, startling her. She immediately turned hostile.

"Don't be this way, Reggie," he said firmly. "We were meant to be together. Now that Dylan is gone, you need someone to look after you."

Reggie pulled her arm away from him. "I'm looking after me!"

He caught her by both arms and forcibly held her. His look was stern and aggressive. "No more games, Reggie. You need to start acting like my girlfriend. You're the only woman I've ever really wanted, and I'm tired of waiting."

She glared into his eyes with an unpredictable look. "You're right. No more games."

Reggie suddenly kicked for his groin. He reacted quick enough to take the shot to his thigh instead. Brady cried out in pain from the sharp thigh shot and released her. She attempted to punch him in the mouth, but he dodged it and shoved her backwards. Reggie struck the glass door, cracking the glass with the back of her head. She clutched her head and appeared unable to move.

Brady straightened and again grabbed her by the arms. "You need to be taught a lesson--"

A low, gurgled snarl was heard from nearby. Brady stared at the dazed woman he held and appeared bewildered by the sound. Something slowly rose above him from behind. He uncertainly released Reggie and slowly looked behind him. The seven-foot tall, black creature towered above him, snarled through exposed fangs, and stared directly at him. Its large, long tail thrashed against the patio like a bullwhip then slashed for Brady. He leaped out of the tail's path. Its tail struck the second glass door and shattered it. Brady rolled across the patio and looked back at the creature with a horrified stare. Reggie slowly lowered her hand from her head and also stared at the creature as her mouth hung open. She was too frightened to move. The creature again whipped its tail at Brady. He dove from its path and scrambled to his feet. The tail struck the patio with a thunderous crack.

The creature's tail rotated and whipped sideways, striking Brady across the buttocks. He was thrown several feet and knocked into the backyard. Brady made it to his feet and ran across the yard. The creature lowered on all fours and sprang onto the side of the house. It ran along the stone siding then jumped into the yard, chasing Brady. Reggie turned toward the broken door, felt dizzy, and clutched the doorframe for support. The low, painful wail she'd heard earlier from the woods was now behind her. Reggie slowly turned with fear. The large creature sat in a condensed lump on the porch railing and stared at her. It appeared almost pitiful and again wailed softly. Reggie stared at the creature while clinging to the doorframe. Despite her fear, she was curious.

"What are you?" Reggie asked softly. "Why do you sound so lonely?"

The creature gurgled a soft response and continued to stare at her. Reggie touched the back of her head then looked at the blood. The creature wailed once soft and short. She looked at the creature.

"Blood," she gasped softly. "God, I hope you're not hungry."

The creature slowly crawled from the railing on all fours and moved a few feet closer. Reggie tensed. The creature stopped and again collected itself into a condensed lump, as if cowering before her. Reggie watched the creature and attempted to relax. She slid down the doorframe to its level and slowly extended her hand toward the creature. The creature extended its tail to her. It could touch her with its tail if it wanted to but held back. Reggie appeared startled and stared at the long tail before her. She slowly reached out and touched the tail, running her hand along it.

"Reptilian--like snakeskin."

The creature slowly eased its way closer to her while she held its tail. Reggie watched the creature closely but didn't move. It stared at her and gurgled softly. She uncertainly reached out and touched its head. It again gurgled softly. Reggie smiled then laughed while running her hand over its smooth, dark head.

✝

Reggie sifted through the refrigerator and removed some fruit and meat. She eyed the meat then quickly replaced it and grimaced.

"Pray for vegetarian," she muttered.

She shut the refrigerator door, turned, and looked around for the creature. She could hear its claws tapping on the floor as it scurried across the kitchen on all fours behind the island counter.

"I have fruit for you. No meat," she said firmly. "I don't want to give you any ideas."

The creature rounded the island counter and came into view. She stared at it and marveled at its size.

"Jesus--"

It approached the pantry, straightened on its hind legs, and opened the door with its tail. Reggie watched with surprise. The creature used its clawed hands to remove a box of Twinkies. It dropped the box on the floor and tore into the box of snack cakes. Reggie stared with a look of shock as the creature ate the Twinkies, wrappers and all. She dropped the fruit.

"Dylan--?"

The creature suddenly spun and straightened. It stared at her and sharply gurgled. Reggie slowly approached the tall creature. It sank to five feet as she approached. She stared into the creature's eyes. Dylan's eyes stared back at her.

"Oh, my God! Dylan!"

Reggie suddenly threw her arms around the creature's neck and hugged it. The creature placed its paws around her waist and wrapped its tail around her. It buried its large head into her neck and wailed softly. She sobbed softly onto the creature's shoulder. A little while later, Reggie paced the kitchen while unwrapping a Twinkie. Dylan-creature sat near the island counter and patiently waited. She tossed the Twinkie to him. He caught the Twinkie in his mouth and waited for another.

"I wish you could explain how this happened." She removed another Twinkie from the crushed box and opened it. "This is just too X-Files for me," she said. "Maybe we can reverse it somehow."

She tossed the Twinkie to him. He caught it in his mouth, swallowed it, and waited for another.

"We certainly can't tell anyone. They'll lock me up for sure," she muttered then looked at the creature. "Think of some way to tell me what happened to you."

Dylan-creature tapped his tail to the Twinkie box on the counter.

"All gone," she informed him.

He made a sound similar to a horrified gasp.

"I'll get more tomorrow," she insisted.

The creature moved toward the Twinkie box and pushed it around with its tail while attempting to peek inside.

Chapter Three

Dylan's bedroom had been cleaned after the incident but otherwise remained untouched. His bed was made and the room had been preserved as it was prior to the attack. Dylan-creature scurried into the room and leaped onto the bed. Reggie followed him into the room and was surprised to see him already on the bed. She was having a tough time keeping track of his fast movements.

"Something in here might tell me what happened to you. I need you to help--"

Reggie looked toward the bed. Dylan-creature burrowed his way beneath the covers, circled beneath the sheets, and then poked his head out enough to rest on the pillow. He took a deep breath, shut his eyes, and immediately fell asleep. Reggie stared a moment longer then smiled.

"Well, maybe it is getting late."

As she watched, Dylan-creature twitched and took several, labored breaths, as if indicating he had been through hell the last couple of weeks. Reggie stared a moment longer, fought her tears, and then offered a smile to the sleeping creature.

"Good night, Dylan."

The following morning, Reggie entered Dylan's bedroom and approached the peacefully sleeping creature still beneath the sheets.

"Come on, Dylan. Time to get up," she informed him. "We have answers to find."

The creature opened one eye, glared at her, and snarled. His long tail appeared and flipped the pillow over his head. Reggie stared with some surprise then laughed.

"Well, I see some things never change," she scoffed. "I'll give you another hour."

Dylan-creature was still fast asleep when Reggie returned that evening. She stood over the bed and watched the sleeping creature.

"You must have been be exhausted," she said sadly. "Come on, Dylan. Time to get up." Reggie revealed a plate of Twinkies. "I have Twinkies."

Dylan-creature suddenly opened his eyes, looked at the plate of Twinkies, and leaped out from under the covers. Reggie set the plate on the bed. He immediately devoured the Twinkies. She approached the closet door and opened it.

"As good a place as any to start."

Reggie routed through the closet and dresser drawers over the next hour. Boxes lie scattered across the floor. Dylan-creature lie on the bed with his head hanging over the side and watched her while she routed through items. His tail occasionally poked her in the side just for laughs. She cried out each time and batted at his tail. Reggie tossed the last box aside and groaned with disgust.

"This is hopeless." She looked at the creature. "We've played charades before. Isn't there any way for you to communicate what happened that night?"

Dylan-creature rolled playfully onto his back with all four legs in the air and swished his tail. He appeared to be playing dead. Reggie groaned lowly.

"You're absolutely no help, Dylan."

He turned his head to look at her and playfully snarled with his teeth bared. Reggie frowned and shook her head. She straightened her legs and kicked something just beneath the bed. She pulled her legs back, reached under the bed, and removed an old leather-bound book. Dylan-creature suddenly sprang to his feet and whipped the book from her hands with his tail. The book flew across the room and struck the opposing wall near the closet. Reggie stared at him with surprise.

"That certainly struck a nerve."

She stood and headed across the room. Dylan-creature leaped from the bed, scurried past her, and picked the book up in his mouth. He attempted to crawl up the wall to escape with it. Reggie grabbed the book and tried to pull it from him. He snarled and pulled on the book with his teeth while hanging from the wall. Reggie pulled back with all her weight. Dylan-creature whipped his tail and knocked her feet out from under her. She fell onto her backside. He scurried along the ceiling with the book in his mouth.

"Dylan, come back here with that!"

He scurried along the ceiling for the open bedroom door. Reggie slid across the floor and kicked the door shut. Dylan-creature struck the closed door, appeared dazed, and fell from the ceiling with a thud. She grabbed the book and backed away from him.

"I'm trying to help you. What's the matter with you?" she demanded then reconsidered. "Well, besides the obvious."

Dylan-creature flipped over and onto his feet, stared at her, and snarled. His tail pivoted over his body in what appeared to be an attack stance. He whipped his tail for the book. Reggie cried out with surprise and leaped out of its path.

"Stop this!"

Reggie opened the book. A brilliant flash of light flew out of the book. She cried out and dropped it. Dylan-creature wailed and darted under the bed. Reggie was slightly stunned, hesitated, and then looked across the room. A handsome, well-dressed man, Kahn, stood only a few feet from the book. His attire suggested great wealth, possibly royalty, and nothing from this world. She stared at him with surprise. He shared her surprise then smiled.

"Well now, this is a pleasant surprise," Kahn said.

Reggie kept her distance and continued to stare at him. "Who are you?" she demanded. "How did you get in here?"

Kahn maintained his charming smile and casually paced the room. "My name is Kahn, and I'm a Rottiwelt."

"A what?"

He chuckled. "A sorcerer of sorts."

Reggie continued to stare at him and remained uncertain. "A sorcerer?" she questioned. "Why are you here?"

"You invited me."

"I don't think so," she protested. "I just opened that book."

"Same difference."

Kahn uncertainly looked around the room, appeared curious, and then waved a finger toward the bed. The bed suddenly slid across the floor to the opposing wall and exposed Dylan-creature hiding beneath it. Dylan-creature squealed and scurried back toward the bed. Kahn pointed his finger at the creature.

"Not so fast."

Dylan-creature was captured in an invisible bubble. He attempted to claw his way out of the bubble then finally gave up.

Kahn shook his head with a look of disappointment. "How did you manage to get away?" He waved his finger and the creature vanished.

Reggie suddenly gasped and took a step forward. She stopped and looked at him. "What have you done with my brother?"

"That was your brother?" His grin mocked her. "I can't say I noticed any family resemblance."

Her expression turned hostile. "What did you do with him?"

Kahn appeared humored by her hostility and aggression. "He decided to join my society."

"You sent him away against his will," she snapped. "I don't think he had much of a choice in the matter."

Kahn maintained his charming smile and casually approached her. Reggie stood her ground, despite her fear. He paused before her.

"Your brother contracted my services," he informed her. "I granted his wish, but he was unable to repay me. In accordance with our contract, he's legally bound to serve me in my world. It's quite cut-and-dry."

"Contract? Show me this contract."

"Sorry, the details of a contract are confidential," he replied. "Business ethics."

"How convenient," Reggie scoffed.

Kahn studied her with some surprise then appeared humored. "Oh, you are a feisty one," he announced. "Obviously you're not satisfied with the end result of my contract with your brother."

"No shit."

"I could return him to his former state, but that would involve you entering into a contract with me as well," he remarked.

"What sort of contract?" she asked suspiciously.

"I'll restore your brother to his mortal state if you complete the simple task he failed to complete," he replied.

"If it was that simple, my brother wouldn't be a seven-foot tall lizard."

Kahn chuckled softly and paced before her. "Nothing is ever as easy as it first sounds, but I doubt you'd have much trouble completing the task. Your brother simply lacked passion."

"What's the task?" she demanded.

"You travel to my world where you're then sent off on a little treasure hunt. You bring the specified object back to me in the allotted time, and your brother will be returned to his mortal state. If you fail, you join your brother as one of my subjects." Kahn flicked his hand and a contract appeared in it. "All you have to do is sign the contract--" He hesitated and gasped softly. "Oh--" He again flicked his hand and a pen appeared between his fingers.

Reggie eyed the paper in his hand then looked back into his sinister eyes. "I'd like to read through it first, naturally."

Kahn handed her the contract. "Be my guest. I'll give you one hour."

He suddenly vanished. Reggie jumped with surprise and looked around the room. She uncertainly looked at the contract in her hand then quickly tossed it aside and ran across the room. She rummaged through several boxes in the closet.

Chapter Four

Reggie sat quietly and comfortably reclined on the plush sofa with the contract in one hand and a pen in the other. She studied it in great detail. The clock chimed midnight. She glanced at the fireplace mantel clock and slowly sat up. Kahn suddenly appeared in the living room doorway, startling her. He casually leaned against the archway and wore his usual charming smile.

"Have you had a chance to review the details of the contract?" he asked.

Reggie casually stood, held up the paper, and eyed him. "I don't care for a few of the terms. They're a little vague," she said. "I'd be much more comfortable with a few minor word changes."

Kahn eyed her with some surprise. He straightened, flicked his fingers, and the paper appeared in his hand. He looked over the contract with several scribbles on it. Kahn looked back at her with surprise. "You're correcting my grammar?"

"I just graduated college," she said with a shrug. "It's all still fresh in my head."

He rolled his eyes, groaned, and tossed the contract over his shoulder. It again appeared in her hand. "If it pleases you, you can have your grammar corrections. Do we have a deal?"

"I'll abide by the terms of the contract, yes."

Kahn again smiled charmingly. "Splendid. Just sign the contract, and we'll be on our way to Neverland."

She approached him with the pen. He gave her a strange look. "If you'll just initial the changes--"

He stared at her and appeared completely baffled. He snatched the pen and initialed the changes. It again appeared in her hand. She took a deep breath and signed the contract. She barely finished her signature when he was about to make it disappear.

Reggie held out her hand. "Ah, I need to make a copy of that for my records," she announced firmly.

His look conveyed his surprise. "This is the hardest I've worked in centuries," he muttered. You have got to be the most controlling, manipulative female I've ever come across."

Reggie offered a pleased smile. "Thank you."

"That wasn't a compliment."

✝

K ahn's world was that of a tropical island but with bizarre, seemingly haphazard terrain. It was unlike anything Reggie had ever seen. Parts of the island appeared rocky, parts appeared deserted, and still other parts resembled a jungle. There was no transition between areas, just a sudden, drastic change. The island was something from another world. Along the beach like setting, there was an amazing fairytale castle straight from a gothic horror book. As Kahn and Reggie stood on the sandy beach, she was left wondering how they even got to wherever it was they were.

"Where are we?"

"We're in my world," he informed her and grinned proudly. "Beautiful, isn't it?"

"I rather doubt I'll have the opportunity to appreciate it."

He chuckled lowly. "I love your sense of humor. You're going to need it," he remarked. "In accordance with the details of the contract, your task is to find the dagger or Zagaball and return it to me." Kahn pointed to Reggie's wrist. An elegant digital watch appeared. "You have three hours to find the dagger and return it to its rightful place in the library. Just to be fair, I've provided a map." A detailed leather map appeared in her hands. He smiled pleasantly. "Happy hunting." Kahn suddenly vanished.

Reggie looked at the map then headed along the beach. "Map my ass. Detailed description of where *not* to go."

✝

R eggie hurried along the worn path within the jungle and looked around cautiously. "Too easy so far," she muttered. She

133

paused and looked at the map. "According to the map, the dagger is just down this path within the ruins of the old temple." She assessed her surroundings then eyed the path behind her to the left. "The map says to go straight, so that tells me I should go left."

She headed for the path to the left and hurried along it. The ruins of the old temple were covered with thick vines and vegetation. Reggie appeared just behind the temple and climbed the crumbling building. She approached a pile of stones, crouched down, and looked down to the temple's main entrance. Everything appeared quiet, which bothered her, so she watched a moment longer. Big, burly ape-like creatures patrolled the entrance, remaining hidden within the thick plant life. They watched the path she was supposed to take according to the map.

"An ambush," she muttered. "Who didn't see that coming?"

Reggie carefully walked along the side of the temple above the opening. Stones were heard falling into a cavern beneath her feet. She hesitated then looked at a small opening in the stone. She removed a pen flashlight from her pocket and shined it down the hole. She smiled deviously.

"Hmm, the back door appears to be left open and unattended."

Within the temple ruins, the small, empty room of stone was lit only by the remaining sunlight from an opening in the broken stone. A golden dagger rested on the old, stone altar. Reggie let out a tiny, shrill scream. She plummeted through a narrow opening in the stone above, taking down a thick layer of cobwebs with her body, and gracefully landed on her feet before falling onto her backside. She was covered in a cocoon of cobwebs. Reggie jumped to her feet and frantically pulled the cobwebs from her body.

"Oh, disgusting," she cried out softly. "I hate spiders!"

As she pulled the last of the cobwebs from her body, she saw the golden dagger on the altar. Relief swept over her. She hurried toward the altar, hesitated only a moment, and reached for the dagger. A large spider crawled across her arm. She gasped and frantically shook it off. Reggie groaned softly then snatched the dagger from the altar. Despite that it was probably worth millions in her world, she barely even looked at it. Getting her brother back was the only thing that mattered. She looked at the main entrance and considered her options.

"Now I just need a way out."

The ape-like creatures attempted to remain still and hidden along the path not far from the temple entrance. They were keeping close watch for her arrival. Little did they know that she was just inside the entrance behind them. Reggie quietly slipped out of the temple through the main entrance and kept close to the vine-encrusted wall.

✝

The castle's broad, marble hallway seemed to extend forever, passing dozens of doorways and a sea of suits of armor. Kahn stormed along the hallway with an ape-like creature grunting as it hurried after him, attempting to keep up.

Kahn appeared furious. "I want her found immediately!"

The creature grunted a response, hurried past him, and left through the front door. Kahn approached the library with disgust, threw open the door, and suddenly stopped in the doorway. Reggie casually sat on one of the leather chairs with a book on her lap. She looked up at Kahn, glanced at her watch, and smiled.

"You're early," Reggie casually announced. "I wanted to finish another chapter before collecting my brother and heading home."

Kahn stared at her with surprise then looked at the golden dagger in its rightful spot above the fireplace mantel.

"That's not possible," he snarled. "My troops didn't see you pass through the temple opening."

"You mean your ambush party?" Reggie shut the book, carelessly tossed it aside, and stood. "Please--" she scoffed. "There's your dagger. Task complete." She glared at him through evil eyes. "Now get my brother."

Kahn's surprise quickly turned to hostility. "How did you get into the temple?"

"Through the back door."

"There isn't a back door."

"I beg to differ," she scoffed. "Where's my brother?"

"The rules of the contract specifically stated *through the temple door*. You didn't complete the task appropriately." Kahn held out his hand. The contract appeared in it. He pointed to one of the paragraphs. A sentence was immediately highlighted. "Right here," he announced firmly. "*Through the temple door*. You didn't complete the task. You lose."

"You cheat," she snapped. "The task was to retrieve the dagger and return it to the library. I did that."

"The contract is the contract."

135

Reggie boldly removed her copy of the contract from her pocket and shook it straight. "Is that so?" She held up her copy of the contract. "Then allow me to draw your attention to paragraph four, addendum two," she announced.

"Addendum?"

"So long as the dagger is returned in said allotted time frame," she read, "any means necessary shall be considered binding."

She eyed him and raised a cocky brow. Kahn looked at his contract, saw her scribbled writing, and appeared stunned. He suddenly sneered and glared at her.

"You added that yourself."

"And you initialed the change, thereby agreeing to it."

Kahn appeared speechless. His look suddenly turned harsh. "If you want to play that way, we're both in violation of the contract. That voids it. Your brother stays right where he is, and you're not going anywhere until I figure out what I'm going to do with you."

Before she could protest, she suddenly vanished.

Chapter Five

The elegant yet medieval looking bedroom was decorated with antique, Victorian furnishings. Reggie paced the bedroom and felt the concern for her situation rising. Kahn was never going to admit defeat, and if he didn't uphold his end of the bargain, there was little she could do in retaliation. She and Dylan were at his mercy, of which he had none. There was a faint knock on the door. Reggie turned toward the door and attempted a calm, collected attitude. No matter what the outcome, she wasn't about to let Kahn know how frightened she was.

"Come in."

The door opened to reveal a docile looking butler in his early fifties. "Good evening, madam," Begley said. "Your presence is requested in the dining room for dinner."

"Thanks, but no."

"Begging your pardon, madam, but I added the part about that being a request," he informed her. "You may not refuse. He'll just bring you on his own, and you really don't want that."

Reggie frowned. "I knew it couldn't be that easy."

"Your evening attire is hanging in the closet," Begley said. "I'll return in twenty minutes to escort you to dinner. The others should be arriving shortly."

"Others?"

"Yes, madam. It's Lord Kahn's weekly dinner party." Begley turned to leave, hesitated, and then looked back at her with an oddly sincere look. "The wine is a very bad year. Very *bitter.*"

Reggie stared at Begley with a look of bewilderment. His words were puzzling. He fidgeted then sheepishly left the room. Reggie sank into thought.

✝

The elegant dining room was adorned with fine china, silverware, crystal glasses, candles, and large floral arrangements. Several well-dressed men and women entered the dining room. All appeared distracted and not a word was spoken. Reggie was shown to the dining room by Begley. He pulled out her chair for her and indicated for her to sit.

"Please, be seated," Begley announced to everyone. "Lord Kahn will be along momentarily."

The others took their seats. Reggie appeared to be the only one curious enough to look at the other dinner guests. None spoke, and they kept to themselves. She was curious but remained silent. Including Reggie, there were seven guests.

Begley stood by the doorway and spoke, "Lord and Lady Kahn."

Reggie looked at the doorway and was the only one interested. Kahn entered with a beautiful, young woman attached to his arm. Lady Chrissy was dressed in an evening gown with perfectly placed hair and make-up. She appeared to snub everyone while taking her seat at the end of the table. Kahn took his place at the head of the table, smiled proudly, and lifted his wineglass.

"Good evening, everyone. It's an honor to have you here at this special dinner party. I hope you will enjoy the feast," Kahn announced. "I'd like to propose a toast--"

Everyone took their wineglasses and stood as Begley shut the dining room doors. Reggie stared at her wineglass, uncertainly took it, and stood as well. The dining room doors suddenly opened to reveal a handsome, well-built man in his mid-thirties. He was dressed less formal then the others. Kahn eyed the man and lowered his glass with a frown.

"Do you ever call first?" Kahn demanded. "I'm in the middle of a dinner party, Helsing."

"Far be it for me to interrupt one of your distasteful parties, but I want to talk to you--now," Helsing growled.

"It can wait. Either join us or come back another time."

Helsing sneered and collapsed into the vacant chair between Reggie and Chrissy. Chrissy snubbed him as well. Kahn eyed Helsing and made a face. Helsing remained seated while the others stood. Kahn was obviously unhappy but put on a false smile.

"To old friends, new friends, and those we haven't met yet," Kahn announced.

Helsing snorted a soft laugh. Kahn glared at him. Everyone drank their wine. Reggie raised it to her lips but didn't drink. Everyone took their seats. Helsing looked past Reggie to Kahn.

"Just because you're my brother, that doesn't mean you have free roam over my estate," Helsing remarked.

"I could say the same to you."

Reggie looked at Helsing with some surprise. She was still the only one paying any attention and was starting to question why. Helsing noted Reggie's curious stare then looked back at Kahn.

"There's an entire colony of your little pets living in my territory," Helsing announced. "They didn't get there on their own."

"Just a minor mistake. I'll correct it in the morning," Kahn said. "You're spoiling our evening, Helsing."

Helsing glared at Kahn then eyed Reggie, who still stared at him. "I doubt there's anything I could do to lower the integrity of your little dinner party," he replied dryly.

Reggie wondered what he knew.

"I really wish you'd mind your own business, stop insulting my guests, and go home," Kahn remarked.

Helsing again met Reggie's gaze and finally addressed her. "Something you'd like to add?"

Reggie's mind reeled. Did he hate his brother enough to sympathize with her?

Helsing snorted, "I didn't think so."

She knew she had to say something fast. "Your brother is a liar and a cheat," Reggie scoffed.

Kahn tensed then smirked. All eyes, including Chrissy's were now on Reggie. The other guests appeared almost frightened by her tone.

Helsing chuckled and smirked. "Tell me something I don't know."

"She's just upset over losing our little wager this evening," Kahn remarked.

Reggie glared at Kahn with hostility. "I didn't lose anything. You changed the rules, because you're a sore loser. I beat you."

Helsing appeared interested and eyed Kahn. "Is that true? You were beaten at your own game--by a woman?"

"She didn't beat me. She didn't abide by the rules."

"No one can play and win by your rules," Helsing responded.

Kahn appeared insulted and possibly embarrassed in front of his guests. Chrissy glared at Kahn from across the table. There was something strange in her expression. The guests at the table suddenly gasped and choked. Reggie looked at the other guests. Only Chrissy, Kahn, and Helsing weren't affected. Kahn eyed his guests then glared at Helsing with annoyance.

"You're ruining my favorite part of the evening," Kahn remarked.

"You *are* pathetic."

Reggie watched the other guests with concern. Chrissy sipped her wine and appeared disinterested. Kahn signaled Begley. He approached and removed the lids from the serving trays. Mounds of live maggots, leaches, assorted worms, and other crawling creatures covered the trays. Reggie stared with horror. The other guests no longer choked and appeared equally horrified. Chrissy minded her own business and casually sipped her wine.

"I don't mean to be rude, brother dear, but I have guests for dinner," Kahn remarked.

"She's right, you know. You've always been a sore loser," Helsing announced. "Must really chafe you to be outwitted by a woman."

"She didn't outwit me," he said with annoyance.

Reggie was too busy staring at the serving trays to participate in the conversation. The other guests breathed heavily and stared with horror at the banquet before them.

Helsing chuckled lowly while glaring at his brother. "Sure sounds that way to me. By right, you have to throw her back."

Kahn glared at Helsing with annoyance then looked at Reggie. "Reggie, do we call it even? Or would you like a rematch?"

Reggie couldn't tear her eyes away from the slithering, crawling creatures on the serving platters.

"Reggie?"

She snapped out of her daze and looked at Kahn. "Huh?"

"Do we call it even, or do you want a rematch?" he demanded.

Reality struck her. "I'm not going anywhere without my brother."

Kahn looked at Helsing and smiled. "There you have it. We'll have a rematch."

Helsing shook his head and glared at Reggie. "Stupid girl."

Reggie looked back at the live entrees. The other guests suddenly reached for the creatures and rapidly consumed them. She gasped and watched with horror. All six guests appeared unable to control their hunger for the crawling creatures. Chrissy looked away and grimaced with distaste.

Helsing eyed Reggie's expression and raised a brow. "Their fate will soon be your own."

Kahn sat back and watched the mass consumption with a pleased grin. Reggie watched the guests devour the slithering, slimy critters like starving animals. She suddenly clutched her stomach, jumped up from the table, and ran from the room.

Chapter Six

Reggie left the hall powder room and held her turning stomach. She saw Helsing and Kahn in the hallway outside the dining room.

"I said I'd take care of it," Kahn growled. "Now please leave."

Kahn slammed the dining room doors on Helsing. Reggie hurried toward him just as he was about to disappear.

"Please, wait," she called out.

Helsing gave her a curious look as she stopped before him. "Something I can do for you?"

She was slightly uncomfortable about the prospect of begging but stood proudly. "You're not like your brother. You're far more compassionate and intelligent, I can tell."

Helsing appeared humored and snorted a laugh. "You've got it half right. Compassion would be a stretch."

"I'll give you whatever you want if you get me and my brother out of here," she blurted out. Sadly, she had been aiming for sexually enticing and completely missed the mark.

"Isn't that what got you into trouble in the first place?" he asked.

"Please, I'm begging you," she said while choking on her emotions. "You're probably the only one who can help me."

"There's nothing you have that I want."

Reggie tensed but attempted to retain her pride. "I saw the way you were looking at me tonight."

He stared at her a moment in silence. "You got the wrong idea," he replied. "I'm not mortal, and I don't subscribe to mortal pleasures. You mistook pity for lust. I gave you an opportunity to get out, but you didn't take it. You made your decision."

Helsing was about to vanish. Reggie placed her hand on his lower arm, stopping him. He looked at her hand as if she dared to touch him, causing her to pull back quickly.

"My brother is all I have. Yours took him from me. Maybe you don't care about your brother, but I love mine," she informed him. "I'd never be able to live with myself if I allowed him to suffer a fate worse than death. He'd give his life for me, and I'd gladly do the same for him."

Helsing stared at her a long moment in silence. "It's exactly that sense of compassion that will be your downfall."

"Please, help me."

"Sorry, I don't interfere with my brother's lifestyle even if I don't agree with it."

Helsing was again about to vanish.

Reggie's sorrow turned to anger. "I guess I can't blame you for being afraid of him. He's quite powerful," she retorted.

He glared at her with surprise. "I'm not afraid of Kahn. He's just a warped and twisted little rodent with a god complex."

"Just seems to me, if you were half as powerful as he was, you wouldn't be *afraid* to help me."

He glared at her and took a step closer. She stood her ground and appeared bold, but she was sure he saw the fear in her eyes. He stared at her a moment then a smile crossed his face.

"You're resourceful, I'll give you that."

"I have little choice. I'm not leaving without my brother."

Helsing appeared curious. "You'd really sacrifice yourself to save your brother?"

Reggie nodded.

He appeared to be toying with an idea then glared at her. "Your problems with my brother are *your* problems, just so we're straight," he said firmly. "But if you would go through all this *for* your brother, then you should go through it *with* your brother."

Helsing gave a simple wave of his hand. Dylan in full creature mode suddenly appeared in the hallway. Dylan-creature appeared bewildered, saw Reggie, and immediately gurgled a cheerful response. He leaped onto her and wrapped his tail around her legs. Reggie was nearly knocked to the floor. She hugged him in joyful response. The dining room doors were suddenly thrown open to reveal Kahn. He looked at the creature clinging to Reggie. Dylan-creature released Reggie and scurried behind her in an attempt to hide.

"What's the meaning of this? How did that get in here?" Kahn demanded.

Helsing casually leaned against the hall wall. "She's willing to sacrifice her life for that of her brother. Her request to have her brother by her side sounded reasonable to me."

Kahn appeared furious. "You have no right interfering in my business, Helsing."

"Guess I slipped, huh?" Helsing straightened and sighed. "Oh, well. It's too late. What's done is done. They're a team now."

"You did this on purpose!"

"Her devotion to her brother is noble and commendable," he announced. "You're damned right I did it on purpose. And now we're even."

"Is that what this is all about?"

"A lesson to be learned; don't piss me off," Helsing snapped.

Kahn sneered, returned to the dining room, and slammed the door.

Helsing appeared pleased with himself. "That worked out rather nicely." He looked back at Reggie. "You're on your own now."

Reggie smiled warmly and again placed her hand on his lower arm. "Thank you. This means a lot to me."

He appeared uncomfortable. "I didn't do anything," Helsing firmly insisted then disappeared.

Chapter Seven

Reggie paced the large bedroom chamber while Dylan-creature appeared to sleep peacefully on the excessively large bed.

"We need to come up with a plan. He cheats," she insisted. "There's no way we can win this thing playing by his rules."

Dylan-creature opened one eye and watched her pace.

"Who knows what he has planned for tomorrow," she said. "I don't know what to do, Dylan. I even offered myself to his brother."

Dylan-creature suddenly perked up and appeared displeased.

"What kind of sick world is this? The one time I try to use sex as a bargaining chip, and I'm shot down. It's just wrong I tell you." There was a faint knock on the door. "Now what?" she groaned. "Come in."

The door opened to reveal Begley. He entered with a small basket of fruit, shut the door behind him, and timidly smiled. "I thought you might be hungry."

Reggie eyed the fruit, snorted, and shook her head. "Thanks, Begley, but I think I'll pass on anything to eat and drink while in this place. After this evening, starvation never sounded so appealing."

"I understand, madam, but I assure you, it's safe."

Begley removed an apple and took a bite out of it. He extended it to her. Reggie uncertainly accepted the apple. She studied it with distrust then took a small bite from it.

"Thanks, Begley. I appreciate your tips on surviving a formal dinner party."

"I don't have that much to lose these days," he replied. "Looking out for pretty, young women is becoming a hobby of mine."

Reggie eyed him and became curious. "You don't work here willingly, do you?"

He set down the bowl of fruit and sighed softly. "We're all prisoners, madam. At some point in time, we all made a similar mistake and gave our lives and souls to Lord Kahn. Some of us have it better than others, but we're all at his mercy." Begley straightened his jacket, stood proudly, and appeared proper. "If I don't want to end up the main course at next week's dinner party, I'd better mind myself and return to my duties."

Reggie appeared slightly sickened. "Don't even joke."

His look was serious. "I wish I were joking."

Begley turned and left the room. He was about to close the door when Chrissy appeared in the doorway and stopped him. Begley and Chrissy exchanged looks. He quickly left. Chrissy entered Reggie's room and casually shut the door behind her.

"He just stopped in to check on me," Reggie said.

Chrissy approached the bowl of fruit, took some grapes, and quickly ate them as if starving. "You don't have to worry about me. Begley and I are in this together. We look out for each other." She casually sat on Reggie's bed and eyed her. "You can't win, Reggie. No matter what you do, you'll never beat him."

Reggie leaned against the bedpost. "Thanks for the vote of confidence."

"I'm not trying to crush your hopes," she remarked then groaned. "Look at me; I'm you."

Reggie studied Chrissy with a curious look.

"I'm little more than his play toy," she remarked while raising her brows, "and I can be replaced very easily."

"According to Helsing, they don't--"

"Helsing and Kahn are very different, but neither can be trusted," Chrissy informed her. "I saw you in the hallway with Helsing tonight. I don't know what he said, but you can't appeal to his compassionate side. He doesn't have one."

"Yeah, so he said."

"I didn't come here tonight to discourage you," she insisted. "I'm here to give you a fighting chance. You seem to have a little more spirit than Kahn's usual breed of client. You're frustrating him, I can tell." She held herself proudly. "Two things. First, when faced with one of his little tasks, be ready for anything, anticipate the worst, and rationalize the situation from the perspective of an egotistical sorcerer with a superiority complex. You've outsmarted him before; you can do it again. Second, whatever happens, don't let him con you into replacing me as his love slave. It's not a position you really want; trust me. Being with Kahn is truly disgusting. I'm not telling you this because I don't want to lose my prestigious position. There's nothing prestigious about it. I just wouldn't wish my hell upon any other poor woman." She seemed concerned for Reggie. "I've seen the way he looks at you. He wants to break you in the worst possible way. Your strength turns him on. I used to be strong. I used to be a fighter. Now I just exist."

Reggie attempted to read Chrissy then frowned and looked away. "I don't intend to give up. I won't ever be a part of his world. I *am* a fighter. And I intend to fight him to the death if necessary."

Chrissy stared at Reggie and appeared bewildered. A strange smile crossed her face. "I guess I was wrong. You're not me. You're a standup fighter." Chrissy's smile brightened and a low chuckle escaped her throat. "While I patiently bide my time and wait." She stood and appeared enthusiastic. "I think my day is finally here. Good luck. Begley and I will be praying for you."

Chrissy left the room. Reggie stared at the door long after she had gone. She looked at the creature lying comfortably on the bed.

"Do we trust her?"

He gurgled a soft response.

Reggie nodded. "You're absolutely right."

✝

Reggie entered Kahn's study the following morning. The medieval room resembled a throne room more than a study. Kahn sat in his lavish chair toward the back of the massive room near the wall of windows. He looked like a king sitting on his throne. A smug smile added to the illusion. Reggie paused midway across the room before the massive desk. Dylan-creature crept in behind her in an attempt to hide his massive body from Kahn. Kahn indicated the chair several feet away from him. Reggie eyed him with distrust and reluctantly sat. Dylan-creature hid behind her chair and peered out.

"Since my brother amused himself by granting your brother's assistance in the challenge, I've decided to raise the stakes," he said.

"I didn't agree to that."

"Nor did I agree to your brother helping you. The challenge is the same. You must find the dagger and return it to the castle. You will have thirteen hours to complete the task. There will be no maps. It's hidden within the old pirate ship along the coast on the far end of the island. You can't walk the beach the entire distance, because a rock ledge prevents passage. You must travel through the center of the island. The rules are; there are no rules."

"What's to stop you from transporting me back here the moment I reach the pirate ship?" she demanded. "You have the ability to stop me with the snap of your fingers. I can't compete against that."

"Fair enough. I'm not permitted to use my powers to prevent you from completing your task. The dagger must be inside the castle before the end of the thirteenth hour. It just has to pass through the doorway. We'll keep it simple to avoid any misunderstandings," he said. "If you return the dagger to the castle within the allotted time period, your brother will be restored to his mortal state. You and he will be returned to your home as if none of this had ever happened. But if you don't complete your task, your brother remains as he is, and you will replace Chrissy as my mistress for all eternity."

Reggie felt her entire body twitch with fear but kept an emotionless expression. "What happens to Chrissy?"

"I suppose she'll carry out her life sentence elsewhere in my kingdom."

She shifted with discomfort then boldly glared at Kahn. "I guess you have upped the stakes. Sounds a little unbalanced to me. I'd assume eat bugs the rest of my life then be your mistress."

Kahn appeared insulted and sneered. "That can be arranged." His warped smile soon returned. "Do you have a counteroffer?"

"If I lose, I will assume Chrissy's position by your side only if she is returned to her former life along with my brother."

Kahn stared at Reggie and appeared slightly surprised by her bold request. "Hardly a fair trade."

"Neither is allowing you to paw me," she scoffed. "The choice is yours."

Kahn and Reggie stared at each other in silence for a long, tense moment. Neither flinched. Kahn's fingers began to tap on his throne, indicating some tension. His fingers stopped.

"Done."

He quickly stood from his chair and pointed to her wrist. The elegant watch again appeared. The digital numbers were set at thirteen hours with zero minutes and zero seconds.

"You have ten minutes to prepare before the countdown begins." Kahn suddenly vanished, startling her. Dylan-creature slowly crept from behind the chair. Reggie looked at him and appeared suspicious.

"I think I really struck a nerve this time." She uncertainly stood, looked around the room, and then back at Dylan-creature. "I think he's nervous. We can beat him, Dylan."

Reggie and the creature hurried along the grand hallway toward the front doors of the castle. Begley stood near the foyer, watched her approach, and offered a tiny, sly smile.

"Good luck to you, madam," Begley said.

Reggie returned the smile. "Thanks, Begley."

He hurried down the hall to avoid being seen. Reggie waited by the main doors and watched the counter on her challenge watch. She fidgeted, took a deep breath, and collected herself. Helsing suddenly appeared, casually leaning against the door.

"Going through with it, huh?" Helsing asked.

"I have no choice."

Helsing straightened and took a step closer. Reggie watched him with concern. He took her hand, studied the stone in her ring, and brushed his thumb past the opal. The colors in the stone began to swirl. He released her hand. Reggie gave him a bewildered look.

"Consider it a mood ring," he said. "Black indicates something dangerous ahead. White indicates non-dangerous territory."

Reggie smiled gratefully. "I can't thank you enough."

"That's all the help you'll get from me."

Reggie threw her arms around his neck and kissed him quickly but passionately on the lips. Helsing tensed with surprise. Reggie pulled back almost as quickly and smiled with embarrassment.

"Sorry. I got a little carried away."

Helsing stared at her frozen with surprise then suddenly vanished. Reggie appeared startled then looked at Dylan-creature.

"I hope I didn't scar him for life."

Dylan-creature bared his teeth with disapproval as his long tail vigorously swished. The counter on her watch suddenly flashed. The front doors unlocked and slowly opened inward. Reggie looked at Dylan-creature, took a deep breath, and sighed.

"This is it. Let's tempt fate one last time."

Chapter Eight

Despite the daylight hours, the forest was predominantly dark, almost as if cursed. Reggie walked along the path in the woods with added caution. Dylan-creature crept alongside her and appeared possibly more frightened than she was. She glanced at her watch and groaned softly. It was taking longer than she had hoped. She uncertainly looked at her opal ring. The color remained white. Somehow, that didn't comfort her.

"I don't think we're in Kansas anymore," she muttered.

Dylan-creature let out a soft wail in response. Reggie again looked at her ring. The color almost instantly changed to black. She stopped on the path and quickly looked around.

"There's something out there," she whispered.

Dylan-creature used his tail to push her closer to a tree, as if indicating for her to remain there. He then scaled a nearby tree and jumped to the next one. Reggie watched in silence as he jumped from tree to tree until she lost sight of him. Dylan-creature suddenly wailed loudly, as if he were in trouble. Reggie felt alarm sweep through her. She looked around then crept through the woods. She could hear faint chatter. She paused near one of the larger trees and looked around. Dylan-creature was heard wailing a warning. Reggie looked up the tree. He clawed at a large net, which contained him. As she looked around, the chatter stopped. Some sort of creature was hiding nearby. She cursed softly to herself then darted for the safety of another tree. The rope holding the net containing her brother was tied securely around a tree near her. She scanned the area then darted for the rope that would free her brother.

Several creatures suddenly leaped out of hiding and surrounded her. The four-foot tall creatures resembled two-legged geckos. Reggie appeared startled and let out a slight cry. She looked at the six creatures surrounding her. They chattered, bared blunt teeth, and held large sticks. Reggie spun into a series of karate kicks as the creatures approached and swiftly knocked them backwards across the forest floor. She had four of the six down when five more appeared. Four of them tackled her to the ground while snarling. Reggie punched and kicked them from her position on the ground, knocking a few off, but they continued coming at her until she was overpowered.

✝

An hour later, Reggie was being held within a crude cage on the ground below where Dylan-creature hung in his net. Her wrists and ankles were tied with crude ropes made from plant life. She struggled to free her wrists tied behind her back from where she sat in the cage. Dylan-creature wailed from his net above. The gecko creatures chattered excitedly while building a bonfire. There were at least twenty creatures surrounding the camp now. A couple of the creatures played crude instruments in musical rhythm, while others appeared to be singing and dancing around the bonfire. Reggie continued to fight her ropes then looked up at Dylan-creature, who had fallen suspiciously silent. He chewed on the rope netting. Reggie stared with surprise then smiled. A large, black hawk landed on a low hanging branch near Reggie, startling her. The hawk whimsically transformed into Helsing. He casually sat on the branch with his back against the tree and one leg dangling while observing her situation. Reggie stared at him with surprise rather than relief.

"Not off to a very good start," Helsing teased.

"You noticed?" she scoffed. "I'm working on correcting the problem. I don't suppose you'd be willing to--" Reggie nodded to the ropes that bind her.

Helsing grinned with humor. "That would be cheating."

"Kahn's rules specifically stated there were no rules, therefore, it's not cheating if you untie me."

"You'll try anything, won't you?"

Reggie continued to struggle against the ropes that bind her wrists behind her back then glared at Helsing. "Yes, so save me some time and tell me what will work on you."

151

"Where would the fun be in that?" Helsing teased.

"We'll have fun later." Reggie stopped struggling and glared at him with disgust. "You know, you're not much of a gentleman."

"I'm not mortal. I'm not any kind of man."

Reggie snorted a laugh and again fought her ropes. "A comment like that would get you seriously teased in the men's locker room."

Helsing appeared bewildered. She stopped struggling, groaned with exhaustion, and rested her head against the bamboo cage bars. Helsing jumped down from his tree branch, approached the cage on the ground, and crouched down to her level where she sat.

She glared at him. "Haven't I amused you enough for one morning?"

He studied her then grinned. "You're unlike any mortal woman I've ever met before."

"It's probably the little cage and the bondage scene that's throwing you off," she announced. "It's not that I don't appreciate your earlier assistance, but if you're going to just leer at me outside my cage, I'd prefer it if you left."

Helsing continued to smile and chuckled softly. As he straightened, the ropes fell from her wrists and ankles. Reggie rubbed her wrists then looked at him. The four-foot gecko creatures swarmed him as he turned. They vigorously shook their big sticks at Helsing. He offered a casual smile and waved his hand toward the nearby bonfire. The bonfire erupted into huge flames. The creatures ducked and squealed with fear. Helsing then waved his hand across the camp. The musical instruments played on their own. The tune was lively and upbeat. The creatures appeared fascinated and marveled at Helsing. They motioned him toward their bonfire. Reggie slowly straightened within her cage and stared with shock and amazement as Helsing danced with the lizard creatures. She looked at Dylan-creature. He had several links of rope chewed through, but it would require more gnawing.

"Come on, Dylan. You can do it," she cheered him on. "Pretend the ropes are Twinkies."

Dylan-creature stopped gnawing and glared at her. She smiled timidly. He returned to gnawing on the ropes. She glanced at the bonfire several times. The creatures were preoccupied with Helsing. He appeared to be having a good time with them. Dylan-creature suddenly fell from his netting and landed gracefully on his backside with a thud. He scurried for her cage and thrashed the bamboo with his tail in time with the drums. The sound of his tail striking the cage was barely heard above the drums. He got into a good rhythm then cracked it hard on the last beat. The bamboo cracked. Reggie pulled the broken pieces away and slipped through the opening. She looked back at the bonfire, watched Helsing dancing with the creatures, grinned, and then hurried away with her brother.

Chapter Nine

Despite the daylight hour, the woods remained dark as night. Reggie and Dylan-creature approached a stream. Reggie knelt along the bank and took a drink. Dylan-creature leaped into the water. Reggie collapsed onto her backside and watched him playfully splash around within the water. She allowed her head to fall into her hands and softly sobbed.

"Missed one hell of a party," Helsing announced.

Reggie gasped while wiping her tears then stood and turned to face Helsing. She maintained a calm outward appearance.

"I can't say I cared for my accommodations," she remarked then managed a smile, "but you were a hit."

"They're just trying to make the best of it," he replied. "They lost everything that ever mattered to them."

"You're starting to sound sympathetic to your brother's tortured souls."

"I never said I agreed with my brother's hobby, but I don't feel sympathy toward any of them," he announced. "It was their greed that condemned them in the first place."

"Love and devotion damned me to this place," Reggie scoffed. "Greed had nothing to do with it."

"You're the exception."

"You don't know that. The truth is you don't know what your brother does," she replied. "If he lied and cheated to condemn me, who's to say he didn't do the same for the others."

"It's really none of my business. I'm not responsible for him or his actions," he informed her. "We just try to stay out of each other's way."

"Your compassion is overwhelming," she muttered. "I'm having a tough time understanding why you're helping me."

"You're mistaken. I haven't been helping you."

Reggie smiled and held back her laugh. "If you say not. No matter, I like having you around."

Helsing appeared slightly bewildered. She gently ran her hand along his lower arm, smiled, and then turned toward the stream. Her brother continued to splash around.

"Dylan, time to go."

Helsing watched her a moment longer and remained bewildered. "Why would you like having me around?"

She looked back at him and smiled warmly. "Despite your superiority complex, you're actually cute. Something about you puts me at ease. I can't say I get that from a lot of guys." She hesitated and considered the comment. "Maybe it's because you're not a mortal male. Although, that does make me wonder why your brother is sexually attracted to woman and you're not."

"My goals are a bit higher than his," he replied. "Kahn wants instant gratification, whether it be emotional or sexual. There's nothing spiritual about Kahn. He wants to rule his pathetic little world and be worshipped by frightened creatures."

"And your goals?"

"It would be tough for you to understand."

"Try me."

"My goal is to be a Light Force. Our version of gods."

"Can't say I've ever heard that before," she announced. "You and Kahn aren't so different. He wants to be a god too, but his is the evil kind."

Helsing offered a tiny smile and appeared almost humored.

"Almost like studying to become a priest, I suppose," she said then smiled with embarrassment. "I feel bad about kissing you now."

"You don't have to feel bad about that. Over half of our Light Forces have children."

"Oh, I just assumed--" She hid her smile. "Never mind."

He appeared humored then indicated a path in the woods just across the stream. "That path looks friendly. I wouldn't doubt it leads to the beach." He looked at Reggie and grinned. "You'd better get going." Helsing suddenly transformed into the black hawk and flew away.

Reggie watched him fly into the darkness and raised a brow. "That's pretty damned hot."

Chapter Ten

Reggie and Dylan-creature walked onto the bright, sandy beach. In the distance, a battle worn pirate ship was stranded in the lagoon. It was an imposing and eerie image. Reggie felt relieved for the first time and looked at her watch.

"We're making good time," she remarked. "Look alive, Dylan. There has to be a catch. This was too easy." Reggie then looked at her ring. It was black. She nervously looked around. "Definitely a bad sign."

Reggie and Dylan-creature walked along the beach and kept close watch for trouble. Both slowed as the ship was seen more clearly. What appeared to be rocks lying on the beach were actually skeletal remains in tattered clothes embedded in the sand. Some had partially rotted flesh, indicating a more recent death. Dylan-creature stopped midstride and appeared reluctant to continue. Reggie stopped as well and looked across the large area littered with partially buried remains.

"To kill so many, it has to be a motion sensor trap." She looked at the water between them and the ship. "We could swim, but who knows what's under the water."

Reggie looked back at the distant ship. It appeared to be slowly sinking before their eyes. Horror crossed her face.

"That little cheat," she proclaimed then looked at her brother. "Stay here."

Reggie maneuvered through the maze of skeletons and partially decayed bodies. As she looked toward the ship, it sank faster. She picked up her pace. Dylan-creature suddenly wailed a warning. Reggie looked back while in the middle of the beach battlefield. The skeletons and decayed bodies were pulling themselves from the sand and to their feet. She gasped with horror and hurried for the ship. They grabbed for her while rising. She cried out and attempted to avoid them. There were several now on their feet between her and the ship in the lagoon. As they grabbed her, Reggie fought them while darting and dodging past many of them. Dylan-creature continued to wail while she fought the overwhelming number of decayed men before her. She made it to the water's edge. Decayed hands suddenly erupted from the wet sand and grabbed her ankle. She screamed and attempted to free herself by kicking her leg. The hands pulled her into the wet sand. Dylan-creature ran for the water, leaped into the surf, and vanished beneath the water.

"Dylan--no!"

Reggie's entire right foot was now beneath the sand. More hands erupted and attempted to grab her left foot. The standing decayed bodies continued their approach. Her left foot was now pulled beneath the sand. She screamed and fought the hands. More hands grabbed her hips and waist. She fought her descend and clutched at the loose sand. Dylan-creature exploded from the water near her and whipped his tail at a hand on her hip. The skeletal hand shattered. He tossed his tail to her as a lifeline. Reggie grabbed his tail with both hands. He clawed at the wet sand in an attempt to pull her out as the creatures continued their approach. She barely budged from her trapped position. He pulled his tail from her and whipped it at the approaching creatures. They shattered and fell but were magically put back together. Reggie attempted to remain above the surface of the sand but it was now up to her waist. The decayed bodies jumped on Dylan-creature. He knocked them off but they continued to swarm him. The sand suddenly turned to dried, cracked dirt, locking the hands and Reggie in the ground.

The water rapidly pulled back several yards, formed into a large wave, and then crashed to shore. Reggie cried out, covered her head, and screamed. The water rushed past her, Dylan-creature, and the decayed bodies with tremendous force. The water rapidly pulled back to the lagoon and carried the creatures with it. Dylan-creature dug his claws into the hard ground and left long scratches while avoiding being sucked out by the powerful undertow. When the water returned to the lagoon, Reggie, Dylan, and the trapped hands were all that remained. Reggie attempted to free herself from the ground, but she was stuck. Dylan-creature staggered dizzily and collapsed with exhaustion. Reggie looked at the lagoon and couldn't believe her eyes. The pirate ship was trapped in the solid ground as well. Reggie again attempted to free herself with renewed vigor, but it appeared hopeless.

A man's hand was offered to her. Reggie looked up and saw Helsing standing over her. She accepted his hand. As he gently pulled her upward, the ground broke free, and she was easily pulled to her feet. He released her hand and met her gaze. She stared at him with surprise then suddenly threw her arms around his neck and clung to him. He appeared momentarily stunned and seemed uncertain how to react. As Reggie sobbed softly into his neck, Helsing uncertainly placed his arms around her waist and held her. He shut his eyes and gently nuzzled her head.

"I can't beat him," she sobbed. "I'm no match for his powers. I can't win."

Helsing gently touched Reggie's face. She suddenly tensed, sniffed softly, and pulled back to meet his gaze. Although he showed little emotion, he gently wiped the tears from her cheek. She uncertainly looked around the beach then back at Helsing.

"You did this? This was you," she said with conviction. "You stopped them, didn't you?"

He offered a tiny smile. "Well, there are no rules."

Reggie smiled and laughed with relief. She again hugged Helsing in a warm embrace. He returned the embrace with less forethought. She then pulled back to meet his gaze with a puzzled look.

"Why the sudden change of heart?"

"I guess you're growing on me," he teased. "Maybe I'm not actually above mortal pleasures after all."

She stared at him with surprise then smiled timidly.

Helsing reluctantly released her. "You'd better get your dagger. You still have to get it back to the castle."

✝

The dagger was embedded in the helm of the pirate ship on the main deck. Reggie glanced at Helsing then uncertainly approached the helm. As she placed her hand on the dagger hilt, large spiders erupted from every crack in the wood and rapidly crawled toward her in a massive flood of black spiders. Reggie cried out with horror and pulled the dagger free. She quickly backed up to Helsing and looked around as they closed in on them. She was nearly paralyzed with fear as she watched the spiders rapidly approaching.

Soon they'd be crawling over every inch of her body. Her body subconsciously shuddered. Helsing stared at her with a puzzled look.

"Don't like spiders?" he asked.

"I'm terrified of them," she gasped faintly. "Especially the big, *hairy* ones."

"How do you feel about snakes?"

Reggie suddenly glared at Helsing. He casually pulled a handful of snakes from his pockets and dropped them on the floor near their feet. The snakes slithered for the spiders, which immediately retreated. Reggie watched the snakes chase the spiders from the deck then looked at Helsing with surprise.

"You can't imagine all that I have up my sleeves," he announced while grinning proudly, "--and within my pockets."

Dylan-creature suddenly scrambled across deck and bolted behind Reggie to hide. Both looked across the main deck. Kahn stood several feet away and looked displeased.

"You have no business interfering in my affairs, Helsing," Kahn snarled then looked at Reggie. "Outside help. You forfeit."

"There are no rules, remember?" she snarled. "Which includes help from your brother. I seem to recall you weren't supposed to interfere and use your powers. Those zombies and spiders were all you."

"That was before I found out you had enslaved my brother into helping you," Kahn said then glared at Helsing. "You're not exactly living up to the high standards of a Light Force, brother. Did she offer herself to you to solicit your help?" His tone sounded almost jealous. "You know you can't become a Light Force while indulging in mortal pleasures."

"My reasons for helping her are my own," Helsing said. "I've accepted nothing from her."

"Then that makes you a bigger fool than I thought," Kahn scoffed. "You can't possibly expect me to believe you're just helping her for the sheer joy of it. You lack compassion, so something is motivating you."

"I admire her loyalty and devotion toward others," Helsing replied. "I think she's worth saving. And if it pisses you off in the process, all the better. You can't interfere. Other than that, there are no rules. So leave us. We have a dagger to return."

Kahn suddenly sneered and appeared enraged. "I won't allow it!"

"You have no say," Helsing announced casually. "We're playing by the 'no rules' policy."

"Then let the games begin," Kahn snarled. "I may not be allowed to interfere with her task, but that doesn't mean I can't stop you." He suddenly vanished.

Reggie looked at Helsing with concern in her eyes. "Your powers are equal to his, I hope."

"That's not the problem. He plays dirty, and I'm not permitted to. I'd be sacrificing my Life Force rights," Helsing replied. "We'd better go. It's going to be a long trip back, I'm afraid."

Chapter Eleven

Several hours later, Helsing, Reggie, and Dylan-creature walked along a worn path in the woods. Reggie appeared exhausted and Dylan-creature was lagging behind. Helsing looked at his weary travel mates and stopped.

"Perhaps we should stop and rest a few minutes," he said. "It's safe here. Rest while you can."

Dylan-creature collapsed and immediately drifted to sleep. Reggie reluctantly sat against a tree. Helsing joined her and waved his hand. A fire appeared a few feet before them and burned in the air. Reggie enjoyed the warmth then glanced at Helsing, who groomed his fire.

"I'm really glad you decided to join me. I don't know how much longer I could have lasted on my own," she said gently. "With Dylan as he is, I have little emotional support. He was always my strength. We had to depend on each other to survive."

"I can't say I've ever depended on Kahn for anything," Helsing informed her. "He's always been hell bent. He wasn't exactly fun to be around all these years. Probably why I avoid him."

"Is it because of his evils that you want to be a Light Force?"

"No, it has nothing to do with him," he replied. "I suppose one of us should make our parents proud."

"Where are they?"

"They're Light Forces," he announced then pointed up with a grin. "Out there somewhere. I'd really like to see them again."

"I'm sure you will."

"I'm beginning to wonder," he said with a sigh. "You've managed to completely throw off my focus and scatter my priorities."

She laughed and playfully clung to his arm. "Dylan says women curse men in the nicest possible way."

Helsing stared at her nestled against his side and the playful smile on her face. He smiled and shook his head. "I've been in contact with mortal women before without any conflict, so naturally I'm having difficulty understanding my behavior around you." He uncertainly placed his hand on hers and gently caressed it. "I'm bothered that I'm enjoying it."

Reggie smiled timidly, removed her hand from his arm, and straightened. "I'm sorry," she said gently. "With all your help, it's not fair that I should compromise your moral commitments."

Helsing studied her a moment longer, moved closer, and kissed her warmly but passionately. Despite her surprise, she returned the kiss. He slowly pulled away, met her gaze, and smiled gently.

"I just needed to get that out of my system."

She blushed and hid her grin "Happy to have helped."

✝

Helsing, Reggie, and Dylan-creature continued along the path in the woods with less exhaustion. Dylan-creature suddenly stopped, looked around, and smelled the air through his open mouth. A soft gurgle escaped his throat. Helsing and Reggie stopped and looked around to his warning. There was no sound and nothing moved. Several creatures no more than two-feet-tall seemingly stepped out of the background they blended against and jumped on top of Helsing. Four of them tackled him to the ground. As he kicked and tossed them off him, one bit him on the neck. He held out his hand and the creatures were violently projected off him and through the air. He held his bleeding neck and slowly moved to his knees. Reggie hurried to his side and attempted visually to assess his injury.

"Helsing, are you okay?"

He looked at the blood on his hand then appeared concerned. He quickly stood and pulled her to her feet alongside him. "Kahn fights dirty. That thing bit me for a reason."

"Some sort of infection?" she suddenly asked.

"We need to hurry," Helsing announced. "Having me turn on you would be just his style."

Reggie stared at him with a look of horror. He hurried her along the path and for the nearby beach. They ran along the sandy beach behind the fast moving Dylan-creature. Helsing suddenly slowed, clutched his head while swaying, and then collapsed to his knees. Reggie attempted to pull him to his feet.

"It's just another mile or two, Helsing. You can fight it."

He slowly shook his head. "You need to keep going. Get as far away from me as possible."

"I can't leave you like this," she gasped.

"You have too. Your freedom depends on you getting that dagger to the castle."

Dylan-creature nervously paced before them. His tail swished as if in panic.

Reggie suddenly groaned with frustration. "This isn't fair."

"You're right," Kahn announced. "It's completely unfair."

Reggie and Helsing looked at Kahn, who casually leaned against a nearby tree. He frowned and shook his head while watching Helsing. Dylan-creature darted behind Reggie and hid.

She glared her loathe for him. "He's your brother. Look what you're doing to him. What kind of monster are you?"

Kahn straightened and appeared innocent. "Not me. I'm not the beast who bit him." He sighed deeply. "Sad, though. That poison is lethal and the only antidote is back a mile."

"Poison?" she gasped with horror.

Helsing appeared equally surprised.

"You probably saw some purple flowers growing on that ledge back there," Kahn said. "He'll need to ingest those within sixty minutes or he's finished. I can't imagine he'll make it back that far in his condition."

"You'd kill your own brother?"

"Again, it wasn't me who bit him."

Reggie knelt in the sand alongside Helsing, who glared at Kahn. "Can you use your powers to get back there?"

He slowly shook his head. "No, I'm too weak."

"You'd better hurry, my dear," Kahn teased with a mocking grin. "You only have one hour to return that dagger--unless you're feeling sympathetic toward Helsing."

Helsing glared at his brother. "She's not that stupid, Kahn, and you wouldn't be so bold as to kill me."

"Again--not me," Kahn said while smirking.

Reggie looked back at Helsing with concern. He met her gaze with a stern, serious look.

"Return that dagger, Reggie," he said firmly. "Don't worry about me. Just go."

She slowly stood while studying Kahn's mocking smile then looked back at Helsing.

Helsing glared at her and sharply raised his brows. "Take the dagger back *now*."

She turned and ran in the opposite direction for the antidote. Helsing appeared horrified while weakly attempting to stand.

"Reggie, no!"

Kahn laughed and vanished. Dylan-creature slid beneath Helsing's hand and helped steady him as he stood. He leaned heavily on the creature and stumbled along the beach. It was nearly an hour later. Reggie ran along the beach with a fistful of purple flowers. Helsing lie motionless on the sand while Dylan-creature lie sadly at his side. Reggie fell to her knees near him and extended the flowers.

"I got them, Helsing," she gasped while out of breath. "You have to eat them--please."

He weakly took a flower and ate it. A bright light approached them on the beach. Helsing stared with surprise, weakly lifted his head, and watched the light get closer. Reggie clutched the dagger and appeared concerned. Dylan-creature scurried behind Reggie and hid. The light appeared in the form of a woman with only light as her features.

"Mother?" Helsing gasped.

"Yes, my son," his mother, Leola, replied. "You've made your father and I very proud today. You took the final step toward securing your future as a Light Force by willingly sacrificing your own life for another. You will be joining us for eternity."

Helsing slowly sat up with Reggie's assistance and stared at the female light before them. "I'm honored, mother, but I can't." He weakly pulled himself to his knees. "I have to deal with Kahn in the only way he'll understand, which means I'll have to forfeit my rights to become a Light Force. I'll see him dead before I ever allow him to harm Reggie."

Leola suddenly groaned. "What did your brother do this time?"

Chapter Twelve

Kahn was casually seated in an elegant chair in the hallway while watching the grandfather clock only seconds away from noon. Begley anxiously stood near the kitchen doorway and stared at the front door with anticipation. Chrissy peered over the second floor railing near the stairs while wrenching her fingers together with her attention on the door. Kahn grinned while waiting for the minute hand to move to its final position. The front door suddenly opened to reveal Reggie with the dagger in her hand. Kahn stared at her with shock and bolted up from his chair. Begley and Chrissy appeared stunned while making their way closer then abruptly stopped.

"That's not possible. You couldn't have made it back in time," Kahn announced then turned angry. "You cheated!"

Reggie stood calmly within the foyer and showed no emotion. "There were no rules. How could I cheat?"

"Helsing transported you here," Kahn announced. "He brought you back. You needed to come back on your own."

"Helsing didn't transport me here," she informed him while playing with the dagger. "I came back on my own."

"That's not possible! How could you have gotten here so fast?"

"If you must know, I ran," she replied while grinning.

"You let Helsing die?" Kahn suddenly asked with surprise.

"No, he'll be along shortly."

Kahn shook his head with hostility. Begley and Chrissy slowly closed in from both the hall and the stairs to witness the scene.

"You couldn't have run that fast," Kahn informed her. "You cheated. You lose!"

"I didn't. I win," she calmly announced. "You're the one who cheats. Dylan told me about his deal with you. He pledged his life to you if you'd spare me from the fire that killed our parents. I wasn't even aware I'd been home when it happened. Some sort of memory trick you used on me. You saved me from the blaze when he couldn't reach me." Her eyes suddenly narrowed as she approached him. "But then he found out that you were responsible for starting the fire in the first place." The look in her eyes was venomous. She stood only a few feet away from him and stared into his eyes with hatred. "You killed my parents, you son-of-a-bitch, just to claim my brother's life for your pathetic kingdom. It's over. My brother and I will be leaving just as soon as he gets here."

Reggie carelessly tossed the dagger on the hall table near the stairs. It clattered against the marble top. Chrissy paused on the last step, glanced at the dagger, and then stared at Reggie. Kahn paced before her and raised his brows while mocking her with an evil smile.

"He couldn't prove any of that and neither can you," Kahn announced then shook his head. "You won't be going anywhere. You'll take your rightful place by my side as you were always meant to. As for your brother, I'll have his head mounted on my wall."

She stared at him with surprise. "This was never about Dylan, was it? It was always about me," she suddenly gasped. "You used Dylan to get to me, and I played right into your evil plans."

"Even if you could prove that, there's nothing you can do about it," he announced. "You'll be mine. And if you're thinking my brother will come to your rescue, think again. He can't harm me or he'll forfeit his right to become a Life Force."

Kahn raised his hand to Reggie with a threatening sneer. A bolt shot from his hand toward her. Reggie defensively raised her own hand with a startled gasp and the bolt of energy suddenly dissipated. Kahn stared at her with astonishment. Reggie looked at her hand, flexed it, and grinned.

"That tingled," she said with a giggle

Chrissy and Begley appeared almost as shocked as Kahn was. Both were now only a few feet away from the show. The front door burst open to reveal a panting Dylan in human form. All eyes were upon him.

"Damn, I'm really out of shape," Dylan said while hunched over and clutching his knees.

"A steady diet of Twinkies will do that," Reggie casually replied.

"What's going on?" Kahn demanded. "Who turned him back?"

Reggie looked back at Kahn and grinned. "It's a funny story, although I'm not sure you'll find it all that amusing."

Helsing half fell through the open doorway, leaned his back to the wall while gasping, and slid down the wall into a sitting position. "I've decided I don't care for running," he gasped.

Dylan continued to breathe hard while holding his side. "Join the club."

Kahn stared at Helsing then looked at Reggie as she approached him. Her sly grin was enough to rattle him.

"Helsing and I were each granted one wish from your mother as a wedding present," Reggie informed him.

Kahn appeared stunned and looked from Helsing to Reggie. "Wedding present? You and Helsing?"

Helsing smiled wearily and gave a tiny wave. "My wish was for my powers to go to Reggie temporarily for her own protection."

"And my wish was for all the people you'd enslaved to be returned to their mortal lives," Reggie announced.

"No, that's not possible," Kahn protested then looked at Helsing. "If you marry, you can't be a Light Force."

"I've already been chosen," Helsing replied. "My Light Force status takes effect after Reggie's tour of life ends."

"Mother would never interfere," Kahn scoffed. "This isn't over!"

The female light, Leola, appeared in the hallway. Begley took Chrissy's hand in his as they moved closer together and watched the light. Kahn appeared stunned.

"Mother?" he gasped with surprise then turned angry. "Mother, what's the meaning of this? How could you interfere?"

"I'm sorry, Kahn. You abused your power," Leola said. "All the mortals you enslaved will be returned to their world as they were. I'm afraid your behavior calls for severe punishment. The council has agreed to strip your powers starting now. You will live your life as a mortal among mortals. I hope you will learn from your mistakes."

Leola waved her hand. Vapors flooded from Kahn. He suddenly grabbed onto the table for support and looked at his mother.

"This isn't fair!"

"You know it is," Leola replied then vanished.

Helsing smiled and pulled Reggie into his arms.

Dylan glared at them. "Can we go home now?" he demanded.

"Yes, I'd like to see our mortal home," Helsing announced cheerfully.

Chrissy and Begley approached them while barely able to control their grins. Chrissy hugged Reggie. "I can't thank you enough for setting us free."

"From both of us," Begley added.

"When you're ready to leave, meet the others on the beach," Reggie said then smiled. "Be happy." She turned to Dylan and Helsing. "This should be an interesting trip with me driving."

Dylan smirked at Kahn in his weakened condition and gave him the finger. Reggie waved her hand and all three vanished.

Kahn frowned with disgust. "It's not over; not by a long shot."

He turned and nearly collided with Chrissy. Kahn gave her a stern, dirty look. "My powers will eventually be restored."

Begley proudly appeared behind Chrissy and placed his arm around her shoulder. He gave her a reassuring squeeze, kissed her on the cheek, and walked away from her. Chrissy stood proudly before Kahn and smiled as if the world was lifted from her shoulders.

"I never thought this day would come, Kahn, but I'm glad this relationship can finally be terminated," she announced and sighed deeply. "I hope there are no hard feelings." Chrissy smiled sweetly and revealed the golden dagger in her hand by her side.

Kahn appeared horrified and let out a startled gasp. She thrust the dagger upward into his abdomen without emotion. He suddenly cried out with pain, clutched the golden dagger as she released it, and stared into Chrissy's expressionless eyes. Begley and Chrissy watched with no reaction as Kahn collapsed to the floor. She turned to Begley and offered a tiny, pleased smile. Begley took her hand in his, suavely kissed it, and returned the smile.

"Now that you're officially a widow, can I call you?"

She sank into his arms and clung to him.

The End

Holly Copella

Already Dead

Chapter One

The ocean was peaceful and tranquil as the sun set on the horizon. A commercial airliner suddenly flew past only a few hundred feet above the water, rippling the glassy surface from sheer wind force in its wake. Within the fuselage, nearly two hundred passengers clung to their seats, some screaming; some in silent terror, as the interior vibrated with tremendous force. Luggage and passengers' carry-on possessions were strewn throughout the aisle along with a motionless man, whose condition appeared grave. A loud banging sound came from the flight deck door. A neatly dressed businessman in his late twenties pounded on the cockpit door. Despite his mild-mannered appearance, Dane Wolfe was adamant in his quest to gain access to the cockpit.

"You don't have to do this," he shouted through the door. "Let me in!"

Something outside the window caught his attention. Dane looked out the nearby galley window. Horror filled his eyes as the color drained from his face. He bolted for the window and saw the ocean rapidly getting closer. Dane dived into the flight attendant's jump seat and strapped himself in. He glanced at the once attractive, dead flight attendant on the floor just inside the galley then shut his eyes and braced for impact. It never came. The jet skimmed the water beneath it for only a moment before the nose crested the water in a huge wake then completely disappeared beneath the surface. The passengers were jerked and jolted within their seats as more objects flew from overhead bins and crashed down upon them. Dane looked back at the window and saw only water beyond the glass. For a moment, the irony of surviving the crash only to drown crossed his mind.

✝

Six months later. The island was a tropical paradise with its soft, white sandy beach and clear waters. The setting sun bid farewell to another beautiful sunny day in paradise. A worn and defeated Dane stumbled out of the woods as he panted with exhaustion. The last six months had hardened and rapidly aged the once sophisticated man. Although six months had passed, he only had a few days' worth of stubble on his once clean-shaven face, and his hair was only slightly longer than it had previously been. His worn and moderately tattered dress shirt was covered in blood. Despite the scrapes on his exposed, lower arms, the blood didn't appear to be his own. He clung to an old revolver, now hanging down at his side, and placed his blood-covered hand to his face in an attempt to control his emotions. He suddenly hesitated, staring at the blood as his hand trembled, and then sobbed softly.

"Forgive me for not doing what I should have," he softly cried.

Dane regained control of his emotions, drew a deep breath, and placed the gun to his temple. His finger tightened on the trigger. A strange thumping sound was heard in the near distance. Dane slowly lowered the gun and looked into the evening sky. A helicopter approached from a distant freighter just beyond the horizon. The helicopter flew past the tail end of the crashed jet protruding from the ocean just half a mile from the beach. Dane stared in silent shock at the approaching helicopter. He suddenly looked at the gun in his hand and the vast amount of blood covering him. His mind appeared to race. He ran across the beach and into the surf, discarding the gun as he dove into the water. Once he surfaced, he waved to the approaching helicopter from the water.

174

✝

The following day, every newsstand in every corner of the country contained several papers all with the photo featuring the tail end of a jet protruding from the water. All headlines read: 'Missing plane found! One man survives!'

Chapter Two

Five years later. The massive, stone library was the showpiece of downtown Harkesville. As old as the city itself, the building was a living work of art and continued to draw in locals despite the internet age. A dashing yet moderately lanky man in his late twenties hurried up the stone steps two at a time for the large, solid wood doors. Although not outwardly a strikingly handsome man, Porter Hendrix had a certain appeal most women found attractive in a hard to explain way. Possibly his baby face, his athletic build, or his flowing, Greek god, sandy golden hair.

Porter headed straight through the massive computer lounge and for the basement archives. He hurried down the less impressive basement steps and entered the massive archives, consisting of rows of old books, sections of newspapers, and piles of old magazines. The deeper into the archives he went, the narrower the corridor became. He entered a back room at the opposite end of the basement archives and looked toward a desk in the back. There were large mounds of books piled on a desk seemingly hiding someone who was busily working. Porter entered the deserted, dingy room and hurried toward the desk while panting out of breath.

"You won't believe what I found," Porter announced, barely able to contain his grin.

An attractive woman in her mid-twenties poked her head up from behind the wall of books and stared at him. Murphy Landon was the classic 'fresh-faced girl next door' beauty. She was attractive, but only to the sort of men who appreciated a less 'flashy' woman. Her expression suddenly dropped and her mouth fell open as she stared at Porter.

"You didn't--" she gasped.

Porter nodded excitedly and could barely stand still. "I did. I found him!"

Murphy shut the book she'd been reading and leaped up from her chair with excitement. Half the books fell to the floor with a clatter, although neither seemed to care.

"Where?" she nearly cried out as her eyes lit up.

"He's been living like a freakin' hermit the last five years at some secluded lake house in the woods," Porter announced and vigorously ran his fingers through his flowing, sandy hair. "The son-of-a-bitch changed his name and everything. Calling himself Max these days." He held back his laugh. "Your boy really wanted to disappear."

"Not exactly easy to do in this day and age," she announced, "but he made one hell of an effort."

Porter's look turned less excited and somewhat serious. "You know he's not exactly going to be happy to see you," he informed her.

She gave him a playful smile. "Why? He doesn't even know me."

He groaned and rolled his eyes at her attempt at humor. "Dane Wolfe refused to tell his story to anyone in the media and fell off the grid two months after his rescue," Porter remarked lowly. "I don't think he wants to talk about Flight 220." He gave her a quick once over then reconsidered. "Although, if you wore something low-cut and sexy he might talk to you."

"I have to write this book, Porter," Murphy declared then folded her arms across her chest. "I'll wear a thong and garter belt if it'll get me an interview."

The mood turned serious. "What if he wants something *else* in trade?"

She glared at her friend. "I think you know me better than that."

"Considering you won't even sleep with me--" he playfully pouted.

Murphy collected several notepads and her laptop then stuffed them into a bag. She smirked her response then resumed her enthusiasm for the news.

"How long is the drive?" she asked.

"Six hours," he boldly announced. "Pack your overnight bag and a sleeping bag."

Murphy was set back by the comment, although uncertain if he had been serious. "There aren't any hotels nearby?"

"I have a call into a guy about a cabin on the lake, but it might be you, me, and a pup tent for two if he doesn't get back to me," Porter informed her. "Cell phone service is non-existent in that area."

"Charming," Murphy announced with a soft snort.

†

The small, log cabin was barely noticeable in the mostly dark woods near the lake. A tiny light fixture on the crude front porch allowed just enough light to see the old door. A car's headlights shined on the cabin then went out as Murphy and Porter uncertainly approached. Only the sounds of nature could be heard, and it was almost deafening.

"Okay, this is creepy," Porter muttered while looking around.

"It looks better in the daytime," a man announced from nearby.

Murphy and Porter suddenly jumped with surprise to a man standing in the shadows on the porch. He straightened and approached them while grinning.

"Didn't mean to startle you," the man in his late fifties teased, although his moderately creepy grin suggested otherwise. "I live across the lake, so I came by boat."

He opened the door without unlocking it and flipped on the lights. Murphy and Porter followed him into the cabin. The interior was surprisingly modern, considering the dated exterior. Both looked around and marveled at the cozy living room as the creepy owner skillfully built a fire in the fireplace. He straightened and turned toward them.

"There are two bedrooms and a bathroom down that hallway," he informed them while pointing. "You can't see it, but you're right on the lake. There's a boat dock. Boat rental will cost extra."

"I think we'll manage without one," Porter replied and flashed a knowing grin. "How much to rent the place for two nights?"

"Oh, I only rent by the week."

Porter eyed Murphy. She smiled and indicated the odd man with a slight nod.

Porter groaned softly and removed a money clip from his pocket. "I don't know how I always end up paying for everything," he muttered while shaking his head.

"I've given up trying to figure that one out myself," Murphy replied as she casually looked around.

Chapter Three

Dane's elegant, A-frame lake house had floor to ceiling windows on the first and second floor. The large, multi-level deck gave the house a certain class and an even wealthier appeal. Just a short distance from the house, there was a modern dock attached to a large boathouse just off the lake. Murphy and Porter stood on a path within the woods and stared at the million-dollar property with some surprise.

"Not exactly roughing it," Murphy boldly announced.

"No, I'd say he did pretty well for himself after the crash," Porter informed her as he casually leaned against a nearby tree.

"He received a sizable settlement from the airline," Murphy remarked while studying every detail of the house. She'd been on a quest to locate Dane Wolfe for years, yet now that she finally found him, she was overwhelmed with the thought.

"How big is 'sizable'?" Porter asked while casting a sideways glance at her.

She shrugged with little emotion. "Ten million--give or take a grand."

Porter eyed her and straightened, slightly surprised by the settlement amount. "What else do you know about this guy?" he asked.

"Nothing, really," she replied with a defeated sigh. "Only what I read in the papers after the rescue, which wasn't much." She couldn't take her eyes off the house, waiting for a sighting of the elusive recluse. "He has no living close family members. Served in the Air Force after high school and was honorably discharged after his tour ended. At the time of the crash, he was working as a consultant for some software company. The only photo I was able to find of him was when he served in the military."

"I think I should go with you," Porter suddenly announced. "You don't know what sort of whack job this guy is."

She looked at her friend with surprise and possible concern by the comment. "No, I'll have a better chance without you lurking over my shoulder."

"You mean he's less likely to proposition you with me by your side," Porter snapped hotly.

"Seriously?" Murphy demanded while sharply eyeing him. "Do you have any idea how many times I've been propositioned?" Her brows raised. "Twice. Both times by you." She shook her head with disbelief. "I don't know who all these guys are that you think want to get in my pants, but they don't exist."

"You're hot, Murphy," he insisted. "Surely, you must be propositioned all the time."

"I think I give off some vibe that repels men," she casually replied.

"You are a bit standoffish."

"Yeah, well, the last five years may have had something to do with that," she remarked. "You can wait here and keep an eye on things, if it makes you happy."

"Oh, I'm not going anywhere," he announced. "You scream, and I'm on him."

Murphy smiled, snorted a laugh at his tough guy act, and patted his chest. "My protector."

Porter smirked his disapproval. Murphy inhaled a deep breath and headed toward the house. She couldn't deny she was trembling inside. It seemed as if she waited her entire life for this moment, and now she was intimidated by it. She walked onto the porch, her legs turning to rubber and her lite breakfast threatening to purge from her stomach. Murphy boldly knocked on the door and waited for a response, her heart pounding harder with each passing second. She wasn't sure if it was disappointment or relief when no one answered. She uncertainly looked around and saw a car just outside the garage. A parked car meant very little when a boat would take residence just about anywhere. Murphy held her breath and again knocked.

"If you're looking for Max--" a man announced from nearby.

Murphy held back her startled gasp and turned with surprise to see a man in his mid-thirties at the bottom of the steps.

An older version of Dane casually leaned on the post with his foot propped on the bottom step. "--he's not home." Although only in his mid-thirties, Dane's six-month tour on the island had aged him.

His once brown hair was almost entirely gray, and his eyes lacked any sparkle of life.

Murphy attempted to relax after her overreaction to the unfamiliar man. She forced a smile and took her time down the steps to greet the stranger. She was shaken from her already frayed nerves, and the neighbor's sudden appearance didn't help any.

"Are you a friend of his?" she asked, maintaining a high level of friendliness.

"I suppose so. He's not exactly the friendly sort--particularly to strangers," he informed her then attempted a smile that came off as more of a smirk. "You could leave a note on the door. I'm sure he'll be back this evening."

"That won't be necessary," she announced and finally felt her heart rate slowing. "I'm renting the house next door. I can stop by later."

"Oh, so you're here for the summer?" Dane asked while cocking his head to one side.

"Yes," she easily lied.

Dane suddenly smiled, revealing a friendlier version of himself. "That's wonderful." He approached her and extended his hand. "I'm Ben. I live on the lake too."

Murphy smiled and shook his hand. "I'm Murphy."

"Murphy?" he questioned then chuckled softly. "I'm guessing your father was hoping for a son."

"I guess he was," she replied. "Murphy was my grandfather's name. He died a few weeks before I was born."

"I suppose you should be grateful his name wasn't Bubba," Dane teased then casually indicated the path near the lake. "I was just taking my morning walk around the lake. Care to join me?"

Murphy looked at her casual yet non-practical shoes and offered a humored smile. "In these shoes?" she teased. "I wouldn't get very far."

"Or I could walk you as far as your rental cabin."

She studied his handsome smile and immediately relaxed. "Okay."

Murphy walked with him toward the path in the woods, noting Porter was suspiciously missing. Murphy and Dane walked along the path toward her cabin. For the first time, she admired the lake to their right. She had to admit, it was a tranquil place. Dane kept close watch of her and appeared interested. Since her nerves had settled, she hadn't even noticed he was staring.

"So how do you know Max?" he finally asked while maintaining his grin.

"Through my father."

"Oh?" he chirped. "And who's your father?"

"Arkin Landon."

Dane casually nodded and now focused on the path before them. "You seem like a nice, young lady," he remarked as his smile quickly vanished. "I almost feel bad."

She gave him a bewildered look. "About what?"

He still didn't look at her. "For how uncomfortable I'm about to make you."

Dane suddenly turned toward her, startling her and stopped her in her tracks. His eyes turned hateful, and his look frightened her.

"I don't know your father, and I don't talk to the press," he snarled and then took a step closer with an unpredictable look in his eyes.

Murphy instinctively backed up and struck a tree. She kept her eyes locked on him. A series of thoughts and emotions exploded within her.

"Consider yourself officially warned," he growled as his eyes narrowed. "If you bother me again, I'll personally toss you into the lake. If you weren't a woman, you'd already be treading water for lying about knowing me."

He turned and walked back toward his cabin. Murphy stared after him, slightly stunned, but quickly collected her emotions.

"I didn't lie, and I'm not a reporter," she boldly announced before he could get too far from her.

Dane suddenly turned and took two quick steps toward her. He was nearly on top of her, startling her with his stealthy reactions. She was quickly reminded that he wasn't as old as he looked and probably only half as sane as he seemed.

"Now you're just pissing me off," he snapped. An evil smirk crossed his face. "Lucky for you, I'm feeling particularly playful. I've never thrown a woman in the lake before."

Murphy felt her entire body twitch with thoughts of physical harm. She could have left it go, but she'd waited too long and come too far. She boldly straightened, locked eyes with him, and cast her fears aside.

"My father died on Flight 220," she announced in a firm, commanding voice.

Dane's expression suddenly dropped. He took a step back as the fight drained from him

"I'm sorry about that," he replied softly.

"Yeah, me too," she almost whispered.

"I can't help you," he offered with less aggression. "I didn't know him. He didn't make it to the island."

"I know, I already interrogated the FBI," she replied and fidgeted slightly. "They told me he wasn't among the ten crash survivors who made it to the island, and that's all they would tell me from your accounts of the crash." She drew a deep breath while staring at him. "I don't know any more than anyone else about what happened on Flight 220, and that's not fair."

He stared at her with a somewhat sympathetic look in his eyes. "Life *isn't* fair."

"I deserve to know how my father died."

"You already know how he died," Dane informed her. "He drowned with the others."

She studied him a moment then ran trembling fingers through her hair. "I know what the government told the press," she boldly announced. "At 1:15 PM terrorists attempted to take control of Flight 220 and killed both flight attendants in the process. At 1:32 PM, a handful of passengers stormed the flight deck, defeated the terrorists, and attempted to keep the jet in the air. At 1:37 PM, Flight 220 crashed into the ocean, drowning the remaining 186 passengers and crew. Only ten made it into the emergency raft. Once on shore, two died from their injuries within twenty-four hours of the crash, and the other seven died within the months that followed. Dane Wolfe was the only survivor of Flight 220."

He stared at her with little expression. "That's almost word for word from the FBI report of my accounts."

"I know," she replied. "I've read it enough times."

"Your father didn't suffer, Murphy," he gently informed her. "Most of those who drowned were unconscious at the time. It happened very fast." He hesitated while studying her. "I hope that brings you some peace."

Dane then turned and walked away. Murphy stared after him with some surprise then hurried after him.

"Peace but not closure," she announced while on his heels. "I've done nothing but obsess over that plane crash for the last five years, and you're my only lifeline."

Dane continued to walk briskly away without looking back at her. "What? Are you writing a book?"

"Yes."

Dane suddenly stopped, causing her to stop. He groaned then glared at her while shaking his head. "You were so close." His hostility immediately rose. "I don't talk to the media," he lashed out. "Media includes would-be authors." He attempted to control his rising temper. "I'm really sorry about your father, I am, but that's not going to be enough to keep me from throwing you in the lake if you continue to pester me about Flight 220."

He again turned and continued toward his cabin. Murphy hurried after him in relentless pursuit.

"I have to write this book," she cried out. "It's all I can think about."

"No one's stopping you," he casually replied without stopping or looking back.

"You're stopping me!"

He snorted a laugh and shook his head. "No, I'm just not helping you."

"I need you!" She stopped on the path and stared at him as he continued to walk further away. "I don't sleep. I barely have a life. If I can write this book, I'll have my closure." He was almost to the edge of the woods. "Please, I'll give you anything you want in exchange for the whole story about Flight 220."

Dane suddenly stopped on the path but kept his back to her. She held her breath and awaited a response. He finally turned and looked at her.

"I've been offered millions for my story," he boldly announced. "I doubt you can top that."

"You have a price, don't you?" The question was more of a statement. She couldn't back down now. "You wouldn't have bothered to stop if you didn't have something in mind."

Dane frowned. "I've been offered *that* as well," he replied. "And let's be honest, Murphy. You're a little too innocent and naive to play that game."

He turned to leave.

Murphy felt offended by his comment and suddenly felt confrontational. "Did you just call me naive?"

"I'm sorry," he announced, sounding almost sincere. His brows boldly arched. "I meant 'young and inexperienced'. My story isn't for sale at any price. I don't need the money, and I've abandoned sexual desire." He gave her a quick once over and shook his head. "There's nothing you have that I want. If you need closure, see a shrink."

Dane turned and continued onto the sandy beach before his house. Murphy followed him from a safe distance. She couldn't give up, but she wasn't sure what she had left to offer.

"I've invested a lot into this," she informed him.

Dane groaned without stopping. "Don't make me throw you in the lake, Murphy."

"I've interviewed families of the others who died on the island," she announced and elected to play one last card. "There was one female survivor. Her name was Kate."

Dane suddenly stopped but didn't turn toward her. His entire body was ridged. She'd struck a nerve.

"Her mother said she was strong-willed and would never have given up," Murphy pressed. "She showed me photos of Kate. She was a beautiful woman. Her mother wants me to tell her story." Murphy stared at Dane's back. He hadn't moved. He didn't even twitch. She was either breaking through or he was about to kill her. "Were you and Kate close?" She played her last card carefully. "Is she the reason you've abandoned your sexual desires?"

His silence and frozen stance was frightening. She wished she could see his expression. Perhaps she'd know whether to run for her life or not. Dane finally turned toward her. His expression was cold and possibly hostile.

"You want my story?" he demanded. "I'll give it to you, but you're going to pay for *every* single word."

Murphy appeared almost chilled by his words and tone but put on a false front. "What are your demands?"

"*Anything* I want for the next 48 hours," he hissed.

She stared at the seriousness in his eyes and felt the chill run down her spine. Neither flinched.

Dane suddenly smirked. "Reconsidering?"

Murphy finally remembered to breathe and put on a brave front. "What guarantee do I have that you'll keep your end of the deal?"

"I'll give you the story in chapters according to what you've earned," he snarled. "If you agree to my terms, pack an overnight bag and be back here by one o'clock."

Dane turned and headed onto the porch and entered the house without looking back. Murphy stared after him and uncertainly rubbed her chilled arms. She'd never been so frightened in her entire life, but she couldn't turn back now. Could she?

Chapter Four

Porter remained on Murphy's heels as she crossed the cabin living room and headed toward the glass patio doors. He was obviously distressed about the current situation, while Murphy was doing her best to ignore him.

"Are you out of your mind?" he continued with his tirade. "There's no cell phone service here. You'll be completely at his mercy. I can't let you do it, Murphy."

"You think I want to do this, Porter?" she demanded without looking back at him. "The guy scares me to death, but he's also the only one who can tell me what happened on that plane and on that island."

Porter jumped in front of the door and blocked her path, keeping her from leaving. She groaned softly then ran trembling fingers through her hair. His fears were feeding hers, and she didn't need him talking her out of getting the story she desperately needed. His look was serious.

"He could chain you in his basement and torture you for the next two days."

"He's not going to chain me in his basement," Murphy reassured him. "These homes don't have basements."

"Is that supposed to be funny?" he launched back.

"I'm not laughing," she muttered then groaned softly while searching his eyes. "You know why I have to do this." She hesitated then offered a reassuring smile. "In exactly two days, you can storm his house if I don't return, but I can take care of myself, you know that."

"This is different," he snapped. "You've basically given the guy permission to handcuff you to the bed. I can't let you do it."

"You can't exactly stop me either."

"Want to bet?"

"How about I make it a condition that I check in with you every few hours?" she suggested. "If I don't, you can come over and demand to see me."

"That's a little better." He considered the comment then threw his arms frantically in the air. "No, that's not better! He's going to violate you three ways from Sunday, and you've given him permission to do it." He pointed a warning finger at her. "You said you wouldn't have sex with him to get this story. You promised me. This--? This is much worse."

"I need this story. It's the only thing keeping me sane," Murphy reminded him. "Yes, he creeps me out, but I can be pretty creepy myself. This is the one thing I have to do--for me."

Porter frowned and reluctantly moved away from the door.

✝

Murphy stood before Dane's back cabin door with her overnight bag clutched firmly in her hand. She was trembling inside but she forced herself to knock on the door anyway. There was a long silence. Murphy uncertainly looked around. Had he gone back on their deal? Part of her secretly wished he had, but she knew she'd never let it go. She had to see it through. Her nerves twitched as she waited and struggled with her emotions. The door was suddenly unlocked and opened slightly. Murphy stared at the partially open door a moment. She wasn't sure she was up for whatever game it was he was already playing. She uncertainly pushed open the door and looked around the kitchen. Dane collapsed at the island counter and reclaimed his glass of scotch. He was obviously drunk and refused to look at her. Murphy slowly entered the kitchen and shut the door behind her.

"Why am I not surprised?" he muttered into his scotch glass.

"I told you this was important to me," she gently replied and felt a little empowered by his sloppy drunk condition. If she had to overpower him physically, she could. "I'm beginning to wonder how you intend to uphold your end of the deal while polluted out of your mind."

"I'm not polluted," he remarked without looking at her. "I'm wrestling with demons. They're winning."

Murphy set her bag down, approached him, and sat on a stool alongside him. He stared at her with a look resembling fear. Suddenly, she no longer felt afraid. Was it possible she scared him more than he scared her?

"It had been a long day already," he began. "I'd had an early morning flight with 220 as my connecting flight. The company was sending me on another boring trip. I always flew first-class on business. I liked to sleep."

Murphy slowly placed a small tape recorder on the island counter between them. It was already recording. Dane was already back onboard Flight 220 and almost seemed unaware of her presence.

"I was seated alongside a tense woman who had just had a blowout with her boyfriend that morning. Her name was Kate Kramer. All she wanted to do was vent," he announced then frowned and drained the contents of his glass. "All I wanted to do was sleep."

✝

Five years earlier. Dane shifted uncomfortably in his window seat alongside an attractive woman in her mid-twenties. Kate Kramer appeared distressed as she ranted then held her head and glanced at Dane.

"I'm sorry, you're probably not the least bit interested in my problems," Kate remarked and sighed.

"It's been a long day already," he replied with little emotion. "It's nothing personal."

She groaned softly, rolled her eyes, and looked around the cabin. "It never is with men."

Dane eyed her with a look of surprise. She met his gaze and smirked. Kate was devilishly beautiful with silky, long black hair and large dark eyes. Despite her small stature, her body was amazingly toned and athletic in appearance.

"She was so beautiful, but I couldn't see anything past my own petty desire to sleep," Dane continued. "I had no idea how big a role this woman was about to play in my life. She left me alone, and I fell asleep sometime around noon."

✝

Later around 1:15 PM. The sounds of screaming and thumping woke Dane. He looked around the first-class cabin with some disorientation. A man stood in the aisle while holding a young flight attendant against him with a crudely constructed shiv to her throat. The passengers were alarmed but unable to react. Similar noise was heard from beyond the curtain in coach. Dane saw Kate twitch out of the corner of his eye and glanced at the woman in the seat alongside him. Her eyes were locked on the man holding the flight attendant hostage, and her hand firmly clutched the seatbelt latch. It was then he noticed her seatbelt was already disconnected. Dane saw the terrified look on Kate's face, but there was something beyond that terrified look. Despite her fear, she oddly resembled a snake about to strike. He gently placed his hand on hers in an attempt to silently stop her from doing anything stupid. She jerked with surprise and looked at him. They shared an odd exchange without any words.

"I knew she was going to do something stupid," Dane informed Murphy. *"While we were all frozen with fear, Kate was already planning an attack."*

"No one moves and no one dies," the angry man shouted while pressing the shiv against the woman's throat. "We're going to take a little detour. Once we're off the plane, you'll be free to go onto your next destination."

"When I looked out the window, I knew we were already off course. At some point during my all-important nap, terrorists had taken over Flight 220."

The screams from coach escalated, causing half the passengers in first-class to look behind them at the partition leading to coach. The flight attendant in first-class suddenly screamed. When Dane looked back, the terrorist had plunged the shiv into the woman's throat. The flight attendant clutched her bleeding neck and collapsed to the floor. A woman in the front row leaped to the floor to apply pressure to her gushing wound. The terrorist suddenly kicked the woman in the face, sending her backwards into another passenger. A male passenger leaped to his feet and tackled the terrorist. Both struck the wall near the galley with tremendous force.

More horrifying screams were heard from coach. Two more passengers jumped from their seats and attempted to subdue the terrorist in first-class. Kate suddenly sprang from her seat and ran up the aisle toward the galley. Dane was stunned as he stared after her.

Kate darted around the passengers struggling with the terrorist. Several passengers had large slices on their arms and hands, which bled freely. Kate ran into the galley, grabbed the beverage cart, and slammed it into the flight deck door. Nothing happened. She pulled the cart back and rammed the door a second time. Kate was suddenly grabbed around the waist by another terrorist. He pulled her away from the cart and slammed her roughly into the wall. He placed his own shiv to her throat and glared into her eyes.

"That's going to cost you," he snarled.

He was about to plunge the shiv into her neck, when he was suddenly grabbed by the wrist. He looked alongside him. Dane sneered at the man while repeatedly slamming his hand against the corner of the galley until he dropped the shiv. The terrorist threw a punch for Dane's face. Dane blocked the fist with his right and punched him in the face with his left. Without warning, Dane slammed the terrorist's face into the corner of the galley. Blood erupted from the large crack in his face as the man collapsed to the floor.

"Four years in the Air Force, and I'd never killed a man before. All I could do was stare at the opening in his skull and the blood pouring out. Kate had better things to do."

There was a loud bang as the beverage cart again slammed into the flight deck door. The door flew open. A third terrorist leaped through the door and rammed the cart into Kate. She was thrown backwards and painfully struck the galley wall. As he attempted to close the flight deck door, Dane threw himself to the floor, grabbed the shiv, and threw it for the flight deck. The shiv struck the man in the shoulder, missing its intended fatal target. Dane leaped to his feet and lunged for the man as he attempted to pull the shiv from his shoulder. Both men flew into the flight deck. Dane and the terrorist fell over the dead pilot's body on the floor and immediately struggled for control of the shiv now in the terrorist's hand. The co-pilot remained strapped in his seat as blood poured from the gaping wound on his neck. Controls on the panel flashed and began to wail. Kate climbed over Dane and the terrorist struggling on the floor and jumped into the pilot's seat. She put on the headset and flipped several switches.

"Mayday! Mayday! This is Flight 220, pilot and co-pilot are down," she cried out. "We need emergency landing!"

There was no response. Dane punched the terrorist now on top of him several times in the face.

"The radio is dead!" she cried out while glancing at the struggling men.

"Got my own problems!"

"Typical man," she scoffed.

The terrorist gained control of the knife and was about to plunge it into Dane. Dane caught his wrist, twisted his arm, and forced him to impale himself in the abdomen. The terrorist suddenly gasped while staring at him with surprise. Dane cast the dying man off him, securely grabbed him around the head, and broke his neck in one swift motion. Kate heard the crunching sound and looked back at Dane with a stunned expression.

"Well done."

Dane moved to his feet and stared at the controls and blinking lights. "How bad is it?"

The clouds parted and the ocean came into view. Both stared at the water.

"Pretty bad," Kate casually replied then looked back at him with a more serious expression. "You need to co-pilot with me. Get in that seat! We need to pull up!"

✝

Present day. Dane leaned on the island counter and stared into his empty glass. Murphy studied him in silence, waiting for his next words. His silence finally got the best of her.

"Well?" she gasped.

Dane glared at her and raised his brows. "Well, what? You know the story. We crashed."

She frowned her irritation. "I hope you intend to tell me more than 'we crashed'."

"Quid pro quo, Murphy," he casually informed her. "You get a chapter at a time."

Murphy frowned and shut off her tape recorder. "That was the agreement," she muttered. "What do you want?"

"You already know the answer to that." Dane smiled drunkenly while attempting to lean seductively on the island counter. He slipped and fell off the stool and onto the floor. "Okay, no need to get rough," he announced from his position on the floor.

Chapter Five

Murphy helped Dane up the stairs to the second floor. He was unsteady on his feet and weighing heavily on her shoulder. She considered dropping him in hopes he'd hit the floor and pass out, but she couldn't force herself to do it. Dane leaned heavily on her as he stumbled into his dimly lit bedroom. Murphy could barely make out the bed toward the center of the room. She reached for the light switch just inside the doorway, so they wouldn't trip over anything.

"No, leave the lights off," he gruffly ordered then resumed a more docile demeanor. "If it's dark, guilt won't find me."

His comment made little sense to her. She wondered what happened on that island to cause him so much guilt. Murphy helped him collapse onto the bed. He half crawled across the large bed, fell onto his back, and made an attempt to pat the bed alongside him. Murphy uncertainly joined him on the bed. She reconsidered the deal she'd made with him and again wondered if it was worth it. Years of obsessing over the crash that claimed her father's life had consumed her. Ultimately, she needed to see it through. She needed closure and Dane was the only one who could provide that. The price was steep, but she needed to pay it. Murphy drew a deep breath, pushed aside her pride, and leaned over Dane. He didn't move.

"Dane?"

There was no response. She heard him softly snoring. Murphy sat back on her feet and stared at the unconscious man in the dim lighting. A sly smile suddenly crossed her face.

✝

Late morning. Dane slept peacefully on the bed with the covers pulled just above his waist. He was almost certainly naked beneath the sheet. Murphy had changed into Dane's shirt, which she used as a nightgown, believing it would lend more credit to her deception. She sat casually reclined on the other side of the bed and played solitaire on her cell phone. Dane groaned softly and stirred. Murphy set her phone aside and quickly slipped beneath the covers. She casually leaned on her elbow and faced him, mentally preparing for an award-winning performance in the art of deception. Dane didn't wake. Murphy groaned softly now bored, retrieved her cell phone, and resumed her game. Dane again stirred and turned toward her. Murphy slipped the cell phone under her pillow and curled on her side facing away from him, pretending to be asleep. Dane moved against her and clung to her from behind, nuzzling her shoulder. Murphy rolled onto her back as Dane's hand caressed her thigh beneath the shirt she wore. Murphy caught his hand and smiled sweetly.

"Quid pro quo, Dane."

He stared at her with mild disbelief but had a hard time keeping a straight face. "Do you seriously expect me to believe something happened here last night?" Dane remarked then grinned. "FYI, undressing me was a nice touch."

Murphy sat up and clung to her knees over the covers. "I don't know what you're talking about." She spoke in a monotone voice and showed no emotion. "We had an amazing night of passion. You were an animal." She then grinned with enthusiasm. "I'm going to make some breakfast. After you've showered, you can continue with the story."

Before he had a chance to respond, Murphy jumped from the bed, flashed a sly grin, and grabbed her discarded clothes from the floor.

Dane had a strange smirk on his face as he watched her. "That game only works once, Murphy," he warned.

Murphy lustfully raised her brows in response while entering the bathroom and locked the door behind her.

✝

Five years earlier. Within the flight deck, the alarm wailed as the lights flashed their dire warnings. Kate and Dane occupied the pilot and co-pilot's seat while both pulled back on their respective yokes. The plane vibrated and thumped loudly while they fought the controls to level the airliner as the ocean appeared to rapidly rise to greet them. They could hear men and women screaming from the plane's fuselage.

"She's going down," Kate cried out, her arms straining to keep the plane from taking a nosedive into the water. "We'll never get her back up in the air!"

"What do we do?" Dane asked with horror on his face.

"Water landing!"

"What?"

"If we can straighten her out enough to keep her from going under, she'll stay afloat for a few hours," Kate shouted above the loudly vibrating plane. "We need to try!"

"We're going down nose first," Dane shouted back. "We'll never keep her from diving into the water. We're already dead; we're just too stupid to know it."

"I've got this," she cried out and cast a look at him. "You need to trust me."

Dane saw the same determined look in her eyes that he'd attempted to ignore when the terrorist first held the flight attendant hostage. If he hadn't stopped her, things may have turned out differently. Dane collected himself and deeply exhaled.

"Okay, okay," he announced, giving in. "Just tell me what to do!"

"First you need to go into the back and tell everyone it's about to get wet," she cried out. "Then you need to strap yourself in and brace for impact!"

Dane stared at her with a look of horror. "No, you need me up here!"

"If I can't get her nose up, we're both dead," she shouted above the plane's vibrations. "I know what I'm doing! Just trust me!"

"I'll alert the passengers, but I'm staying on the flight deck with you!"

"Don't be an idiot!"

"Don't argue with me," he launched back while glaring at her.

She sneered her consent. "Fine! Go! We're running out of time!"

Dane released his harness, ran from the flight deck, and grabbed the phone on the wall to make his announcement. Despite the passengers clinging to their seats while screaming, all eyes were on him.

"Attention!"

A strange silence fell over the first-class compartment. Everyone stared at him for some sort of hope.

"We're attempting a water landing! Everyone needs to remain belted in their seats and prepare for impact," he informed the panicking passengers. "In an emergency, your seat cushions can be used as a flotation device. Our pilot assures me that the plane will stay afloat, so please remain calm. Once the emergency doors are opened, the ramps will inflate into rafts. We're going to be okay!"

Despite their slim chance of survival, his reassurance was all they needed to hear. The screaming subsided and passengers clung to one another while bracing for impact. Dane returned to the flight deck and discovered the door was closed. He attempted to open it, but it didn't budge.

"Kate, open the door," he yelled through the door.

"Get in the flight attendant's jump seat!"

"Damn it, Kate," he cried out. "Open this door! You're not doing this alone!"

"If I let you in, you're dead too!"

Dane's expression suddenly dropped as he realized what she'd done. She knew her chances for survival were slim, and she wasn't willing to risk his life along with hers. He pounded harder on the door.

"You don't have to do this! Let me in!"

Something outside the window caught his attention. Dane looked out the nearby galley window. Horror filled his eyes as the color drained from his face. He bolted for the window and saw the ocean rapidly getting closer. Dane dived into the flight attendant's jump seat and strapped himself in. He glanced at the dead flight attendant on the floor just inside the galley then shut his eyes and braced for impact. It never came. The jet skimmed the water beneath it for only a moment before the nose crested the water in a huge wake then completely disappeared beneath the surface. The passengers were jerked and jolted within their seats as more objects flew from overhead bins and crashed down upon them. Dane looked back to the window and saw only water beyond the glass. They were sinking! Passengers screamed while leaping from their seats and ran up the aisle for the side doors still above water.

Just outside, the airliner was sinking nose first into the ocean. The inflatable ramp remained attached near the still partially exposed jet wing. Passengers scrambled out of the emergency hatch, across the wing, and attempted to make it into the inflatable ramp. Panicking, screaming men and women trampled one another, tossing fellow passengers into the water. Several people made it into the raft and attempted to pull others in with them, but the plane continued to sink, taking most of the passengers with it. The raft was released from the rapidly sinking jet to avoid going down with it. Eight passengers paddled the raft away from the wing as it slipped beneath the water. Dane's head suddenly appeared above the water not far from the remains of the wing. He gasped for air. Those within the raft shouted to him. He saw the raft and swam backwards while holding Kate's head above water. She wasn't moving and her condition was unknown. The remaining survivors pulled them into the raft. Dane hovered over Kate and started chest compressions followed by mouth-to-mouth resuscitation. She finally gasped, spit up water, and coughed. Dane clung to her and shut his eyes.

✝

That evening, eight of the ten survivors shivered while sitting around a modest bonfire on the remote island beach. They wore only their undergarments while their soaked clothes hung to dry on bamboo sticks embedded in the sand. Dane clung to Kate, who shivered in his arms. They were fortunate the island had been visible from where the jet crashed, allowing them to row to safety. It was already several hours after the crash, and there was still no sign of a rescue. Not far from the small bonfire, two men lay in agony on the sand while a third man, A.J., tended to their injuries. A.J. was a distinguished looking man in his late thirties or early forties. His dark hair was lightly peppered with gray. A.J. sat back on his feet while observing the injured men. He then looked at Dane several feet away and expressed his prognosis without uttering a word. Their condition was obvious. Dane frowned, nuzzled the top of Kate's damp head, and looked away.

✝

Early morning. Still mostly asleep, Dane lay on the sand alongside Kate and clung to her from behind. The others were finally able to fall asleep, although not soundly, as well. The bonfire was reduced to embers, but the sun would soon be rising over paradise. A strange slurping sound followed by soft snarls brought Dane out of his light sleep. He looked around the small camp within the dim lighting and took a quick head count. A.J. suddenly bolted past him while crying out. Dane's eyes fell upon several wild boar tearing into the flesh of the two men who'd been injured. It was obvious they had died during the night, which attracted the wild boar. Dane gasped, grabbed Kate, and pulled her to her feet along with him. They backed away so fast; they nearly fell into the sand. The others were alerted and jumped to their feet as well. Everyone ran toward a rock formation several yards away then turned to watch the horrifying sight.

"There was really no way to know if the two injured men had actually died before the boar began eating them," Dane informed Murphy. "We felt better telling ourselves they were dead. In the days that followed, we became the hunters and it seemed we had the wild boar crisis under control. But none of us was equipped for island survival. Well, maybe Kate was. She didn't ask to be put in charge, it just sort of happened."

†

Within the woods, Kate kneeled over her latest kill. Her newly found skills for killing wild boar with little more than a sharpened bamboo stick was nothing less than amazing. As she gutted the boar with a pocketknife, she swatted away dozens of flies without care. Dane stood several feet away with a look of distaste and watched Kate dig out the animal's innards with her bare hands.

"You, uh, having fun?" he asked while attempting to hold back his grimace.

"Not really," Kate snarled while elbow deep in guts. "Care to grab some intestines and help?"

"Is that a request?" he sheepishly asked.

Kate glared at him, raised her cocky brow, and beckoned him with a blood-covered finger.

He groaned while clutching his stomach. "I think I just became a vegetarian."

"Get over here and get your hands dirty."

Dane took a step toward her then hesitated and looked down. "What the hell--?"

"That won't work."

Dane picked something up from the ground and studied it with a bewildered look. "What is this?"

Kate eyed the object he held, appeared curious, and quickly joined him. She studied the object in his hand then appeared horrified.

"Hell! That's a toe!"

Dane cried out and threw it away. "Christ!"

Kate's expression was alarmed. "That's fresh, Dane," she announced and looked around with concern. "Hours at most. We need to find the others--now."

Chapter Six

Present day. With their dirty breakfast dishes pushed aside and her recorder between them, Dane sat solemnly at the kitchen table across from Murphy. His hands were wrenched together so tight, his knuckles were white. He stared off into another world and a darker time, leaving Murphy wondering if he even realized he was talking.

"Eddie went missing," Dane reluctantly announced. "We never did find his body, just his toe."

Dane reached across the table and shut off the recorder, surprising Murphy.

"Now wait one minute," she demanded. "You're not seriously ending it there."

He leaned back in his chair and returned to his more confident, arrogant world. "I most certainly am," he proudly proclaimed. "I think you've gotten enough free story time out of me."

Murphy fidgeted in her chair. "Just because you were too drunk to remember last night--"

He leaned across the table and met her gaze. "Let's pretend for five minutes that I'm smarter than I look."

Murphy became frustrated. "At least tell me what happened to Eddie."

"I can't," he casually replied and sat back in his chair. "That's in the next chapter. I should say our assumption of what happened to Eddie is in the next chapter."

She groaned softly. "Give me something. Five more minutes."

Dane reluctantly sighed. "Okay, five more minutes." He stood from his chair. "But not here."

She watched Dane leave the kitchen. Murphy groaned, snatched her recorder, and followed Dane into the living room. Dane collapsed onto the sofa, casually reclined in the corner, and patted the spot alongside him. Murphy reluctantly joined him, leaving a gap between them. Dane eyed the gap then her. Murphy frowned and moved against him. She pressed the record button. Dane placed his arm around her and held her against him.

"After Eddie's disappearance, the seven of us decided no one should wander off on his own," he continued with his story. "It was eight days since the plane crashed and hopes of a rescue were looking slim. Despite the mystery surrounding Eddie's toe, my fellow castaways were beginning to compete for Kate's attention." He cast a lustful smile at Murphy and raised his brows suggestively. "Maybe it took them a while to realize how attractive she was, or perhaps it was the realization that she may be the last woman they'd ever see that turned them into steaming piles of testosterone." His hand relaxed on her shoulder and his tone turned more serious. "Meanwhile, Kate was spontaneously combusting into 'one of the boys'. Perhaps it was because I'd saved her life, or more likely that I was like some obedient dog, that Kate chose me as her *sidekick*."

†

Five years earlier. There was a large pond situated in the picturesque clearing within the woods. A tall waterfall cascaded down the side of the cliffs, lending beauty to the already breathtaking scene. Kate entered the clearing with Dane following obediently behind her as usual. Both carried sharpened bamboo sticks for protection from predators, whether animal or human. Kate's hair was now untamed and her skin a golden bronze, giving her a more authentic, exotic beauty. Dane's eight-day growth of facial hair and slightly worn clothes gave him a ruggedly handsome appearance, which was far from his quiet businessman look. He looked around to the trees with some bewilderment then eyed Kate.

"I don't think we're going to find any useful provisions around here," Dane informed her. "Unless you're in the mood for python."

She glanced at him and smiled with what could only be described as a come-hither look. "Sometimes a girl just wants to soak in the tub."

Kate kept her eyes locked on him and maintained her smile while unbuttoning her shirt. Dane stared a moment, tensed uncomfortably, and looked away.

"Would you, uh, like some privacy?" he asked while avoiding looking at her.

"No offense, Dane, but you could use a bath too."

Dane looked at her and appeared surprised by the comment. He uncertainly sniffed his underarm and made a face. "Yeah, you're probably right."

As he looked at Kate, she removed her bra and panties. Dane suddenly tensed at the sight of the naked woman. Kate laughed at the frozen expression on his face then dived into the pond. He stared after her a moment longer then nervously fidgeted. Kate surfaced, pushed back her wet hair, and offered a seductive smile.

"Well, are you coming in?" she playfully demanded.

"I'm afraid I, uh, might make you a little uncomfortable if I did."

Kate's smile beamed for the first time. "Stop being so fucking polite and get in here."

It only took a moment for Dane to realize what was being implied. He practically tore his clothing off and jumped into the pond with her. He no sooner surfaced when Kate pounced on him. She pressed her naked body against his, clung to his neck, and sought his mouth, kissing him passionately and with startling aggression. Dane returned the kiss without hesitation, although it was obvious she was taking charge of the situation.

"From that day on, Kate was mine. Well, technically, I was hers. She pretty much controlled every situation. Although I never admitted it to her, she was hard to keep up with. Despite the fact that we were going at it several times a day, we never let the others know. I'm sure they suspected, but we didn't advertise."

✝

Present day. Dane held Murphy against him where they remained casually reclined on the sofa. Murphy cast a look at him as he stared off in another world. She was almost certain what *world* Dane was reliving.

"I think we're getting off subject here," she remarked and shifted uncomfortably in his unusually tight embrace.

"I'd say we're exactly on topic," he teased and cast a playful look at her. He inhaled deeply and sighed. "Kate and I became lovers." He then reconsidered. "Well, maybe I was her boy toy. It's hard to say. Being with her was the only good thing to ever come from that island."

Dane appeared to drift back out. This time it wasn't a lustful thought but something personal and possibly traumatic. Murphy studied him a moment in silence, uncertain if she wanted to intrude in whatever private thoughts he was having.

"You loved her, didn't you?"

Dane remained distant while staring off. "Yes, very much," he replied softly. Dane became uncomfortable and stood nearly knocking her to the floor, startling her. "I, uh, have a headache. I'm going to lie down a while." He was about to leave then hesitated without looking at her. "Will you lie with me?"

Murphy turned off the recorder and joined him without hesitation. She clung to his arm and offered a warm, supportive smile. "Yes, I'll lie with you a while."

†

Five years earlier. A panic-stricken Kate clung to Dane as they stumbled through the woods together. She clutched her bleeding shoulder while gasping in agony. Dane's shirt and arms were covered in blood as he attempted to hold her up. They heard movement behind them, frightening both. They needed to hurry.

"Just a little further, Kate," he gasped softly. "You can make it. We have to keep going."

"I can't," she whimpered softly. "Leave me."

"No, I won't leave you," he shouted softly. "Now move!"

"I'm dead either way," she gasped while fighting her tears. "Leave me or we both die!"

"No, you're not going to die!"

Dane swept Kate up off her feet and carried her through the woods as fast as he could run with her. The rustling sounds and movement behind them was getting louder.

Kate sobbed while clinging to him. "Please, Dane, leave me! I don't want you to die!"

†

Present day. Dane held Murphy in his arms while they took a nap on the king-sized bed in his room. He twitched in his sleep then suddenly cried out and violently thrashed. Murphy gasped with surprise and leaped away from him. Dane suddenly shot up in bed, clutched his head, and panted, fighting his own horrors. Murphy stared at him a moment while attempting to control her own pounding heart. She uncertainly placed a sympathetic hand on his shoulder.

"Are you okay?"

Without warning, Dane pulled Murphy against him and clung to her. He gently rocked her in his arms while nearly down to tears.

"I'm so sorry," he gasped while sobbing. "Forgive me for not doing what I should have."

Murphy gently caressed his taunt arms around her. "It's okay, Dane. You were just having a bad dream."

He relaxed and attempted to control his emotions. The rocking finally ceased. Dane looked at the woman he held in a viselike grip. She stared into his once dead eyes and saw a flood of emotion he'd kept buried deep inside for the last five years. Dane lowered his mouth to hers and kissed her with amazing passion and aggression, startling her. As she searched for an appropriate response, it was already too late. Dane broke off the kiss, leaped from the bed, and sought refuge in the bathroom. Murphy sat on the bed nearly dizzy from the passionate kiss and it's all too abrupt ending. The sound of shattering glass shocked her back into reality. Murphy leaped from the bed.

Chapter Seven

Murphy sat at the island counter alongside Dane and gently cleaned his scratched knuckles. He remained mostly sedate while staring at the bloody cloth lying on the counter between them.

"Personally, I'd punch the door next time," she casually informed him. "They're more forgiving than mirrors."

When he didn't respond, she glanced at him. She wasn't sure if he was off in another world or residing somewhere on the borderline of insanity. She wrapped his knuckles with light gauze then securely taped it.

"There," she announced and straightened. "Good as new."

"I'm surprised you're still here," he muttered softly.

"We have a deal," she replied proudly. "You're stuck with me for another twenty-four hours."

He finally looked at her and inhaled deeply. "My psychotic episode didn't scare you away?"

"I'd hardly call *that* a psychotic episode," she casually remarked and leaned back in the tall chair. "Four years ago, I flipped out in a crowded movie theater over a promo with a plane crash scene. I had to be escorted out by two burly guards, one of which I dislocated his shoulder when he tried to physically remove me. Now *that's* a psychotic episode."

"Dislocated his shoulder, huh?"

"Yeah, I'm not nearly as sweet and innocent as I look."

He studied her a moment longer. "So you're not mad about my aggressive advance?"

His question eluded her. "I assumed that was part of our deal as well."

"The body is willing, but the mind won't allow it," he reluctantly replied. "I'll never get Kate out of my mind."

She felt more confused now than before. "So why did you make a deal with me?" she asked with surprise. "You're not getting anything out of this."

"Kate deserves to be remembered," he replied softly. "A.J., Eddie, they all deserve to be remembered." He hesitated then ran his fingers through his prematurely gray hair. "I want to be forgotten."

Murphy slid off her chair, placed her arms around his neck, and hugged him. He didn't even react.

"Too late," she announced cheerfully. "You're just weird enough for me to like."

Dane snorted a soft laugh and returned the embrace. "Did you just make me your bitch?"

Murphy smiled and kissed his cheek.

✝

Five years earlier. The six remaining castaways stood on the beach at sunset near a large bonfire. A.J. held a torch and appeared alarmed by the news they'd just received. Kate paced the area before the five men. Dane sat on the beach and watched her pace. The other three men, Lee, Brian, and Pete, looked from A.J. to Kate with shared concern.

"We need to do something before we're picked off one at a time," A.J. informed them, already taking the aggressive approach.

"Can we be serious a moment?" Lee demanded and looked at the others. "Do we honestly think one of us killed Harold and Eddie? That's insane."

"I can't speak for Eddie, but someone definitely killed Harold," A.J. replied. "It wasn't an animal that did that to him."

"We've been on the buddy system since we found Eddie's toe," Kate remarked while glancing at the men before her. "I think we can all vouch for one another." She shifted uncomfortably. "That means only one thing."

Dane drew symbols in the sand with a stick where he sat and muttered, "There's someone else on the island."

"Like some Tarzan jungle dweller?" Pete suddenly asked with concern.

"I don't think so," Kate replied. "That would be preferable. Our killer was wearing shoes with new tread. It's pretty obvious who's out there." She eyed each man with a serious expression. "Someone *else* survived the crash and swam to shore."

"One of the terrorists?" Dane questioned.

"We took out three before the plane crashed," Kate replied. "There could have been another one in coach."

Brian groaned softly. "It was total chaos back there. I saw two men with blades, but I never saw the ones you said were killed. We don't know if it was either that died."

"Okay, starting tonight, we take shifts watching the camp," Kate announced while pacing before them like a drill sergeant. "Two-man details. In the morning, Dane and I will check out the main water source and see if we can find any tracks from our interloper. The four of you need to stay together on the beach. If we find him, there's no telling what he'll do."

†

It was another sunny, humid afternoon but the nearby trees provided shade surrounding the swimming pond. Dane appeared slightly shaken while zipping his pants. Kate eyed him as she slipped into her tank top. A sly grin crossed her face.

"Nervous?" Kate teased.

He glanced at her and attempted the same calm demeanor she displayed but failed. "I have this fear of being killed with my pants down."

"Certainly didn't give you any performance jitters," she proudly announced then smirked, "except for the jackrabbit on Viagra part."

"Sorry," Dane muttered then leaned against a nearby tree and attempted to relax. "I'll admit, I'm a little naive about women, but shouldn't the whole serial killer on the loose ruin the mood a little for you?"

Kate smiled seductively and placed her arms around his neck. "I assure you, we're completely alone," she announced and gently caressed his chest. "The only thing keener then my hearing is my sense of smell, and I can smell you guys a mile away."

"I'm suddenly feeling self-conscious."

"Yeah, you should," she announced and grinned. "You smell like sex."

Dane smiled and chuckled softly. She kissed him warmly, patted his chest, and retrieved her sharpened pole.

"We'll explore a little further this way before turning back," she announced then headed down the path.

Dane took his cue, reclaimed his own sharpened bamboo pole, and obediently followed her.

†

Kate and Dane walked along the old path mostly overgrown with vegetation. They looked around the unfamiliar area with great interest.

"No one's been here in a while," Dane informed her. "Is this some sort of game trail?"

"I'm not sure. It used to be much wider." She eyed the trees and indicated the cut branches. "Tree branches were cut along this path. That means there were people here at one time."

"Still?" he asked with concern.

"No, this trail hasn't been used by people in years," she replied but remained interested. "Those branches were cut maybe twenty years ago."

"Who do you suppose was here?"

Kate suddenly stopped and stared ahead of them. "I think we're about to find out." She indicated the area before them.

Dane looked past her. There was a large, mostly overgrown building in what was once a massive clearing. Both stared at the old building with disbelief.

Chapter Eight

Present day. Murphy and Dane sat outside on the second tier porch railing with the recorder between them. It was early evening and the lake was peaceful after an afternoon of water-skiers and fishermen traveling the lake. Murphy barely noticed the lake backdrop. She remained focused on Dane and the current chapter of his story.

"What was the building?"

"It was an old medical facility of some sort," he replied. "All the good stuff had been removed, but there were some clothes, medical supplies, and functioning indoor plumbing. Some high-tech design. After a month of living on the beach, actual shelter with locking doors and a toilet was like paradise. There was even enough gas remaining in the generator to give us power for a few hours each evening. We finally felt safe and had no fatalities for an entire month, but our need for food forced us to venture outside our fortress." He hesitated a moment and appeared to drift out. He snapped back to reality and shifted uncomfortably. "When Kate became sick, A.J. and I teamed up to collect fruit and vegetation. Pete, Lee, and Brian declared open season on wild boar. We had a particularly unruly family of boar living near the entrance." He managed a soft laugh. "Those three actually constructed bows and arrows from things we found at the facility. Kate was particularly bitchy that she was too sick to play with their new toys."

Murphy shifted on the railing, feeling uncomfortable herself. "What was wrong with Kate? I mean, is that how she--?"

"No," he replied and offered a tiny smile. "It was nothing. Just a bug."

†

Five years earlier. Kate sat hunched over on the generic bed while holding her stomach. The bland room was dimly lit and offered no natural sunlight. The only window was completely covered with plant life stretching up the side of the building. A vase of fresh flowers on the bedside was the only colorful item within the otherwise grim room. Kate stared at the fresh flowers and appeared distant. The bedroom door opened, and she instinctively looked up. Dane entered and approached the bed with a tray of cut fruit and a glass of water. He set it on the nightstand then joined her on the bed and smiled timidly. He affectionately caressed her leg.

"Are you feeling better?"

"I only puked once this morning," she announced then forced a smile. "Definite improvement."

"I thought you might be hungry today," he remarked then indicated the tray. "A.J. and I are going out for more rations. 'The Three Stooges' already left on their wild boar safari."

"Bastards--"

"They made you your very own bow," he interjected cheerfully. "When you're better, you can go out and play."

She glared at him, lacking humor. "I don't like you when I'm sick. You turn into my mother."

Dane smiled and kissed her forehead. "I'll take that as a compliment."

Kate reached for the bedside table, opened the drawer, and removed an old revolver. She flashed the gun and raised her brows demandingly.

"When were you going to tell me you'd found this?" she asked.

"Not much point," he informed her. "There are only two bullets. I thought I'd leave it there, you know, as an insurance policy."

"Insurance policy?" she questioned slyly.

"Yes, Kate," he announced firmly. "An *insurance* policy."

She forced a smile and laughed softly while returning the gun to the drawer. "As if you'd ever be able to use it on either of us," she casually remarked.

"We'll save that debate for another time," he announced then stood.

Kate grabbed his arm and stopped him. He looked back at her with some surprise. Her look was serious, and it was obvious it had nothing to do with the gun he'd found. Dane slowly returned to the bed alongside her and appeared concerned.

"What's wrong?"

"I know what made me sick," she informed him while grimacing.

He stared back fearfully. "What?"

"You."

"Me?"

"I'm pregnant."

Dane stared at her a long moment in silence and possible shock.

She stared at him and shifted uncomfortably while holding her stomach. "Are you mad?"

"Mad?" he gasped then shook his head while attempting to hide his smile. "No, I'm not mad. I'm probably a little happier than I should be."

Kate appeared relieved and managed a soft laugh. "You're happy about it?"

"A little Katie?" he chirped then smiled without covering. "Of course that makes me happy." He placed his hand on her leg and rubbed it. "You'll make an awesome dad."

Kate laughed, wiped her tears, and hugged him.

✝

Present day. Dane and Murphy remained on the porch while the sun set. Dane appeared to drift off in the middle of his story. Murphy stared at him a moment then gently cleared her throat. Dane snapped out of his trance and smiled gently.

"So what was wrong with Kate?"

"Something she ingested, I guess," he casually replied. "She was her old self in a few days. Probably the longest she'd gone without molesting me." He gently cleared his throat. "What were we talking about?"

"You and A.J. were going outside for provisions."

"Oh, A.J., right," he replied then grinned in reflection. "A.J. was one of those even tempered, hard to ruffle types. He came across as someone who wasn't paying attention, but he always seemed to know what was going on."

†

F ive years earlier. A.J. and Dane walked along the path that afternoon with their sharpened bamboo poles and backpacks slung over their shoulders.

"So--what's the deal with you and Kate?"

"Me and Kate?" Dane asked innocently. "I don't know what you mean. We're friends."

"Come on, Dane," A.J. announced with a low groan. "We've been stuck here together for two months, and you're the only one not jerking off. That means Kate has to be doing it for you." He cast a look at Dane and raised his brow. "And, let's be honest, she smiles a lot after your 'evening walk'."

"Fine, Kate and I are a couple. I doubt we'll be able to hide it much longer anyway with our close quarters," Dane announced. "I'd like to share a room with her without sneaking around to do it." He glanced at his friend with some apprehension. "Do you think it'll upset the others?"

"I'm sure they'll be a little jealous, but we pretty much assumed you were doing Kate."

He snorted a soft laugh. "More like Kate's doing me."

A.J. eyed him then laughed as if understanding completely. They heard screaming from within the woods. Both men ran along the path toward the male screams. Several yards away, they nearly collided with Pete, who was covered in blood while clutching his bleeding shoulder.

"He got Brian! Brian's dead!" Pete exclaimed.

"Are you sure?" Dane asked.

"We should find Brian," A.J. announced. "Maybe he's only injured."

"You're insane! He's dead!" Pete cried out. "We need to lock ourselves inside the facility!"

"Pete's bleeding pretty badly, A.J.," Dane informed his friend. "He needs medical attention. We can't go after Brian."

"You take Pete back to the facility. I'll look for Brian," A.J. announced, almost as if looking for an excuse to hunt the killer. "Which way, Pete?"

"You're crazy," Pete cried out. "That's what he wants! He attacked us when we were together! You don't stand a chance by yourself!"

"We need to kill this fucker!" A.J. looked back at Dane. "Take him back. I'll be fine."

Before Dane could protest, A.J. ran along the path in the direction Pete had come. Dane stared after him with a concerned look.

✝

A.J. walked along the path in the woods with his sharpened pole leveled and ready for action. He heard movement behind him, but it was already too late. A.J. turned and was immediately tackled to the ground. He held his attacker back with the stick braced between them. A scruffy, dirtier version of the man from their plane attempted to slash A.J. with the shiv in his hand. A.J. cried out and cast the man off him. The man swiftly sprang back to his feet at the same time A.J. did. As he attempted to slash A.J., the killer was suddenly struck in the face with a pole. He flew backwards and hit a tree. Dane skillfully twirled the pole in his hand and prepared to impale him with the sharpened tip. The man sprang to his feet and ran down the path.

"We ran after him, but he somehow got away without a trace. I'm sure Kate could have tracked him, but A.J. and I weren't that good."

✝

Present day. Murphy handed Dane a glass of iced tea and sat on the railing alongside him. It was nearly dark now. The full moon shined against the lake, creating a double moon effect. Even without the outside lights on, the moon provided plenty of light.

"We tried to save Pete, but his injuries were more severe than we originally thought," Dane informed her. "He died during the night. When Lee couldn't be found the next morning, it didn't take a genius to figure out the idiot went looking for the killer by himself. He and Pete had become close since the crash." Dane frowned and sipped his iced tea. "Kate and I found his body three days later.

213

You don't want to know what three days of decomposition in the jungle does to a body. She positively confirmed it was Lee." He sighed deeply. "I never asked how she was so sure. A.J., Kate, and I were all that was left of Flight 220."

Dane stared at his iced tea and appeared to drift out. His story was rapidly coming to a close and it was becoming increasingly painful. Murphy reached past him and shut off her recorder. He looked at her with some surprise. She warmly clung to his arm.

"Why don't we take a break? How about a moonlit walk around the lake?"

Dane smiled warmly and gently caressed her leg. Murphy gave him a strange look. He patted her leg and removed his hand.

"As I said, the body's willing--"

He stood and extended his hand to her. Murphy placed her hand in his and walked off the porch toward the lake with him. Porter stood by the tree line with his arms folded across his chest. Murphy and Dane stopped when they saw him.

"You didn't call," Porter snapped.

Murphy fidgeted and immediately felt flustered. "Porter, I'm so sorry. We were talking. I completely forgot."

"Is this your overly concerned friend?" Dane asked.

"Yes, this is Porter." She then looked back at Porter. "Everything is fine. We're going for a walk around the lake. I'll call you when we get back."

"You better."

Porter and Dane exchanged glares. It was an uncomfortable exchange. Porter turned and headed back for their cabin.

Dane chuckled softly. "Your boyfriend is a tiny bit jealous," he announced. "Maybe you should tell him there's nothing to be concerned about."

"He's not my boyfriend," she corrected. "If he were, I'm sure he would have killed either or both of us by now."

†

Late evening. Murphy sat alongside Dane on the sofa while they refilled their wineglasses. Dane appeared to drift off at the prospect of finishing the story.

"I don't know if I can finish the story, Murphy," he announced gently. "The three of us made it nearly four months together. When they died--"

214

There was an awkward silence. Murphy watched him a long moment then affectionately clung to his arm.

"It can wait until morning," she gently replied then smiled warmly. "Why don't you finish your wine, and I'll run you a nice hot, bubble bath. Afterwards, I'll give you a back massage that'll put you right to sleep."

Dane hid his smile. "Would you be this nice if you didn't want something from me?"

"You and I share a connection, no matter how slight it may be."

"Does that mean you'll lay with me a little while?" he asked timidly.

"All night if you want me to."

Chapter Nine

Three A.M. Murphy slept peacefully beneath the covers in the dimly lit bedroom with Dane nestled against her from behind. He twitched in his sleep then jerked awake. Murphy didn't stir. Dane reached past her for the recorder on the bedside table and pressed record. Murphy slowly woke and attempted to look back at him.

"Is everything okay?"

Dane again snuggled against her from behind.

"Kate, A.J., and I lived quietly for the next four months without incident from our unwelcomed guest," he continued with the story. "We mostly remained inside our fortress behind locked doors. Two of us would go out to collect food, while the third stayed behind to guard the place from 'unwelcomed' visitors. A.J. was stuck with that job most times. Kate didn't like being cooped up, and she and I made a great team." He drew a deep, shaken breath. "We thought we were careful. Maybe we were too confident in ourselves. I was particularly anxious when we left the facility that afternoon. Looking back, I had every reason to be."

†

Five years earlier. Dane and Kate walked along the path in the woods. Kate wore a scrub uniform left at the facility, which barely covered her five-month baby bump. Despite her 'delicate' condition, she carried a machete and looked more than menacing. Dane had found some old dress shirts, possibly belonging to an on-

216

staff doctor. Despite having found a straight edge razor, he wore a few days' worth of stubble on his face. Dane carried an ax he'd found as his new weapon of choice. For some reason, Dane appeared unusually tense that particular day.

"I'd kill for anything chocolate right now," Kate muttered.

"Store's fresh out," Dane replied then looked to the sky between the trees. "I think there's a storm approaching." He scanned the woods. "It seems awfully quiet today."

"Quiet I can take," Kate informed him. "It's when I hear things that I get nervous."

Dane nervously looked around even though nothing moved. "This was a bad idea, Kate," he announced. "We should wait until tomorrow morning."

"If the weather is bad tomorrow, we'll have nothing to eat by tomorrow night," she firmly protested. "I'm starving now."

"I'll do some rooftop hunting this evening with A.J."

"We're almost there now," she replied. "We'll snag a bushel of bananas and return home."

"All things considered, I think you should let me do the climbing this time."

She eyed him sharply. "All things considered, I'm still a better climber than you."

They appeared in a clearing filled with banana trees. Dane removed a rope with a makeshift grappling hook and tossed it into the tree. It fell back down, forcing him to dive from its path. Kate raised her brow.

Dane caught her look. "I've got this."

He again threw the rope and hook. It snagged a tree branch near a bushel of bananas. He smirked at Kate.

"Don't get cocky," she snapped. "That's more my style."

Kate easily climbed the rope despite her enlarged belly. Dane watched her and grinned. Kate reached the bananas, removed her machete, and hacked them free. They fell to the ground. A large, black spider scurried out of the bushel. Dane jumped with surprise and avoided the fast moving creature. Kate laughed from her perch on the rope.

"Afraid of a little spider?"

"Afraid you might want me to catch it and cook it for you," he remarked.

"Don't give me any ideas."

Dane reached for the bushel of bananas. A pair of dirty feet stood just before the bushel. Dane straightened with alarm. The dirty, ragged man leaped for Dane and slashed at him with the shiv.

Dane cried out with surprise and avoided the slashing knife. Kate looked down and saw the attack. The killer tackled Dane to the ground. They rolled several times while fighting for control of the knife. Kate slid down the rope. Dane managed to kick the killer off him, tossing him backwards and into the rope. As the rope swayed, Kate lost her balance and tumbled the last couple of feet. The killer turned for Kate on the ground. Dane lunged for him with rage and tackled him against the tree. The killer punched Dane several times, grabbed Kate's discarded machete, and lunged for Dane. Kate suddenly appeared in front of Dane with the ax and blocked the blow. The machete struck the ax handle. As the killer coiled back with the machete for another strike, Kate flipped the ax and swung for him. The killer dodged the ax while slashing with the machete. The blade struck Kate's shoulder and cut her deep. She cried out as she was driven to the ground. The killer pulled back for another strike.

Dane threw himself to the ground, grabbed the ax, and swung from his lowered position. The ax struck the killer in the side and knocked him to the ground. Dane pulled back for another swing. The killer kicked him in the legs and sent him back several feet, allowing him enough time to scramble to his feet and take off with the machete. Dane turned toward Kate as she clutched her bleeding shoulder while gasping in agony. Dane checked the wound then applied pressure to it.

"We need to get you back to the facility and take care of that."

Kate slowly nodded while fighting her pain. Dane helped her up and toward the path in the woods. They heard movement from close by.

"We have to hurry."

†

Kate clung to Dane as they stumbled through the woods together. She clutched her bleeding shoulder while gasping in agony. Dane's shirt and arms were covered in blood as he attempted to hold her up. They heard movement behind them, frightening both. They needed to hurry.

"Just a little further, Kate," he gasped softly. "You can make it. We have to keep going."

"I can't," she whimpered softly. "Leave me."

218

"No, I won't leave you," he shouted softly. "Now move!"

"I'm dead either way," she gasped while fighting her tears. "Leave me or we both die!"

"No, you're not going to die!"

Dane swept Kate up off her feet and carried her through the woods as fast as he could run with her. The rustling sounds and movement behind them was getting louder.

Kate sobbed while clinging to him. "Please, Dane, leave me! I don't want you to die!"

†

Moments later. Dane ran through the woods with Kate in his arms. She clung to him while attempting to keep pressure on her bleeding shoulder. The facility was just ahead of them.

"A.J.!"

Dane ran for the closed door fifty yards before them. The door opened to reveal A.J. He saw Kate and Dane covered in blood and appeared horrified.

"What happened?" he cried out while running for them to assist.

The killer appeared alongside A.J. and slashed at him with the machete, slicing him across the chest. A.J. cried out with surprise and genuine agony. Dane continued to run toward them and the open facility door. As the killer coiled back for another swing, A.J. appeared enraged and tackled him to the ground. The machete flew from his hand. A.J. straddled the killer and punched him repeatedly in the face.

"Get her inside!"

Dane carried Kate through the doorway, set her down just inside, and turned back around with his ax raised. The killer threw A.J. off him and reclaimed the machete. Dane ran toward them. The killer swung and struck A.J.'s neck, nearly decapitating him.

Kate stood weakly in the open doorway and screamed with horror. "No!"

The killer turned as Dane approached with the ax and prepared to strike. Dane swung with the ax and struck him in the face. The killer was stopped in his tracks, sinking to the ground. Dane looked back at A.J., who was clearly dead, then ran for Kate in the doorway. He hurried her inside and shut the door behind them.

†

Dane carried Kate into the infirmary and placed her on one of the cots. She gasped while clinging to her bleeding wound. Dane grabbed a rolling cart with supplies and found a needle and some sedatives.

"I'm going to give you something to relax you, so you don't go into shock."

"No, I need to talk you though this," she gasped in protest.

Dane held the needle while staring at the serious look on her face. He slowly nodded, knowing she was right.

"Okay, what do I do?.."

"You need to find a mild numbing solution," she instructed.

Dane found a bottle and showed it to her. She nodded and fought for her breath. He drew some of the solution into the needle, knowing enough to flick the bubbles from the syringe. She painfully removed her shirt and collapsed to the cot. Dane hurried toward her with the needle. He looked at the gaping wound and appeared horrified. He leaned over her to inject the area around the wound.

"No," she gasped, "you need to numb my abdomen."

Dane looked at her and appeared bewildered. "What?"

"You can't save me, Dane." Her look was serious. "You have to take the baby."

"What?" he suddenly cried out and vigorously shook his head. "No, I'm not going to do it. I can't remove the baby. You'll die for sure."

"I'm dead already," she screamed. "Take the baby!"

Dane stared at her and appeared unable to move.

She stared at his frozen, blank expression. "Damn it, Dane, do it!"

Dane suddenly jerked then looked around the room. He grabbed a nearby container and a facemask.

"I'll have to put you out," he insisted. "I can't do what you ask with you awake. I can't do that to you."

Kate gasped several times, appeared exhausted, and nodded. Dane placed the mask over her face and turned the valve. Kate slowly drifted out. Dane stared at her a moment then began suturing the gash on her shoulder.

†

Present day. Dane held Murphy from behind within the bed and remained silent. Murphy just stared across the darkened room while listening to his heavy breathing. She felt her own heart pounding at the story of Kate's final moments. He continued with the story.

"I carried her into the infirmary where she talked me through suturing her shoulder wound," he announced gently. "The painkillers I'd given her knocked her out before I had finished stitching her shoulder. Despite the fact that the bleeding had stopped, she'd already lost too much blood." He hesitated, drew a deep, shaken breath, and exhaled softly. "She died in my arms while I lay beside her. When I realized she was gone, I left the facility that evening and wandered through the woods. I wound up on the beach near the crash site and contemplated ending it all. I was nothing without Kate. I'd never survive without her. Just at that moment, the rescue arrived."

Murphy was about to turn to face him, but Dane held her in place to keep her from moving.

"No, don't look at me." He turned off the recorder. "Go to sleep."

Dane nuzzled her from behind and lay quietly while holding her. Murphy clung to his arm around her and stared across the dimly lit room. A tear streaked her face.

Chapter Ten

Five A.M. the following morning, Murphy was fully dressed and sat on the porch railing. She held a cup of tea and stared at the dark, peaceful lake. She couldn't believe how much his story of A.J. and Kate's death impacted her. She felt his pain almost as if she'd been there with him. Dane appeared in the doorway of the mostly dark house.

"I thought maybe you'd left," he announced softly.

She glanced back at him and attempted a smile. "That would be rude."

"Maybe, but you got what you came for. You have little reason to stay."

"I have little reason to go."

Dane slowly approached and joined her on the railing. "I wish I believed that. I'd be very surprised if I ever saw you again."

"Actually, I'm thinking Porter and I will rent that cabin next door for the entire summer after all," she announced and looked around. "Seems like a nice, quiet place to work on my book. If you're in the mood for some company, you can always give me a shout."

A warm smile crossed his face. "I may just take you up on that."

Murphy slid off the railing and moved closer to him. She placed her hands on his shoulders and smiled warmly.

"I can't tell you how much I appreciate you telling me your story," she announced gently. "I think I can finally come to terms with what happened. I owe you a debt of gratitude, and somehow I'll pay you back."

"We've been down this road before," he replied. "I'm independently wealthy and emotionally impotent. That doesn't leave many options."

Murphy gently caressed his shoulders and chest. "I can offer you some say in the structure of the book. We can dedicate it to Kate and my father." She smiled teasingly. "I can even write you an I.O.U. for the weekend you actually wanted. You can collect at some later date when your mind and body call a truce."

Dane laughed softly, pulled her against him, and held her. "I'd like all of the above in writing please."

"You've got it," she replied with a soft laugh. "Of course, the third will have to come with a one-year expiration date, in the event I actually meet someone and get married."

"Well, I usually demand a five year expiration date on my I.O.U.'s, but I'm willing to be flexible in this case."

Murphy pulled away and appeared humored. "Why do I get the feeling you're serious?"

"Oh, I am. Dozens of people owe me favors," he informed her. "I have an I.O.U. app on my cell phone just to keep them organized and save time."

Murphy stared at him a moment then smiled and laughed. "Show me where I sign."

Dane smirked and removed his cell phone from his pocket.

✝

Morning. Murphy approached her shared cabin with Porter, her overnight bag slung over her shoulder. Porter sat on the porch while drinking his morning coffee. He saw her and quickly approached.

"Is everything okay? I wasn't expecting you for another few hours." He considered the comment. "Actually, I was thinking I'd have to storm his place to free you."

"I'm fine, Porter. I wasn't a prisoner," she informed him.

"Are you sure you're okay?"

"Of course. He never even touched me."

Porter gave her a bewildered look. "Then you didn't get the story?"

"Oh, I got the story--all of it." She sighed softly. "Luckily he has a soft spot for me. I did, however, promise him my first born child."

Murphy walked past Porter and toward the porch. He appeared horrified and hurried after her.

"Wait! What?"

"You take me so literally," she teased. "Nothing quite so drastic. I gave him some say in the book and a dedication to his girlfriend alongside my father's dedication."

"Oh, well that's not too bad."

Murphy continued walking onto the porch. "And a weekend of unbridled passion at some future date, if he so chooses."

Porter stared after her with his mouth hanging open.

✝

Murphy soaked within the deep tub in the cabin bathroom with bubbles covering her entire body. She just about fell asleep when there was an urgent knock on the door. Before she had a chance to respond, the door immediately opened to reveal Porter. Murphy half sat up, appeared alarmed, and covered herself with bubbles.

"Porter!"

"Sorry, this couldn't wait!"

"Unless the cabin is on fire, it could wait!"

"One of the feelers I had out paid off," he announced while grinning. "There's this cruise in Florida offered by this guy. He's taking people to the island."

"The crash site?" she suddenly gasped.

Porter grinned and nodded.

"I thought that location was kept a secret. Agent--"

"Never mind what the feds told you," Porter announced with excitement. "This guy was with the rescue team. It's totally via underground connections and off the government radar. He's charging a small fortune to take a select few out to the island. It's a three-day voyage there with two days on the island then three days back."

"Define a small fortune."

"Within my means," he replied while grinning.

"That's fantastic! When do we leave?"

"Now."

"What?"

"Now," he cried out. "I booked us on a private plan to Florida. We'll have just enough time to make it to the airfield if I break a few speeding laws. The plane will get us there thirty minutes before the ship leaves port."

Murphy held her hand up. Porter threw her a towel and left the bathroom.

Chapter Eleven

The twenty-passenger, luxury yacht was docked at the end of the pier. The unsanctioned cruise had to sail below the radar, so it was no surprise that the yacht was located at a private dock with few prying eyes. Approximately eight people were on deck as the limited crew of four, including the captain, prepared to cast off. Murphy and Porter ran along the dock with their duffel bags.

"Wait!"

Captain Flynn, an athletically built man in his early fifties, stood by the gangplank and saw them running toward the ship. He motioned for his men to wait. Porter and Murphy ran for the gangplank where Flynn helped them board.

"We were about to give up on you two," Captain Flynn announced cheerfully while grinning in an almost sinister manner. "Another minute and you would have missed the boat--literally."

Both smiled and laughed at the tired joke. They didn't care; they made it, and they were on their way. Porter placed his arms around Murphy and hugged her excitedly.

✝

The following morning, Murphy stood on the yacht deck by the railing as the ocean rushed past the vessel. It was a beautiful, sunny morning and a perfect day for the start of a new adventure. Murphy was blissfully transformed into her own world. She couldn't believe that in three days' time they were about to explore the infamous island she'd heard so much about from Dane's stories. Even though her father had never made it to the island, she was anxious to see it. She felt the story about what happened to Flight 220 was about to come full circle, then she could write her book and finally have closure. Porter approached, bringing her out of her tranquil state. He leaned on the railing alongside her and watched the calm waters rush past as well.

"I heard some of the other passengers complaining they'd already lost their cell phone signals," Porter informed her while holding back his mocking smile. "This isn't a cruise ship. I don't know what they were expecting."

"No cell phones? Oh, the horrors of roughing it," she added with a soft laugh. "I don't know how they'll ever survive."

Both laughed at the others' expenses. Murphy's cell phone chirped from her jacket pocket as if on cue, surprising her. Apparently, she hadn't lost her signal yet.

"Huh? Who'd be calling me?" she announced as she removed her phone. "You're the only one who has my cell phone number." She placed the cell phone to her ear. "Hello?"

"Hey, Murphy, it's Dane."

"Dane?" she announced aloud with surprise then eyed Porter. "I didn't know you had this number. I thought I gave you the cabin phone number."

"You did, but there wasn't an answer," Dane replied. "When I saw your car was gone, I thought I'd call you on your cell phone. Porter left the number with the cabin owner as a second contact." There was a brief pause. "If you're coming back soon, I thought we'd take a walk around the lake this morning." He suddenly hesitated. "You are coming back, right?"

"Uh, Porter and I had to run out unexpectedly," she announced while casting concerned looks at her friend, "but I'll be back in a few days."

There was an awkward silence. "You don't have to lie, Murphy. If you've gone back home just tell me," he announced. "It's not as if we're dating."

"I know that, and I'm not lying to you. Porter and I had to fly to Florida last evening," she attempted to explain without offering too much information. "We'll be back in a few days. Probably by Saturday at the latest."

There was an odd silence. She could almost hear his mind processing the information through the phone.

"Florida?" he suddenly asked. "What's in Florida?"

She fidgeted slightly and attempted to remain evasive. "Porter and I had business."

Porter watched her fumble for a reasonable explanation then muttered, "You don't have to explain anything to him, Murphy."

"Please tell me you're not going to that island," Dane suddenly demanded, his tone becoming stern.

"I, uh, no," she fumbled. "How would I even--?"

"My God, you are! You can't go there, Murphy," he suddenly proclaimed through the phone loud enough for Porter to hear. "Where are you?"

"We're fine, Dane."

"Damn it, Murphy, tell me where you are!"

"I'm on a ship," she explained. "We're on our way to the island."

"No, no," Dane cried out in panic. "I don't care what you have to do, just get off that ship!"

"You're being overly dramatic."

"You can't go to that island," he shouted into the phone. He didn't sound angry, he sounded frightened. "No one can ever go to that island!"

Murphy straightened and felt a slight chill from his words. "And now you're being possessive and creepy."

"Listen to me--"

"I'm sorry you're so upset, Dane," she announced firmly, "but I'll see you in a few days."

"I lied, Murphy," he shouted through the phone. "I lied about what happened--"

The phone suddenly went dead. Murphy appeared bewildered a moment then looked at her cell phone. She had lost her signal. She replaced the phone to her jacket pocket and sank into thought. Porter groaned and shook his head while returning to his relaxed state against the railing.

"That was weird," Murphy informed him. "He completely freaked out."

"Yeah, I heard," Porter mumbled then eyed his friend. "He nearly died on that island. He's expected to be a little nutty about it. Sort of like spending the night at the Bates Motel."

"He told me he lied right before we were cut off," she remarked then eyed him suspiciously. "What do you think he meant by that?"

Porter waved her off. "He was just trying to convince you to come back. The guy's highly damaged goods."

✝

The ten passengers relaxed on deck that evening, enjoying the clear warm night. Murphy and Porter played a card game with another couple, Cindy and Toby, while others socialized with drinks they'd secured from the bar in the lounge. Cindy and Toby were a young, adventurous couple, who wanted to explore the island where Flight 220 had crashed. Both were built athletic and probably enjoyed running, hiking, and swimming. They made a cute couple, both having the same sandy brown hair and similarly bronzed skin from spending most of their time outdoors. Although they seemed friendly enough, Murphy had to wonder what their reason for paying such a high price just to see the island. Just to say they were there? To her, it made little sense.

Ron and Shannon, on the other hand, were thrill seeking rich kids with too much time and money. Despite their out-of-the-way destination, Shannon looked as if she walked off the cover of a fashion magazine. Her hair and make-up were nearly perfect, and her clothing was designer. The rugged island setting and the first sight of creepy crawlers would undoubtedly send the woman screaming. Ron was the typical spoiled rich boy who liked getting his way. He'd heard the island was off-limits and had to secure passage for bragging rights. Neither had any real knowledge about the infamous Flight 220 crash or the island. Murphy wondered if either were even aware that the island had no resort or spa. Ron and Shannon were having a particularly difficult time living without their cell phones as it was. What did they expect to find on the island to interest them?

Franklin was the only other passenger Murphy and Porter bothered to get to know. He was the explorer type with a solid build and sturdy features. He made it a point to mention how he enjoyed a challenge and had been on plenty of island adventures in the past, yet he seemed to obsess over the female to male ratio. Certainly not a handsome man by any means, he'd be one of the last passengers Murphy would find attractive. Although he seemed to talk a good game, Porter easily pegged him for a man with limited knowledge on things he claimed to know. They never bothered learning the names of the other three passengers. Whatever their reasons for paying the steep ticket price, they lacked any knowledge of Flight 220. The others were more interested in getting drunk and the thrill of exploring a forbidden island.

An excited crewmember ran onto deck and motioned to the passengers. "Everyone needs to follow me now!"

"What's wrong?" Cindy asked as she and Toby uncertainly stood from their seats at the table.

"There's a military ship coming this way," the young crewman announced. "They must have been tipped off to our destination."

"Is that a problem?" Murphy asked.

"Considering the island is off-limits, yeah, I'd say it's a problem," the crewman replied. "Our ship has clearance to sail through here but not with passengers. We have to hide everyone."

Everyone followed the crewman.

Murphy looked at Porter with concern as he hurried her behind the others. "Did you know about this?"

Porter fidgeted slightly. "Yeah, but I didn't think he was serious."

✝

The passengers were quietly sitting within the dimly lit, dingy room in the cargo hold. Footfalls were heard above them along with garbled voices. Murphy attempted to listen to the voices but could only make out a few words. She was feeling a little betrayed. Porter didn't tell her they'd be stopped by the military and risking arrest for venturing out to the island. Sure, she knew the island was in some secret location, and the government wanted to keep reporters away from the crash site, but she didn't know site was secured by the military.

Within the living quarters, Captain Flynn walked with two military men through each of the staterooms. The officer in charge glanced around, although it was difficult to tell what he was actually looking for.

"There's no one onboard but me and my crew," Captain Flynn informed him while playing innocent. "Can I ask what this is about?"

"We got a call from the FBI with a tip about a cruise heading to the restricted island in this area," the officer informed him. "Someone must have seen your ship and mistook it for an unauthorized vessel. I'm sure it's nothing. Your clearance is good to travel these waters."

"I've been given orders to steer clear of that island," Captain Flynn explained. "We'll reach our research site in a few hours. You can track us, if you'd like. We'll be at the site for three days before returning to port."

"You know we have to track you, just to be safe," the military officer replied.

Flynn nodded and grinned at the comment. "I'm aware of procedure. I wouldn't expect any less."

☦

Everyone slowly returned to deck as the military ship nearly vanished over the darkening horizon. Its lights were nearly out of sight, allowing everyone to relax. Toby approached Captain Flynn and gave him a slightly concerned look.

"So what happens when they track us and we're where we shouldn't be?" Toby asked.

"I have a special buoy with our tracking locator on it," Captain Flynn replied while grinning slyly. "We drop that off in an hour, and they'll think we're anchored a day away from the island. We've tested it several times. They've never returned to check that we were actually anchored where are tracker indicated."

Toby grinned and laughed at the captain's creativity. Porter leaned on the railing near Murphy as she stared at the distant lights of the vanishing military ship. He stared at her with a strange look.

"It was him, wasn't it?" Porter asked. "Dane sent that anonymous tip."

"We don't know that," she muttered softly without looking at him.

Porter straightened his sore back from their lengthy cramped position beneath deck. "Oh, I think we do."

Murphy frowned knowing he was probably right. It was a little too coincidental.

Chapter Twelve

The following day the yacht was docked not far from the tail section of the plane that still remained above water. It had settled a little deeper into the ocean floor, but that it remained visible was an eerie reminder of what had happened over five years ago. As the crew prepared the inflatable launch, Murphy stared at the tail section with a solemn expression. Somewhere beneath the water was where her father died. Porter and their fellow passengers feverishly took photos of the eerie image.

"I can't believe they never retrieved the plane or any of the bodies," Porter remarked then saw Murphy's hypnotic gaze and immediately fidgeted. "Sorry, I didn't mean to sound insensitive. You're probably going through a lot."

Murphy remained sedate while staring transfixed on the massive tail section of the plane. "No, that's okay," she replied. "This is what we came for." She drew a deep, shaken breath. "By the time the rescue arrived six months later, the plane had sunk too far into the ocean floor. They managed to recover the black box, but the passengers were, well, gone."

"You mean fish food?" Ron teased.

Porter glared his disapproval of the rich boy's insensitivity for the situation.

"For lack of a better word, yes," Murphy replied while sighing. "With the exterior hatch open, it would have only taken a few days to a week at most."

"I heard the guy who survived went completely insane," Shannon announced while clinging to her boyfriend's arm.

"Not completely," Murphy announced softly.

"I thought he died," Ron remarked as Shannon cozied up to him. "Didn't he commit suicide?"

"No, that's not true," Murphy informed him without elaborating.

"I think you're wrong," Ron insisted, obviously knowing more from internet gossip than the woman who spent years researching the crash. "He killed himself."

Murphy captured Porter's hand and led him away from the railing. "We should get our gear."

Murphy and Porter walked along the worn path in the woods. It seemed strange walking the path she knew Dane had once traveled over five years ago. Several of their shipmates mulled about in the woods lacking direction then watched them walk with purpose. Porter looked back at the others then to Murphy and grinned at their shipmates' befuddled state.

"Our shipmates look a little bewildered," he informed her. "Probably wondering where we're going."

"Maybe. I'd like to make sure they don't follow us," she informed him. "I want to reach the facility and get some pictures before it becomes the hot tourist spot."

"You want to lose them? No problem."

Porter suddenly grabbed Murphy around the waist while they walked and pulled her against him. He spoke louder than necessary. "The first secluded spot we find, your ass is mine."

Murphy attempted to hide her smile. Porter glanced back at their shipmates to assess the situation. They lost interest and no longer followed.

"Huh, I was expecting at least one pervert hoping to watch," Porter announced then shook his head with disappointment. "The insanely rich are so boring."

She suddenly eyed him. "Aren't you insanely rich?" Murphy asked.

"Not insanely--"

Both laughed.

An hour later, Murphy and Porter appeared in the clearing on the far side of the island. Both suddenly stopped and stared at the massive facility overgrown with vegetation. The structure itself was almost camouflaged with vines, but it was where Dane said it would be. Porter's mouth fell open with surprise at the enormous size of the building.

"Did Dane say it was massive?"

"He conveniently left that part out," she remarked. "He called it a research facility."

Porter approached the main door and pulled plant life away from a bold, bronze plaque. "Not according to this sign."

Murphy hurried to join him. The sign read 'Vexler Island Mental Hospital'. Murphy and Porter exchanged stunned looks.

Porter's expression suddenly dropped. "What did Dane say about a lie?"

"I wish I knew," she gasped softly and looked at her friend. "Maybe the terrorist from the plane was actually a patient who escaped the hospital."

"Okay, what if it was? Why lie about that?" Porter asked with concern. "What would that matter? Why not just admit it was a deranged mental patient? You said he killed the guy, right?"

"That's what he said," she muttered then drew a deep breath. "But that's why we brought the 'special' flashlights."

Murphy removed two baton style flashlights from her bag and handed one to Porter.

"You're scary prepared," Porter remarked while fiddling with his. "Are they fully charged?"

"Shock someone with one of these puppies, and they're going to twitch for days," she announced.

Porter pressed a button. The Taser portion of the baton sparked while making a loud, distinctive sound. It was enough to make him jump.

He chuckled softly. "My money and your devious mind are a wonderful combination," Porter announced then extended his hand to the door. "Ladies first."

Murphy glared at Porter's grin. She shook her head, turned on the flashlight portion of her baton, and pulled the door open the rest of the way. Porter followed Murphy into the large lobby. Both stopped and looked around, marveling at the size of the place. For a mental institution, the lobby was amazingly elegant with marble floors, expensive furniture, and an amazing front desk with detailed trim. Plant life had worked its way inside the lobby as well, giving it a creepy feel. Porter removed his video camera and turned on a massive light, brightening the entire lobby.

"Film everything," Murphy ordered.

"As much as we can before we have to hike back to the ship," he announced while slowly panning his camera around the lobby. He cast a look at her above the camera. "You weren't thinking about spending the night in here, were you?"

"If I was before, I'm certainly not anymore," she muttered. "We need to look for anything that proves Dane and the others were here."

Porter aimed the camera and light at an old, crudely made bow on the floor. "Something like that?"

Murphy followed the light and saw the bow. She became excited. "Yes, exactly like that." She looked around and rubbed her chilled shoulders. "I can't believe we're actually here. Dane's entire story practically coming to life."

"Don't get too excited," Porter remarked. "Remember, you're writing a tragedy."

†

Murphy and Porter entered the large, once sterile infirmary and looked around. Porter continued to film everything. There were old cots lined along the walls of the dimly lit room. Plant life had covered the high windows, allowing very little sunlight inside. Murphy rubbed her chilled arms while looking around. A strange reality struck her.

"This is where Kate died," she almost whispered while feeling an eerie chill.

Dane's story seemed so real now. Both scanned the room for signs to confirm his story. Their eyes fell upon the old cot with a massive bloodstain soaked into the once white sheet.

"I'm guessing that would be where she died," Porter gently remarked. "Did he say he buried her?"

"He didn't say, and I didn't ask," she replied gently. "I assume he did. He loved her."

Porter continued to film the room and paused the camera on the rolling cart near the counter with clean surgical supplies on it. He lowered the camera then glanced back at the bloodstained cot across the room.

"Huh, that's strange," Porter muttered.

She cast a look at him. "What is?"

"You told me he stitched her wound."

"Yeah?"

He indicated the bloodstained cot. "She was obviously laying here, but the surgical supplies are across the room, and they're clean." He looked at both several times. "There's nothing laying around to indicate he even cleaned the wound."

"Maybe he cleaned up later."

"Seriously? He'd clean the surgical tools but leave the blood soaked sheets on the cot?" Porter suddenly remarked then shook his head. "No, that doesn't sound right." He raised a curious brow. "Didn't you say he wandered into the woods grief-stricken after she died and then stumbled across the rescue team?"

"Yes, that's what he said."

"So when would he have had time to clean the tools or even bury her body?"

She sank into thought but the answers weren't coming. "I don't have an answer, Porter." She attempted to brush off her doubts. "Maybe they took her body back with them for burial."

Porter considered the comment then shook his head. "I don't think so, Murphy. Kate's mother never mentioned receiving her daughter's remains."

Murphy fidgeted and vigorously ran her fingers through her hair. "We don't have a lot of time before we need to head back," she announced boldly. "We need to find their living quarters, the kitchen, and the rec room. I want to make sure we get that on film before someone else stumbles upon this place and disrupts things."

"You're deflecting the bigger questions here, Murphy."

She became frustrated and glared at her friend. "I don't have the answers, Porter. I don't know what happened. Okay?"

Porter stared at her a moment then slowly nodded. "Okay," he announced gently then resumed filming.

†

Murphy and Porter entered one of the many staff rooms, uncertain which belonged to the Flight 220 survivors. After entering the tenth room, they realized finding the right room was becoming a challenge. It seemed logical the survivors would have chosen rooms closest to the other living areas, but they were getting further away from those areas.

"This one actually looks lived in," Porter remarked while taking a break from filming. "How will we know if it was his bedroom?"

"Look for anything that indicates a woman slept here," Murphy replied while scanning the room. "Small clothing, small shoes, a hairbrush with long hair in it."

They headed in opposite directions to search the room more efficiently.

Porter glanced around the floor. "This was Kate's room all right," he announced.

Murphy looked at him with surprise. "It is? How do you know?"

"No clothes on the floor."

She groaned softly at his attempt at humor. "Dane didn't leave clothes lying on his floor either," she remarked. "Not all men are slobs, Porter."

Murphy approached the dresser and opened the top drawer. She suddenly hesitated and removed an old bra. "Okay, this was Kate's room."

Porter aimed the camera in her direction and zoomed in on the bra. Judging by its dated style, it belonged to one of the resident nurses.

"Videotape every inch of this room," she ordered. "Everything."

Porter nodded and filmed the entire room. He approached the bed and zoomed in on the nightstand. He hesitated, appeared surprised, and stopped filming.

"That's weird."

Murphy approached and looked around. "What's weird?"

Porter indicated the book on the nightstand. Murphy uncertainly picked it up and stared at the title.

"Yoga for Mommies?" she softly read the title then set the book down with a moderately confused look. "I'm assuming the library is limited."

"You don't think Kate was pregnant, do you?"

Murphy fidgeted. "I think Dane would have mentioned it if she was."

"Maybe he didn't know."

She held her breath. "Then I don't want him to ever see that footage," Murphy boldly announced. "He doesn't need to learn anything that will cause him further emotional trauma."

Porter lowered the camera and studied her expression. "You like him, don't you?"

"Yeah, I like him," she muttered softly then eyed her friend. "He's a less perverted version of you."

"Hmm, the jungle brings out your claws." Porter hissed and scratched the air at Murphy.

Murphy rolled her eyes and walked away.

Chapter Thirteen

The forest was starting to darken just a few hours from sunset. Porter and Murphy left the facility and shut the door behind them. They'd have just enough time to make it back to the ship before the woods became too dark.

"We'll come back tomorrow morning and explore the rest of the place," Murphy announced. "We should have just enough daylight to get some footage of the beach and the plane wreck when we get back. You have a spare battery on you, right?"

"I'm good for hours," he announced cheerfully. "You point, I'll shoot. We better get moving." He looked at the clearing above the trees. "We're losing light fast."

†

Porter and Murphy walked along the worn path in the woods. With his camcorder concealed within his bag, Porter led the way with his baton flashlight as an additional security measure. They still had quite a distance to go before reaching the beach with the anchored yacht when they heard movement from nearby. Both stopped and looked around. Whatever they'd heard sounded big. Shannon suddenly appeared on the path before them. All three jumped with surprise.

Shannon held her chest and laughed nervously. "Jesus, you scared me." She gave them a serious look. "Have you guys seen Ron?"

"No, you're the first person from the ship we've seen all day," Porter replied.

"What a jerk," she scoffed while shaking her head. "We had a little disagreement and he stormed off leaving me here alone." Her eyes pleaded with them. "Please tell me you know the way to the beach."

"It's half an hour along this path," Murphy replied.

"Thank God, my feet are killing me!"

Porter and Murphy looked at the expensive, designer sandals she wore.

"Not exactly my first choice in hiking footwear," Porter announced.

She glared at him and sneered her annoyance. "God, you too?" Shannon scoffed. "What's with you men?"

Shannon walked along the path in front of them, struggling with her sore feet. Porter and Murphy exchanged knowing smirks.

Murphy muttered, "Well, we know what the disagreement was about."

All three walked in silence for several minutes before hearing loud sounds of movement on the path behind them. All three looked around with concern. They heard a woman's loud gasp. She sounded as if she were in pain. Cindy and Toby ran along the path toward them, happy to run into someone. Toby clung to Cindy's hand while she held her bleeding forearm. He had some of her blood on him as well. All three stared at the couple with surprise.

"What happened?" Porter gasped.

We were exploring a cave," Toby announced while panting heavily. "There was some wild animal in there. It knocked the light from my hand and attacked Cindy.

"It bit me," Cindy cried out.

Murphy approached Cindy and examined her wound. There were deep teeth marks along all sides. She was lucky it hadn't taken a chunk from her arm.

"We'll need to clean that right away," Murphy announced. "I'm afraid you're going to need stitches, and you'll probably need rabies shots when we return. Let's get her back to the ship."

All five hurried along the path.

✝

Twenty minutes later, all five explorers appeared on the familiar beach. They saw the deflated launch on the sand with no sign of other passengers or the crew. All five looked around with concern at the deflated launch.

"That's just great," Shannon snapped while removing her uncomfortable, expensive shoes now that she was in the sand. "Now we'll have to swim to the boat."

"Cindy can't swim that far with her injury," Toby announced with concern.

"There's no reason for all of us to swim out there," Porter informed him. "I'll swim to the ship, get the second launch, and come back for the rest of you."

Porter handed Murphy his backpack and flashlight.

"Call me paranoid, but shouldn't the crew have noticed the deflated launch?" Murphy asked then looked around the beach. "Where's the crewman who brought us to the beach?"

"You're paranoid," Porter remarked.

Porter removed his shirt and shoes and headed into the surf. They watched Porter jump into the waves and swim for the distant ship near the tail section of the plane. It didn't take long for Porter to reach the ship and climb the ladder. Nearly fifteen minutes had passed since they watched Porter climb onto the ship, but he still hadn't returned with the second launch. Murphy paced the beach while watching the ship.

"Why's it taking so long?" Shannon demanded from where she sat on the sand rubbing her sore feet.

Murphy removed her shoes and tossed her pack to the sand alongside Porter's pack. "Stay here."

She headed into the surf and swam for the ship. It was an easy swim. Murphy reached the ship and climbed the ladder to the deck above. She looked back at the others on the beach and waved to them before walking along the deck for the lounge. Murphy entered the empty lounge and looked around. She was surprised to find no one there. Murphy turned and nearly collided with Porter. She let out a startled scream and jumped with surprise. Porter barely reacted.

"What happened? Is the launch not inflating?"

The look on Porter's face was almost alarming. "The captain and crew are gone."

"What?"

He fidgeted and appeared unusually tense. "I, uh, found blood on the bridge."

✝

Murphy stared at a large amount of blood on the floor near the helm. Whatever happened had been serious if not fatal. She didn't want to admit that one of the crew had been killed, but the fresh blood told a grim story. She looked back at Porter and the ghostly expression on his face.

"Someone's been severely hurt," Murphy remarked in a soft, nervous tone.

"Fatally, I'd guess," Porter nearly gasped.

"Did you look everywhere?"

He vigorously nodded. "Just about. I mean, I didn't look in the cargo hold or under the beds, but if anyone was onboard, they would have heard me calling."

"We need to inflate the second launch and get the others on the ship. We need to treat Cindy's wound," Murphy informed him, taking control of the situation. "You get the launch, and I'll radio for assistance."

"We're here illegally," he reminded her.

"Right now I don't care," she snapped. "There's no telling what sort of animal bit Cindy or if the other crewmen are hurt. We need medical help."

"You're right," he replied and exhaled with defeat. "I can afford good lawyers for us."

Porter hurried from the bridge. Murphy grabbed the radio handset and switched it on. To her surprise, nothing happened. She attempted several controls then appeared disgusted and cast the handset aside.

"That damned Flynn disabled the radio!"

Chapter Fourteen

Murphy wrapped Cindy's lower arm while they sat on the sofa together within the lounge. Cindy seemed to be in more agony than the severity of her wound indicated. Murphy was almost positive the woman wasn't overreacting, which led her to wonder why a bite wound would cause such intense pain. The woman had broken out into a cold sweat and looked slightly pale. Murphy was almost certain most infection caused a fever, yet Cindy appeared to be losing color and catching a chill. Murphy worried the animal that bit her carried some strange disease, which was causing her odd symptoms. Toby brought his girlfriend a drink along with one for himself. His concern was mounting as well. Shannon barely acknowledged the suffering woman and showed little concern. She was more interested in her own blistering feet. Porter entered the lounge and appeared slightly out of breath, his enthusiasm evident.

"Two more passengers showed up on the beach," Porter informed them. "I'm taking the launch to get them."

Shannon finally became alert as she sprang up from her chair. "Was Ron with them?"

"With the distance of the beach and the setting sun, I couldn't tell," he replied.

As Porter left the lounge, Shannon hurried after him.

"There were ten of us plus four crewmen," Toby informed Murphy. "That means seven of us are still missing."

"They're not missing," Cindy announced and drained the entire contents of her glass. "Something happened to them. Murphy said the bridge was covered with blood."

"Not covered," Murphy corrected her. "Someone's been seriously injured, but I'm sure it was just one person."

"Okay, fine," Cindy remarked, lacking enthusiasm for details while gingerly rubbing her wrapped arm. "So where did they go after this person was injured? The hospital?"

"She's right," Toby announced. "There was no blood in the deflated launch. If they're not onboard, they must have left the ship. They either took the first launch before it deflated, or they went overboard." His look was serious. "When Porter gets back with the others, we should return to the mainland and get help."

"I agree we should leave and see if we can get help, but we can't just assume everyone who didn't show up tonight is dead. What about fixing the radio?" Murphy asked.

"No, it's junk," Toby replied. "At the very least, we should sail further away from the beach and protect ourselves from any unwanted visitors."

Murphy appeared curious and tilted her head with a concerned look. "Are you suggesting there's someone else on the island?"

"No, just that someone may have killed one or all of the crew and we don't want them swimming to the ship without our knowledge."

"You have a point," Murphy reluctantly replied. "Do you know how to weigh anchor and steer this tub?"

"Enough to take us home if need be," Toby replied.

"Okay, start her up and wait for Porter to get the others onboard," Murphy announced. "We'll take her just far enough out to prevent swimmers but close enough that we can still see others if they make it to the beach."

Toby nodded, kissed his girlfriend quickly on the forehead, and hurried from the lounge.

"He's a bit of a conspiracy theorist," Cindy announced while forcing a tiny grimace. She tensed and shifted uncomfortably, again rubbing her sore arm. "What do you really think happened to the crew?"

Murphy stared at the concerned woman and held her breath. "I don't know, but I'm confident whoever was injured never made it to shore." She fidgeted slightly. "Once we're anchored further away, we'll search every inch of this ship for the crew or anyone responsible for what happened to them."

†

All seven remaining passengers had gathered within the lounge looking exhausted from their search of the ship. They hadn't found anyone else onboard either dead or alive. On a positive note, they also didn't find any further signs of blood or that a struggle had taken place. It was possible they only had one casualty, which would allow room for a misfortunate accident. Shannon was concerned that Ron wasn't either of the two men Porter rescued from the beach. Franklin and another man, whom Murphy hadn't gotten to know, were the two men rescued from the beach.

"Not a soul left onboard," Franklin remarked after their search. "She's secure for now."

"I'm glad you have some good news to report," Toby remarked while appearing disgusted. "The ship's been disabled. We're not going anywhere until we figure out what's wrong with the engine."

"A bit convenient, don't you think?" Porter remarked callously. "We find blood on the bridge and both the ship's engine and radio aren't working."

Everyone was uncomfortable despite Porter having stated what they were all thinking. Someone wanted to make sure they couldn't leave. Captain Flynn was high on their suspect list, since it was his ship and only he and the crew had been onboard when everything went to hell.

"We need to guard the port side of the ship and keep an eye on the island," Toby announced, taking charge. "We should post two man teams throughout the night."

"Isn't that a little paranoid, Toby?" Cindy questioned her boyfriend.

"If it gets us through the night, I'm okay with paranoid," Murphy muttered.

Chapter Fifteen

Later that night, Porter and Murphy stood along the deck railing on the port side of the ship and stared at the dark, silent beach. Both shared the same look of concern for their shipmates as well as their own situation.

"You know, it's ironic," Murphy announced.

"What's that?"

"I so desperately wanted Dane to tell me his story, and now I'm living it."

Porter placed his arm around her shoulder and held her to his side. "We don't know that anyone has died, Murphy. It's possible there was another ship nearby that took the injured man for medical attention. The rest of the crew may have taken the launch to the beach, where it deflated. They could be out in the woods right now looking for us."

She eyed him, revealing little hope in his story. "That's really a stretch."

"Yeah, well, it's the best I've got."

Murphy looked back to the beach and saw two crewmen appear from the woods. The men frantically waved to them on deck. Murphy and Porter suddenly straightened, appeared relieved, and waved back.

Murphy managed a soft, relieved laugh. "And maybe you're right after all."

"I'll get the launch," Porter announced excitedly.

The distinctive sound of an approaching helicopter could be heard in the near distance. Both searched the clear, moonlit sky for the sound.

"Is that--?"

Murphy suddenly grinned. "It most certainly is," she proclaimed. "I don't care if they arrest us, we're alerting that helicopter."

Murphy ran for the bridge and turned the massive spotlight on and off in S.O.S.

"That's my girl," Porter announced while grinning.

As the helicopter approached, everyone but Cindy appeared on deck and looked to the sky.

"My God, it's a rescue," Franklin gasped.

"We should meet them on the beach, right?" Shannon questioned.

"That's where they'll be landing," Toby replied with enthusiasm. "I'll get Cindy."

Toby hurried for the lounge. The helicopter circled the ship and shined its floodlights on the deck. The people on deck waved to the helicopter. Within minutes, the seven passengers were already in the launch heading to shore to greet the helicopter. As they jumped from the launch, several of them realized the two crewmen were no longer on the beach. It didn't seem important enough to distract them as they waited while the helicopter circled then lowered to the sand. Everyone shielded their eyes from the blowing sand as it pelted them. The helicopter barely set down when five men dressed in combat gear sprinted from the side door with automatic weapons raised. All seven passengers immediately held their hands in the air. The man in charge approached and lowered his automatic rifle. Bronson was built large and muscular. Everything about the man was intimidating from his bald head to his predominant scar on his cheek.

"Is this everyone?" Bronson demanded.

"There were two crewmen on the beach," Porter responded. "I guess they ran back into the woods. Aside from those two, that still leaves five people missing. Three passengers and two crewmen."

Bronson gave the signal to his men. Two of the soldiers, Jim and Rory, ran toward the woods with powerful spotlights on their weapons. As the helicopter shut down, the remaining soldiers lowered their weapons. Dane climbed out of the helicopter and joined them. Murphy stared at him with surprise or possible shock.

"Dane?" she gasped.

Dane approached her with a stern and serious look on his face. At that moment, he was moderately intimidating. "Are you ready to leave or must I remove you by force?"

Murphy felt ashamed and immediately submitted to his authoritative tone. "I think we've seen enough."

He nodded with little emotion. "Good."

"We have room for four of you," Bronson informed them. "Two of my men will accompany the rest of you on the ship."

"The ship's been disabled," Toby quickly announced.

"Don't worry; my men can fix it."

"No, that's not advisable," Dane suddenly announced. "We need to leave right away."

Bronson turned toward Dane and stared him down. "You called in a favor, Dane, but that doesn't give you permission to order me or my men around."

"No, you're right, it doesn't," Dane snapped while glaring at the intimidating man. "But as your pilot and the man who secured the helicopter, I'm expressing my intent to leave as soon as your men return with the others."

Bronson and Dane stared at each other in an eerie exchange. Murphy didn't think Dane had it in him, but he proved to be more of a force than she originally thought. Bronson frowned, reluctantly giving in.

"We'll attach a cable to the helicopter and tow the ship a few miles away. Once we're clear of the restricted area, we'll radio for assistance and a search party for the missing people," Bronson announced then glared at Dane and raised his brows. "Is that satisfactory?"

"It'll do," Dane replied.

Bronson turned to his remaining two men. "Harry, Webb, take our male passengers back to the ship with the launch then bring it back for the others when they return. The three women will join us in the helicopter. The helicopter will leave as soon as our men return."

Both soldiers nodded and motioned Porter, Toby, Franklin, and their fellow passenger, whose name still eluded Murphy, toward the launch. Porter appeared reluctant to leave Murphy. She offered him a reassuring smile. The four men and two soldiers headed for the inflatable launch. Bronson motioned Shannon, Cindy, and Murphy toward the helicopter. Dane noticed the blood seeping through Cindy's wrapped forearm then saw she was pale and weak. He suddenly stopped her and appeared alarmed.

"What happened to your arm?" he almost demanded.

"Oh, uh, some animal in a cave bit me," she replied and cringed as she touched her wrapped arm.

"What animal?"

"I don't know. We didn't see it in the dark," she responded and appeared puzzled. "What does it matter? I'm going to need shots no matter what."

Bronson again motioned the women toward the helicopter. Dane appeared tense and watched them approach the side door.

"She's not going with us," Dane suddenly announced.

Everyone stopped including those approaching the launch. Toby looked back with surprise.

"What?" Toby suddenly demanded.

"She's already sick from whatever bit her," Dane announced firmly. "If she has a seizure or worse, we won't be able to do anything for her. She could injure herself or the other women. She should go on the ship. Preferably in quarantine."

Everyone appeared stunned by Dane's insistence that Cindy not ride in the helicopter. Toby hurried to Cindy's side and helped her back toward the launch. Judging by his reaction, Toby was going to have words with Dane later.

Bronson turned to Webb and indicated the injured woman. "Take her to one of the cabins and keep an eye on her."

Webb nodded. Just then, they heard gunshots being fired from within the woods, which was followed by men yelling. Everyone on the beach became alarmed and looked toward the woods. Dane wasn't interested in waiting to see what came out of the woods. He grabbed Murphy's hand and pulled her toward the helicopter.

"We have to go--now," he ordered.

Bronson signaled for Webb and Harry to check on their men. Bronson joined the two men as they ran toward the woods to assist their comrades.

"No, get them in the launch!" Dane cried out to Bronson, but his order was ignored.

All three soldiers disappeared into the dark woods, their spotlights dancing around within the trees. The gunfire continued. Dane looked back at Porter, who stood not far from the inflatable launch while staring at the woods.

"Get them to the ship," Dane yelled to Porter while shoving Murphy into the helicopter.

Porter appeared momentarily frozen then snapped out of his daze. He nodded and hurried Cindy, Toby, Franklin, and the remaining passenger toward the launch. Dane shoved Shannon into the helicopter behind Murphy.

"What about the soldiers and the crew?" Murphy asked from inside the helicopter doorway.

"I'll come back for them once we're safely off the beach," Dane shouted back.

The gunfire became louder as it got closer to the beach. Webb appeared on the beach with his wounded comrade, Jim, clinging to him. Bronson, Harry, and Rory backed onto the beach just behind them while firing into the woods. All five soldiers looked as if they'd seen ghosts, the fright clearly in their eyes.

"What the hell are they?" Webb cried out while practically carrying Jim on his hip due to his bleeding leg.

"Get to the helicopter," Bronson yelled to his men.

Dane jumped into the helicopter and it immediately started. Bronson frantically waved for the others to get in the launch while Webb helped Jim into the helicopter. Harry continued to fire into the woods while backing toward the helicopter. Captain Flynn and one of his crewmen suddenly appeared from the woods. Both had a psychotic look in their dead eyes and massive injuries to their arms and necks. They snarled and charged for Harry, who repeatedly fired at them, striking them each several times. They didn't stop their relentless charge. Four severely decomposed men stumbled from the woods, although moving slower than the captain and his crewman. Captain Flynn and his crewman charged Harry as he was about to throw a grenade. They tackled him to the sand, causing the grenade to fly from his hand and roll beneath the helicopter. Bronson saw the explosive projectile fly beneath the craft.

"Out! Out!" Bronson yelled.

Everyone panicked and ran from the helicopter. Dane grabbed Murphy's hand and pulled her behind him while she stared helplessly at Harry, who was being devoured by the crewman. Captain Flynn chased after them while snarling like some wild animal. A shockwave of horror struck Murphy, now realizing they were zombies. The slower moving zombies piled on top of Harry and joined the crewman in his feast. As the helicopter exploded, Dane tackled Murphy to the sand and narrowly avoided the flying rotor. The spiraling rotor struck the nameless passenger, nearly cutting him in half, and narrowly avoided striking the inflatable launch. Harry, the zombie crewman, and the four ragged zombies exploded along with the helicopter. Murphy and Dane lifted their heads and looked behind them from their position on the sand at the destroyed helicopter. Captain Flynn was nearly on top of them. Murphy screamed as Dane pulled her to her feet. Porter suddenly appeared and struck Captain Flynn with a raft ore. The three joined Shannon and Bronson in a mad dash for the nearby launch.

Bronson fired at two more slower moving zombies, allowing Webb time to help the injured Jim to the launch. Captain Flynn suddenly tackled both men to the sand. Webb threw him off and shot him in the chest. Captain Flynn was barely fazed by the direct hit and leaped on top of the wounded soldier. Rory pulled Captain

Flynn off Jim and was about to shoot him when Captain Flynn lunged for him, biting him on the neck while driving him to the sand. Rory cried out in genuine agony as Flynn took a chunk out of his neck. Blood gushed from the gaping wound. They heard a gunshot. Captain Flynn's head suddenly exploded as the bullet passed through his skull. Dane lowered the assault rifle he now held in his hands. Two more zombies were closing in. Dane shot both in the head before they got too close. There was more movement from the woods, indicating it wasn't over. He saw a discarded hand grenade in the sand not far from Bronson's fatally injured man. He snatched the grenade from the sand and secured it in his jacket pocket then removed Rory's gun holster, since he no longer needed it.

"There will be more," Dane announced while looking at the others. "They're attracted to the sound."

Bronson checked on Rory, but he was already dead. He straightened and cursed softly. "We need to get to the boat."

Within minutes, all ten survivors climbed out of the inflatable launch and onto the ship's deck. They'd nearly capsized the launch by overloading the raft meant for six, but they had no choice. They stood by the railing and stared at the devastation on the beach. Cindy could no longer stand on her own and had to be held up by Toby. All ten watched the destroyed helicopter burn on the beach. The fire attracted more zombies, who now filtered onto the beach and feasted on the dead men. There were at least twenty zombies collecting around the bodies. As soon as Rory began twitching, the other zombies lost interest in him. Rory stood with some unsteadiness then joined the others in feasting on the scattered flesh from Harry's blown apart body. Nine of the ten survivors stared at the beach and appeared stunned by what they were witnessing. Dane didn't bother looking and just frowned with disgust. Bronson watched his dead man devouring charbroiled flesh alongside the others. He remained stunned only a moment then suddenly turned toward Dane and grabbed him by the shirt.

"What are those things? What happened to my man?" Bronson suddenly demanded. "He's *eating* Harry!"

Dane glared at Bronson with little reaction to his physical assertiveness and made no effort to fight him. "What do you think they are?"

"Zombies?" Porter gasped.

"Bullshit!" Bronson launched.

Dane remained calm and still while Bronson held onto his shirt. "We have bigger problems right now, so I suggest you take your hands off me."

"I want answers, you fuck!" Bronson screamed.

Dane suddenly broke free from Bronson's grip, twisted his arm, and kicked him in the ribs twice before flipping him harshly onto the deck. Bronson landed roughly on his back and clutched his ribs in agony as he writhed on the deck.

"I did warn you," Dane scoffed while glaring at the once intimidating soldier. "Considering our tarnished relationship, any other time I would have broken your arm, but we're going to need your fighting skills to survive this little ocean voyage."

Webb kept a distrusting eye on Dane while helping Bronson to his feet. Bronson appeared angered but humbled as he straightened his combat jacket. He glared at Dane with an unpredictable look in his eyes.

"There's a good chance I'll kill you later, but I'm guessing we need you right now," Bronson snarled. "Tell us what the hell is going on."

"I think I'd like to hear that explanation too," Murphy announced hotly while folding her arms across her chest.

"The short version? This island was a research facility for viral weapons," Dane informed them. "Apparently things went bad. The human guinea pigs ate the scientists, and they scrapped the project. Not surprisingly, the government did a sloppy clean-up job and allowed several infected people to wander off."

"So you're trying to tell me those things are actual zombies?" Bronson demanded.

"For lack of a better word," Dane replied.

"And you knew this when you fed me that sack of lies?" Murphy demanded.

Dane stared at Murphy but didn't respond. Murphy frowned and walked away from him. Dane appeared tense then looked back at Bronson.

"The infection is spread through blood and saliva. Particularly bites." Dane indicated Cindy, who leaned heavily on Toby. She looked terrible. "She's been infected."

Toby appeared horrified and glanced at the pale woman clinging to him. She barely had the strength to look up at him.

Dane suddenly turned to Jim and indicated his bleeding leg that he'd hurriedly wrapped. "What happened to your leg?"

"Your captain lunged for me in the woods," Jim replied. "I was thrown ground. I must've landed on a sharp rock or branch."

"We need to have a look at that," Dane insisted.

"I wasn't bitten," he assured him.

Bronson appeared stern and glared at Dane. "He's fine."

Dane wasn't convinced but didn't push it. "The girl needs to be isolated for our protection."

"What's going to happen to her?" Toby asked, frightened for his girlfriend's life.

"She's going to turn into one of them."

"How can you be sure?" Bronson demanded.

"I've lived this nightmare before," Dane assured him. "She's already showing signs of infection. The milder the wound, the longer it takes for the infection to destroy the host. Rory was fatally bitten, so he changed almost immediately. She's going to die from the infection and then come back and try to kill the rest of us."

Bronson looked at Cindy. Despite her weakness, she was horrified by the news. Toby pulled Cindy into his arms and held her against him. She clung to him and fought her emotions.

"We'll isolate her in one of the cabins," Bronson replied.

"I'll stay with her," Toby insisted. "She's my girlfriend."

Bronson nodded. Dane just frowned and shook his head. Toby helped Cindy along the deck with Bronson following. Dane cast a look at Jim, who still clutched his bleeding leg. Jim glared at him then limped away.

"We should be safe onboard the ship," Webb informed the others.

"I wouldn't be too confident about that, Webb," Dane announced.

"Yeah? Well, I doubt those things can swim."

"No, but they can walk," Dane launched back. "We're not that far from shore. There's one way on this ship. The stern ladder. We should patrol the deck, keep an eye on those on the beach, and secure that ladder."

"I'll take first watch," Webb offered then walked across the deck to the port side.

Franklin and Porter approached Dane. Both remained concerned for their situation.

"You think that soldier is infected, don't you?" Franklin asked.

Dane nodded. "We'll know for sure in a few hours."

"Yeah, but will that be too late?" Porter asked while fidgeting.

Shannon uncertainly approached them. "I'll offer to patch his wound. I can tell you if it's a bite wound or not."

"That's a good idea," Franklin announced.

"He's already on the defensive," Dane informed them. "I don't think you want to test him."

"What's he going to do?" Shannon asked while cocking her head to the side.

"If he's hiding the fact that he's been bitten, he might snap your neck on principle alone," Dane remarked.

Porter indicated the men in combat gear. "Who are these guys?"

"The only men I could find to come along on this unsanctioned mission," Dane informed him. "They're mercenaries. I called in nearly every I.O.U. I had." Dane looked at Murphy where she leaned on the railing further down the deck. "And it still wasn't enough. Excuse me."

Dane approached Murphy as she stared toward the beach while watching the devastation.

Murphy didn't bother looking at him. "You lied to me."

"Even if I was allowed to tell you the truth, would you have believed me?"

Murphy glared at him. "You told me an emotion packed tale of lies. If you couldn't tell me what really happened, then you should have kept your mouth shut."

"I took nothing from you," he insisted.

"Nothing?" she snapped. "You played on my sympathies. You made me feel sorry for you."

"No, I made you feel better."

"You used me like some perverse security blanket," she launched back.

"For the record, it wasn't all lies," he informed her. "Most of what I told you did happen. I just substituted a serial killer for ravenous flesh eaters."

"Go to hell." Murphy leaned on the railing and avoided looking at him.

"You're mad, I get it, but maybe you should be seeing the bigger picture," he announced while showing little emotion. "I risked my life and the lives of five soldiers to save you. Grant it, my plan backfired and we're all probably going to die here, but I think you should show a tiny bit of gratitude for the effort and drop the attitude."

Dane turned and walked away.

Porter slowly approached and watched him leave. "What has him pissed?"

"Me, I suppose," she replied then groaned softly. "I'm just so mad at him."

"The man came here to rescue you," Porter reminded her. "I think you should cut him some slack. At the very least, give the guy a blowjob."

"You're not helping."

"How many men would have done what he did?" Porter demanded. "The fact that he put himself back in this situation is amazing in itself. He's obviously willing to die for you."

"Exactly why I'm mad at him," she scoffed then looked at Porter with a sad expression. "If he dies because of me, I'll never be able to live with that."

"So tell him that," Porter insisted. "He has major feelings for you. Let him know you have some for him."

She sighed softly. "You're right."

Chapter Sixteen

Murphy entered the ship's lounge and briefly glanced at the far end of the bar. Shannon attempted to talk to Jim, but he didn't appear interested in letting her care for his injured leg. She had to give the woman credit for trying. All things considered, Shannon seemed as if she'd be the first to lose it under the circumstances. She was holding up rather well. Dane sat at the bar with a glass of brandy in his hand and the bottle within reach. Murphy held her breath a moment then approached Dane and sat at the bar alongside him. He didn't bother looking at her.

"I made a mistake by coming to this island, I realize that," she informed him without awaiting an official greeting, "but you never should have come after me."

He sipped his drink and refrained from looking at her. "If you're apologizing, it needs work."

"I didn't ask you to risk your life for me," she continued. "I don't want to be responsible for you dying."

"I'm not dead yet," he muttered.

She groaned softly with defeat. "You're not making this easy."

"I'm sorry," he announced and finally looked at her. "Were you making a point?"

She stared into his eyes and held her breath. "I care about what happens to you."

"It's possible I care about you too."

Murphy stared into his eyes a long moment feeling sorry for herself. She gently touched his face without taking her eyes from his. He placed his hand on hers, caressed it gently, and then kissed the back of it with great affection. Her heart seemingly skipped a beat to the warmth of his kiss. He'd swooped in to rescue her. Despite having failed, she couldn't deny it made one hell of an impression on her. Porter ran into the lounge and appeared highly excited and not in the good way.

"You guys have to see this!"

Everyone followed Porter from the lounge.

✝

Several zombies bobbed around within the water just off the beach in an attempt to reach the ship. They didn't appear to be making much ground, but the current was gently pulling them out then pushing them back to shore. Eventually, they could make it to the ship. The seven passengers, minus Toby, Cindy and Bronson, stared at the sight and appeared uncertain how to react.

"What are we going to do?" Shannon gasped.

"I have an idea," Franklin declared then ran along the deck.

He removed an ax from a security box on the wall then hurried toward the stern. Webb and Dane hurried after him with concern.

"What are you doing?" Dane suddenly asked.

"What we should have done right away," Franklin cried out.

Webb suddenly appeared alarmed. "No, stop!"

Franklin approached the gear holding the anchor and swung the ax, chopping through the thick rope. The anchor plummeted into the water and the ship floated freely.

"You idiot!" Webb cried out.

Franklin turned toward him and glared at him with hostility. "I'd rather be adrift at sea than eaten alive by zombies!"

"We're not going to drift out to sea," Dane snarled. "We're going to drift toward the island!"

Franklin appeared alarmed while staring at Dane. "What?"

"It's the current flow, you idiot," Webb shouted out. "You're going to take us right to them!"

Toby appeared on deck with a solemn look about him. Bronson followed behind him as he approached Dane.

"You were wrong," Toby announced sadly. "She didn't turn into one of them. She died."

Their current situation aside, Dane looked at Toby and appeared alarmed. "Did you lock her in the cabin?"

"Lock her in?" he practically gasped. "I told you, she's dead."

Dane turned to Bronson, who stood just behind Toby. "We need to take care of her now before she turns."

The ship started drifting toward the island.

Bronson suddenly looked around and appeared concerned. "Are we moving closer to the island?"

"Some idiot cut the anchor free thinking we'd sail further into the ocean," Webb snapped.

"What sort of idiot--?"

Dane interrupted Bronson with limited patience. "Bronson, we need to do something about the girl!"

Cindy slowly walked onto deck and joined them. By the vacant expression in her lifeless eyes, she had already turned. Everyone stared at her with surprise.

Toby ran toward her. "Cindy--?"

Porter suddenly grabbed Toby and pulled him back just as Cindy lunged for him with her teeth exposed while snarling. There were several screams and gasps. Webb removed his pistol and shot Cindy in the head. She immediately collapsed to the deck. Toby appeared horrified and pulled free from Porter, falling to Cindy's side.

"We're no longer safe on this ship," Dane informed the others. "We have to leave while we still can."

"And go where?" Bronson demanded.

"The facility," Porter gasped with enthusiasm.

"It's the only safe place left," Dane reluctantly replied.

"What facility?" Webb asked while looking from Dane to Porter.

"I'll explain on the way," Dane announced.

"On the way?" Murphy suddenly gasped. "That's an hour trek through the jungle in the dark with those things. We'll never make it."

"We'll take the launch to the nearest beach," Dane informed her.

"That launch only holds six," Webb remarked. "We nearly capsized it on this short trip."

"I'm not leaving the ship," Bronson informed them. "I can fix it. I just need time."

"You don't have much time, Bronson," Dane remarked.

"It'll take at least an hour or two for this tub to reach the shore. Jim can keep watch," Bronson informed him. "Webb, you go with them to the facility. The ship has portable two-way radios. I can radio when the engine is running, and we'll come and get the rest of you."

"We can make it with seven people in the launch," Webb informed them. "It'll hold."

Toby remained kneeling over Cindy's dead body. He finally looked up. "I'm staying."

Dane reluctantly gave in and eyed Bronson. "I'll draw you a quick map to the facility by land and sea, just in case."

"I'll get the radios," Webb announced then hurried away from them.

"Porter and I will get some supplies," Murphy offered.

"Just a day's worth," Bronson warned. "We'll need the rest of the food for the journey home."

†

The inflatable launch with the six survivors reached the beach on the other side of the island. All six jumped out and pulled the launch to shore for their return to the ship after it was fixed. Webb and Dane carried their assault rifles fixed with powerful flashlights and kept watch as they approached the woods. They also carried semiautomatic pistols for added measures. Dane had secured his from the dead man on the beach before they'd made their run for the ship. Murphy and Porter carried their stun gun batons while Shannon had a pool stick from the lounge and Franklin carried a baseball bat he'd found onboard the ship.

"It's only a few minutes along this path," Dane informed them. "We go fast and quiet."

Dane turned on the high-powered light attached to the rifle and aimed it along the path. It brightened a large area before them.

"I'll bring up the rear," Webb announced and turned on his light as well.

"Let's go," Dane announced and led the way.

All six hurried through the woods brightened by the assault rifle lights. They heard faint sounds of someone moving around in the darkness. Shannon and Franklin clung to each other and looked into the dark woods beyond the lights.

"They're out there," Shannon gasped softly.

"Quiet," Dane growled.

They arrived in the clearing before the facility and discovered a man standing just in front of the facility door.

"Ron," Shannon gasped with excitement and hurried past the others toward the facility.

Ron stepped into the light to reveal massive chunks of flesh missing from his blood-soaked body. He snarled and lunged for Shannon. She cried out with horror and momentarily froze. As Webb tackled Shannon to the ground, Dane struck Ron in the face with the butt of his assault rifle. Once he was on the ground, Dane repeatedly struck him in the head until he no longer moved. Webb pulled Shannon to her feet. She stared at her dead boyfriend, his face almost completely bashed in from the assault rifle. She sobbed softly and looked away.

"Why didn't you just shoot him?" Franklin demanded.

"Because we'll have an entire herd of them coming to investigate the noise," Dane snapped. He then noticed the partially closed door and hesitated. "Someone's been here."

"That was us," Murphy confessed.

Dane appeared unconvinced and slowly pushed open the door. He raised his rifle and cautiously entered with the light brightening the way. The other five followed him inside. The facility lobby was nearly dark with the only light coming from Dane and Webb's rifles. Murphy and Porter turned on their own baton flashlights and helped brighten the lobby.

"We'll secure the doors on all ends for tonight, in case any got inside," Dane announced to the others. "We'll worry about securing the rest of the facility tomorrow morning. I'll check on the generator then. There may still be enough gas left to run it a few hours in the evening."

Chapter Seventeen

The hallway doors were tied shut that night to secure the lobby area. The six survivors attempted to relax on the worn sofas, but it was obvious no one was going to get more than a few minutes of sleep. They kept a fire burning in the large fireplace to brighten the lobby, since the generator was in a different part of the facility and traveling to it in the dark was unwise. Webb was preoccupied with the two-way radio, clutching it like a security blanket, hoping to get some word from Bronson. Murphy took a bottle of water and joined Dane on his sofa. She handed him the bottle. He took a swallow from it then returned it to her. She set it aside, clung to his arm, and rested her head on his shoulder. Dane placed his arm around her and held her firmly against him.

"I'm sorry you had to come back here," she said softly while nuzzling his shoulder. "Are you okay?"

"I'd be lying if I said I wasn't more than a little haunted by this place."

"Your heart is racing."

"And yours isn't?" he countered.

"I'm terrified out of my mind," she replied softly, "but it won't do anyone any good to freak out about it right now."

"Sound advice," he replied then patted her arm around him. "Why don't you try to get some sleep? I'll keep an eye out for intruders."

Murphy sank into some dark thoughts while staring blankly across the dimly lit lobby. "We're going to die, aren't we?"

"Not tonight," he replied without hesitation.

"That part was true, wasn't it?" she asked softly.

He attempted to look at her where she rested against him but couldn't see her face. "What part?"

"What you and Kate shared?" She glanced up at him and met his gaze. "That wasn't a lie, was it?"

"That I was her sex toy?" He grinned and chuckled softly. "Yes, that part was fairly accurate."

She smiled with embarrassment and lightly slapped his chest. "That's not what I meant." Murphy again nuzzled his shoulder, keeping him from seeing her face. "I wouldn't mind one last night of passion before I die," she whispered softly.

Dane strained to look at her, but she refused to look at him. He nuzzled the top of her head and sighed softly. "I promise you will," he replied softly. "Because you're not going to die; not here. I'm not going to lose anyone else I care about to this island again. That's a promise."

It was a beautiful sentiment, but she was actually hoping he'd cash in his last remaining I.O.U. She wasn't sure why it was important to her, but somehow, now that they were facing possible death, it was important.

†

Jim patrolled the yacht's deck while keeping watch on the beach as the ship slowly drifted closer to the island. Several zombies were seen in the water; their heads bobbing like buoy markers. Although unable to swim, they were slowly getting closer to the ship. Nearly a dozen more paced the beach and watched the ship in the near distance, waiting for their meal to come to them. Jim frowned and continued to patrol the deck. He paused by the streak of dark blood on deck where Cindy had fallen. He stared at the blood and appeared almost sickened by the sight then insecurely rubbed his injured leg.

"Christ--"

†

Toby was slumped over the bar with an empty glass before him and a nearly empty bottle just within reach. It seemed as if he had passed out after having a few too many drinks. Jim entered the lounge, saw Toby sprawled across the bar, and shook his head. He wasn't going to be any use on guard duty in his condition.

"Come on, Toby," Jim announced as he approached the bar. "Your watch for the next two hours. I need a drink."

Toby didn't respond, obviously out cold.

Jim groaned softly. "Don't tell me you're drunk, man. That's not cool." He placed his hand on Toby's shoulder and firmly nudged him. "Wake up, asshole."

Toby slowly lifted his head from the bar, turned toward Jim, and suddenly snarled. His dead eyes conveyed he'd turned sometime during Jim's shift. Before Jim could react, Toby bit his hand. Jim cried out and attempted to pull his hand free from the clenching teeth.

✝

Bronson continued to work on the ship's engine despite the late hour. He took a moment to pause and study the engine, casually picked up a large wrench, and angrily pounded on the engine. While pounding on the engine, he didn't hear the faint sounds of gunfire from the deck above.

"Stupid piece of shit!"

Bronson suddenly stopped pounding and listened a moment, thinking he'd heard something. He didn't hear anything. Bronson drew a deep breath and returned to the engine with less hostility.

"I swear, Dane," he muttered to himself, "if we survive, I'm going to kill you."

There was a faint thumping sound from above him. Bronson again hesitated, looked toward the ceiling, and listened. Something didn't seem right. He picked up his two-way radio.

"Jim, do you copy?" he announced into the radio. There was no response. "Jim?"

There was still no response. Bronson grabbed his assault rifle and hurried from the engine room. He ran up the steps, unlocked the engine room door, and appeared on deck with his assault rifle aimed. He cautiously headed toward the stern, rounded the corner, and came face-to-face with a soaking wet Rory. Bronson stared at his dead comrade, who now stood before him with chunks of flesh missing from his face and neck. Bronson leaped back and attempted to aim his rifle, but he was too close. As Rory lunged for him, both men fell to the deck. Bronson attempted to hold Rory back as he

263

tried to bit his throat. Bronson fumbled for his firearm in the holster on his side, but it was partially pinned beneath him. He attempted to reach his knife stowed inside his boot. Rory snarled with his teeth exposed and got closer to his neck. There was movement along deck. Toby suddenly leaped onto Bronson's leg and bit his boot. Bronson screamed and kicked Toby in the face several times before freeing his foot. He secured the knife from his boot and stabbed Rory in the head. Rory tensed and fell limp on top of him.

Bronson shoved Rory off him while kicking Toby once more in the face, sending him onto his backside. Bronson scrambled to his feet as Toby pulled himself up. Bronson grabbed his holstered pistol. He stared at zombie Toby, frowned his disgust, and then shot him in the head. A slower, severely decayed zombie appeared around the corner and approached while snarling. Bronson looked at the approaching zombie and was about to raise his gun when a gunshot rang out. The zombie took a shot to the head and fell to the deck. Jim stepped around the corner and into view with his assault rifle. He was exhausted and the infected bite wound on his hand bled freely.

"Are you okay?" Jim gasped softly, clearly in agony.

"Yeah, barely," Bronson replied and attempted to control his breathing. "What happened to Toby?"

"He must have been infected and didn't know it."

"More like he was bitten and didn't admit it," Bronson scoffed.

"I don't believe anything Dane says," Jim gruffly retorted. "He doesn't know shit."

Bronson indicated Toby's body. "Check Toby for a bite wound."

Jim hesitated a moment then kneeled over Toby's body and searched for a bite wound. There was a tell-tale bite wound on his lower leg.

Jim looked behind him at Bronson. "That doesn't prove--"

Bronson's gun was already aimed at Jim's head. Before Jim could even gasp, Bronson pulled the trigger. Jim's head snapped back as blood exploded out the back of his skull. He collapsed to the deck.

Bronson frowned. "Sorry, man."

The ship suddenly jolted nearly throwing Bronson off balance. He clutched the railing to keep from falling then ran for the bow. Bronson stopped by the bow railing. The ship had run aground and several zombies within the water were already pawing at the side of the ship.

"Fuck me!"

Bronson slung his rifle over his shoulder and neck and hurried for the stern. As he approached the stern, several severely decayed and soaking wet zombies were already climbing the ladder and falling onto the deck.

"Shit!"

Bronson turned for the nearby railing and looked into the water. There were a few zombies bobbing around near the ship, but it appeared clear just a few feet out. Bronson climbed onto the railing and dived into the water beyond the zombies. He surfaced with a soft gasp and looked back at the ship. Several zombies were only inches away staring back at him. Bronson screamed and attempted to swim away from them. They clutched the assault rifle strap around his shoulder and neck and pulled him back. He struggled against them and the water while screaming.

Chapter Eighteen

Murphy slowly woke to sun shining on her from a small clearing in the vegetation growing outside the window. She was nestled in the arms of a man while partially reclined on the sofa. Murphy lifted her head and saw she was sleeping against Porter. He remained asleep while reclined in the corner of the sofa with his head propped on his fist. Murphy slowly sat up waking him.

"What? Who--?" He groaned softly while looking around then appeared disappointed. "Oh, we're still here."

Murphy looked around the lobby as well. Franklin and Shannon had fallen asleep on other sofas within the lobby. Dane and Webb were both missing.

"Where's Dane?" she asked with concern.

"Lord of the undead went on an outing with Webb," Porter replied as he stretched with some stiffness. "They thought the radio wasn't working, so they went to the beach to contact Bronson."

"Not working?" she scoffed. "More like there's still no word from the ship."

"Yes, that's probably more likely."

She groaned softly and held her head. "I'm so sorry I got you into this, Porter. It's all my fault."

He stared at her with surprise. "In what life did you ever talk me into anything?" he almost demanded. "Face it, Murphy, I'm the ringleader. I drug you out here, not the other way around."

"But you did it because of me," she protested.

"Oh, you poor, naive little girl," he announced with a deep sigh. "This has never been about you. This has always been about plane crashes, conspiracies, and government cover-ups. You're just fun to hang with. If it wasn't you, it'd be someone else."

She laughed softly. "Nice try."

"You are going to be *so* devastated when you finally realize I've never been in love with you," he teased.

"I'm sure I will."

Both laughed softly.

✝

Murphy paced just outside the facility while scanning the woods with every sound. There was no sign of zombies or live people alike. It was almost unfair that the island seemed so peaceful on such a beautiful, warm morning. Porter leaned within the open doorway and watched her pace.

"Do you really think that's going to make them return sooner?" he asked with little emotion.

"No, but it makes me feel better."

"Well, that's what's important," he muttered.

Shannon poked her head past Porter and watched Murphy pace several feet outside.

"Is that wise?" Shannon asked.

"I'll hear them long before they see me," Murphy replied without looking back.

She heard movement within the woods. All three bolted inside behind the door. Murphy glanced back outside. Dane and Webb hurried along the path toward them. Their faces told a worrisome but familiar tale. Murphy approached Dane and studied his expression that conveyed her concern.

"What happened?" she asked.

"We could see the ship from the cliffs," Dane announced while frowning. "It's aground near the beach. The infected are crawling all over deck."

"Don't sugarcoat it, Dane," Webb announced. "They were *eating* someone."

Webb hurried to the facility door where Shannon and Porter waited. He entered the facility and disappeared.

"So Bronson, Jim, and Toby are dead, and we're officially stuck here," Murphy reluctantly announced.

"I'm sorry, Murphy."

"Why? It's not your fault," she replied and frowned. "I did this to us."

"Once the infected lose interest in the ship, they'll work their way back to the island," Dane informed her. "Webb wants another shot at fixing the engine and possibly the ship's radio."

Murphy stared at him with surprise. "I think he's insane. If they come back to the ship now, he's trapped."

"When men feel they're backed into a corner, they all react differently," Dane replied. "In Webb's case, he's hell-bent on exhausting every option before he accepts defeat."

"So what do we do?"

"Well, we only have enough food to make it through today, so I'm going mango hunting."

"By yourself?" she nearly gasped. "Don't you think that's dangerous?"

"So is starving to death," Dane assured her. "Don't ask why, but they don't move around as much during the day. As long as I'm back before evening, I'll be okay. I'll only be gone an hour or two." His words didn't comfort her any. "That'll leave plenty of time to search the facility, so we'll have more room to spread out and access to bathrooms. Hopefully the water still works."

"I'm going with you," Murphy suddenly chirped.

"Why am I not surprised?"

✝

Porter and Franklin collapsed onto a sofa within the lobby and appeared exhausted after their search of the first floor.

Shannon stared at them with concern while fidgeting. "Are we safe?"

"This level is clear," Franklin informed her. "We secured the stairways until we can make sure the rest of the place is secure."

"There's running water just like Dane said. It seems to run on either solar power or waterpower. Pity it wasn't hooked up to the electric as well, but we can also run the generator enough to give us some power at night." Porter announced. "There are extra linens, towels, clothing, and non-perishable goods. Whatever that mess was that we found in the pantry, though, is rotted beyond recognition."

"So that's it?" Shannon nearly choked on her words. "We're officially moving in?"

"Unless Webb has better success with the ship's engine and radio, we're probably here for life," Franklin replied with little emotion.

"Let's be honest," Porter announced. "Webb is going to be served up buffet style long before he gets that ship running."

"That's awful," Shannon cried out.

"No, that's male pride and stupidity," Porter informed her. "I'm going to sit outside and wait for Murphy and Dane."

"Better keep an eye on her," Franklin remarked.

"She's safe out there with him."

"Not what I meant," Franklin continued. "He knows the situation. I wouldn't doubt he's already staking his claim on your girlfriend."

"Seriously, Franklin?" Shannon suddenly lashed out. "Who's thinking like that after just one day of being stranded?"

"All of us."

"Murphy and I are just friends," Porter assured him.

"You may rethink that after a few months alone with your thoughts," Franklin teased.

Shannon rolled her eyes and walked away.

Porter watched her leave then eyed Franklin. "Considering you just disgusted the only other woman on this island, I'd say you're the one who's going to be spending a lot of time alone with your thoughts."

"Oh please," Franklin snorted. "I stand about as good a chance with Shannon as you do. She'll eventually settle for Webb, providing he's not eaten before sunset." He reluctantly sighed. "Face it, Murphy is your only shot at getting any, but not if you let Dane get in her pants first."

"Well, I don't know about Dane," Porter announced while glaring at Franklin, "but there's no chance I'm letting you get in her pants." He then walked away.

Chapter Nineteen

Dane placed fallen mangoes into a sack while Murphy climbed down the nearby tree. She joined him on the ground and helped collect mangoes. Dane stopped and watched her. Murphy placed several mangoes in the bag before realizing he was staring at her. Their eyes met. He suddenly tensed and looked away.

"Tomorrow I'll show you a nice banana tree," he announced then closed the sack and turned away from her.

Murphy held up a mango. "Mango for your thoughts?"

He seemed unable to look at her. "We should probably save intellectual conversations for when we're safely indoors."

Murphy eyed the area and shifted uncomfortably. "You and Kate have a few afternoon delights here?"

Dane looked at Murphy with surprise then appeared embarrassed. He managed a tiny smile. "More than a few."

Murphy casually leaned against the tree, played with the mango in her hand, and smiled warmly. "It's okay if you have erotic feelings regarding this place. You don't need to hide anything with me."

"I appreciate that, even if you have the wrong idea." He shifted uncomfortably.

"And what's the *wrong* idea?"

He glanced at her. "That I was indulging in a sexual fantasy with Kate."

"You weren't?"

Dane approached her and let the bag fall to the ground as he stared into her eyes. "No, not with Kate."

Murphy stared at him in silence as her heart pounded. There was something in his eyes that she hadn't seen before. It was a spark

270

of life. Dane grabbed Murphy around the waist, pressed his body against hers, and kissed her passionately and with aggression. Her heart nearly pounded through her chest. Despite their current situation, she felt compelled to return the kiss knowing it would only encourage bad behavior. Her senses were alert to every sound within the woods. The fear of falling prey to a ravenous zombie only increased her heart rate. As his hands firmly traveled her body with uninhibited desire, she was suddenly aware of his intentions. It was possible he would take her here and now without regard to what was lurking just within the woods. She had to admit, it was a bit of a thrill, but her fear was greater than her desire. Dane grinded against her as his hand ran firmly across her buttocks. Murphy broke off the kiss while attempting to hide her fear for their safety.

She managed a moderately lustful smile while gently running her hands along his chest. "Can I assume the mind and body have finally gotten together?"

He stared into her eyes. "From the moment I thought I'd lost you."

They heard movement within the woods, forcing them to jump apart. Dane had his assault rifle in his hand and aimed into the woods at the sound with amazing speed. Bronson suddenly appeared in the clearing. He was out of breath, damp, and covered with scratches. Murphy let out a startled scream.

Bronson jumped to her scream then stared at them with relief. "Thank God."

"I can't believe you're alive," Dane remarked with surprise and lowered the rifle. "What happened?"

"Toby was infected but didn't say anything," Bronson informed them. "He turned into one of them and attacked Jim." He frowned while inhaling a deep, shaken breath. "I had to do Jim. I couldn't leave him, and I certainly couldn't risk bringing him along." He trembled slightly. "God help me, I shot Jim."

✝

Bronson sat on one of the sofas with a bottle of water in his hand and a distant look on his face. The others sat or paced the lobby, feeling there was no longer any doubt of their fate.

"We're all going to die, I know it," Franklin muttered with defeat.

"Just shut up, okay," Porter snapped lowly.

Bronson suddenly looked around and appeared interested. "Where's Webb?"

"He insisted on going back to the ship and attempt to fix it," Dane informed him.

"Idiot," Bronson suddenly exploded. "Why didn't you stop him?"

"He had an AK-47," Dane replied. "How would you propose I stop him?"

Bronson resumed his distant look and continued to stare. He was starting to twitch with anxiety. "Is this place secure?"

"This level is secure," Porter assured him. "There are two more floors and the basement that need to be checked."

"The basement is the lab," Dane informed him. "I doubt any of those things got through that door. They're not that smart."

"Anything useful down there?" Bronson asked with a glimmer of hope.

"Yeah, and I used it when I was stuck here," Dane replied.

Porter stood with a sigh. "Since you feel it's secure, I'm going to have a look around down there. Maybe there's something that will tell us what happened on this rock."

"I can tell you what happened," Dane announced. "The government created a superbug that reanimated the dead. They were attacked, they came in and wiped most of them out, and shut the facility down. My shipmates and I came along, discovered a few infected they had missed, and subsequently died before coming back to life and eating one another. After my rescue, the government came back to finish the job they botched years earlier. Judging by the number of infected, I'd guess they did another piss poor job of it. There's more now than there were five years ago."

"Story time over," Porter remarked. "I'm still going to have a look for myself."

"I think I'll go with you," Murphy replied with a sigh.

"I may as well go too," Shannon remarked. "I've seen enough of these four walls for one day."

"Better get used to them," Dane muttered. "This is your new prison."

Shannon glared at him while placing her dainty hands on her hips. "Aren't you the ray of sunshine?"

As the three left, Dane groaned, snatched his discarded assault rifle, and followed them. "If you insist on going down there, at least let me start the generator, so we'll have some light."

✝

Porter, Murphy, Shannon, and Dane entered the sterile, white lab within the basement. The room had some high-tech equipment remaining, which appeared more modern than the facility. There were several closed doors near the back. Shannon and Murphy checked out pieces of equipment that required electric to run, but the generator wasn't widely connected. Porter picked up a flash drive on top of a stack of folders, eyed it, and then looked around for the computer. A laptop was smashed on the floor.

"That's too bad," he muttered and set the flash drive aside. He then looked over some files stacked on the end of the counter and picked one up.

Dane, with his assault rifle slung over his shoulder, leaned against the doorframe and folded his arms across his chest. He appeared bored.

Murphy walked along the opposite side of the room and picked up an unusual looking gun. "What's this?"

"Looks like a gun," Shannon replied while making a face of distaste.

"There's no chamber," Murphy informed them while studying it.

Dane approached and took the gun from her. He briefly examined it and appeared surprised. "This wasn't here during my stay."

"You said the government came in to clean up," Murphy reminded him.

Dane pressed the trigger. A rod was expelled from the barrel nearly four inches then popped back in place in one, swift motion.

"This is a cattle gun," Dane suddenly remarked. "Used to kill steer for butchering."

Shannon grimaced. "Oh, that's disgusting."

"Sort of like a bullet to the head," Dane continued. "A more humane way to kill them."

Porter found something of interest in the file he held. "Oh, you're going to love this." They approached Porter, who studied some papers. "According to this file, the test subject was destroyed six months *after* Dane's rescue."

Dane snatched the folder and looked at it. Porter picked up another and casually flipped through it.

"This one too," he continued. "Looks as if our government didn't come here to destroy but to study. Anyone else not surprised?"

"I don't believe it," Dane gasped with surprise. "After what I'd told them, they should have known better."

"They did know better," Porter informed him. "You gave them access to free biohazard weapons."

Shannon stared at one of the stretchers in a darkened corner of the room. Something moved on the stretcher beneath the sheet. She slowly approached then appeared horrified.

"There's one of them under that sheet!" she cried out.

All three hurried toward her. Dane armed himself with the cattle gun as Porter cautiously reached for the sheet and pulled it off. Several large rats jumped off the stretcher containing a badly decomposed body and scurried across the floor. Shannon, Murphy, and Porter all screamed while avoiding the rats. Dane frowned and shook his head.

Porter collapsed against the wall near one of the doors. "I'm so ready to go home."

A zombie suddenly struck the shatterproof glass on the window near him. Porter jumped, spun toward the door, and cried out. Everyone jumped back with alarm. Several zombies pounded on the glass window of the solid door.

"Can they get through?" Shannon gasped.

"No, that glass is shatterproof," Dane informed them. "That's a holding tank."

Porter looked into the room beyond the zombies collecting at the door. "There must be a dozen or more in there." He looked back at the others. "One is wearing a lab coat."

"Someone on the team must have gotten bit," Murphy announced.

"With the way they abandoned this place, I'd say a lot of them were infected," Dane replied.

"And they still didn't think to wipe them out?" Shannon nearly gasped.

"All in the name of science," Porter muttered.

"Just to be safe, we should keep all doors between here and the upstairs locked," Dane informed them. "No one should come down here. If they don't see us, they won't become agitated and aggressive."

They all agreed and left the lab. Dane took the cattle gun with them. The zombies continued to pound on the door.

Chapter Twenty

Bronson paced the lobby while periodically looking out the thick glass window between the plant life growing in front of it. It was getting dark outside, and the zombies would soon be prowling around the woods in search of a meal. Porter, Franklin, and Shannon played a card game with limited enthusiasm. There wasn't much else to do by candlelight. Dane entered and placed a plate of sliced mango on the lobby desk.

"Dinner's served," Dane announced in an attempt to sound cheerful.

"I don't get it," Bronson said while pausing before the window and peering out through the vegetation. "Where are they? I haven't seen one all day."

"They're out there," Dane informed him. "They don't come out as much during the day. We never came up with a satisfactory answer as to why. Perhaps the sunlight hurts their eyes, temporarily blinds them. Who knows?" He casually leaned on the lobby desk. "They move much slower during the day. Maybe it's the heat and humidity. I'm not sure it really matters."

They heard the handheld radio crackle from its position on the lobby desk.

"Hey, anyone listening?" came Webb's familiar voice.

Bronson sprinted across the lobby and pounced on the radio. "Webb? Is that you?"

"Bronson?" Webb exclaimed. "You son-of-a-bitch! I knew you'd find a way to survive."

"Where are you, man?"

"Fixing this piece of shit ship," he replied from the other end. "It's been quiet here all day."

Dane became alerted. "Tell him to lock himself someplace safe," he quickly announced. "It's almost dark. They'll be coming back for him."

He nodded and conveyed the message. "Dane says to lock yourself in for the night. You're going to have visitors soon."

"Way ahead of you," Webb replied. "I'm locked in the engine room. The good news is I should have this bitch fixed before morning."

"Really?" Bronson cried out with enthusiasm. "That's great!"

Everyone suddenly became interested in the conversation and stopped what they were doing.

"Yeah, I found the part I needed in the helicopter wreck," Webb informed him. "Someone deliberately sabotaged the ship. It doesn't make any sense, but someone didn't want to leave the island on the scheduled departure date."

Everyone appeared surprised and exchanged looks.

"You mean there's a part missing?" Bronson demanded through the handheld radio.

"Exactly," Webb replied. "My first guess would be one of the crew. I wouldn't doubt the part is on this mother somewhere."

"Radio us at daybreak and give us the status on the ship," Bronson announced.

"We'll need to get creative," Webb informed him. "The ship is still grounded. If we're lucky, the tide will loosen her up, but she may need some help to get unstuck."

"We have enough rope on the ship and tools here to make a winch," Dane offered. "We can attach it to the tail of the plane and pull it free."

Bronson nodded then spoke into the radio. "Hey, Webb, we have that covered. Just get the engine fixed and call us in the morning."

Everyone appeared relieved. Bronson finally collapsed in one of the chairs now able to relax.

"So that's it," Franklin announced. "Now we just sit and wait."

"Aren't you forgetting the part where someone sabotaged the ship?" Shannon announced boldly. "Who would do that?"

"Does it matter?" Porter asked. "They're probably dead, well, or dead-ish."

"That captain was shifty," Franklin remarked while tossing his cards onto the table. "I wouldn't doubt he had his own reasons for coming here in the first place."

"We should probably take turns on guard duty tonight," Dane informed them while casually glancing around the room. "Just in case."

"In case of what?" Porter nearly demanded. "In case one of us disabled the ship?"

"He's right," Bronson announced and sprang to his feet. "We don't trust anyone. I'll take first watch. We should breakup into pairs."

"I'll take second shift with Shannon," Franklin quickly offered.

Shannon made a face at Franklin's enthusiasm. "I'll take first watch with Bronson."

Bronson grinned at Franklin and mocked him. Franklin appeared disgusted and stood from the table. Dane and Porter looked at Murphy as if secretly suggesting she pick one. She suddenly appeared uncomfortable.

Porter managed a tiny smile at his friend. "If you want to take last shift with Dane, I'll be okay on second shift with Franklin."

Murphy was surprised he gave her up without a fight. "Are you sure?"

Porter smiled with a hint of lust and nodded.

Murphy was slightly uncomfortable by her friend's knowing grin. She fidgeted then gently cleared her throat. "In that case, I'm going to turn in early and get some sleep before my shift."

She caught herself casting a glance at Dane as she headed for the connecting corridor leading to the staff bedrooms.

Dane shifted slightly and attempted to act casual. "Anyone for a few hands of poker?"

Porter rolled his eyes and groaned with disgust. "Everyone knows you're slipping into Murphy's bed, Dane. Drop the chivalry act and go already."

Dane glared at Porter with moderate disapproval. He then considered the comment, turned, and casually followed after Murphy.

†

Murphy lit a candle to brighten the dingy, bland bedroom.

She didn't know how the nurses and doctors on staff lived in such depressed quarters, considering how depressing their jobs were to begin with. Her thoughts were interrupted by a soft knock on the door. She couldn't help but smile.

"It's open, Dane."

The door slowly opened and Dane slipped into the room. He smiled timidly and appeared almost as nervous as she was.

"Were you expecting me?"

Murphy withheld her laugh, approached him, and ran her hands along his chest while on their way around his neck.

"What do you think?"

Dane groaned softly and kissed her passionately, nearly knocking her off her feet. She attempted to return the kiss while keeping up with his rising passion, but she was no match for him. Dane nearly tackled her to the bed. She let out a startled yet playful scream.

Chapter Twenty-one

Murphy and Dane writhed around wildly beneath the covers by the glow of candlelight. Moans of pleasure coincided with the creaking of the old bed with its sagging springs. Once their passion had subsided, Dane clung to Murphy while she rested against his chest and gently caressed his shoulder. Both panted softly and appeared pleasantly exhausted.

"I'm a little out of practice," Dane informed her while breathing heavily. "I hope I didn't disappoint you."

Murphy laughed softly while running her hand along his bare chest. "If that's 'out of practice', I'd love a rematch when you get back into the swing." She lifted her head and met his gaze. "You were romantic and *very* passionate."

"I enjoyed taking it slow, you know," he teased, "without fear of something taking a bite out of my ass for a change."

She returned her head to his chest and lovingly kissed his shoulder. "Certainly sounds like a lot of pressure," she replied then held her breath. "Sort of like living up to your *past* expectations."

Dane attempted to look at her where she rested against him and appeared bewildered. "How's that?"

She gently ran her fingers through his light coating of chest hair. "Just that I know how you felt about Kate, and, well, I'm not her." She sighed softly. "You'll probably never get over her. Honestly, I was half convinced you'd reconsider and back off."

There was an odd silence in the dimly lit room. "You're right," he announced soft but firm. "You're not Kate, and I probably won't get over her. But our relationship was more complicated than that of typical lovers." He gently caressed her shoulder. "I'll admit I loved Kate. We were survival companions. We needed each other. I probably felt about her the same way you feel about Porter."

Murphy lifted her head and met his gaze. Her smile mocked him. "Porter and I are just friends. There's never been anything romantic or sexual between us," she informed him. "I hardly think the two relationships compare."

"If you initiated, Porter would jump you without a second thought."

"True, but it's still different," she protested.

"No, it's not different," he stated firmly. "Kate and I were you and Porter, but with a lot of sex. I wouldn't have been Kate's first choice of sexual partners if we hadn't been stranded together." He hesitated a moment. "And, in the real world, I never would have chosen someone like her for a serious relationship either. She wanted sex, and I was the only man she could tolerate being around. Just as you chose me over Porter, I would choose you over Kate."

She stared into his eyes with some surprise. "Really? You would?"

"I came back to this place. If that doesn't proclaim me your fool, nothing does."

She offered a warm smile. "I have no desire to rule over you," Murphy informed him. "I love you the way you are."

Dane stared at her a moment, soaking in the comment, and then pulled her against him, kissing her passionately. Murphy sank into his arms and returned the kiss without hesitation.

†

Franklin slept reclined in the corner of the sofa within the dimly lit lobby. A strange clunk caused him to stir with some disorientation, realizing he'd fallen asleep while on guard duty. His eyes opened. A zombie's face was directly before his. It snarled, exposing its discolored teeth and lunged for him. Franklin suddenly cried out with surprise and horror.

†

Dane and Murphy carried their weapons while they walked along the hallway toward the lobby, clinging to each other in a loving embrace. Murphy was almost positive the permanent smile etched on her face would give away their earlier antics to Porter and Franklin on guard duty.

"So much for sleep, huh?" Dane announced with a boyish grin.

"I got an hour here and there," she replied. "When you'd let me."

Dane chuckled softly. "That's not entirely my fault," he announced. "Something tells me Bronson and Shannon were having a pretty good time in the room next to ours."

"I can't say I heard that."

He eyed her with some surprise. "You're kidding right? They went at it half the night."

"Yeah? Well, so did we," she teased, causing him to smile with boyish embarrassment.

They suddenly heard a terrifying scream from the lobby. Both clutched their weapons and ran for the nearby lobby. The zombie was on top of Franklin, clutching and clawing at him while tearing into his bleeding face with its teeth. Franklin thrashed beneath the zombie while screaming. Porter stood directly behind the zombie with a rope around its neck and attempted to pull the zombie off Franklin. His baton Taser was on the floor out of reach. Dane ran across the lobby for them, placed the cattle gun to the side of the zombie's head, and pulled the trigger.

The rod impaled the zombie's head exploding its brains out the opposite side. Porter finally managed to pull the zombie's lifeless body off Franklin and tossed it across the floor. Franklin, who was missing most of his cheek, spit up blood while clutching his bleeding neck. He gasped one last breath, causing Murphy and Porter to jump back out of fright. Dane frowned his disgust, placed the cattle gun to Franklin's head, and pulled the trigger. The horrifying sound caused Murphy to gasp and shut her eyes. Only a few minutes later, Porter was pacing the lobby while Dane and Murphy wrapped a sheet around Franklin's body. His blood was already soaking through the once white sheet.

Porter continued to pace and eyed the dead zombie. "I don't know what happened," he practically exploded while flinging his arms in the air. "One minute I was talking to Franklin, and then we both must've fallen asleep. Suddenly I hear Franklin screaming. When I looked up, that zombie was on top of him tearing chunks of flesh from him. I tried frying it, but it wouldn't let go." He vigorously shook his head. "I didn't know what else to do."

"How did it get in?" Murphy gasped.

"The front door was shut," Porter insisted almost defensively. "There's no way it could have gotten in."

"The basement door is still locked," Dane remarked. "It must have been trapped on the second floor somewhere, and we just missed it. I noticed the stairway door was open."

Porter stared at Dane with surprise and vigorously shook his head. "No way! That door was locked. I swear it was!"

Dane straightened and stared at the dead man wrapped in the blood-soaked sheet. "I think we'd better check on Bronson and Shannon."

†

Several minutes later, Bronson paced the lobby before the two, sheet-covered bodies and shook his head while the others watched.

"No, I had watch before Porter and Franklin," Bronson insisted. "That door was shut and locked. The lock isn't broke. That means someone unlocked that door."

"But the door to the lab is still locked," Murphy insisted. "Who'd want to open that particular door and for what reason?"

Dane groaned softly with disgust. "I'm going down to the lab and have a look around," he announced then looked at Murphy and extended the semiautomatic pistol to her. "I want you to lock the stairway door behind me."

She uncertainly accepted the handgun and stuck it down the back of her pants.

"What are you thinking?" Porter suddenly asked.

"I just want to make sure our friends in the lab are still locked in the holding tank," Dane replied.

"I'm going with you," Porter suddenly announced. "I'm not letting Murphy alone in that hallway. What if more are running around?" He cast his flashlight stun gun aside. "Obviously these don't do any good."

"Fine," Dane announced. "You're with Murphy."

Porter, Dane, and Murphy left the lobby with their weapons. Dane left the cattle gun behind and opted to take Franklin's baseball bat, which didn't require getting as close to effectively use on the undead. They didn't have much ammo left for the assault rifles, so he left his behind with Bronson. As long as Murphy had the semiautomatic, that was good enough. Despite Porter's insistence that the baton stun guns didn't work on the zombies, Murphy felt better keeping hers as added protection and followed the men to the basement.

Chapter Twenty-two

Dane cautiously walked across the dimly lit lab with the baseball bat in his hand and headed toward the holding area near the back. Despite the generator running, it only provided sporadic lighting throughout the lab area. Something clattered within the room, causing him to spin around with the bat prepared to swing. Nothing moved and there was no other sound. He attempted to relax then continued across the lab. He saw several stacks of folders were rearranged and the flash drive was no longer where they left it. A puzzled look crossed his face. He continued his way across the room. Nearly halfway across the room, he was able to see that the door to the holding tank was open. Dane was momentarily frozen with alarm then quickly turned to leave.

A zombie in a lab coat stood directly behind him, softly snarling and drooling. Dane barely had a chance to cry out as the zombie lunged for him. He swung the baseball bat, connecting with its head, stopping its attack, although only stunning it. Dane struck it in the head two more times, dropping it to the floor with its head smashed in. He heard movement and faint snarling from all corners of the lab. Dane ran for the lab door and a hasty departure. As he approached the door, Murphy and Porter arrived and looked around with concern.

"What happened?" Murphy cried out.

"Someone left them out!" Dane practically shouted as he joined them outside the main lab. "We need to seal off the entire basement!"

All three entered the corridor while Dane slammed the door shut and flipped the lock. It seemed as if it should hold, but enough of them would eventually break it.

"I know what we can use to seal off the basement in case they get through," Porter announced excitedly and then turned to leave.

Dane suddenly tackled Porter face first into the wall, surprising Murphy. Dane then spun him around, shoving his back into the wall with a loud crack. Murphy cried out at the sudden attack on her friend. Before she could protest, Dane punched Porter in the face then kicked him in the ribs and flipped him over his hip onto the concrete floor. Porter writhed on the floor in agony. Murphy drew her gun and aimed it at Dane with a look of horror on her face.

"What the hell--?"

Dane stared at the semiautomatic pointed at his face. "He let them out," he launched with anger. "He was the only person unaccounted for when that door was opened!"

Porter slowly pulled himself to his feet while dabbing the blood on the corner of his mouth. He glared at Dane only a few feet from him.

"You're insane!" He looked at Murphy. "Shoot the bastard! He's insane!" Porter wildly gestured with his hands. "I was with Franklin! That means it had to be Bronson!"

Dane sneered at Porter and shook his head. "Bronson was with Shannon. They were screwing around while Murphy and I were trying to sleep," Dane launched back. "And he may be a prick, but I've known that prick most of my life. He's into combat and women. If he had come down here, it would have been to destroy every last one of those things."

Murphy kept her gun aimed at Dane while fidgeting. "There has to be another answer, Dane," she protested. "I know Porter. He wouldn't set them loose to kill Franklin. He's a spoiled rich boy with no stomach for violence."

"The flash drive is missing from the desk," Dane informed her. "He wants the information on the virus for himself or for someone else."

She vigorously shook her head. "No, he wouldn't do that, Dane."

Porter slowly moved closer to Murphy while gingerly dabbing his lip and glaring at Dane. "He's trying to turn you against me, Murphy." He then pointed excitedly at Dane. "He just admitted he was awake around the time the zombies were set free. If he was awake, he could have been the one down here releasing those things. I think he was the one who stole the flash drive, so he'd have the virus." Porter cast a glance at her then resumed glaring at Dane.

"He lied about everything else. I mean, hell, he never even told you he let his pregnant girlfriend turn into one of them."

Murphy suddenly looked at Porter with surprise. Dane appeared almost horrified by the comment. Murphy's look turned hard as she aimed the gun at Porter and shook her head with disbelief.

"Oh, Porter, no," she gasped softly. "Tell me it's not true."

Porter appeared surprised while starting at Murphy and her sudden distrust of him.

Dane's look hardened and appeared mildly unpredictable. "How would you know whether or not I terminated her?" he suddenly demanded with a slight growl in his voice. "The only people who would know that were the government guys who promised they'd take care of her for me."

Porter groaned softly, shook his head, and smirked almost evilly. "I was so close--"

Murphy stared at him with horror to the admission. "Why, Porter?"

"Isn't it obvious?" Dane demanded. "He wants to sell the virus to the highest bidder."

She shook her head in protest. "No, he's a conspiracy theorist. He wants to expose criminal government activity. He's been helping me."

"Has he, Murphy?" Dane asked while raising a brow. "Was he really helping you, or just using you to get to me? Think about what really happened."

She uncertainly looked at Dane while flexing her grip on the gun. Porter suddenly lunged for Murphy. She hesitated pulling the trigger. He grabbed the gun from her hand and spun behind her, holding her against him from behind with the gun to her head. Dane flinched while staring at them with concern.

"Any closer and I'll blow her brains out," Porter snarled to Dane. He smirked and laughed softly. "Yeah, I've been helping you, Murphy. Dane was right. You were my best bet on getting information about what really happened on this island. I knew about the virus, but I couldn't get any information on this island. I needed someone who could get close to Dane. You were my ticket."

She gripped his arm around her neck and held back her emotions. "I thought you were my friend."

"It's not as if I don't have some feelings for you, Murphy," he announced, "but I did warn you that you'd be surprised when you realized I wasn't in love with you. I have my priorities straight. I need a new revenue source, and this virus is going to make me a very rich, powerful man." He grinned and glanced at her profile while keeping his lips close to her face. "Lucky for you, I'm sentimental. I'm going to give you another chance to survive this nightmare." He glared at Dane and indicated the door. "Inside, lover boy."

Murphy cried out, "No!"

Porter glared at Dane and pressed the barrel of the gun into Murphy's temple. "Inside or I kill her."

Dane frowned and approached the locked door alongside him. As he flipped the lock, they could hear the zombies just on the other side clawing at the door. Dane pulled open the door and slipped inside, vanishing behind the door.

"Dane, no!"

Porter forced Murphy closer to the door and reached to lock it. The door was suddenly thrown open to reveal Dane holding a zombie around the neck from behind, using it as a shield. The zombie snarled and snapped at Porter while attempting to free itself from Dane's grip. He forced the zombie closer to Porter and Murphy. The zombie snarled and fought Dane's arm while attempting to bite him. Murphy screamed with horror, uncertain of Dane's endgame. Dane forced the zombie closer to Porter's arm around Murphy. He was going to make certain the zombie got a hold of Porter first. Porter cried out with fear, removed the gun from Murphy's head, and fired several shots into the zombie Dane used as a shield. On the fourth shot, the bullet penetrated the zombie's head, stopping it.

Murphy cried out while stomping on Porter's foot then rammed her elbow into his ribs behind her. As she bolted away from him, Dane allowed the zombie to fall to the floor then spun into a high, roundhouse kick, striking Porter in the head before he could get another shot off. He was thrown into the hallway wall, dropping the gun. Porter clutched the wall and appeared momentarily dazed. Murphy grabbed the discarded gun. Dane grabbed Murphy's hand and pulled her away from the zombies now pouring out of the lab. Porter straightened from his position alongside the wall, appeared horrified at the sight of the zombie mob, and attempted to bolt ahead of Murphy and Dane. Dane kicked Porter in the knee, driving him to the floor and directly into the path of the zombie mob. The zombies pounced on him as he screamed. Dane took the gun from Murphy as they ran along the hall for the stairwell to escape the basement. They ran up the stairs and out the door, slamming it behind them. Dane attempted to lock the door, but the lock was now bent.

"Son-of-a-bitch! He sabotaged the lock," Dane cried out then looked at Murphy. "Find something to block it!"

Murphy nodded and ran down the hallway. The door was suddenly hit with force, tossing Dane across the hallway and into the nearby wall. Murphy stopped and looked back with surprise. A badly bitten and bleeding Porter charged through the door and tackled Dane harshly against the wall. He'd been bitten multiple times, but that didn't stop him from seeking his revenge.

"If I'm going to hell, I'm taking you to hell with me," Porter shouted.

Murphy could hear the zombies in the stairwell getting closer to the door. They'd soon find their way through and swarm them. Murphy ran for the door and slammed it shut, knowing she had no way to keep it closed. The zombies shoved against the door and nearly pushed it open. Murphy braced the door shut and looked at Dane, who fought with Porter for control of the gun.

"Dane, I can't hold it!"

Dane attempted to keep the gun away from his face. "Get out of here!"

"No, you can't take on that many," she cried out.

The door thumped against Murphy's body.

Dane slammed Porter into the wall, although he still refused to give up the gun close to Dane's face. "You need to trust me, Murphy! Go!"

Murphy stared at Dane with concern. It was hard to tell which man was winning the power struggle with the gun. Neither would survive the zombie mob. Murphy cursed softly and released the door. She ran for the fighting men and punched Porter in the kidney. He gasped with surprise more than pain from her surprise attack. That split second was all Dane needed to knock the gun from his hand. He punched Porter in the face, tossing him back several steps as the zombies flooded into the corridor just behind him. Dane stared at the mob of zombies behind Porter and suddenly froze with horror.

"A.J.--?" Dane gasped.

Despite the large slice through his neck, a severely decayed A.J. approached Porter from behind. As he snarled, Porter spun to face him with alarm. Murphy grabbed Dane's hand and pulled him with her then looked at A.J. as well. Her face drained of all color.

"Dad?" she gasped with surprise.

A.J. lunged for Porter. He attempted to hold him back, but he already sank his teeth into her former friend's throat. Porter cried out with horror and pain as A.J. tore a large chunk from his neck.

Dane pulled free from Murphy, who stood frozen with horror, and dived to the floor near a group of zombies. He grabbed the discarded semiautomatic and swept the legs out from under the nearby zombies. As the zombies fell, Dane sprang to his feet with the gun.

"Sorry, buddy."

Dane aimed the gun at A.J.'s head as he chewed on a mouthful of flesh and pulled the trigger. A.J.'s head snapped back as his head exploded from the shot. Murphy cried out with horror. Dane grabbed her hand and pulled her along the corridor as the horde pursued them. Within seconds, Dane and Murphy ran into the lobby, startling Bronson and Shannon. They ran through the lobby past them without stopping.

"Time to go!" Dane cried out.

They could hear the moaning of zombies as they relentlessly pursued them. Bronson grabbed his assault rifle, prepared to fire, when he saw more than two dozen zombies spilling into the lobby. Shannon screamed and ran after Dane and Murphy. Bronson shot several, attempting to slow them down, but it was no use. He turned and ran from the lobby after the others. Bronson slammed the door shut behind them while Dane returned with a vine, attempting to tie the doors shut as the zombies struck the glass. Shannon jumped back while screaming at the zombie horde. All four backed away from the doors and watched them slam their decaying bodies against the glass. It wasn't going to hold long.

"We are so screwed," Bronson cried out.

"Head for the launch," Dane ordered. "We can make it to the yacht."

Bronson looked at him with disbelief. "We don't know how many are waiting onboard for us."

"Would you rather stay here?" Dane demanded and motioned wildly. "Go!"

Bronson grabbed Shannon and ran for the path to the beach. Murphy was about to follow when she realized Dane wasn't behind her. She turned to see Dane running alongside the building just on the other side of the lobby doors. He turned a green valve, causing a soft hissing sound. As the zombies rammed against the glass doors, the glass cracked behind their weight. Dane hurried toward Murphy and stopped. He removed the grenade from his jacket pocket, pulled the pin, and looked at her.

"You may want to run now."

She suddenly gasped with horror and ran toward the beach after the others. Dane threw the grenade for the valve and ran after her. The grenade exploded, igniting the remaining fumes from the old gas line.

Chapter Twenty-three

Bronson, Shannon, and Murphy reached the beach and slowed near the inflatable launch. Murphy looked back and witnessed Dane running onto the beach just behind her. There was a second, much louder explosion that rocked the island beneath their feet. All four were thrown to the sand. They slowly moved to their knees and looked at the burnt woods not far from them. Smoke and flames shot up high above the tree line.

Bronson nodded with approval. "Not half bad."

Several zombies appeared from the nearby woods in the opposite direction, apparently attracted to the noise.

Shannon pointed and screamed. "There's more of them!"

Bronson shoved her in the direction of the launch near the tree line. Murphy and Dane ran after them and helped carry it toward the surf.

Murphy looked toward the ocean and the rising sun. She suddenly pointed. "The yacht!"

All four looked where she pointed. They could see the yacht cruising toward them.

Bronson suddenly chuckled and shook his head while tossing the launch into the surf. "Webb, I could kiss you, you son-of-a-bitch!"

Bronson and Shannon waded through the water with the launch then jumped into it. They could hear the zombies closing in as they trekked through the sand in an attempt to reach them. Without bothering to look back, Dane pulled Murphy into the water behind him. Murphy felt compelled to look back in fear of how close they were to them. She suddenly stopped, jerking him to a halt as well. Dane appeared surprised by her sudden stop and looked just across the beach in the direction she stared. Kate stumbled at a decent clip across the sand toward them. Her eyes were glazed over, a large amount of stained blood remained on the glaring wound on her shoulder, and her enlarged belly revealed her still pregnant state after five years. Dane stared with horror and pulled his hand free from Murphy.

"Don't do it, Dane," Murphy cried out. "That's not her anymore. She'll kill you!"

Dane waded through the surf back to the beach and approached Kate. His look was as transfixed and blank as hers was. She snarled at him and bared her teeth. He stopped in the sand a few yards from her, looked at her pregnant belly, and fought the tears in his eyes. Dane took a few steps closer and reached out to touch her belly. She snarled with a hideous growl and lunged for him. Dane raised the gun and pulled the trigger. Kate's head snapped back, momentarily stopping her in her tracks before she sank to the sand. The remaining horde of zombies rushed for him. Murphy suddenly stood alongside Dane, who could only stare in horror at the dead woman on the beach. Murphy gently removed the gun from his hand.

"I'm sorry, Dane, but we have to go," she whispered.

Dane couldn't look away from Kate's lifeless body and her pregnant belly. There was movement from her belly. Dane covered his eyes and sobbed softly. He turned away and looked at Murphy, who stared at the moving belly with horror.

"Do it," he gasped softly.

Murphy grimaced, fought her tears, and shot Kate's belly. The movement stopped. The other zombies were nearly upon them now. Murphy grabbed Dane's hand and pulled him into the surf toward the inflatable launch now several yards away. Bronson and Shannon screamed at them while frantically waving. As they hurried for the launch, the zombies slowly waded into the surf behind them. Dane and Murphy dived into the inflatable launch and helped row away from the beach. As they rowed toward the yacht, Dane stared back at the beach in silence.

✝

Once safely onboard the ship and headed toward their destination, Dane leaned on the railing and stared into the dark water behind them. The island had been gone from their sight for quite some time, but he continued to stare, off in his own world. Murphy approached him and gently caressed his shoulder.

"Are you okay?"

"Not really."

Murphy clung to his arm and rested her head lovingly on his shoulder. He immediately placed his arms around her and held her against him. She nuzzled his chest and endured the pain he must have been feeling.

He drew a deep, shaken breath. "After Kate was bit, she begged me to take the baby. There was a chance, you know. The baby may not have been infected," he announced then sniffed softly. "God help me, I couldn't do it. I couldn't do what I should have done. I couldn't destroy her to save our baby." He exhaled while trembling. "I let her turn instead of destroying her. What sort of man does that make me?"

She lifted her head and met his gaze with her own tears in her eyes. "It was a highly emotional situation, Dane. No one can judge your actions unless they've gone through it." She hesitated then gently touched his face. "The baby was infected. You couldn't have saved it."

"I'd like to believe that, but I don't know that I can."

"Her wounds were severe. She was bleeding out," Murphy assured him. "She would have turned before you finished the C-section. In the time it took you to return to the facility, the virus had already spread to the fetus. It was already too late for both of them. They were already dead."

He stared off a moment in silence as if contemplating her comment. "You know, I was so happy when she told me," he gently announced and forced a smile. "I wanted to be a daddy so badly--"

"You will be one day," she informed him then smiled warmly. "You'll be an awesome father."

Dane managed a smile while clinging to her, wanting to believe her. He finally pulled away from her, sighed deeply, and gently caressed her hand on his chest.

"Incidentally, I have the perfect ending for that book of yours," Dane announced surprising her.

"Oh?" She couldn't believe he was actually thinking about her book at a time like this.

Dane removed the flash drive from his pocket and held it up. "How about an anonymous tip providing proof that the government is experimenting with viral weapons on that island? In their panic to avoid a scandal, they lit up the facility."

"Where did you get that?" she gasped with surprise.

"I liberated it from Porter's pocket while we were fighting," he replied. "I figured I needed one, last I.O.U., and it needed to be big."

She held back her laugh. "I think that's a great ending to my book."

Dane grinned, pulled her into his arms, and kissed her warmly on the lips. He broke off the kiss and replaced the flash drive to his pocket.

Murphy ran her hands along his chest and met his gaze with a tiny smile. "If I recall correctly, you do still have one I.O.U. left."

Dane met her gaze, appeared slightly surprised by the grin on her face, and then hid his embarrassed smile.

"It's going to be at least two days before we reach land," he remarked in mild suggestion.

"I'm free for the next two days," she casually replied.

The End

Other books by Holly Copella!
Reviews left on Amazon are appreciated!

"The Battle for Andrea Marie"

A cruise ship attack turns six survivors into overnight celebrities after they take credit for the heroic act of a stowaway who died saving them.

The cruise is just what Jess needed--a bit of harmless fun far from her daily grind. But what begins as a relaxing vacation turns into a desperate fight for her life when terrorists take over the ship and start piling up bodies. Teaming up with a mysterious stowaway, Jess attempts to send out a distress call but knows they cannot wait for help to come. If she or the few remaining passengers have any hope for survival, Jess must act now. The papers dub it "The Battle for *Andrea Marie*," but to Jess it is the moment she fought side-by-side with her enigmatic Romeo, saving the ship--and losing him. She thinks the story ends there, but really, the nightmare is just beginning...

"Insanely Deadly"

When the dead return to life, it's up to an admiral's daughter and a mildly insane, former war hero to save their small town.

Jetta Cross, a Navy Admiral's daughter, is tasked with keeping her father's comrade, a former war hero turned town crazy, grounded in the real world. Capt. John Hunter is still fighting the war in his head, where imaginary dead people are part of his world. When a viral outbreak brings about a zombie uprising, Hunter is left to his own devices. He must resume his role as a one-man commando unit in order to destroy the ravenous undead. With Hunter still fighting his own inner demons as well as the undead, the townspeople fear their zombie neighbors may not be the only threat. Stranded at the island's luxurious resort with a handful of workers, Jetta is forced to live up to her father's reputation and take charge of the deteriorating situation at the hotel. She must wage her own war against the infected before the government declares her hometown a total loss.

"Deadly Institution"

A town recluse suspected of killing his wife teams up with a young woman in order to stop a killer.

After being accused of murdering his wife, Konrad Asher turns his back on the town that once adored him. Ten years later, he still holds his grudge and the title of the most feared man in town. With the reopening of the burned mental institution, where his wife had died, former employees are now murdered one-by-one, throwing suspicion back on Asher. A young local reporter, Jacey, is forced to reveal her long-time friendship with the infamous recluse in order to clear his name not only in the recent murders but to exonerate him in the death of his wife as well. Will Jacey's relationship with Asher invite the killer closer to her? Or is the killer already in her life?

"Screenplays: The Island Collection"
"Jungle Princess", "A.L.F. Resort", "Brighton Island"

Discover how romance and fun in the sun can be downright *chilling*!

"Jungle Princess" is a romantic/thriller that leaves a teenage girl stranded on an island with two male shipmates and a creature of "unknown" origin. She soon discovers the island is home to an abandoned prison with several prisoners roaming free. What really killed over one hundred prisoners? And is it still out there--?

"A.L.F. Resort" is a romantic/thriller set on an island resort with Artificial Life Forms as the main draw. At this resort, all your fantasies come true...until a malfunction removes safety inhibitors on the A.L.F.'s. Zombies, biker gangs, and mobsters run amuck, turning fantasies into nightmares. A young reporter gets more of a story than she anticipates, but will she survive long enough to write the story?

"Brighton Island" is a romantic/thriller set on a private island. When the owner's niece brings her psychic friend to the mansion, his presence awakens the spirits' tortured souls. As the psychic attempts to solve the old murders, the niece is confronted with the possibility that she's next to join the mansion ghosts. Stranded on the island with a crazed killer, her uncle wages his own war to save them. Will his "shock and awe" tactics actually save them or get them killed?

"Death Displacement"

A grief-stricken man travels back in time to seek revenge on the woman who murdered his girlfriend but inadvertently falls in love with her.

Kane is about to marry the woman he loves. His life is perfect. A few weeks before the wedding, a vindictive woman from his girlfriend's past mysteriously arrives and kills her. He learns of a traumatic accident that happened five years earlier, which triggers Riley's hatred for his girlfriend. Distraught over his girlfriend's death, Kane uses an antique time machine to travel into the past in order to find and destroy the woman responsible. When he runs into Riley's younger self, he realizes she's not the monster she later becomes, and he can't bring himself to destroy her. With a little help from his oddball friend from the past, they formulate a plan to prevent the accident that sends Riley down her destructive path. Kane's plan backfires when he falls for the younger Riley. His new tortured existence is further complicated when future Riley, his girlfriend's killer, shows up with her own devious agenda that doesn't include him. Will he be able to stop the time ripple, which ultimately ends with his girlfriend's death? Or will future Riley take him out of the timeline forever--

"Dead Village"

After strange happenings isolate a small resort town from the rest of the world, nearly one hundred residents seek refuge at the closed hotel. Only eight survive the night. And that's just the beginning...

One day after the entire population of Fox Ridge Village disappears, a car wreck forces several unsuspecting crash victims to seek help at the closed summer hotel. Within the hotel, they discover the grisly aftermath of a brutal slaughter. Crash victims Vander and Devon, a reluctant clairvoyant, team up to solve the riddle of the "haunted hotel" and the mass hysteria plaguing the remaining survivors. By the time they discover the hotel's secret, they're already drawn into the hysteria. As the body count continues to climb, it's a race to isolate the source and bring everyone back to reality before they kill one another. Will Devon be able to communicate with the traumatized spirits before their fate becomes her own?

"Misfits, Inc."

A seemingly ordinary, young woman meets four misfits who claim she has given them supernatural powers.

While on a business trip to a remote island paradise, a bored secretary, Hailey, has her world turned upside down when her path collides with a psychic freak, Skyler. He attempts to convince her that they had met in his dreams, and she had chosen him as one of her four mystic warriors. After Skyler foresees a woman's death, they discover an unidentified creature has killed one of the guests. They are joined by a lounge pianist and a rich playboy, who also claim they had met her in their dreams. If Skyler's prophecies are genuine, the evil entity controlling the ravenous creatures needs to destroy Hailey to ensure its survival. Reluctantly accepting her fate, Hailey has to locate the last and most powerful of her chosen warriors, The Guardian. Their fate is in doubt when The Guardian turns out to be a self-absorbed, former cat burglar with a bad attitude. Can Hailey turn her company of misfits into an elite team of mystic warriors? Or will The Guardian's secret agenda destroy them all?

"Basement Dwellers"

A viral outbreak at a hospital leaves a mortician, sheriff, and coroner fighting for their lives against a horde of undead and the CDC.

After a massive car wreck leaves several survivors in critical condition at the local hospital, a surgeon uses experimental drugs on his critical patients and accidentally causes a zombie outbreak. When local mortician, Lexx, receives an infected corpse as her client, she becomes stranded in the hospital basement during CDC quarantine along with the local sheriff and the coroner. The infamous surgeon struggles to find a cure for his infectious blunder by using the other survivors as test subjects. Meanwhile, Lexx and the sheriff attempt to locate his missing sister, who's stranded somewhere in the battle zone that once was the emergency room. It's a race against time and the ravenous undead. Can they survive the undead before CDC sanitizes the hospital of all infection?

"Witness Protection"
Also available in audiobook!

After witnessing an execution, a resourceful young woman attempts to disappear while being pursued by a hitman and a handsome federal agent.

A helicopter pilot, Jackie Remus, reluctantly agrees to go on a date with one of her clients, but her date is unexpectedly cut short when she witnesses a man being murdered. After narrowly escaping with her life, she is placed into protective custody. When the safe house is breached, Jackie makes a daring escape from both the hired killers and the handsome FBI agent, who wants to return her to protective custody. With a little help from her sly and crafty friend, Monroe, Jackie is convinced she can disappear until the trial. While on her journey to meet with her friend, she solicits help from a few shady but lovable characters along the way. Although she manages to stay one-step ahead of the hired killers, the federal agent remains in hot pursuit. Will Jackie reach Monroe before she's captured by the FBI and returned to protective custody? Or will the hired killers silence her first?

"Town Darling"

After surviving a brutal attack that claims the lives of those she loves, a young woman seeks revenge on a corrupt town.

Going back home is never easy, but for Casey, it means returning to her corrupt hometown where she barely survived a brutal attack. Accompanied by two family friends, she seeks justice for the night that destroyed her life. Her physical scars are nothing compared to her emotional ones, forcing the local sheriff to believe that the town darling is back for revenge. As the conspiracy for her revenge appears to be leading up to the coveted town fair, the sheriff is determined to stop her from fulfilling her vengeful scheme...but guilt over his role on that fateful night continues to haunt him. Will his desperate need for Casey's forgiveness be his undoing? Or will Casey's desire for revenge destroy them both?

"Unconditional"

A young woman puts her life on hold to care for an unstable, highly skilled combat soldier, who believes someone is trying to kill him.

A botched military coup leaves a team of elite fighters injured with one clinging to life in a coma. When Harlan wakes from his coma, he's left with no memory of his past life. His commander's daughter, Indy, takes it upon herself to care for the fallen war hero. She's challenged with more than just his physical care as she combats with not only his memory loss but also his newly found desire for her. His infatuation with her becomes the least of her worries when he sinks back into his role of a combat soldier. Believing his life is in danger, his fighting skills surface, turning him into an unpredictable and dangerous man. Will his memory return to him before Indy is forced to commit him? Or will he finally find his nemesis, "the coyote", and possibly claim the life of an innocent person?

"Witness Protection 2"
The Return of Whiskey Tango Foxtrot

Believing she holds the clue to millions in missing laundered money, a young woman is placed into the protective care of a former Navy SEAL team.

Feeling sorry for her recently separated co-worker, Leeann invites Wiley to join her and her friends on their night out. Little does she know that finding her co-worker murdered is just the beginning of her nightmare. Leeann unknowingly holds the key to fifty million dollars in potentially laundered mob money. With hired killers pursuing her, the FBI places her into a different kind of protective custody. Former Navy SEAL team Whiskey Tango Foxtrot reunites to keep Leeann alive at their secret hideaway. What should be an easy assignment takes an unscheduled turn when secrets, lies, and betrayal threaten to derail their mission. Is the team prepared for a war on their own doorstep? Will Leeann's misguided trust endanger the lives of those sent to protect her?

"Deadly Institution 2"

When blackmail turns into murder, a young woman finds herself caught in the killer's crosshairs.

The small town of Stony Ridge is no stranger to scandal and persecution of the innocent. When a brutal killing shakes the town's prestigious country club, Jacey McMurray seeks help from a self-proclaimed vigilante, Konrad Asher. As her professional and personal worlds collide, Jacey fears the stress of the country club killings have finally taken their toll on Asher. Can a stressed out vigilante stop the killer before he strikes again?

"Witness Protection 3"
Alpha Mike Foxtrot

A helicopter pilot risks her life to help a team of retired Navy SEALs rescue two girls from a killer.

When former Navy SEAL team Whiskey Tango Foxtrot asks for a simple favor, Jackie reluctantly offers her air-taxi services. What could go wrong? What begins as a search and rescue for two girls turns into a fight for survival against a heavily armed drug cartel. Wanted by the law with the cartel in hot pursuit and their home base breached, the team is forced to call in a favor from a questionable ally. Unfortunately, their new safe house isn't what it seems. Without knowing who the real enemy is, can Jackie and the team save their young witnesses from the hands of a killer?

"Awaken the Dead"

A grieving innkeeper struggles to keep her haunted hotel out of foreclosure.

After losing her parents in a suspicious boating accident, Harley Brandon is determined to keep the family hotel out of foreclosure. Unfortunately, the hotel ghosts have other plans. Built with tainted money, the century old Horizon Hotel thrives on a tradition of murder, scandal, and suicide. As the paranormal activity increases to alarming levels, Harley discovers the truth about the hotel and its residents. Can Harley save her friends from the hotel's frightening hidden secrets?

"The Pen Pal"

In order to save her friend, she must enter the mind of a serial killer.

When her best friend is abducted, no one believes Jolynn saw it in a psychic vision. With nowhere to turn, Jolynn reluctantly joins Agent Harris Slade and his team on their hunt for a sadistic serial killer known only as "The Pen Pal". Finally confronted with the killer, Jolynn realizes she must enter the mind of the psychopath in order to stop the brutal killings. But when her vision reveals a particularly disturbing death, can Jolynn sacrifice her lover for her friend?

Coming Soon!
"Witness Protection 4"
O-Dark-Hundred

ABOUT THE AUTHOR

Holly Copella has been writing since the age of twelve when her frustration at a book's poor plot drove her to author her own story. Over the last decade, she's written a number of screenplays, some of which she's now adapting into novels. Her fascination with zombies and other darker material lends an edge to her writing, which tends to lean toward horror. As a fan of Agatha Christie, she appreciates the craft of a good plot and the importance of creating significant characters.

Hailing from Pennsylvania, Copella lives in the Endless Mountains on a farm with her rescue horses and other animals. In addition to writing and reading fiction, she enjoys riding horses and traveling to Las Vegas and Disney World.

www.ingramcontent.com/pod-product-compliance
Lightning Source LLC
Chambersburg PA
CBHW061130200626
46817CB00016B/520